I0657300

Vasily Mahanenko

THE QUEST

Books are the lives
we don't have
time to live.

Vasily Mahanenko

DARK PALADIN

BOOK#2

Magic Dome Books

The Quest
Dark Paladin, Book # 2
Copyright © V. Mahanenko 2017
Cover Art © V. Manyukhin 2017
English Translation Copyright ©
Alexandra Tussing 2017
Published by Magic Dome Books, 2017
All Rights Reserved
ISBN: 978-80-88231-29-5

TABLE OF CONTENTS :

CHAPTER ONE

THE SANCTUARY

S/TRIVE FOR THE benefit of my class to the extent of my strength, knowledge and ability, refraining from inflicting any harm and injustice to my class. I shall, honestly and forever, transfer the excess of my personal resources, in the amount of ten percent, for the needs of the class. Whatever dwelling I enter, I shall enter as a guest, for I shall know no other home than the Citadel of my class.

Whenever I see or hear that with respect to my class which should not be disclosed, I shall keep silent and treat that thing as a secret. May I who follow the oath steadfastly receive good fortune in the Game and glory with all Paladins for eternity; and the one who violates it or whose oath is false may suffer the opposite. So be it!"

WHITE LIGHT washed over me from head to toe, indicating that the Game accepted my oath. From now on I was a full-fledged Earth Paladin, the only survivor out of five recruits sent to the Academy, the only one whom Archibald had been able to pull out of the mages' hands.

The catorian was standing nearby, looking too pleased for someone who had just been chewed out, first by the blue-skinned Viceroy, and then by a weird bearded Judge. Due to recent events a scandal had broken out in the Game, and Paladins had spared no effort to inflate it.

It was not like hunting recruits was not allowed, but killing noobs before official presentation was sort of bad sport. In our case it had been plain genocide. Everyone was indignant and demanded that the Viceroy and the Supreme Judge make a resounding statement and adequate response. As soon as Archibald pulled me out, the case initiation suggestion had popped up and I immediately accepted it. My soul craved blood and revenge.

But those plans were not to be. The odd-looking Judge, who looked like an overgrown gnome, had taken this right away from me simply by showing up.

The case you initiated and investigation thereof have been transferred to Supreme Judge Koni

No reward, no punishment, no satisfaction from righteous revenge. It felt somewhat frustrating. The high-born elven upstarts deserved a good spanking. Would someone, please, fetch me a belt!

The ceremony of being made a Paladin of Earth, however, had turned into a one-man show. Oh, it's my first night, oh I am so nervous! Glancing at the spectators, I noted how few my brothers in class were. There were only about forty players in the hall; most of them were elves. I would bet a hundred to one that I would not hear from them today anything like "Long live new Paladin Yaropolk!"

Not as though I really wanted to. One glance at Nartalim's father Garlion really filled me with certainty of how "glad" they were to see me here. The elf kept staring at me, and I understood really well the way he felt.

You became a full-fledged player
8 artifact properties are available for
redistribution
Check your choices carefully

The defense and attack amulets bought in the Academy worked fine, improving the properties "Defense" and "Weapon" by 5 points, so there was not much sense in putting lots of available points into them. One point for each would be enough, just so that the properties would not disappear, making the amulets purely decorative.

The situation with the "Spiritual integrity" was somewhat more complex. Given that for the next three years no one could take me under control it was not necessary. In the short run I could drop it and then start using it again in a couple of years. So, the only two left for further development and upgrading were "Context Search" and "Neuronal network". Knowing full well what an advantage the "Neuronal network" would confer, since at level 15 it was capable of automatically analyzing the video it recorded in 24x7 mode, I invested 4 out of my 6 points available into it. The remaining two went into "Context Search", thus making available to me not only comparisons of the surroundings by the Book of Knowledge, but also navigation and an alphabetical index.

"Welcome to the family, brother Yaropolk!" As soon as I confirmed redistribution of artifact properties, the gray-haired head of class for Paladins on Earth nodded approvingly to me, completing the ceremony. Gerhard van Brast's bright blue eyes shone with such incomparable wisdom and understanding that I could not but respect him. You rarely meet a person whom you can't help trusting as soon as you meet his eyes. Gerhard van Brast was one of those. He looked sort of like Sean Connery in *Highlander*. He was as regal and steadfast.

Nodding again, to the Paladins this time, Gerhard left the room, followed by two guards. His departure broke the dead silence that had hung over the entire ceremony. To the right of me I heard a snuffling voice loudly speculating on Gerhard's sudden public appearance. Now, that was interesting! During the last three years the Head of class had never appeared at any public events. Already rumors and tales were circulating among our people, each stranger than the next. But Gerhard's appearance today stopped all the wagging tongues. He was alive, strong and, importantly, of sound mind. I doubted that it was my humble self that had caused the head of the class to appear here.

"Come with me, brother – we need to anchor you to the Citadel." Sharda was dragging me out of the hall and I couldn't hear what else that snuffling guy was saying. "After that you have an appointment with the Judge – he wants to hear your version of the events. Also, brother Garlion wants to talk to you about the death of his son Nartalim. Then you are expected in the Sanctuary for assignment. There you will also receive your first quest and access to the Dungeon."

There were many more "thens" and "afterwards". As Sharda clarified, no matter where I am assigned, the Citadel will pay for rent and transportation and provide a stipend for the first three months. I will receive access to the Citadel library after living in the main world for at least six months. If I had not had such a high level – eleven – I would have had to first spend some time at the special training range for newbies, upgrading and leveling up to an acceptable point. In that case I would have been in debt to the Citadel, because the class training ranges were not free even for class members. One granis or one year of working for the benefit of the class was the price of not being very successful in the Academy.

"Anchor point," Sharda said curtly, pointing inside the large hall and letting me come in first. In the center, without any apparent support, a sphere was hanging. It was about two or three meters in diameter, and pulsing with blinding blue light, creating quite an unreal picture. It felt like a fairy tale. It seemed like the sky itself had descended, washing the hall with its innocent pure light, shying away from the dark corners. Menacing shadows lurked there, waving threateningly in the same rhythm as the pulses, trying to reach the center and vanquish the small blue sun.

"WHO?" A resonating voice reverberated through the hall. The surface of the sphere visibly rippled, and my body responded with acute pain. I trembled, trying to endure it silently: it would not do to betray my weakness. The voice fell silent and the pain subsided.

"Brother Yaropolk!" Sharda introduced me, bowing his head slightly to the ball as a way of greeting. Rightly considering that it wouldn't do me any harm, I copied his gesture. "Newly graduated from the Academy."

"THE SOURCE WELCOMES THE NEW PALADIN!"

I tried to brace for the new wave of resonating pain. But it didn't work. First I bent down, and then fell on my knees. I didn't fall on the floor only because I had thrust out my hands. It took the Source forever to finish its greeting!

Finally the voice faded and I was able to catch my breath. The gnome was standing next to me as if nothing had happened.

I wanted to ask why the voice affected me in that way, when the agonizing pain pierced me once again:

THE YOUNG ONE MUST JUDGE THEM AND
DISCOVER HIS TRUE PAIR
TO FIND WHAT IS LOST AND DEEM
IF THE WORLD'S PUNISHMENT IS FAIR

Anchoring to the Paladins' Citadel is complete

"Charades again!" Sharda said with displeasure, as he wrote something down in a small book that was floating in the air. "From all that was foretold, brother Yaropolk, all I understood was that you might become one of the Panel of the Judges of the Game. Become one of the Arbiters. The rest you'll have to figure out for yourself."

"What was that?" As the darkness in front of my eyes faded, I rose to my feet and hastened to peek into the book over the gnome's shoulder. The book fluttered a page with a calligraphy drawing on it in front of me, shut itself loudly and disappeared into a portal.

"The first prophesy," Sharda answered laconically, as if that statement was supposed to make it all clear to me. My silence was his answer: "Did you not know about it? Oh yes, you weren't there at the first class of training before the Academy! So, we will repeat that lesson. Before anchoring to the class citadel, each new player receives a personal prophesy. Some are told clearly what they need to do, some are given an elaborate hint that changes are needed and indications regarding the path of development. You, brother Yaropolk, were told what you could become or what you might be able to

7

accomplish in your life. Only your prophesy has more that is not clear than is clear. Oh well: that's your luck... What does it mean, "discover his true pair"? Are you going to become a part-time matchmaker? He-he-he!" Sharda laughed at his own guess, but immediately turned serious again, "I hate charades."

The bluish tinge of the "sun" floating in the middle of the room faded and gradually turned to white. The anchoring was over. There was a dull click, and the door opened with a protesting squeak, as if no one had oiled the hinges for a millennium or two.

"I see that all the mandatory procedures are over. Yaropolk, may I congratulate you? You are a free player now." The Supreme Judge appeared in the doorframe.

I shrugged my shoulders, considering the answer was obvious. The Judge addressed the gnome:

"I'll see Yaropolk to the departure area. May I?"

Even I figured out from Sharda's grimace how "glad" he was at the Judge's proposition, but in some situations there is simply no choice:

"It will be my pleasure to palm off to you a novice who has not completed training," the gnome responded, trying to look indifferent, and then took off to mind his own affairs.

"Yaropolk." The Judge gestured, inviting me to walk with him down the hall. As soon as I approached Koni, the Game informed me of the status "witness", beginning the procedure of examination and the impossibility for a third party to interfere with this process. The broad-shouldered Judge grinned, seeing my displeased face, and slowly started along the long hallway. There was nothing I could do other than follow him. At the last moment I looked back and met the eyes of the gnome, who peeked out the door. It seemed someone was way too curious.

"I would like to reassure you from the start – there is no threat in this for you," the Judge had a low and pleasant timber of voice, enveloping one's mind and making one feel relaxed. "I know practically all the circumstances of the case; I just need to clarify some details. But first of all, as one Judge to another, I can offer you some advice: never deliver a verdict on a case with which you are familiar less than ninety percent. Even if you deliver a correct verdict, it is not good practice; it will have an adverse effect later when the Panel of Judges of the Game makes the decision regarding your membership. I hope professional advancement is part of your long-term plans?"

"I don't know yet." I responded honestly, trying to overcome the euphoria that was washing over me from talking to the Supreme Judge. I had never felt reverence or obsequious urges towards the high and mighties until now, so I doubted that I had developed a bout of idol-worshipping all of a sudden. My experience of dealing with Dolgunata only fueled my doubts. To counteract this, there was still a thought buzzing in my head that it was forbidden to exert mental control over novices during the first three years after they graduated from the Academy. Understanding how dangerous it would be to start an open confrontation with the Supreme Judge, I squashed my indignation. I would do better to use my accumulated ardor for self-control.

"Tell me, what happened at the mages'?" Koni stopped right in the middle of the hallway and nailed me with his stare. He was shorter than I, yet had perfected the skill of "looking down" at people. I started answering, choosing my words carefully:

"We were kidnapped immediately after our return from the Academy, and then those kidnapped were sacrificed, one after another. Then Archibald appeared and pulled me out of that hell. Monstrichello had the worst luck of all... What did they do to him?"

"They destroyed him without the possibility of respawn. The soul of the being, immune to magic, was supposed to activate the artifact, but for some reason it did not happen. What do you know about it?"

"About the activation? I don't know anything," I was surprised at that question, and from Koni's pursed lips figured out the Game told him I was telling the truth. I really knew nothing, either about the activation, or about the mysterious artifact... Had anyone even mentioned anything about Madonna's Diary? "I was sitting in the cage and thinking how great it was that I had reached level 11 in the Academy. That's the reason I survived and am standing here now."

"Which of the high-born mages ordered the beginning of the sacrifice?"

"Emm..." I even opened the Book of Knowledge to review that episode. "They did not mention names. It was some elf. Ask Devir – he would certainly know. Or Levard. I think he does know what actually happened there."

"I already spoke with the beings you mention. I am interested in your opinion."

"What opinion could I have? Devir commented on everything he did. Two Paladins were killed to get two mage slots. Monstrichello was killed to activate the artifact and then to receive a slot for another mage. By the way, what artifact are we talking about here? Levard interrupted Devir and demanded that the sacrifice be started immediately, as if he were in a hurry to get somewhere."

"How did Zangar die?" Koni changed the topic abruptly, ignoring my question.

"I killed him." I was not going to deny the obvious, but noted to myself how quickly the Judge showed who was who here. He did not last long with all that flirting like "as one Judge to another", "professional advancement", and all that. So be it, colleague, and I will respond in kind. "The Chancellor ordered us to have a duel, and I won."

"How did you manage to beat a being that was much stronger, wiser and more experienced than you?" The Supreme Judge would not relent, but by now I was ready to fight back:

"Does this have anything to do with the mages and the case you took away from me?" I raised an eyebrow quizzically. Inside I was bursting with desire to tell it all, about the duel, the initiation and Monstrichello's soul. But I had to resist. I had already guessed that by repeating my manipulation of Madonna's Diary after Zangar's teacher I had somehow managed to activate my artifact, while the necromancer got nothing. Perhaps it had happened because I was closer to the sacrifice. What I could not understand was Koni's interest in this matter. I seemed a little paranoid, but after the Academy I was planning to check even myself from time to time. Nothing and no one could be trusted in the Game.

"No, that's a personal request from the Viceroy – to find out what happened to the student of his closest advisor. After all, an experienced fighter was killed."

"I killed Zangar in honest battle. The Chancellor can confirm that." I was not going to back down.

"Did you kill Marinar as well?" Koni demonstrated that he was rather well informed about what had happened in the Academy.

"Yes. They wanted to kill me."

"How?" The broad-shouldered Judge was puzzled. "Two against one. One was an excellent fighter, the other a pretty good mage. I would like to see the video of that battle. You are an explorer and have the Book of Knowledge for an artifact, right?"

"True, but, unfortunately, I can't help with this." I decided to pull a trick of my own. "I cannot download the video – the artifact is not leveled up enough for that. As soon as the "Context Search" levels up, we can get back to this. Unless you provide to me an express course now so that it could upgrade," I suggested, knowing very well what the answer would be. Koni grimaced in displeasure, and my bout of euphoria passed. I had no more desire to tell him everything I knew. At that moment the Game informed me that "witness examination was complete", and I felt very silly. How could I have not guessed that it was not Koni pressing me, but the Game itself. Being an official witness turned out to be unpleasant. I must have looked really dumb talking back to the Supreme one, when I was a Judge myself.

"Find Judge Redel in the Sanctuary," Koni said curtly a couple of moments after the examination was over, not even looking in my direction. "He is the Head of the Judges' Panel. As for the video: it was just a request, nothing more. If you can't download it, I'll ask the Chancellor."

Without saying goodbye, the Judge rapidly walked back down the hallway, leaving me alone in the middle of it. The moment he disappeared behind a corner, Archibald appeared out of nowhere.

"Go straight – second door on the right." He looked me over, and shook his head in displeasure. "You held well, but made one mistake. Declare the information on the battle with Zangar to be confidential. You have the right to refuse to disclose information if it directly affects your safety. Go to the Sanctuary. Dolgunata is already waiting for you there. Do the Dungeons with her, both yours and hers. It will be useful for both of you. Take this – it will help you feel you are a player in your own right.

Archibald handed me a small glimmering rectangular card. The moment I took it, it disappeared with a blinding flash. Archibald commented on the system message that appeared before me:

"This is the mentor's permission to obtain a game communication device. Without it they won't sell you one in the Sanctuary. My number and

Dolgunata's will be automatically programmed into it. Get in touch with her and arrange to meet."

"When did she receive hers?" I was suddenly struck by a horrifying thought. "Before the Academy, or after it?"

"Before," Archibald took a long time answering. His permanent smile left his cat face while he was silent. "What does that give you?"

"She got in touch with you immediately after we were attacked," I started speaking bluntly. "Surely you are able to teleport to a place if you know the coordinates. But you did not appear when the mages took us. It's unlikely that Levard held you back – he was too busy to deal with you. Then all of a sudden you appeared right the middle of the cage without having any idea as to where it would be. There was no marker from Dolgunata on me – Devir stated that right away. So that means you were with us from the start under invisibility, just as you were just now."

"That's a funny conclusion, but let's suppose it's true. So then what?"

"Then?" I frowned. "You allowed the mages to kill the Paladins who had just came out of the Academy. Logir, Sartal and Monstrichello were killed right in front of you, and you did not make the slightest attempt to save them. But as soon as Levard started cursing about..."

Case initiated: Improper Behavior of the Paladin (Slots available for: 9 more cases)
Description: You consider that player Archibald behaved in a manner unworthy of the name of

Paladin by allowing the mages to kill your brothers in class
Task: Investigate this case and deliver a verdict
Case investigation: Not applicable; the case was initiated by the Judge himself
Period of limitation of action: None

I stopped, seeing the system message. I had a strong urge to send the catorian to respawn forever right away, but talking to the Supreme Judge had been useful to me; I decided to postpone further investigation till a more suitable occasion. I will use this ace in my sleeve later. No matter how good Archibald's intentions were, it is still unworthy of a Paladin to watch in cold blood as his brothers are being sacrificed. A cold shiver ran through me with my subsequent understanding: Archibald had actually been in that cage! He could see full well my manipulations with Madonna's Diary, and as soon as I activated it, he revealed his presence to everyone! He knows about restart!"

"Right, I decided that there was no point in hiding any longer. I got what I wanted," the catorian completed my thought. "Do you seriously consider that I should have sacrificed my interest for the sake of some half-baked not-quite- Paladins? They were already condemned as unworthy. Whether it was me or someone else, it didn't matter: I believe you get the point. Let's consider that you observed natural selection in action. As for Levard and his cursing – we'll talk about that later. I repeat – you answered Koni's questions well. Levard climbed too high using his artifact, and those who fly high fall long and hard. On his own or with some help. Right? The Viceroy does not forgive failures. I hope it's clear to you at what level the interested parties sit. Now you will go to the Sanctuary. Dolgunata will keep an eye over you. Do disappear for a couple of months so that even if they don't forget about you, they will at least stop mentioning you at every turn. You do understand how important this is for our COMMON effort? You got it right: I see very well in the dark; also I know a lot, and can surmise the rest. For example, who and where SHE could be. I'll be waiting for you after you are done with the Dungeons. Now go straight down the hall, second door to the right; I will sort things out with Garlion myself. Go!"

Archibald vanished as suddenly as he had appeared. His monologue provided plenty of food for thought, but first I needed to figure out what to do right away. Should I listen to the cat and go with the flow? Or listen to the cat and do the opposite? I liked the second option better, for I really hated following the demands of this flea-ridden beast. Catorian knew about restart a lot more than I did, but was in no hurry to share the information. Therefore, he was planning to use me while keeping me in the dark, forcing me to do whatever he needed for his own ends. I saw no difference between him and Koni. The latter at least told me openly that he was doing the Viceroy's bidding. I liked more and more the scenario where I ignored the catorian's direction: if he suggested that I go ahead, I needed to go back and catch Sharda. The way I saw it the gnome had owed me training ever since our first encounter before the Academy, so it should be possible to make him answer at least a couple of questions.

I found the Paladin I needed in the anchoring hall. He was sitting in the lotus pose in front of the darkened "sun", and presumably was contemplating things lofty and eternal. At least the expression on his face suggested precisely that. I felt awkward to distract the teacher, yet I cleared my throat a couple of times to attract his attention. The gnome startled and roused himself. The moment he opened his eyes I realized: the valiant Paladin was simply sleeping soundly.

Sharda blinked calmly a few times, then nodded:

"Have a seat, brother, we have just a few minutes before they notice you went missing and start looking for you. I need to tell you something."

I had the impression that no matter what I did, this Paladin would react as if he had known it in advance. Copying Sharda's pose, I settled next to him and became all ears.

"Archibald has reported to the Head of class that you have activated Madonna's Diary. The rules of the Game forced him to do that. Gerhard will hold the information back from the Viceroy to the extent possible to avoid unnecessary hullabaloo. Restart of the entire Game is looming close. You will be hunted. There are a lot more those who want to get the activated notes than we initially thought."

"We?" I could not help asking.

"It was foretold that I would find the Keymaster

when the Immune one appeared," ubiquitous Archibald stepped out of the shadows, not surprised in the least by my disobedience. "The mages were the first to find Monstrichello; they followed him for a couple of years until they made sure that he was precisely the one they needed. Then Devir started the hunt. The plan was to make the Immune one a mage; that way it would have been easier to kill him later. Devir decided that the quickest way to do it would be to impress the stupid ape with special effects. Actually, it could have worked if he had not become carried away. So, now we have what we have. Devir went to respawn and the Immune one decided to become a Paladin. It would be a shame not to use that situation to find the Keymaster. I sent just three Paladins in during this enrollment: Sartal, Nartalim and you. You were just an accident, a random pawn. Sartal and Nartalim both failed, but the pawn turned out capable of the knight's move. So we had to change all our plans quickly and bring new variables into the equation. You were so lucky and quick, that with Zangar's help you were able to grab the needed object. After the Immune one's death some scapegoats were needed, because the Game is very particular about its creations. Four extra mages were not too high a price, particularly since we were promised compensation for them. We would not be able to avoid killing them anyway: Paladins cannot betray their brothers-in-arms.

"Why are you telling me this now? What has changed in the last fifteen minutes? I could already be in the Sanctuary."

"Because you are closely watched by our wonderful Judge," Sharda grimaced. "You are wearing more bugs than a gypsy wears baubles. That's not even counting three headhunters who are following you. This is the only place in the Citadel protected from eavesdropping and unwanted ears. But you had to come here on your own accord and not because you were ordered. If you had gone to the Sanctuary, we would wait for the next Keymaster. We were not going to put our necks on the line without a good reason. After a year, ten, a hundred or a thousand, sooner or later Archibald would find him. Prophesies always come true. By the way, Archie, where are my granises? I told you he'd run to me rather than the Sanctuary, just to spite you."

"We'll settle it, you old trickster!" grinned the catorian.

It was so disgusting – feeling like a puppet in the paws of those two puppeteers.

"I was already running a risk, letting everyone know that I have some information," Archibald continued to enlighten me. "They already got in touch with me and demanded that I immediately present myself for interrogation. Now to the most important part: information on where to find Merlin's Diary and who could be Madonna is kept in the library in the restricted section. You need to get in there. Neither Sharda nor I will be able to help you with this. The guards will not let us in. Garlion, the Librarian, has access. And you killed his only son, just by sheer luck. So far it's the only way we know. Your task, as you might have already figure out, is to convince the elf to help you. Don't count on Sharda and me – that would be pointless. If we try to hustle too much, it will attract attention and bring up questions about you. Now all Garlion can think about is revenge, so it's better not to approach him directly. Find some method to pressure him. Of his own volition he will not help you, and it's not only because of his son. If he's caught disclosing information from the restricted section, he'll be stripped of his Librarian title and exiled from the Citadel in disgrace. So you have something to think about. Right? Just don't take too much time thinking. Gerhard will tell the Viceroy about you in six months — that's the time the Head of class has to prepare his report. So during this time you'll have to find Madonna and Merlin's Diary.

"Who was the third player?" Information was flowing like a river, unsettling me, but I was still able to ask the most important question. Without the answer to that it made no sense trying anything else.

"Pardon?" The catorian's face looked puzzled. "Two players restarted the..."

"Three. Madonna's Diary states it directly, but there is no mention of a name in it. The third player survived, that's why the world came out defective. Two players cannot accomplish full restart – it takes three."

"Sharda?" Archibald stared at the short Paladin.

"I will find out," the gnome grumbled, moving his lips as if recalling a text he had memorized. "If I could take a look at the notes..."

"No!" Archibald cut him off. "You will be forced

to inform Gerhard about what you saw. Yaropolk has little time as it is, and there is no need to reduce it further. Find the information regarding the third player!"

"Here you are!!" The door to the hall opened with a deafening squeak as one of the Paladins appeared in the doorframe. "Brother Yari, everyone's been looking for you! New Paladins need to be sent to the Sanctuary right away. This is a directive from Gerhard van Brast! Brother Sharda, don't delay him – I don't want to suffer just because you are slowpokes."

"He's all yours, brother Langirs," the gnome nodded, and resumed his meditation. Archibald was long gone – the head hunter had disappeared again.

Langirs was practically dragging me, trying to make it in time. The corridor and a few rooms flashed by so fast that I never had a chance to take a good look at them. All that I had time to do was to cast a quick glance around, letting my camera record the video and place it in the Book of Knowledge. I would review it in detail later. The Paladin dragged me into a small room with a flaming portal and pointed at it without too much ceremony or words of farewell. He shuffled his feet impatiently, hoping to be able to quickly report to his superiors that his task was accomplished. Funny – in the Academy I had thought that once one became a player, one ought to be regal, full of dignity and look at everyone with the eyes of a being who had attained true wisdom. Because, in essence, you would have gained immortality. But in fact, as it turned out, nothing changed. Some did not wish to stay at the bottom of the food chain, and desperately climbed back over the heads of their colleagues, meanwhile brown-nosing to the higher-ups or doing something nasty to them from envy; some simply used others to advance... The world cannot change or become different if we stay the same. Wherever we come, we bring our vices with us and then reap the results of our deeds.

"Come on!" Langirs sort of twitched towards me to push me into the portal. At the last moment he checked himself, but it was obvious that his impatience and desire to deserve some praise from his superiors was growing.. It seemed so funny to me that I dared play on my guard's vanity to extract some information from him.

"I so appreciate you helping me find the portal." I started working on implementing my ploy. "Next time I see Gerhard van Brast I will make sure to mention you to him as a conscientious and responsible Paladin."

"You... you know the Head?!" Langirs exclaimed in surprise, stuttering, as he was overcome by feelings. I could not lie – the Paladin could request confirmation from the Game – so my response was elaborate:

"Just a few hours ago I had a meeting with him, so yes, I can certainly say that we know each other. Is that so unusual?"

"N-no, it's just not so many brothers-in-arms know the Head of class personally." Langirs was stuttering from excitement, but still kept pushing me. I needed to build on my success before he decided that a bird in the hand in the form of immediate praise for sending me into the Sanctuary quickly was better than some hypothetical advantage from establishing an acquaintance with me. "Are you serious about mentioning me?"

"Sure, that's not hard for me," I grinned to myself as I heard confirmation of what I was thinking. NPCs, players... manipulation psychology works the same with all of them. So, let's use the rule of "you scratch my back and I'll scratch yours"... "But I have a question: what will I get in return? Because Gerhard will surely ask why I am telling him about you. I need to know how to respond to him."

I deliberately called the head of the Paladins of Earth by first name, causing Langirs to suffer yet another culture shock. Because for him Gerhard van Brast was the Head and there was no other way. I was looking at the Paladin, and did not share his feelings in the least. It felt like Gerhard was everything to him. Father, god, brother and devil only knows what else. Maybe I have just not been in the Citadel long enough, and with time I'll become the same. By the way! I wonder if there are devils in the Game?

"In our world they had been exterminated a long time ago; mostly, they live with the demons in their locations," Langirs responded. Apparently recent events had taken their toll on me: I was talking aloud without noticing it. I had to quickly review the record of the last minute, and only then sigh with relief: the only thing I had actually said to Langirs concerned the devils. I would have to pay more attention. "As for the question – yes, we can be of use to each other. I have access to the Armory and I can help with enhancement. But only after you talk to the Head."

"Enhancement... what is it...?" I frowned. "Additional plates for armor?"

"No, no – not at all," a patronizing smile flickered across the Paladin's face, and he hastened to demonstrate his knowledge: "Each class has just five sets of armor: the standard (the one you were issued before departure to the Academy), the Zharkee set that you are wearing now, Klifand, Daro and, finally, the Imperial set. It's possible to buy the first three, while the other two sets, Daro and Imperial, are only granted for special merit. So the majority can access only three types of sets."

"In the Academy the teacher spoke about twenty types of armor, and the best of those was Charleston armor. There was no mention of any Imperial set," I said with surprise.

"It's a popular misconception." The Paladin was practically glowing with self-importance. "You are confusing the kinds and types of armor. There are only five types, as I mentioned. But each type can be enhanced, leveling it up to Charleston armor. As you understand, this is true only for knights; other classes have their own kinds of armor. But in any case, the players must make sure to enhance their existing protection. Not all the classes have armor, but all want to live. You catch my drift?"

I mumbled something negative, amazed at the paucity of the class armor. In all the games I knew, armor was one of the key components for a successful fight against high level monsters. In reality I was in for a nasty surprise. Five types with twenty kinds each seemed like too few for the infinite Game, even to my inexperienced view.

"Intaglios!" Langirs said the unfamiliar word with great reverence and stood still, apparently expecting an excited reaction. But all he got was my stare without a spark of understanding. The Paladin was forced to launch into more explanations, making the best of what he was offering:

"The most popular method of improving armor is using enhancers: intaglios – otherwise called gems. These are gemstones with various properties. For example, they enhance defense, attack, or whatever else. Just a couple of well-selected gems and your chances to face a respawn pleasantly drop. I am sure that you have encountered them previously, before you became a player. Most symbols of power used by the NPC have them. You think crowns are purely decorative? Not so! They provide strong protection and suppression of will! An NPC with such a crown suppresses the will of people and drives them like a herd. Just gems, nothing complicated. Or charisma... But that is quite rare."

"Are you offering me some gems?" I asked immediately after the Paladin fell silent.

"No, no, I am just an ordinary Paladin of modest means, whereas gems don't come cheap at all." The Paladin pulled back. "I can help with installing them on the armor. It's not easy to install the gems just so – it requires skill. If we strike an agreement and you put a word in for me, I'll take you to the armor shop to the master of installation. But the gems themselves you will have to buy at an auction. Or find somewhere."

I felt as if I had been deceived, or at least disappointed. In my mind I already had a couple of gems settling in my pocket. So much effort just for some piddling middleman.

"Thank you for information. I will think about it," I said briefly, and noticed how Langirs pursed his lips. The Paladin had obviously expected a different answer. Well, it would be fair if we parted mutually disappointed. Since we could not be of use to each other, I did not waste time, and bravely stepped into the portal. A bout of dizziness was followed by the system message:

You have arrived at the Sanctuary of Game world: Earth
Quest available: Registration. Access the Registrar to receive the Dungeon token and initial tasks for class and specialty
Have a nice game!

The space around me solidified; right in front of me two creatures materialized, covering my entire field of view with their fat bodies; their sex was indeterminable, but they were baring their teeth in friendly grins. From the noise around I surmised that we were in some city, but I was unable to see any details. Directing all my attention to the greeters, I was trying to figure out their sex. Short hair, loose checkered unisex coats and army boots could confuse anyone, but seeing the makeup on their faces I decided to give this world a chance, and decided to consider them female. Of course, even in my time of being an NPC I had met men who quite confidently discussed recent trends in makeup. However, I hoped that here all normal guys would sock you one in the kisser for trying to use anything other than a shaving kit on their face. There was a time once when I contemplated why normal guys would decorate their faces. But then I looked at the girls drawing surrealistic eyebrows and pumping silicone into their duckface lips, and figured it out. The guys decided to save the world using their own beauty, before the victims of female logic do it in completely. Or they could be... different. What can I say? Tolerance is everything to us these days!

"Guten Tag! Möchten Sie Grossmünster besuchen?" the creature on the right asked, and I was glad as I realized two things. First, I was not wrong about the sex. Second, she was speaking German. That was the end of my rejoicing, since all the German I had was barely enough to identify the language.

As I was thinking what to do, other faces appeared among us. A small well-groomed man pushed himself in between the ladies somehow; he was wearing an elaborate green Renaissance period jacket.

"Ja, ja," the man was pushing with his elbows with great diligence, fighting for more space. From the effort his little face turned bright red, making an excellent contrast with his snow-white lace shirt-frill. Not in the least embarrassed by his ludicrous appearance, the man clicked his fingers right under my nose, puzzling me even further. Was there anyone at all here who was not completely bonkers?

"Sorry, mademoiselles, but this specimen of tourist fauna is mine. Sorry to disappoint you!"

"We have a quota!" The madam on the right barked. "We need to bring three more tourists to the church! Else Herr Schulz will be angry! He needs to visit Grossmunster!"

"He'll certainly visit it and have a chance to look at everything there in detail. Herr Schulz will be pleased with you," the shorty kept going, while I enjoyed the dialogue, now understanding why he had clicked his fingers. It's a pity the rest of my problems could not be resolved this way. "We'll be on our way then. All the best to you!"

The weirdo bowed and scraped for those broads so much it seemed they were just one step away from royalty. In turn, they transformed right in front of us: their cheeks blushed, their eyes started shining, and their coquettish smiles turned them into some cozy and homely gals into whose laps children would settle to listen to a fairy tale. They smiled, dropped their eyes and retreated, stepping slowly like respectable matrons, minding their own business, removing their coats as they walked – apparently to demonstrate to the short guy that they were not devoid of some beauty: it turned out that both were wearing boho dresses. What I didn't understand though, is why those women always look the same? Well, at least I was not wrong about their sex.

"Oh, those cute NPCs." My liberator looked

after the retreating women, then turned back to me. "One never knows what riddles the Game hides when it brings us close to these creatures. Allow me to introduce myself: Count Lefer de la Gant, a nobleman by birth, a bard and, if you would allow it, your guide and companion during your first visit to the Sanctuary, Paladin Yaropolk."

With a smooth move of a professional dancer Lefer stepped to the side, and, with a funny old-fashioned gesture, invited me to follow him. Seeing my confusion, the count added:

"Please forgive my forgetfulness. I should have explained everything to you from the start. We are now within the Sanctuary, otherwise called Zurich; it's one of the most splendid cities of this game world. You can consider this city an oasis in the desert of darkness and strife. Here you will not be threatened: neither by other players, nor by NPCs, who periodically try to inflict damage on each other that is incompatible with normal life. Nor is there a threat of cataclysms, floods or other natural disasters. The Game itself monitors compliance with the rules. You can safely rely on my talent as a guide. It would be unforgivable to leave Zurich without taking a look at all of its landmarks. Believe me, there are plenty of them here. I can confidently tell you that you are lucky to have me as a guide. I know this city like no one else. And we... is something bothering you?"

Lefer seemed to have stepped out of a fascinating historical adventure novel. With his manners, speech and gallantry he could have been the main hero and lover or a breakneck adventurist.

All he lacked to complete the image was a wide brimmed hat and the inevitable peacock feather. I could easily assume that right now Lefer was in fact wearing one, but had simply rendered it invisible. However, whatever he looked like – it was not that which bothered me. There are plenty of those who like cosplay, after all.

"I apologize for my inadvertent discourteousness; however, I have to admit that I have some insurmountable doubts with respect to our joint promenade in this wonderful place," I said suddenly, without expecting this kind of thing from myself. Damn – apparently this is contagious. But Lefer was impressed. I guess reading all those Dumas novels as kid had not been for nothing. His moustache twitched a couple of times, and then he spoke in a normal tone, without extra flourishness:

"Let's proceed to specifics. It will save us time. What are you unhappy about?"

"I will be glad to. I have a couple of questions for you. I am not going anywhere till I receive the answers. Why is the Sanctuary in Zurich? Should it not be in some hidden place, surrounded by force fields and high fences so that ordinary NPCs cannot access it? Something like Shambala or Eldorado? But Zurich? Then, I don't quite understand your role as a companion. Please clarify: who assigned you this role? And if so, why there were first two ladies who greeted me, and not you? Why should I believe you that it's safe here? And in particular, why should I go anywhere with you?"

"The monks of Shambala would not be

particularly happy if members of other classes were to appear at the doorstep of their Citadel," Lefer smiled, not fazed in the least by my speech. "Neither would the vampires of Eldorado. By the top-level decision of Heads of classes several hundred years ago Zurich was chosen as the Sanctuary, being the only city which is equidistant from all of the Citadels on Earth. The Game confirmed that, and now we have this incredible opportunity to enjoy peace and quiet in Zurich. I hope my answer to the first question is satisfactory to you?"

"More than satisfactory," I nodded.

"As for companionship, there is only one thing to tell you: it's a community work assignment, and I enjoy it no more than you do." Lefer was speaking in a calm and serious tone of voice. "Periodically every player receives a task like that; it just needs to be completed, regardless of anything, and then forgotten. Normally the meeting occurs in the central square, but you were delayed, and the arrival point coordinates shifted. Just about anyone could have met you there. Everything I said about the safety I can confirm with an oath. May the Game bear witness that I am speaking the truth."

For just an instance white fire flashed around the bard, relieving the enormous tension I had felt in my soul. I really was wondering why this green embroidered coat was following me. If this is his task, he may as well perform it well.

"What did you mention about a tour?"

Zurich turned out to be a rather interesting city. One could not say that its beauty compared to

Rome, Paris or London, yet it had its own charm. I was particularly impressed with the people – nobody was in a hurry to get anywhere. In my previous life I happened to live in a huge megalopolis, where time was quite valuable. Everyone was in a rush: to work, from work, to eat, to sleep, to die. In Zurich it was different. All the NPCs, local residents and tourists alike, wandered around the city slowly, in a strange melancholy, like someone in love after a successful date. Tired from walking for a long time we decided to have some coffee in a cozy little café. Watching it being made slowly, I realized that only those who know they have an eternity in store for them could be cooking that way. At some point the informational tables appearing above the NPCs heads were flickering in front of me so much, particularly when groups of tourists passed by, that I opened the settings and turned them off. My chest contracted: the world seemed practically the same as it had been before the Game. If I were to think that the players dashing back and forth were simply historical re-enactors or cosplayers, it would be as if nothing had happened to me. As if I were simply traveling and did not have an eternity before me.

"Let me consider my mission completed." Five hours after we met, Lefer sighed with relief, and with the familiar old-fashioned gesture pointed at the doors of the three-storey Town Hall. "I dare hope that your tour around Zurich will not fade from your memory for a long time, and during interminable winter evenings, as you enjoy a glass of wine in front of the fireplace, you would recall yours truly, wistfully and gratefully. I wish you a nice Game, monsieur Yaropolk; Count Lefer de la Gant is always at your service."

Nodding farewell to the count I waited till he turned a corner and opened the doors of the Town Hall.

"Purpose of your visit?!"

Two NPC guards blocked the way.

"Registration," I said, expecting to be let in right away.

"What registration? This is the City Council!" The first guard was not going to give up easily.

"I need to visit office number twenty-three." I started with a new approach.

"Introduce yourself. I need to see if you are on the list." The second guard brought out his tablet.

"Paladin Yaropolk!" Fatigue was taking its toll, after all; it had been a very busy morning. I was becoming irritated. That was not at all the kind of welcome I had expected.

"Right, there you are." The guard noted something in the tablet. "You were scheduled for twelve thirty; it's two forty-two now. You can sign up for tomorrow... wait, no – we are all booked. The soonest appointment available in office twenty-three is the day after tomorrow, at five thirty. Shall I book it for you?"

"No! I need it today! Now!" My temper boiled over.

"Calm down, or else we'll have to call the police. You are late. Other visitors are being seen now. Are you signing up for the day after tomorrow?"

"Yes," I barked, not even trying to calm down. I wondered: did Lefer know that the registration was time-specific? Most likely he had – yet he still dragged me on that tour. The door opened, and a hunter dressed in leather armor appeared. Glancing at me briefly, he approached the guard, introduced himself and easily received a pass for that very office number twenty-three. I cursed silently, turned around and took my anger out on the door. What was I supposed to do in Zurich for two days?

"What an encounter! What a pleasure seeing you again! I take it you had some issue with the registration?" Grinning Lefer was waiting for me at the entrance to the Town Hall. Now I will very likely find out what was all this elaborate setup for. Surely not just for the fun of it. "I could offer my humble services and help to speed up the process. As it happens, the Registrar, Claude, owes me a favor. For a modest fee of half a granis it will be my pleasure to help you complete your registration now, rather than in a couple of days."

"How nice of you," I grinned. "Are you sharing with Claude? Will I have to pay him separately, or will half a granis cover all the expenses?"

"It's a pleasure when your vis-à-vis understands you so well. Another half a granis will be Claude's compensation, as he'll have to stay at work late. If you don't have this sum, we could make an agreement."

"Guarantees." I cut off the eloquent bard. He was quite a sweet talker. A plan was gradually taking shape in my mind.

"Is my word not enough?" Lefer's indignation was quite sincere. "Have we not become friends during the time that we have known each other? Why would I deceive a friend? Well, it was unfortunate that I forgot about the time of the appointment. But this kind of slip could happen to anyone. I am willing to extend a helping hand. Lefer never abandons his friends! Just half a granis and I will solve the problem!"

"A granis," I clarified. "You seem to be continuously forgetting Claude's share."

"Really, it is so fortunate that your memory is so powerful," Lefer regained his cheerful mood. "You are right – it will be a granis altogether. I understand; to a beginner player this amount may be excessive, so we could make an agreement to complete the Dungeon. Take us along! This will be enough to cover all our obligations under the agreement."

Now I understood the true purpose of the affair. In effect, those conmen were not running any risk. Attacking players in the Sanctuary was prohibited, so there was no danger of physical damage. Then, not all newbies knew that it was possible to initiate a case for extortion, besides which, they would be unlikely to want to spend their time dealing with it; Lefer must not really hope for granises, because normally a new player would be a poor player. So here's the conclusion: either a player would just quietly wait it out and register a couple of days later, or take this whole bunch along to the Dungeon. The part that was not clear was why were they were all so eager to go through the Dungeons with the newbies.

"I want to talk to Claude first." I decided to pretend that I was ready to agree, but still had some doubts. The Game had not yet offered to open a case, but I was certain that it would do so at any moment now. These conmen were quite unlucky to try and snag a Judge. "If he confirms that he is ready to help me register today rather than wait for two days, then we'll talk about agreements."

"That's reasonable. Would you perhaps like to have a seat?" Lefer pointed at the nearest bench. An enamored NPC couple suddenly jumped up, yielding their seats to me. I looked at the bard with a different eye: he was obviously using a will suppressor.

Five minutes later Lefer returned from the Town Hall and happily informed me that all the formalities had been settled and Claude had kindly agreed to see me even though he had been working with another visitor at the time. Of course he would, when the prey was practically begging to be skinned.

This time the guards paid zero attention to me and Lefer, and I freely ascended to the second floor, into the realm of bureaucracy. Clerks were running to and fro everywhere, pitiful in their attempts to look important by looking grim and wearing dark blue business suits. It's funny, but the lower a clerk's position is on the career totem pole, the more effort he puts into pretending he is exceedingly busy, checking his watch every minute or continuously pressing buttons on his smart phone. And you will never guess that he is checking his watch not because he is hurrying along with his important clerk business, but because it's time to set his slaves to work in yet another computer game, or he is already expected at an online casino; and he is fiddling with his phone because you are distracting him, and he is having a hard time aiming his angry bird at the target. While if you see grey people, listlessly leafing through never-ending piles of paper, you may count on that being someone who will definitely help you. Because he is wearing grey not because that's the color he prefers, but because he long since lost his taste for life, having to work hard to cover for all those nincompoops. But those true slaves of the office are few and far between.

"This is outrageous!" The hunter I had seen previously was yelling when Lefer and I opened the door to office twenty-three. He was hanging over the desk and screaming at the gnome, who was impassively looking at the player over his glasses. "I will complain!"

"It's up to you, random assignment is not subject to control." The gnome shut his notebook and turned to us. "Lefer, is everything all right?"

"You could say so," the bard nodded, pushing me into the office and shutting the door. "Yaropolk wanted to talk about the details in person before entering into the agreement."

"Just a moment; I'll just finish with this," the gnome said, and returned his attention to the previous visitor. He rose slightly from his chair and leaned towards the hunter, who had been taken aback by us barging in. "Please leave my office! Your registration is complete! Continue on to the assigner! Office number thirty-one!"

I smiled bitterly: bureaucracy! Bureaucracy

everywhere! One registers, the second assigns, certainly the third does the paperwork and the fourth signs and approves! No – it should be the fifth who approves! I seem to confer too much responsibility on the fourth one.

"I did not...," the hunter started, but was cut off immediately:

"Shall I call security?!" The gnome was getting really worked up. Another moment and he'd start spitting fire! "Get out of my office!"

The hapless visitor, as he was leaving, took his irritation out on the door, just as I had a few minutes earlier. Immediately making a friendly face, the gnome, smiling as if nothing happened, offered me the armchair:

"What is it that you want to discuss?"

"Is it possible for me to choose the location where I am registered?"

"Well...," the gnome hesitated but his furtive eyes and quick exchange of glances with Lefer told me that it was possible, even though not included in the original price.

"Lefer will get his share," I promised, and the registrar smiled with obvious relief and leaned back in his chair. He didn't want to share with his accomplice. "But I need guarantees. Just your word is not enough. I don't know you."

"Neither do we know you," the gnome immediately quipped.

"That's right. My conditions are as follows: you register me today to California, assign me to two of the most interesting Dungeons, send me to a Judge, provide me a communication device, since I have my mentor's permission already, and give me extra complex class quests, the quests to explore something interesting... and for this each of you will receive..." I fell silent, and looked at Claude questioningly.

"You take us along to both Dungeons," the registrar named his price.

"And for this you will receive one Dungeon and a granis each," I responded in kind, outlining my conditions. "And you will receive them now, without any extraneous loan agreements or other delays. One granis to each. Here and now. Agreed?"

"One and a half," Lefer came to the pensive registrar's aid. "A granis and a half each, but after we complete the Dungeon. You don't have to do it now, we'll wait."

"One and a half," I agreed easily, noting the unexpected comment. "Or do you prefer three hundred kilos of gold each?"

"No! We want it in granises!" the gnome said worriedly. "We don't need gold. Only granises! And only after the completion of the Dungeon!"

I was starting to like the Game more and more. A Judge calmly bargaining about the amount of the bribe – that's the way it was; that's what I was used to.

"Agreed. So then I look forward to receiving the agreement from you stating all that we have just specified. May I wait here?"

Case initiated: Zurich Conmen (Slots available for: 8 more cases)

Description: You believe the actions of the bard Lefer de la Gant to be unlawful; there is clear evidence of criminal conspiracy between him and registrar of players <hidden> Claude de Leur.
Task: Investigate this case and deliver a verdict
Case investigation: Not applicable; the case was initiated by the Judge himself
Period of limitation of action: None

The information on initiating the case appeared at the moment when the agreement was handed to me. Actually, I had expected the case would appear much earlier, but apparently my subconscious waited for us to proceed from discussion to action. As they say, you can't put the words into a case. A quick glance at the agreement confirmed that I received guaranteed assistance in selecting registration location in case of voluntary contribution to provide aid to the poor and starving Lefer and Claude amounting to three granises, to be paid following our joint completion of the Dungeon. The document was already signed by the other party, and I rubbed my hands in anticipation. It's time to show these jerks who is the hand of justice here!

"For abuse of official capacity and extortion, I sentence Lefer de la Gant to stripping of his 'guide' status, to prohibition from occupying such a position in the future, and impose on him a fine, to be paid to the Game, in the amount of ten granises; Claude de Leur shall be stripped of his position of registrar and prohibited from occupying any administrative position within the Game in the future; I also impose on him a fine to be paid to the Game in the amount of ten granises. The verdict is final and not subject to appeal!"

Verdict is confirmed
Verdict is deemed optimal
The case "Zurich Conmen" has been closed.
Sentence has been executed by the Game
Award for correct verdict: basic Energy level
increased by 100

Oh, this scene was worth all the trouble and nerve-wracking. I enjoyed the moment of triumph without even trying to conceal my broad smile. The gnome kept gulping air, trying to say something, unsuccessfully. Lefer was outwardly calm at hearing my verdict; in any case, only his twitching right moustache betrayed his state outwardly. But I could not care less about their feelings. In addition to my satisfaction from the righteous revenge, I felt internal satisfaction with myself at a professionally investigated case. At least so it seemed to me.

A portal suddenly opened in the room, and a sleepy leprechaun wearing flower-patterned pajamas fell out of it. Blinking to clear his vision, he was looking around, trying to assess the lay of the land. Seeing the pantomime "two in a state of shock", he hemmed, looked at me, hemmed again, then sat down at the desk and pushed the intercom button. A secretary ran in at once.

"Two cups of coffee, please." The leprechaun's voice was high and light. "I need to wake up."

The new owner of the office turned out to be active and down-to-business. Presenting me with one cup of coffee, he asked me to wait while he dealt with urgent matters: procedure for being confirmed at the new position, preparing an inquiry for a list of all the players registered by the previous occupant, clarification of the rules and specifics of registration. Finally, having donned a classic dark blue suit that concealed information on class, the leprechaun proceeded to deal with me.

"I don't even know where to start. Thank you, first of all... I applied for an administrative position several decades ago and it has only been granted now. Even though it's in such a second-rate game world. Earth... What a weird name... So, let's start. I know your preferences, but I cannot help you: registration and assignment are performed by the Game. It is the only one who knows where you can best use your skills and abilities. You are assigned to Moscow. You have been allocated a studio apartment at the address... 16 Nth Street, Apartment 48. You are assigned to complete level 2 Dungeon 'Alveona'. The keys to the apartment and access keys for the Dungeon will be issued to you by the assigner. Then, in the Sanctuary you should see Judge Redel to receive initial Judge quests, Paladin Grizdan to receive initial class quests and archivist Taleem at the Sanctuary library to receive initial explorer's quests. That's about it. Oh, no, not quite – you should also visit office thirty-one. More coffee?"

CHAPTER TWO

PREPARATION

I LEFT THE TOWN HALL building a couple of hours later! It took me two hours to complete all the procedures before the Game informed me that I was officially registered in the game world "Earth". Those clerks had run me ragged, and I craved just one thing: a soft and warm bed. The Book of Knowledge got its bearings instantly and a green arrow appeared I front of me, pointing to the nearest hotel.

Zurich met me with cold evening air. Six o'clock!

"Young man wants to enjoy himself?"

It was not immediately obvious to me that this hoarse smoker's voice was addressing me. Pulling my tired eyes away from the blinking pointer, I concentrated on a bedraggled plump woman way over forty. I grimaced involuntarily: checkered tights, short leather skirt, red blouse with only one button closed and bright makeup clearly indicated this NPC's occupation.

I stopped, taken aback. The woman interpreted my stopping as being interested; she hastily exhaled a stream of cigarette smoke and continued with her lively invitation:

"Girls and boys of all colors and ages will fulfill your every whim!"

This bedraggled peddler of sex stared at me unblinkingly, like a fish. It made me sick to my stomach. It was not as though I really hated people of her profession, but I was always overcome with disgust when I encountered such characters. I did not bother them, they did not bother me, and everyone was happy with that. But now, looking at this forward pimp, I wished like never before to make sure that this filth would never exist anywhere again.

Case initiated: Moral Degradation (Slots available for: 8 more cases)
Description: You consider it is not acceptable to engage in prostitution and provide sex services in the Sanctuary
Task: Investigate this case and deliver a verdict

Puzzled, I read the message at least three times. What did that mean? The Judge was supposed to judge players and minions. The Game took care of

NPCs on its own. So what was I supposed to do now? I thought for a minute, decided that at that point I had no choice anyway, and stifling my disgust, started the investigation. The best place to start would be to interrogate her:

"In the name of justice I demand that you speak the truth and nothing but the truth! You are being detained as a suspect in the case "Moral degradation". For the duration of your testimony you are released from all physical, moral and emotional bonds. Anything you say can be used against you when producing the verdict."

The NPC's eyes glazed.

"I acknowledge your right to administer justice," the woman drawled in an emotionless voice, and stilled, waiting for the next question.

"Name?" I gingerly started with the simplest part. NPC tourists passing by pretended that we did not exist and only a few players stopped nearby, intrigued by the show. Who cares! First I needed to deal with the pimp.

"Samantha Durs. Also known as Firefly."

"Age?"

"Twenty-seven."

I hemmed: the young woman looked so old and bedraggled, even though her life had been so short.

"How long have you been working as a prostitute?"

"Since I was fourteen. For the past two years I've been working as a pimp."

"Why did you become a prostitute?"

"I was thrown out of my home. First my

stepfather raped me. I told my mother, but she didn't care about me, all she cared about was downing another glass. She screamed like crazy that it was my own fault, that I seduced her dear hubby so that I could have him all to myself. Then they threw me out into the street like a dog. Then Rick found me there, had fun with me and then gave me to his friends; then he took me to the brothel to work for him. They always like young girls there."

"Why did you not go to the police?"

"Never had a chance. First Rick locked me up, beat me up and had me gang-raped to make me more agreeable. When I gave up, he sent me out to work the street. I was sixteen, and that was all the life I knew. Who would need me here? I had no education, no money, no connections. There was no reason for me to go to the police, so I stayed with the 'Lush Garden'. Now I am fine here."

"So you would not want to leave the streets?"

"Not really. I am fine with what I do. I don't get gang-raped or beat up any more, now I can arrange that for the young new ones. I like to whack the new kids. I like smoking grass with Rick and I sniff coke. I like feeling important. In a different life I wouldn't have any of this."

I grimaced in disgust and practically forced myself to say:

"I don't have any more questions for you. In the name of justice I release you from the obligation to speak the truth and nothing but the truth." Samantha's eyes cleared. But there was no erstwhile indifference in them. Her eyes, faded from long use of drugs, were full of fear. The NPC was so afraid of me that her knees were shaking; she seemed completely unconcerned by a trickle of wetness that started down her stockings.

"Samantha Durs! I pronounce you guilty of engaging in prostitution and violence towards minors, and sentence you to death! This verdict is final and not subject to appeal!"

Initially I had planned to fine the woman, or sentence her to community work, or devise whatever other punishment, but Samantha's statements had sealed her fate. There was no place for her in the world into which I came!

"I beg you, don't!" Samantha barely had enough strength to crumble down to her knees. She had no doubts of my right to sentence her to death; she just vainly hoped to receive mercy by begging. "Don't! I beg you, take this, that's all I have!" "The woman quickly took something off her neck and pushed it into my hands. "Just don't..."

**Verdict not confirmed, case investigation
incomplete
Case "Moral Degradation" is relegated to the
nearest Judge. Remaining verdict error limit: 99**

The world exploded in blinding white shards. The left side of my body became both numb and fiery hot, making me scream with torturing pain. My legs went out from under me; I crashed down on the pavement and rolled around trying to beat down the flames. The pain was so extreme that I lost all self-awareness.

"So in addition to everything else you are a Dark one?" It felt like I was burning for an interminable time before it all ended, leaving behind just a phantom of the pain. Breathing heavily, I realized that I was next to Samantha, who was frozen in place like a stone statue. We were both lying on the ground. "Get up – enough of soiling the title of Judge."

Shaking off the residue of pain I stood up sharply. A leprechaun was standing next to me, looking at my dirty armor in disgust. In his hands he was twirling a small object; the Book of Knowledge identified it as Samantha's cross on a chain. In her pleadings the woman had pulled it off and shoved it into my hand as a bribe.

"It's amazing how many true believers there are among prostitutes." The leprechaun followed my gaze and relaxed his fingers; the cross and chain fell to the ground. "A common cross pendant turned into a source of Light and nearly sent for respawn a Dark one playing a Judge. Congratulations! You failed this case most spectacularly."

"Would you perhaps at least introduce yourself?" I did not like the tone of the leprechaun as he started this dialogue. Of course, kudos to him for taking the cross away and all. I am filled with gratitude and such, yet my pride would not allow me to forgive someone openly mocking me even so.

"Of course I will – what else?" The leprechaun pulled out a vial from virtual space and sprayed the air around him, grimacing in displeasure all the while. The fragrance of lilacs floated on the air. "Judge

Redel at your service. I hope you will take care to clean your armor? Well, do it later, as now we need to deal with poor Samantha. Aren't you a hero: just barely showed up in the city and already found yourself a prostitute and sentenced her to death. What did she do – deny you service?"

Without waiting for me to respond, Redel approached the immobilized Samantha, donned rubber gloves, pulled out a small pair of pincers and lifted the woman's left eyelid. She did not even twitch.

"Well, well, well. A procurer, thirteen years in the profession, lately business has not been too good, not making enough money to get a dose... Where's the interrogation record?"

A shining scroll appeared out of the air. The leprechaun perused it quickly and stared at me in amazement:

"And that's all you found out from the suspect?!"

Redel was obviously used to asking rhetorical questions. Without waiting for me to answer again, he started his own examination:

"Tell us, madam, how many minors do you have in your care and where are they now?"

"Thirty two." The prostitute regained just enough mobility to be able to answer. "They are locked in the brothel's basement. I need to feed them at least once a day, or else they'll croak."

"Who else knows about them other than you?"

"Only Rick does, but if they were to croak he'd just find new ones. He was never worried by the bodies."

49

"And the keys to the basement are...?"

"In my pocket. I don't trust anyone, so I carry them with me at all times. If something happens to me, at least I'll not die alone."

"Where do we find Rick?"

"He spends his evenings in the 'Lush Garden' with his gang."

"Now that's really it," the leprechaun said, pleased; then looked at Samantha, pulled out a small vial, put a drop from it on the woman and commanded: "Die!"

Her eyes opened wide as she tried to scream but failed: her vocal cords did not work anymore. I grimaced from the sight: the NPC started imploding as if dissolving from inside.

"Since you are new, I'll give you a couple of free lessons." The leprechaun was not very original, and started with his advice, paying no attention to what was going on. He bent down to the remains and pulled a bunch of keys from the dead NPC's pocket. "Lesson number one: for a Judge all cases are equal. There cannot be a case that you like or don't like. Emotions have no place in this. All the cases need to be investigated most thoroughly. Any error will result in a fine. The Game doesn't care about the kids locked in a basement – so what if they die? – but the Judge must do his job thoroughly. Forget the distributed judiciary system. From now on you are a Judge in the Game! You are the investigator, the prosecutor, the attorney, the Judge and, well, an executioner if need be. We have a singular right to judge. Lesson number two: if new facts appear in the course of investigation, you need to initiate an additional case and investigate it as well. You found out about Rick. Why did you decide to pretend that this did not concern you? That's why the Game punished you, and not because you decided to sentence the prostitute to death. Even if you were to kill her without any trial at all, no one would say a word to you. Within the Sanctuary players are completely safe, and the police turn a blind eye to things like that. If need be, the Game will simply generate new residents. Oh, and lesson three: cut that out – all those high-flown statements – "in the name of justice", "the sentence is final" and such. It is enough if you say them in your mind – no reason to entertain the public like a clown. Those phrases belong in the courthouse, not in a dark alleyway. And last: if you decide the person should die – kill them yourself, don't wait for headhunters."

A street cleaner slowly approached us and began putting Samantha's remains away into a trash bag. The NPC's face showed no emotion, as if he were dealing with a pile of leaves.

"Here's a good remedy I am happy to recommend." Redel showed me the vial he had used on the prostitute. "Alrian oil. Dissolves bones and tendons and pumps the body full of adrenalin, so that the victim does not lose consciousness and its heart only stops half an hour later. Even now Samantha is alive and feeling all the aspects of her unenviable situation. Criminals should be punished, but no one said the punishment should be painless. She tortured the minors, so now she may suffer herself. In this world Dark ones need to generate emotions themselves to replenish their Energy. In this respect, just in every other, actually, Judges' hands are not tied."

"What do you mean by 'in every other'?" I caught the phrase, but the answer came to me unbidden: "So it means that in the Game there are no regulations and laws that we may follow? Only the internal feeling of being right? But this is complete anarchy!"

"You only figured that out now? The Game doesn't care about any laws players invent for themselves to fit their needs; all it cares about is self-preservation. Judges have the right to judge in whichever way they please. Why do you think I am sitting here in the Sanctuary? It's not just me – the entire Panel of Judges of Earth would not dare take a step out of Zurich!"

"Because a Judge is target number one for any player," I grumbled heavily, feeling just how unenviable my situation was. "Since we have the right to judge in line with our current perception of the world, we become extremely undesirable figures. Because today we may think one way, tomorrow another, the next day something else, and every time we sincerely believe in what we are thinking. No one knows what to expect from us, what will wander into our heads... But then what does the Emperor confirm? What for? Or is it all fake?"

"The Emperor checks whether a Judge sincerely believes his verdict is just, whether he sincerely believes that the punishment is commensurate to the crime, as well as whether the

Judge took into account all the circumstances when delivering the verdict, as it was in this case. If Samantha had not mentioned Rick, your investigation would have been deemed successful. So... I took the keys, tomorrow morning I will generate a quest – send some young players to release the kids. As for you – it is preferable for you not to show up in my office tomorrow. As you understand, the life of Judges is not easy in our world, so without a high-level protector it is not a good idea to advertise what you do. Level up some, find someone who will stand up for you; then you will be able to present yourself to the world as a Judge. Registrars will keep silent; nobody else on Earth knows who you are."

"Some players saw me questioning Samantha."

"You'll have to deal with them yourself. If you want, find them and make arrangements. Or forget about it if that's what you prefer. That's for you to decide. But I do need to assign some kind of case to you. Let it be the one about the stolen pendant. There is a similar quest – we'll use it to cover up the investigation. Go to the bank tomorrow morning; I will leave an envelope for you under a new name with a description of the case and the quest. What is your name now?"

"Evgeniy Frolov," I responded. The new name to be used with NPCs had been assigned to me in the Town Hall together with the "legend" for life on Earth. From now on I was a fitness instructor at one of the gyms in Moscow. There was no reason to even bother to remember my new name; while talking to NPCs "Evgeniy Frolov" would transform into "Paladin

Yaropolk" and vice versa. In this sense the Game took great care to preserve the NPCs minds: to them my game name would have sounded silly and strange.

"Fine. What else? Oh, of course! I forgot to tell you one of the most important things: stop judging NPCs! The teachers were supposed to have told you: anything NPCs do is predicated by the algorithms of the Game and a Judge does not need to bother with them at all. Even if they were to all exterminate each other, we care only about the players and minions. But still, if you decide to level up using NPCs, do it skillfully and professionally. Remember why you initiated a case against the prostitute: because you decided that she was a criminal. You evaluated her in accordance with your moral system. As a starting point that's fine. For small cases that are judged correctly the Game will enable you to increase Energy, but that only works in the beginning. And don't forget the limit of 10 concurrent cases. The more you disapprove, the more you suffer. For example: is that young man not committing a wrongdoing?"

Redel pointed out a young guy jaywalking. The NPC had supposed that in the falling darkness no one would notice his transgression, but my view differed: a message on initiation of a new case flashed in front of me immediately. Redel hemmed: he had expected my reaction.

"That's exactly the situation against which I am trying to warn you – you should not let your internal self control you. Jaywalking, being noisy at night, flashy clothing, aggressive behavior – you should dispense with internal evaluations. Every time you disapprove of an NPC, the Game perceives this as a signal to open a case. It's more complicated with players. I'll tell you about that later, after we finish the case with the pendant. Let's see how good you are at learning lessons. Perhaps Koni was too hasty when he sent you to me."

Seven hours later I was sitting on a bench in a Zurich courtyard and contemplating. I really wanted to find a nice bed and get some sleep, but life was conspiring against me. Redel was right: the problem with an internal assessment of whether others' actions were right or wrong was real and something needed to be done about it. I punished the jaywalker with a couple of days of community service and received a unit of Energy. The verdict was deemed correct. Then there was an arrogant woman who pushed me because I was standing in her way. Again community service and a unit of Energy for me. A young girl with a dog who crapped on the sidewalk. Same thing. A loudly laughing couple, a group of slightly tipsy friends. A punk, striding peacefully somewhere. A policeman smoking on duty... The moment I thought that an NPC was doing something wrong, the Game instantly initiated a case which needed to be immediately investigated.

Another problem appeared that I had not thought of previously: correct verdicts increased my Energy level by twelve units, yet the bar was not even close to being full. As the interface informed me, the game world "Earth" had practically no available Energy! It would take a week to reach full level with the crumbs that were available from the surroundings! In the Academy I was used to relying on shields that were active all the time, and now I felt unprotected and vulnerable. Something needed to be done about that. It was impossible to continue on elixirs alone, I needed regeneration. I hoped Gromana would explain how Dark ones survive in the Light worlds. I did not feel like continuously torturing NPCs, extracting emotions from them as it had happened with Samantha.

"Would you like some coffee?" A sweet voice jerked me out of my slumber. I had fallen asleep unawares. "It's cool; you've been sitting here all night and must be chilled."

A huge woolly sweater was standing next to me; above it was a lovely face framed in blond hair. Smiling, the blue-eyed charmer extended me a cup from which the exhilarating fragrance of freshly made coffee was floating.

"Warm yourself! It's fresh here in the mornings."

"I do love coffee." I beamed, took the cup and tensed. The girl was perfect. Her appearance was so close to my ideal of beauty that there was no doubt: our meeting was no accident. Particularly since the girl was an NPC and spoke Russian to me.

"How long have you been in Zurich, and where are you from?"The girl's voice was so sweetly delicate it made her even more attractive.

"From Moscow." The red flags in my mind were flapping madly. "Thanks for the coffee, but I have to go. It has been a pleasure to meet you." I slowly retreated from the girl.

"Helen!" The girl extended her hand, not in the least embarrassed. "We have not introduced ourselves yet. And what is your name?"

"Good bye!" I ignored her hand, put the cup on the nearest bench and quickly left the courtyard. I heard a disappointed sigh behind me, and it took me an effort to not look back. The girl was really good, but I valued my own hide more.

Avoiding crowded locations since I did not want to incur more cases, I went to see the archivist Taleem. Before meeting Dolgunata or Gromana I needed to research something in the Sanctuary Library.

"How can I help the new player?" Taleem was a short and plump warlock. He continuously adjusted his glasses that kept sliding to the tip of his nose, and periodically cast a menacing glance around the reading room looking for potential disrupters of the order. There were no players among the visitors; just a few random NPCs were leafing through the books and surreptitiously photographing the richly decorated hall. Tourists: what do you do...

"I would like to receive a quest..." I gave the information letter to the librarian. "I decided to become an explorer, like you."

"Explorer, hm," Taleem looked at the papers briefly and ordered the closest NPC: "Keep an eye over the room. I need to step out."

The warlock calmly took off for the internal rooms of the library, inviting me to follow him.

"Are you interested in something in particular? Or would you prefer to have the Game select a quest for you?" Taleem asked laconically. That is an enviable level of skillful handling of information: clear and to the point. If you need to issue a quest, why waste two hours following the social norms talking about weather and politics? Come, receive, leave. Perfect time management.

"I have no specific predilections," I responded cheerfully. "I would prefer something simple to begin with. I would like to understand the principle of exploration quests. The second quest may be more complex."

"Second? The librarian was surprised. This is a library, not an almshouse. If you need a second quest, you'll have to pay."

We entered a small room filled with books. Taleem dug into the pile and extracted a dusty tome.

"Here! That's your quest. Find out what it is and for what purpose it exists in this world."

All I was able to notice before I carelessly took the object in my hands was that the tome was ancient, and that it was made of human skin. As I took the book, I once again felt the whole range of feelings I had experienced yesterday as I encountered a source of Light.

"Are you Dark then?" the warlock asked in disappointment, releasing me from the hellish flames. He dropped the book back onto the pile "That's a shame; I would like to have found out about this thing. So, then, take this map, it needs to be completed. You are being sent to Moscow; that's good – this map is from Russia. So, this will be your quest."

I took the scroll, unrolled it carefully and stared

at the so-called "map". Some child, on a piece of paper bearing food stains, had scribbled carefully "Home" "Treasure" "Road" and connected them with a dashed line. There were squiggles, presumably indicating trees, and a "scary" skull in the right corner. I stared at the librarian skeptically and waved away the message concerning the quest.

"The author's coordinates are on the back of the scroll," Taleem said as if nothing had happened. "Your task is to find out everything about the "Treasure". You will receive three additional Book levels as a reward."

"But those are just scribbles!" I was unable to contain myself.

"That's right. And you will turn them into a serious document. The minds of NPC children are not capable of original creation; the Game uses them to send us riddles. The more careful you are about the details, the more reliable and precise the research result will be. So your disdain for these 'scribbles' is inappropriate. For your information, America was discovered that way as well. This completes the mandatory part. Anything else?"

"Also, I have some questions," I started habitually.

"And I have some answers." Taleem smiled in a predatory manner. "One twentieth of a granis apiece."

"Accepted," I sighed. What do you do – "those who own information, own our granises", so it made no sense to bargain. "I have two questions. First: what books will help me level up my artifact? Second: what do players receive for successfully completing a

---

Dungeon?"

Taleem grimaced in displeasure, pursed his lips and replied:

"The answer to the first one: those you have not read yet. Answer to the second one: players receive a reward. You owe me one tenth of a granis.

I lifted my eyebrow questioningly.

"That's not fair! It's not an answer!"

"The answer corresponds to the question!" The warlock raised his voice. "Some explorer, aren't you! Is that how you treat information?! Your questions are supposed to bring precise and concise answers that would bring you one step closer to your goal. Just one step! Any leap in knowledge can rob you of significant detail."

I sniffed in disappointment but had to admit the comment was fair.

"The money's gone," I took into consideration all that was said and decided to approach it from a different angle: trying to elicit pity. "That's why I am here – no one taught me the basics; I had to study everything myself. As for exploration, all I have..," I stumbled remembering the present from the Chancellor of the Academy. I didn't want to reveal all my secret trumps. It was possible that the Explorers' Book was not unique in the least and it was possible to buy one at every street corner, but before exposing it I should study it myself.

"So what is it that you have as an explorer?" Taleem asked with interest.

"My interest to explore and desire to develop my artifact," I reported quickly. "Dear Taleem, I would be glad to pay you a quarter of a granis, if you share the information. You did understand what I was trying to ask, right?"

"Half," the warlock started haggling. "In addition I'll teach you how to ask questions properly."

"One third," I decided to dig in my heels. "I am smart; over time I would figure it out myself, so your assistance is not really unique. And it's way too expensive for a poor explorer.

"Two fifths," the librarian resisted. "Or hit the road and try to find another keeper of knowledge. I am sure in Zurich there are tons of those who want to help you for free."

"Two fifths and you'll provide me the books to develop my artifact." I gnashed my teeth inwardly and decided to give some. I needed information like air, and there was no other place I knew to obtain it. When I tried to access the Temple of Knowledge at night the request was denied. I still had enough granises but they were evaporating at an alarming rate.

"Agreed. The answer to the first question: yes, an explorer can develop his artifact through books. But only through those that describe the game world. You can't take a book, say, on physics and level up. Our library has one hundred and seventeen of the books you need. I will provide seven of them for you to explore. There are twenty more that I can make available for an additional granis. Thirty two books you will be unable to use since they are sources of Light; the rest you could only access by permission of their owners. I can tell you their names, but none of them are on Earth any more. As for the second question: the player, or players, depending on the situation, receive the final prize; sometimes it's granises. But it's not always a treasure chest. It could be gems, or an artifact enhancer, or some other unique object. The power of the Dungeon monsters and value of the reward object are directly related to the number of the party, up to ten – that's the limit for the group. I suppose I don't need to mention the importance of the final prize for the player and how heated things become after the last boss is downed? It's simpler to pay a fine for breaching the agreement and go for respawn rather than let someone take a gem that's a ten times enhancer."

"Lovely," I drawled. I had guessed, of course, that the erstwhile registrar had a reason for wanting to join me in my Dungeon. Dolgunata was not resisting the idea of a joint raid too much either, but of course no one told me anything about the final prize. In her Dungeon Dolgunata would take the final loot by right; in mine she would force me to give it up using her charisma – I did not need a witch to figure that out. Speaking of witches. I should not forget about Gromana!

Taleem gave me some time to think about the situation, then suggested:

"Have you already promised a joint Dungeon raid to someone?"

I nodded sadly.

"I can provide advice, but it will cost you. How to prevent someone else from taking your reward. It will cost you a granis and some information."

"This looks like a scam," I snorted. "You must understand that a cat in the bag for two hundred kilograms of gold is a luxury a beginning player simply can't afford."

"I do understand. So, you can pay me the granis after you complete the Dungeon. As for information – that's simple as well. Your doll. As an explorer I am interested to know what your ideal woman is like."

"Doll?" I tensed. "My ideal woman?"

"You don't know yet?" Taleem was upset. "That's odd. Normally players meet their Doll on the first day."

"What doll?" I insisted.

"After you complete the Academy, the Game gives each player a gift," Taleem started explaining. "During registration it pulls out of your head the ideal image of your 'other half', and then emulates it. The point of the Doll's existence is to adore its master and fulfill his desires. It's impossible to give it to someone else, but it's possible to refuse it... Even though those cases are few and far between. Teachers normally don't mention Dolls, making it a surprise to their trainees. I was interested about what is your ideal in that respect. There was one elf explorer here before you – he got a male black orc for a Doll. It was funny how he was trying to explain his extremely non-traditional sexual predilections to his parents – that was too much even for the tolerant elves." The librarian tilted his head back and laughed heartily. "The Game never misses the mark with Dolls."

"It's more or less standard for me," I mumbled,

a little shocked, and Helen's image appeared in my head. I felt sympathy towards the elf. It's really wrong to expose one's most secret desires to be mocked by everyone. "It was a woman, a human... No horns or tails or anything like that. I really didn't know about Dolls."

Taleem did not look upset by my confession. On the contrary, he seemed pleased; then he continued on a more serious note:

"One of the seven books is actually about , their rights and relations with players. Do make sure to read it before you fall for yours head over heels. It's important to understand that Dolls are a vehicle created by the Game to satisfy the main needs of the body, nothing else. You can do whatever you want with it."

I nodded in gratitude. The librarian then resumed his entrepreneurial approach:

"Have you decided – are you going to buy my advice on completing the Dungeon?"

"What advice? Bring the number of players up to ten, make agreements with everyone and the loot is yours?" I asked sarcastically. "And esteemed Taleem, just by chance, happens to know some reliable players, with whom he has no sharing agreements whatsoever, but who would never cheat and who would definitely comply with all the provisions of the agreements?"

"We can consider that you have saved a granis, and I have received information regarding your Doll," the warlock shrugged. "Anything else?"

"You gave up so quickly and don't even seem

upset," the warlock's complacency kept bothering me. "If the loot in the Dungeon is so attractive, it's surprising you are not trying to convince me of the reliability of your players."

"My offer for paid advice is still standing," Taleem was practically shining with self-content.

"No, thank you. If I was wrong about possibility number one, there is still possibility number two: no one may get it. You mentioned that the more numerous the group, the stronger the bosses will be, and the harder it will be to kill them. Maybe even impossible." And then it hit me. Registrar, Lefer and myself. Dolgunata, her brother and myself again. Three in each case. There are no coincidences in the Game. "The best number is three players! Right?"

Taleem sighed, went to a book shelf and retrieved seven brochures from it, about thirty or forty pages each.

"As promised," Taleem said dryly and handed them to me. "Go ahead and study those. Once you are done, return them. I will look forward to seeing you with the updated map."

The warlock strode proudly back into the hall, leaving me alone with the books. My hands were itching with impatience, but experience suggested that haste makes waste. Who knows this guy? There could be many a source of Light in the office; one wrong book and I would not be able to get away with just a granis for sure. Settling in the armchair, I decided to start with the book on Dolls.

It took me an entirety of ten minutes to finish this work. Now I knew everything about Dolls. The

Game gave each player a present: a Doll, the living embodiment of his ideal, which only wanted one thing: to love and serve its master, and pleasure him in every way. The players were supposed to perceive Dolls as objects in a beautiful package, no more. These creatures had no rights. The present could be smart, stubborn, sarcastic, depending on the player's wishes. All Dolls bore the mark of the owner that identified them among normal NPCs. Once the player became bored with the Doll, the Game removed it, as it was no longer needed. Until rather recently it had been possible to turn Dolls into players; however, even after becoming a player, those creatures were not free from their inherent desire to belong to their owner. The Game considered that was not humane, and thus the conversion was prohibited. Players who would still dare such a thing would be destroyed together with the Doll. In addition, the Dolls were mortal: if one were to be killed it would respawn as a different NPC. There were even certain rules of etiquette with respect to them. For example, appearing with your Doll in society was bad form. A pet was supposed to bring joy to its master only at home. Well, at least there was no need to return to that little courtyard to pick up Helen. We would run into each other again and again until I either accepted or rejected her. In case of the latter the Doll would be destroyed.

An hour later I was going to the archivist with a clear understanding: now I would voluntarily become one granis poorer. I needed all the information that I could get on the Game that I could obtain from the local library in order to develop my artifact. The brochures raised the level of the Book of Knowledge by two units, thus bringing the "Neuronal network" attribute to an incredible level 6. Figuring that Taleem had another twenty books in store, I considered the effects of upgrading the artifact by another six levels. The probability was close to 100 percent, and losing such a chance for development so early in the game would be stupid. Those were the thoughts I had as I went to part with my very own granis.

From the standpoint of game mechanics the books provided by Taleem for the additional fee did not contain anything particularly important. History of class wars, game worlds, the rules of conduct for hunters in Lubot Forest and other "highly relevant" information. I swallowed book after book, breaking only for food and restroom breaks. As an experiment, I read several normal textbooks on quantum physics, about which I knew nothing at all. Taleem had not lied: the experience bar for the Book of Knowledge did not increase one bit; neither did my knowledge about quantum physics. Finally, my labor was rewarded: the Book of Knowledge received the six levels I had hoped for.

I left the Library puzzled by new considerations. Neither Archibald nor Dolgunata had contacted me yet. We were supposed to have set out for the Dungeon yesterday, but my "allies" kept mum and apparently were not worried about my precious self. The conclusion was obvious: the markers had done their job very well and the headhunters stayed very well informed of my location. Something needed to be done about that. But first the bank: Redel was supposed to have left me an envelope.

"How can I help you?" The bank, just like similar establishments in most games, was run by goblins. Green men with huge ears wearing stuffy jackets dashed to and fro, seemingly in a chaotic way. But once you took literally a minute, the Book of Knowledge identified the main directions of movement, which did not cross; a few moments later it informed me that the whole pattern was anything but chaos. The goblins seemed like ants capable of fulfilling multiple tasks without the constant control of their superiors, which I, actually, did not even see.

"There should be an envelope left for me." I turned around and met the eye of one of the workers, who separated from the stream to find out the reason for my visit.

"Is this your first visit to the bank?" The goblin requested verification, and once I confirmed it, broke into a merry speech: "Let me tell you about the promotions our bank is running and work, on your behalf, on the financial aspects of the Game. My license 'D' enables me to complete transactions of up to seven granises..."

"Envelope." I cut off the chatty clerk harshly. I was not in the mood for being too polite. "For Yaropolk. A Paladin."

"Please wait." The goblin's perked ears flopped again and he merged back into the fast moving stream of the bank clerks. Seeing an information desk nearby I decided not to waste time and studied the areas of the bank's activities.

Banks in the Game played one of the key roles with respect to interaction between NPCs and players: they converted granises to gold or bank notes and vice versa. There were no differences between a Game bank and an ordinary one in all other respects.

Having received the coveted envelope, I did not open it. Who knew – the case could have a time limit for completing it, and I had things to do now. First I wanted to test a theory I had, so I made sure that all the regulations and charter documents for the bank were brought to me. I spent twelve hours of game time, and certainly the goblins now had more grey hair; but I received an excellent confirmation: my artifact developed in the process of reading any papers that had to do with the Game. And even though the bank provided only one level of "Neuronal network", it was enough to highlight half of Zurich in green. I strolled down the streets and noted with delight how many things were hidden from ordinary players. I was surprised to discover that the Sanctuary had three levels: sewers, ground and roof. Out of curiosity I looked into a manhole and noted the active life of players who did not tolerate daylight.

In this leisurely and interesting manner I reached the Paladins' residence. A grey three-storied building was sitting inconspicuously on the bank of the Limmat, and only the sign "Temple of Truth" helped me figure out that the defenders of truth resided there. In a dim empty hall a portly elderly Paladin sat; he tiredly lifted his head as I approached.

"Paladin Yaropolk, reporting to obtain a quest," I grinned, pleased with my fruitful walk; the old man sighed heavily. "I need Grizdan!"

"Took you quite a while to get here," the gatekeeper said with displeasure, and pulled his notebook out of the desk. The old guy was blind in one eye, which was rather strange: normally during respawn the Game would completely restore the body. Either he had not respawned for a while or his was an abnormal case. I immediately felt a hope that it was the latter and I made a mental note to myself to try and ask if an opportunity presented itself. You never know – what if it proves useful knowledge. "There are not many quests now, all we have... My lord!"

The registrar of Paladins – it was he – jumped up and bowed reverently. It looked somewhat clumsy, as it turned out that the old guy was missing not only an eye but his right leg as well. I turned around and saw a procession exiting a portal. The hall quickly filled with all sorts of Paladins. The shine of their armor dispelled the gloom in the hall, and it became so bright it hurt my eyes. It was the first time that I had seen members of my class in full battle outfits, so I was awed by their beauty. A golden Paladin was striding at the head of the procession. He was moving so fast it was possible to feel the air parting around him, and his aura of power was so thick it was almost palpable. Even though he was not just standing out from the crowd because of the armor, the latter fit very well with the image of a "tough boss": terrifying spikes; elaborate decorations and engraving. The Book of Knowledge hesitated for a moment, then clearly identified the armor as the Imperial set. Some players were wearing Klifand and Daro sets as well, but the artifact was unable to identify on its own which one was which, so it marked each armor set with two notes as a possibility.

"Grizdan, take this one," the golden Paladin said briefly, and another three fighters stepped out of the portal. Two huge Paladins were carrying a tied-up squirming monster similar to an octopus, that had a head at the end of each tentacle.

"Hydra," Grizdan said with awe, and pressed several buttons on his tablet. I stared at the legendary monster. The Earth legends described Hercules killing another one like that, only a larger one. Either the legends lied or the Paladins had managed to catch a younger relative of the well-known monster. But in any case they were seriously cool.

Several rods extended from the wall, and a force field activated around them.. The Paladins who were holding the monster exhaled noisily. "Good catch, My lord!"

"Brothers Dungard and Rivier have been affected by chimera's breath. Put that in the report. Oh, a new one? — The high-born Paladin deigned to notice me. The force field lifted the hydra in the air and took it away somewhere near the ceiling.

"We've been waiting for him for three days, and he showed up only now," Grizdan nodded. "Archibald's protégé."

"Hunter as well?" The "golden" looked me over head to toe with disdain.

"Explorer." I felt awkward. The helmet was completely closed, preventing me from seeing the race of the Paladin, but from his manner of speech I decided he was an elf. His arrogant tone reminded me of Nartalim.

"Did you issue him a quest?" the Paladin asked Grizdan.

"No, My lord. Yaropolk arrived here just a moment prior to your triumphant return."

Turning around, as if he had just forgotten about our existence, the head of the troop ordered:

"Send him to retrieve the pendant. This quest will teach him manners."

He started to the furthest door, without doubting for a second that his order would be fulfilled immediately. The troop followed.

"Weeeelll, lad...," Grizdan drawled and extended a sheet of paper to me as the group was moving further away. "I see you don't consider the rules to be written for you? Here: that's the description of your quest. Sign here and here."

"What do you mean, 'weeeell'?" I was not even making a move to accept the document that was extended to me. "What rules did I break, and who was this?"

"Where do they even find twits like you?" Grizdan sighed. "You've had the rare honor of personally hearing Milord Iven, the Head of the Battle Wing of the Paladins of Earth, the right hand of Gerhard van Brast," Grizdan's voice filled with reverence as he listed the titles of the high-born Paladin. Apparently Iven was really a worthy Paladin, as there was no obsequiousness or flattery in Grizdan's voice. The gatekeeper really did respect and honor the Head of the Battle Wing.

"So what was I supposed to do?" I asked, losing all my joy. I would really hate to have the encounter with Iven prove to be a bad strike of fate.

"What do you mean? Do I need to remind you of class rule number five?" Grizdan was indignant.

"I don't even know number one, let alone number five!"

"Liar! They would not have let you out of the Citadel without teaching you the rules of the class," Grizdan started, but faltered, seeing the expression on my face. "That's impossible! Archibald would have never framed you like this!"

"May I be blown to smithereens on this spot if anyone provided the Paladins' rules to me in the Citadel," I barked angrily, considering this to be another strike against the catorian. The Game accepted this improvised oath and showered me with white light.

"Oh, what is this world coming to?" Grizdan was taken aback."That's so against the order."

"Please enlighten me, an explorer unfamiliar even with the basic rules of behavior: what was the reason why Archibald did not train you?" I heard Iven's voice behind me. The "golden" one reappeared in the hall as quickly as he had departed previously. "Figaro Here, Figaro There", no less.

"I think the mages were the reason. Archibald was busy with the investigation initiated by the Viceroy. I even had to be seen off by the Judge from the Citadel." I felt disgusted having to justify Archibald, but it made no sense to lie in order to make the catorian look bad. When the time comes, I will pay back to him for everything, including the gaps in my training and my family.

"Grizdan: issue the young Paladin a book on the rules of the class. It's not right to loose an untrained one on the world," Iven fell silent, looking at me intently. It gave me the impression that he was taking all my qualitative measurements and deciding whether I was worthy of the name of Paladin. With a capital P. Whether I was clean in mind and body. I wiped my palms on my sides quietly, just in case.

"There is a book mentioned in Archibald's report," Iven stretched out his hand. "I want to take a look at it."

My breath caught at this demand. My thoughts rushed to my head. The pause was lengthening, and the chief fighter was starting to show traces of displeasure. I could not stall any longer, and decided to take the risk. The gift of the Chancellor of the Academy plopped into the golden one's hand. The Paladin turned it around in his hands.

"The book has not yet been activated. Why?"

I really loathed this interrogation, and so confined myself to brief explanations:

"No time. First there were the mages, then the trial, then I was quickly transported to the Sanctuary. I had no chance to work with the book nor with my pet."

"The pet is of no interest to me." Iven returned the book and ordered the nearest Paladin: "Ask Yaropolk about his training with Archibald and completion of the Academy. I will see your report tomorrow. Grizdan, did you issue the quest?"

"Yes, I just have to give him the paperwork."

"Take that." As soon as the document was in my hand the Game reminded me of itself:

Quest received: "Stolen Pendant". Travel to the estate of Lady Lecleur and find out from her the circumstances under which the "Pendant of Joy" was stolen

"A week should be enough for you to finish the quest. After that I'll be waiting for you here. Go!"

"Yaropolk, tell me how you became a player." The player that Iven had selected decided not to drag things out, and started his questioning immediately. I frowned, not expecting such an outcome to that conversation, but regained my normal disposition quickly. Despite his high station, I did not like Iven as a player: it does not look good to so openly and brazenly crush everyone around. So then, following the principle "every action has a reaction", I rolled my eyes up poetically and started off on a tangent:

"It all started in the high and far-off times when I was still an NPC. It was a drizzly Tuesday. We were thundering down a country road, clinging to the side of our hard mean steel machine, swallowing the dust and looking forward to just one thing: seeing our beloved ones. Surely you must know: every soldier must have his beloved, the one in whose name he would do fair deeds and who will soften his coarse manner. Even Cervantes wrote in his Don Quixote: cherchez la femme! How's your French? You want me to translate that?"

The player who was questioning me first honestly tried to absorb this river of nonsense that I was pouring onto him; he tried to find traces of reason in these floodwaters, but as his converging eyes indicated that he was not going to hold up for very long. I chuckled inwardly: no one had promised him a rose garden.

"Listen, from where did you drag up that hydra? And what are you going to do with it in the Sanctuary?" As soon as I heard "enough!" I attacked the Paladin with my own questions. I had been wrong about Viltar. His patience was enviable. For two hours he stoically listened to my ravings; at the end he put in snide comments instead of questions. In other words, we found common ground. And I needed to take advantage of that.

"The hydra is from Altair," Viltar still could not believe that his torture was over. He checked his notes again, stuck them into the inventory and added: "Just cannon fodder for the Games."

"Ah, the Games," I pretended that I was well informed about the event. "Will Milord Iven take part?"

"Of course!" Viltar perked up once we started talking about his boss. "Next year he'll surely get the gold! He caught this hydra himself – we didn't even help him! In the arena he'll kill it with his bare hands! Since the berserkers won't be there, he'll have no competition."

"What about them?"

"They were banned from participating. They gobble up shrooms with vodka before the tournaments – turn into total animals. That's not good sportsmanship. Of course, they don't all do it, but it's too much bother to sort them out. So the whole class was punished outright. It's kind of a weird story; I don't really know what happened there."

The Games... Gold medal... 2016 ... The Book of Knowledge tentatively, as if not quite certain of its conclusion, presented a suggestion: 2016 Olympic Games.

"Yeah, it would be cool to see the Games. How much is the portal to Brazil?" I asked, based on this guess, and was right:

"One tenth of a granis. Plus accommodation. If you want to go, make your reservations now. The prices will skyrocket later."

"Thank you! Really, it hadn't occurred to me... And what happened to brothers Dungard and Rivier? Is chimera's breath something dangerous?"

"Oh, it's nothing much," Viltar grimaced. "A chimera binds the player to his world for a period of time; it's impossible to take him out of there either by teleport or respawn. There's no Paladins' base on Altair, so the brothers will have a tough time. Milord Iven said that we could just forget about them for a month, and then we'd go pull them out. It's a pity, Dungard was a cool guy."

"Why 'was' If you are going to bring them back?"

"Milord does not forgive mistakes. They were affected by the breath; that means next time they could let you down in something more serious. Battle knights are only allowed one mistake. The second one will not be pardoned."

"You have a tough setup, but that's the only way to train true fighters." I was playing to butter Viltar up, but it produced no visible reaction. "And where..."

"I have to go," the Paladin cut me off. "I need to prepare the report. Good luck in the Game!"

That was it for questions. Viltar went outside, and the Paladins' headquarters was once again empty. Grizdan was dozing with his head on his hands. The elderly Paladin couldn't care less about breaching his work discipline. Apparently the job of gatekeeper was so attractive that the only one who had agreed to do it was this one-legged one-eyed old fellow. I settled on a bench and decided to follow Iven's advice and work on the Chancellor's present.

Explorers' Book is not activated. Do you want to perform primary anchoring?

Once I opened the cover, the system showered me with messages. I looked through them and cursed elaborately at the librarian and all his relatives. There was no other way to express it: as it turned out, over the last two days I had lost at least eight levels of the artifact. All because the blasted librarian had never bothered to tell me about his "favorite" source of knowledge.

The Explorers' Book proved to be a treasure. The first thing it did was request an anchor to the character; that made it an inherent part of my artifact and increased all the available properties by 10% of the basic level. While that had no effect on "Weapon" "Defense" and "Context Search", the "Neuronal Network" jumped to 16. Simple math told me that each 10 levels of the properties would bring me an additional unit. What I learnt next, and one of the things that caused me to react so much, made me delve deeply into the character settings. Explorers were given a great bonus: a doubling of artifact experience points. To achieve it, once a month you could select a "preferred" method for obtaining information: books, scrolls, music, exploring the surrounding world... there were lots of options. All I could do was sigh, deploring my lost opportunities, and scold myself for tardiness: no one had kept me from studying the book in the Citadel.

"What are you doing lazing around here?! This is not a hotel!" Grizdan's irritable voice yanked me out from my dreamland. Tired and pleased with my work with the book I had fallen asleep sitting in the armchair.

"Good morning to you, too!" I stretched with gusto. The armor had worked like a soft bed, so I was spared feeling battered. On the contrary, I was bubbling with desire to commit great deeds and feats.

"Milord gave you a week, one night has already passed, and you are not a step closer to completing your assignment." The gatekeeper was not at all as enthusiastic about the new day as I was. "Get out at once!"

I did not feel like arguing, so I left the headquarters quickly. I had had a very interesting thought at night, and I spent a couple of hours to find the teacher I needed.

"Greetings, apprentice Yaropolk." A short guy with a moustache welcomed me. I thought at first that I was seeing a gnome, but the snake-like face could not really belong to an inhabitant of the kingdom under the mountain. I stared at the player to the point of being rude. The master, not abashed in the least, inquired: "So how long are you planning to stare at me without saying a word? Normally I don't charge granises for looking, but I could make an exception for you."

"Please forgive me – I have never seen people of your race. I hope that's not too forward a question, but who are you?" As I had found out, honesty tends to overwhelm your opponent in ninety nine percent of cases. This master was no exception from the rule:

"I am a kobold." He was flattered by my interest. "Our race is not numerous but it is tightly knit. What can I do for you?"

"Is it possible to write incantations down on scrolls only, or on any object?"

"Depends on the object." The master was thinking. "Most important things are the area – it should be large enough for the spell and... well, have the surface affinity for writing on it. As you understand, it would take something special to write, for example, on a water surface. Even though some are skillful enough for that. Tell me in more detail though."

I described my idea to the teacher. He only laughed:

"Those who come from technogenic worlds are

so predictable! Every one of you arrives at this idea sooner or later, but you forget about the specifics of the Game. The laws of physics on Earth and, for example, on Saldan, which is my home world, are completely different. What burns here is used as a coolant there. There are tons of similar examples. The method you came up with would be fine on Earth only; in any other world it won't work. That has been tested thousands of times."

"Even in Dungeons?" I asked in dismay.

"Well, that depends." The master fell to thinking. "If the Dungeon is in this world, it should work. If it's in a different one, it won't. Which one are you thinking about?"

"Alveona. Level 2."

"Wait a minute, I'll take a look now." The kobold reached into the desk and pulled out a huge reference book. My hands literally started itching from my desire to borrow this treasure from him for a couple of hours. Given that I had chosen books as my "preferred" way of leveling up, this would have given me something like ten levels.

"Actually, you know, the first and second levels of Alveona are located on Earth. Classic Dungeon for new players, nothing special. One monster and a huge crowd of its companions. Your method might work."

"The one problem I have is time," I sighed. "I just completed the Academy; there during training we were placed into extratemporal pockets. Is there something like that in the Game?"

"It's very good that you mentioned the Academy," the kobold replied seriously, even seeming to perk up somewhat. "Because your question is so naïve and stupid that a player just could not have asked such a thing. I had even thought you were an 'echo', and wanted to call the guards. Think about it: You became an apprentice. To reach this level you had to produce over seven thousand scrolls. In order to become a master you will have to create over a hundred billion scrolls. If there were no pockets, how would the players have an eternity?"

"With each word you utter I have more questions than answers," I said slowly. "What's an 'echo'? Who are the guards? How does one gain access to a pocket like this?"

"Man, slow down!" The kobold cut me off. "as for an extratemporal pocket: I can provide one. This service costs three granises. As for the rest, figure it out for yourself, I don't have time."

Three granises were such a huge amount for me that I did not try to bring it down to a reasonable level. I was sure I could find plenty of other masters in Zurich who would charge much less for a private eternity. My eyes fixed on the reference book again:

"What is the book you have? And could I read it?"

"Do you want to borrow my wife for an hour as well?! He wants The Book – oh really! Go... say hello to Shevran! I can sense a trap a mile away! Really, who would have thought! To distract me with a stupid idea in order to get close to the book! Well, that will never happen! I need to work – get out of my shop!"

Puzzled, I went outside and the door shut behind me with a resounding crash. The kobold even shut the bolt, demonstrating his desire never to see me again. All that remained to me was to move on to the auction, to buy the stuff I needed.

The Game auction was comfortably located in the building of the Swiss Exchange, and its attitude towards visitors was most commendable. The core idea of the auction was simple: nothing at all was supposed to interfere with the client's concentration. All the transactions were completed using a terminal with a clear and intuitive interface. Several times I received offers of food, drink or rest, but I resisted the tempting offers steadfastly. It's not as though I didn't trust the local hosts, but... oh well. No – I did not trust anyone.

The first thing I did was find information on completing Dungeons generally, and the second level of Alveona in particular. Minus a granis, plus an artifact level and understanding that there is nothing seriously scary in the Dungeon for newbies.

The next thing I bought were weapons. A couple of AKs with unlimited ammunition would be a hefty argument in disputes with minions and the main boss of my Dungeon. However, while a machine gun is excellent for killing monsters, for energy armor I needed a net launcher. Had I not been an active gamer in the past I would not have even guessed about such a thing existing. Buying licensed weapons was expensive, but I had no time to look for dealers selling things like that under the table. So the weapons took two granises; they came with a warning that it was not desirable to use my purchases against NPCs.

I was able only to drool looking at gems, enhancing elixirs and scrolls with the spells prepared by advanced players: the prices started at ten granises. Instead I extended my inventory to the maximum extent (as it turned out it did have a limit, after all), and filled it halfway with the Energy elixirs. My stash for a rainy day. The attack and defense amulets that I had received in the Academy were all but worthless; I nearly threw them away after replacing them with +20 each. In the end I put them up for auction for one hundredth of a granis, since they would not yield more. The only worthwhile item from the Academy was the Energy amulet: +500 was rare at the auction and cost 4 granises or more.

Having solved my issues with respect to weaponry and outfit, I got stuck on the tab "Services". Because I needed to find nine volunteers willing to join me in a hellhole called "10-th level Dungeon" who would not try to take the final loot. I did not even bother to think of Dolgunata and her brother; those two would not even come close to my Alveona.

I decided.

CHAPTER THREE

ALVEONA

"YARI, YOU OUGHT to lower the fines." Miltay tried once again to appeal to my conscience, but all he got was a negative gesture and an invitation to sign the agreement. Or move on and find business somewhere else: there were plenty of mercenaries at the auction.

"You think that'll stop us if we are really hard up?" The warrior surrendered. The Game provided information about entering into an official agreement with the team of mercenaries named "Zeltan" for rendering services with respect to completing my Dungeon. Minus three more granises.

"I wouldn't really care at that point," I honestly replied. "At twenty granises from each body I'd be able to buy myself such a bauble that all the loot in

Alveona would look like child's play by comparison. So if you get an irresistible urge to stiff me, go right ahead."

"Reach the boss first, then put on airs," snorted the mercenary. "Completing level ten is not like downing a six-pack."

"That's what I have you for, along with all your weaponry."

"Are we setting out for Earth?" Miltay perked up as soon the upcoming work came up.

"That's right – that's the ticket. One boss, tons of small crap. Here's the overall layout for the Dungeon," I extended the document I had prepared. Miltay started reading, whistling contentedly from time to time. Of course. I had not spent two hundred kilos of gold on this book. At this point I was a theoretical guru for completing Dungeons. By the way, I put the book back into the auction right away: I would like to recoup my money and check how the Game functions work. It was still not clear to me: if one had to come here to retrieve the objects they bought, what happened to the money? Will my account be credited immediately or will it be stuck somewhere in virtual space waiting for me to come back? That was an interesting question; immediately a plan for getting rich appeared in my head.

"Let's take a look at what we've got here. We provide a force field dome. Support and backup is also on us. We'll provide the Energy. How are you planning to remove their shields? While they're up, you can't even scare these guys with ammo. They have good protection against magic as well as physical damage."

"Sticky net with spells. Here, I have explained its principle of operation here to the extent I could." I handed yet another document to Miltay.

"The shield will come back up in seven to eight seconds," the mercenary was thinking. "There are ten of us, so we'll have time to fire about twenty shots each, no more. Look, most of the monsters have chitin armor; bullets may not pierce it. We'll soften it up with magic, but it takes time. How many nets do you have?"

"There'll be enough nets; how do you enhance the bullets?"

"We don't. How could one enhance them?"

"There are ways." I sensed an opportunity to reduce the cost of hiring these mercenaries. "Shall we talk about it?"

Miltay did know about the possibility to put a spell on each bullet, but had no idea how to actually implement it. Too many things would have to come together at the right time: a ton of Energy for charging, an infinite amount of patience to engrave each bullet, an available draftsman willing to spend several years on monotonous and tedious work, and most importantly, one needed to prevent the spell from deformation once the bullet hit its target. Given that opponents were clad in tough chitin that sometimes resisted even bullets with an iridium core. There was another condition, and Miltay remembered that: 5 seconds had to pass between the shot and spell activation; that was enough time for a monster to kill us flat out. However, the force dome and decelerators were supposed to help against that.

"Check this out." I pulled out three shells and handed them to the mercenary. "If it doesn't work, the agreement is void, and I'll pay the fine."

Miltay looked at my creation with interest. It had taken me almost two years, as far as I could tell personal time, to experiment and continuously test the results. My first bullets with the Templar's Blow engraved on them would not detonate: the engraving deformed on impact. I created models again and again, trying to figure out one problem after another, and plodded back to the auction for more knowledge. I was happy with the result; even in case of deformation the bullets enabled me to activate the spell engraved on them. Funny that one of the teachers in the Academy had mentioned that it wasn't profitable to sell knowledge in the main world – that people rarely buy it. Ha! All I do is shell out one granis after another trying to become smarter. The only conclusion that could be drawn from that is that for a teacher a hundred granises is mere change. Gromana had made a generous gesture and presented me with a handful of Game money, obviously without much hope of return on this investment.

"Hm...," Miltay reacted meaningfully to the explosion that destroyed the nearest tree. "Did you make it yourself?"

"So I did." Let's drop the price by half a granis, and I'll make a thousand of those little jewels for each of you." I was quick on my feet, catching Miltay's drift.

"That's expensive," he cringed. "This way we'll be going in for nothing."

"Tell that to someone else. I know very well what experience you get in the Dungeons," I pointed out. "So shall we make an agreement?"

The book on the Dungeons helped me understand one important nuance of the Game: why the players were so concerned about their levels. One could think that the lower the level, the less experience it would take to increase it. However, the Game had decided that would be too trivial. There were two types of levels: current and global. The current one controlled the number of available respawns, access to abilities and enhancements, opened doors to different places, etc, etc, but there was one most important thing it did not do: it did not advance you to the next stage of development. That's where the global level came into play. The amount of experience needed to advance to the next level was calculated using a simple formula: the global level multiplied by 1000. So it took 2000 experience to attain level 2, 10,000 to attain level ten and so on. The problem was that the global level never dropped: if the player was sent to respawn, his current level diminished while the amount of experience needed to attain the next level stayed the same. So it was problematic for players to live with a low level count: the risk of being killed was too high. That's what the Dungeons were for! Dying there did not have any repercussions for the players; all you got there was experience. Access to Dungeons cost players a pretty penny; it was compensated by just one granis one received from the Game for entering a Dungeon; so various mercenaries grabbed every opportunity that would bring them in there. By the way: each participant received a reward for taking part in the Dungeon raid: a granis or more. However, the "more" part started with level ten Dungeons, so I was still a long way away from that.

"Smart one, aren't you," the mercenary sighed. "Look. You provide a thousand enhanced shells to each plus three granises for the raid. We provide help in completing it and half a granis for ammo. If we fail – there's no claim against the group unless we, like, do some kind of an epic fail on purpose there. Loot fifty-fifty. Is that right?"

"So then... We have little time, so we are setting out today. Bring the ammo and I'll decorate it."

The gears of the machine called "Dungeon preparation" were set in motion at full speed. Miltay was dealing with materials, food, enhancements and other important things, in accordance with the contract. Meanwhile I was sitting in my eternity to which I had bought access for a month and worked on the shells. When I was there last I had polished my routine to the point when I could do it on autopilot. So now my hands and my head could be engaged in two different things. I preferred to occupy my head with thinking. I was turning over and over in my head everything I had found out about restart. Now was a great time to pick the wheat from the chaff and figure out for myself who was who.

So, let's start from the very beginning. It was foretold to Archibald that he would find the Keymaster once the Immune one appeared. Suppose that's true. So then neither I nor any other potential

Keymasters of whom Archibald spoke received no help? We were given no potions, no enhancements, no information. Nothing! At the same time Dolgunata, mages, and even the necromancer were equipped for the Academy as if they were heading to war. Everyone except Keymasters, who were so vitally important to the Paladins. Strange.

The other thing that was unclear was something Sharda had said in passing: that if I had gone into the Sanctuary without talking to him, it would have been no big deal. They would have just waited for a new Keymaster. Why would it be preferable for them to wait another thousand years than to arrange a private meeting within the Sanctuary? There were plenty of opportunities. Take the auction, for example! Protection there must have been as good as at the anchoring point in the Citadel. Instead, the Paladins calmly let the Keymaster with his activated Madonna's Diary go into the wide blue yonder, not bothered in the least that he could give that Diary to someone else, for example. All of the above would have some logic and meaning in one case only: I was not the Keymaster, and Sharda and Archibald were simply using me to protect the real one. Now all I had to do was to fit the activated Diary into this theory. At this point there was not enough information about it to draw any conclusions. It could turn out that it had no value whatsoever.

The only question that remained was: who was the real Keymaster? No matter how you put it, Dolgunata was an excellent candidate. Covered by invisibility, the druid could have very well sat in our cage together with Archibald and activated the book nearest to her just by being there. Maybe that's why it was my Diary that activated rather than the Councilor's, and being closer to Monstrichello had had nothing to do with it. Actually, that sounds like a plausible solution. The trained Keymaster is sent to the Academy, the mages and Zangar shift their attention to me while Dolgunata completes her training and no one harasses her. As Archibald mentioned, no one counts collateral damage in those cases. But still: why was I allowed to keep Madonna's Diary? Maybe they thought I was Merlin!

That would be quite a nasty outcome. I really hoped that I was not he. Otherwise, during the real restart, Paladins would expect that I would voluntarily, like a lamb, lay myself on the altar together with Madonna and whoever was the third one. Who still remained to be found. While I was so far from that idea that I wouldn't venture to take a crap in the same field with that suicidal gang. I snorted in dismay and redoubled my engraving efforts: I had plenty of work for the next year. At this stage it was impossible to receive any answers to the questions that bothered me anyway.

"What kind of a gypsy band is that? You should have brought a bear and balalaika with you too, to entertain the boss!" Dolgunata was waiting for us at the door of the building where the Dungeon portals were. I decided to ignore her as long as my patience would allow. Instantly figuring out who the head of the mercenaries was, the druid addressed him first, then turned to me again: "You are free to go. We'll deal with this from now on. Yari, I hope you brought elixirs, food and enhancements? Come on, time is short – we are already late by waiting for you. My brother will catch up with us."

Dolgunata had no doubt that her words would be taken as instructions, so she turned around and calmly proceeded towards the building. Miltay raised his bushy eyebrows, puzzled.

"Never mind her," I reassured the mercenary. "This girl is in her stage mode. Let's humor her."

"I am waiting!" The druid screamed from the door. "Come on!"

"Her stage mode is kind of lame," Miltay drawled. "This pest has marked everyone in the group now!"

"Once we get inside the Dungeon, would you take them off me? By the way, I ran into a few more besides. Could you take them off too?"

"Why not help a good man? I'll take the hunters' ones off for free – I don't like their ilk. So what about this chick?"

"I ran into her in the Academy," I said under my breath, unwilling to go into this in any detail.

"I can tell... the markers on you are quite something," Miltay laughed. "Look here – six different ones. I guess all from random encounters, eh? Oh, and how did you manage to cross Archibald so badly?"

"Does this affect our contract in any way?" Miltay was teasing me mildly, but I felt uncomfortable.

"Nah, everything stands. Your affairs are yours

alone. It does not concern us at all. It's good to be a mercenary: the Game itself protects us from vengeance and from harassment. Oh, and aren't you a truly lucky one! You even managed to run into Devir."

"So I did." All I could do was sigh. "There was never time to remove all these disco lights. I don't like being so conspicuous myself."

"Yari, I don't get it – what are we waiting for? Say your goodbyes already! The shorter the parting, the fewer tears." Dolgunata appeared next to us.

"Nata, I changed my mind." I decided to cut to the chase "I'll complete the Dungeon on my own."

"Even so." The druid was taken aback for a moment, but regained her composure immediately. "Will you make it on your own? I won't offer twice. You owe me a fine for breaching the agreement."

Miltay looked at me with interest, and the druid immediately started fueling the fire.

"Yes, he is a right out bastard," she sighed theatrically. "First he begs me to help him do the Dungeon, signs the contract and all, and then: 'Sorry dear, it was all a big mistake!' So keep your eyes peeled, warrior."

"She's actually rather cool." Miltay looked at the girl. "Lively and with a sharp tongue. Baby, come join us. You want to be the tenth? I'll find a spot for you. Miltay won't hurt you.

"I am not that easy to hurt. Right, Yari?" Receiving no answer from me, the druid added, "It's up to you. See you later," casting a disdainful parting look, Dolgunata disappeared into the building again.

"She is damn good," the mercenary watched as

she retreated. "Is she your ex?"

"No, it just never happened.

"So it goes. Shall we now? Time is wasting and we are still alive. We need to work on this."

The guard at the door checked my access, clicked his tongue considering the composition of the group, then pushed a few keys on his laptop, and a portal appeared in front of us. An empty room, guard, desk, chair and a portal. Minimalism at its best. The good thing was that there were no magical rituals or shamanic dances; the process was fully automated.

"Tomcat!" Miltay called, and a completely inconspicuous player stepped forward. "Tomcat" was so totally unremarkable that it was hard to keep one's eyes on him. In case one managed to do that, it would still be quite problematic to remember and describe him later. Without saying a word, he sank into the portal, and Miltay's phone beeped immediately.

"It's all clear!" He read the message and pointed out to me two fighters with machine guns. "Yari, here, hang next to Beast and Burst. Rast, forward!"

A shooter hung with odd-looking coils went into the portal next, practically immediately followed by Beast and Burst. Remembering the instruction to keep close, I stepped in after them, and was engulfed in cool fog. It dissipated a moment later, and I found myself under a powerful force dome. Rast's coils were generating a visible flow of energy that covered the area around the group with a three-meter umbrella.

Alveona was a classic Dungeon comprised of five levels. Glum dark brown walls of unhewn stone, hanging stalactites, an echo of dripping water, semidarkness dispelled by the greenish glow of the moss – making players look like horrifying green zombies – the atmosphere of the desolate caves inhabited by all sorts of monsters was done to perfection. The monsters, as well as the final second level boss, were ordinary crabs; the only difference from their normal earth counterparts was their dimensions. The smallest arthropod was about half a meter in size.

"Tomcat! Bring the first one!" Miltay commanded, as soon as he had taken all the marker bugs off me and the group completed its preparations for battle. The scout covered with chainmail pressed something on his outfit and seemed to just disappear into thin air. The Book tried to visualize the player's movement from slight traces of floating dust, but soon gave up: the fighter moved fast, and left barely any trace. I heard dull bolt clicks: the team was preparing for battle. Not wanting to lag behind, I took out my weapons and attached the detonator to my forearm. Even if I were to die, the others would still be able to push the "red button" to destroy the crabs' protection.

The group stilled, waiting for the enemy. The oppressive silence was broken by a raspy screech and a quickly approaching staccato, as if someone were hitting the stones with a small hammer with lots of enthusiasm, but without any pattern.

"Wasn't able to get one – catch three! Their spit's toxic!" Tomcat appeared about three meters away from the dome; it took him one leap to get under the protection. A bubbling black splotch covered the chainmail on his thigh, spreading with each second.

"Hang on!" one of the players commanded, and aimed his flame thrower at Tomcat. Flames leaped; we smelt burning flesh – the scout arched in horrible pain, but made no sound except a short moan of pain. This fiery cleansing lasted but a moment. With one gulp Tomcat downed half of the elves' potion, then poured the other half on the leg, and finally sighed deeply with relief. There was no splotch and no other visible signs of the burn. I really did not want to think what was going on underneath the scout's chainmail: I knew how the "elven ointment" worked. It did not heal wounds like the life elixirs in all games or fairy tales. The potion dulled the pain and maximized the body's own ability to regenerate by providing the necessary microelements. So at the moment the scout's leg must look really horrendous.

The warrior with the coils switched something and the dome's color changed from white to greenish. That was when the "hammers" crescendoed, and the first group of monsters rolled out from around the nearest boulder. Three young crabs: level 5, enhancement 10. They were immediately caught in the traps that had been prepared.

"Straight ammo! Fire!" Miltay ordered. Three fighters brought up their weapons and the "hammers" were silenced by a sound similar to stones sinking into the water. All three machine guns had silencers. I pursed my lips, looked at my AK, and put it back on the shelf until better days: during my preparation for the Dungeon it had not occurred to me that the echo of the shots would attract all the monsters in the level.

The shooting had completely no effect. As I had seen with Devir, the bullets ricocheted in different directions, deflected by the force field appearing in front of the crabs. Tired of struggling with the space slower, the nearest monster spat heartily, wishing to get rid of the intruders at once. The force dome started pulsing: a black splotch was rolling down it slowly.

"That eats up Energy pretty fast! Rast reacted immediately, looking at the data on his PDA screen. "Avoid spits!"

"Yari! Net!" Miltay's next order was addressed to me. Bringing up the net launcher and assessing the distance, I took a shot and immediately activated the detonator. Months of training really did help: two crabs were caught. Their claws started moving immediately, but the monsters were too slow. Five short seconds later Alveona was perceptibly shaken. I integrated into each net two hundred scrolls with the Templar's Blow, so the outcome of the explosion was expected: the force field around the crabs did evaporate. So did the crabs themselves: their pieces were rolling down our dome in black bits. The Dungeon inhabitants tried to get rid of the intruders even after death.

"Don't do that!" Rast hissed, madly typing something on his pilot. The coils reacted, changing connections in a complex pattern, and the field around us compacted by a meter, forcing us to crowd tighter. "The field will not withstand another explosion if it doesn't come back fully before it!"

"Let's finish off this critter," Miltay's reaction

was instantaneous. The explosion affected not only us, but the third crab as well; it was madly rotating in place, clawing at its own bubbling chitin. The remnants of its kin entirely covered it with black mucus; it went through its force field like butter and ate away at its body. Several bullets shot at the crab met no resistance, ending its agony and providing bits of experience for us.

"Replenish it now," Miltay patted Rast on the shoulder approvingly, and went to take a look at the remains of the crabs. Tomcat was nowhere in sight. The scout had taken off to look at the consequences of the explosion and check if it had alerted the other monsters. "Yari, do you need any of this?"

The list of our first batch of loot appeared before me. We had decided that we would share everything right away. I scrolled down the list and did not see anything worthwhile: black mucus, chitin and white crab meat. My Book of Knowledge showed the approximate value of those ingredients: all of that could yield no more than one thousandth of a granis. Visiting the auction was not a waste of time: having leafed through various offers for several hours had provided the artifact with quite a bit of knowledge on game objects and their value.

"Nothing from that." I came out from the dome and approached a claw that had been severed. "Did you check out the first two as well?"

"Sure I did," Miltay smiled for the first time as he cast a proud glance at our restored dome. "You know, don't give up. Ten times enhancement is not easy to find; there's definitely nothing like that at the auction. They'll sell like hotcakes even for a tenth of a granis."

"You are too kind and spendthrift for a mercenary," I pointed out, picking up a piece of twisted chitin. I turned it around and threw it away: the Game perceived it as "useless trash" with zero value and time to disappearance of "10 minutes". I looked around – there was a fair amount of similar "useless trash" strewn around on the stones.

"So then I can afford it," Miltay shrugged offering me some black mucus carefully collected in a vial. Look, there are plenty of crabs here, it's clear how to destroy them; even if they all die from the explosions, Tomcat will pick it all up. Loot is a good thing, but one's got to support reputation as well. You didn't pick us out just so, right?"

I nodded in agreement. Before selecting a team I had to go through a veritable mountain of very similar information. I shuddered to imagine how much time this would have taken me if it had not been for my Book of Knowledge that singled out the main points in reviews and complaints for mercenaries. Miltay's group suited me like no other, but I did not remember any mention of their "generosity".

We cleaned the small fish out of the first cave within an hour. Chose the place for an explosion, which was enclosed with large boulders, and spread the slower in it – it looked like brown goo pumped from a portable tank – then brought the crabs in threes into this improvised trap. Tomcat had learnt his lesson, so he avoided the spit thoroughly. Burst, who took away the net launcher from me, acted as the spearhead. I did not even bother to protest. The guys had signed up for that, so let them work for their reward.

"Miltay, stop! There's something here. The wall," I said with interest, staring at one of the walls of the cave we had just cleaned. I was used by now to a green highlight appearing around objects, but here the highlight was red.

"Gere," Miltay was not wasting time on questions, and sent his tracker forward. I looked at my almost colleague. It would be silly to suppose that a group of mercenaries would not have a fighter specializing in finding treasures, and I was interested to see his method of work. A device with a little screen that appeared in the fighter's hands puzzled the Book of Knowledge – it was not familiar with this device. Using it as radar, Gere slowly approached the wall – like a sapper on a minefield – looked around, carefully felt the wall itself and the floor next to it, then turned to us and shook his head to indicate there was nothing.

I did not argue and approached it myself. Making sure that there was no threat coming from the wall, I went toward the point that was apparently only visible to me. The glow intensified with every step, and once I came close its color changed to blue. I pressed the stone lightly. It moved aside and a familiar object fell into my hand: a steel hexagon. Attribute stone.

Silence fell over the Dungeon, and the rustle of the crabs' claws could be heard in the adjacent cave. I looked at Miltay. His eyes had narrowed; he was intently staring at the hexagon. The group as one man trained their weapons on me. If the head of the mercenaries were to say a word, or even if a stone were to fall somewhere, they would shoot me full of holes. Finally Miltay tore his eyes away from the stone:

"Put it away, out of harm's way." He was speaking slowly, as if with difficulty. "Or, look, it might happen that the Dungeon will end right here."

I nodded slowly and exhaled, releasing the tension. Despite relative immortality it was unpleasant to stare at the silencers of eight machine guns ready to spit out death at any moment. The Book of Knowledge did not provide any additional information on the hexagon: there was no object like that at the auction. Either they sell immediately upon appearing regardless of the price, or players never offer them for sale – just use the stones themselves. I turned the loot around in my hands, decided that even ten granises would not bring me luck, I activated my find.

Luck increased by 1
Luck of your group has been increased
(Level 2 Luck). Effect duration: 72 hours

The mercenary coughed, attracting my attention and, having made sure that he had all of it, said in a businesslike way:

"Going through the Dungeon with level 2 Luck is good. No arguing that. Only, look, you did not even ask how we should divide the stone, and used it yourself. That's not so good, Yari. Or you think there's another hexagon hanging out here?"

"I remember our contract." I saw no point in denying it. "And I think that we'll really benefit from doubling our luck. And you – can you guarantee that using that luck we won't find something ten times better than the stone? This way we have at least increased our chances to complete the Dungeon. Besides, if it hadn't been for me, no one from your team would have found it."

Miltay said nothing, and neither did his group. There was nothing they could object to that.

"After all, if we receive nothing, I'll find a way to return half the price of the stone. The Game is my witness!"

Light washed over me: the Game accepted my obligation. Miltay hemmed – he had not expected such a turn of things:

"Look here, and I'd thought you weren't so stupid as to hang a debt of ten granises on your neck. That's settled then. Since you will pay it back – no issues on our part. I won't even ask how a novice player got activated Luck and why is it that he sees what our tracker can't see. I don't really need no extra info like that. The Dungeon'll be done and that's the last we'll see of each other."

Having settled the problems, the fighters were looking for a good place to set the next trap, and I continued exploring green highlights in the cave, trying at the same time to find common ground with Gere. I had no luck in either. There were no more caches, and Gere would not even speak to me: either he was mute, or mad at his slip, or I wasn't good enough for him.

"Holy mother," Miltay suddenly barked in irritation, and followed with a command:" "Circle up! We've got visitors!"

At first I wasn't sure what to do, as I didn't know my position, but Beast and Burst, who were watching over me, helped me figure it out. I was shoved behind the mercenaries' back to be out of the way. Only then did I notice that Tomcat's frame was not in the group: the scout had disappeared from the Dungeon. That could only mean one thing: for him this trip to Alveona was over. The mercenaries bristled with weapons, but the threat had come from an unexpected quarter: Behind us, just a step away from the force dome, the floor bulged and immediately exploded like a volcano. Stone shrapnel was pelting the dome. The shields held, but then a monster started climbing out from the crater it had created: an oversized crab as big as a large truck.

"Rast, turn it up all the way!" Despite our unexpected guest the mercenaries exhibited no signs of loss or panic. As soon as the monster from down under climbed out of its crater, it was covered with a dozen activated nets, its legs were stuck in the brown space slower and a bright blinding sun was hanging next to each eye. Rast cursed, pressed several buttons and suddenly the cave faded: the force dome became completely solid.

"Turn on personal protection!" Miltay kept commanding. "Let's see how good the nets are."

"Three. Two," Burst had launched the nets, and

now his lips were moving with the countdown to detonation. Everything happened so fast that there was not even time for me to get properly scared. Wrapping myself in the "Energy armor" and having replenished my Energy to the max, I listened to the fighter: "One." Boom!

The force dome was crushed, and a huge piece of stone hit me right on the head. The shield held, but nothing protected me from inertia. Darkness fell over me in an instant.

"Yari? Hear me?" Miltay's very funny voice penetrated through the blessed darkness. Through the din of a plane engine – how did that thing get in the Dungeon? – it sounded dull, as if from a metal drum, but I could still hear it rather clearly. The mercenary must be using an ability of some sort: it's unrealistic for a common person to be heard over a plane's noise.

"He's moving now," Rast was talking from the same tin drum as the head of the group. "Elves' ointment doesn't help against shell shock. He has to come to on his own."

My thoughts moved around my skull as listlessly as the parents of a teething baby. Shell-shocked? Me? A bright thought suggested that it may be so dark because my eyes were closed. So I tried to correct that problem immediately. A flicker of light showed up somewhere far away, but I immediately bent over in a crippling spasm. It felt like I was being turned inside out for real.

"Like hell we needed that kind of luck," Rast said, irritated, and once again cursed elaborately. "At least this one's... alive. Drink!"

Someone forced my mouth open, and a warm and astoundingly delicious fluid poured down my throat. I choked, gulped, coughed, but kept swallowing: I did not want to miss a single drop of the wonderful nectar. Ambrosia, no less!

My ability to see clearly returned instantly, as if someone had flipped a switch. I was sitting among the stones in a huge crater. All was left of my left leg was a good memory and my flattened armor. It was not clear what had happened to the right one: it was under a pile of stones. I tried to move my toes – seemed as though they were still there. I had no other visible injuries, and finally I noticed the other participants in our raid. There were not that many left: Miltay, Rast and Burst. While the first two looked intact, the net wielder looked much worse than I did: he was missing both arms and legs. However, the mercenary was far from despondent. The elves' ointment had removed the pain and now he was lounging on the stones grinning happily: since he was alive he could still do something. As to what specifically – the lead would think of that, that's his job.

"So, look, what did your luck bring us?" Miltay settled down next to me. "One third of the group is alive, one fighter is only good for acting as a living bomb. The net launcher went down the same road as Burst's arms. There's no access to the next cave: the stones have collapsed. The good news are experience, loot and the passage that monster dug through."

I must have not fully recovered from the shell

shock, as it took me a while to realize that now I was a 14th level player. Now I understood why Burst looked so pleased: his level had increased as well. Then I looked at the loot list and frowned: it was not clear why Miltay considered it a benefit. Same stuff: meat, chitin, and now instead of black mucus there were two crab eyes. The Book of Knowledge kept silent: it had not encountered such a thing at the auction.

"I could take the other eye to offset your debt for the attribute stone," Miltay's words completely dispelled the haze. I looked at the two bloody balls with different eyes.

"What are they for?" My voice was still hoarse.

"They're enhancers," he clarified. "The lenses in the eyes are enhancement gems. Frightfully expensive, they are, just like that stone of yours. That creature wasn't weak, so the gem would be good too. Just about ten granises, if you don't look to trade precisely. But if you do, we'd have to look."

"May I ask you something?" Finally the moment came when I could obtain an answer to something that had been bothering me for a while. "You seem to be operating on the basis of numbering dozens of granises per item, yet you agreed to go with me for a ridiculously low price. Three granises is nonsense for a high-level team of mercenaries! I can't figure out what's at the core of the cost of things in the Game. For the sale of a granis people commit crimes, and here we are, calmly sharing the loot, and no one has any issues with that. Where's the catch?"

"Look here," Miltay drawled in surprise. "When

did you come out of the Academy? With this enrollment? Yet you nailed the problem right on. Rast, tell the kid the way things are while I'll check where that hole leads."

"There's not much to tell here," the mercenary started reluctantly. "The more granises a player has on hand, the more trouble he encounters. If you are rich, you have to pay for personal security. Or die. Traders don't count – they have their own setup – but in quests for killing ordinary rich guys; during local events their residences become the number one target; they shine in space like beacons in the night. No way to hide. That's the main source of income for head hunters, for which they are so universally disliked. Blasted cleaners. The Game tolerates it if you have up to three granises in your hands, but once you go a little above – it starts quietly reminding you that it's time to spend some. Players like you are tasty morsels. If you had not been sitting in the Sanctuary, you would have died a couple of times by now for sure. You shine like you have over twenty granises on you."

"Oh, now it has all become clear as mud," I replied testily. "What's a 'local event'? Where do I 'shine'?"

"You shine where you ought to!" Rast said curtly and turned around to look at the hole in the stone just in case. Miltay was not there and Burst only scowled sarcastically. After a pause the mercenary continued quietly: "Trader's license. It enables one to see the client's wealth. What, you think Miltay continued the raid out of the kindness of his heart when you ate the stone? He could see that you'd be able to pay him."

"The license is also what shows the hunters' marks as well?" I guessed. I recalled the hearty welcome I received from the trader in the Academy. I had thought he treated everyone like that, and actually the swindler just could see how much I was able to pay.

"That's why there's so much barter in the Game," Rast avoided the question. "You help me, I help you, and granises don't even enter into it. Dungeons are good for us because half of the loot is always ours. Loot, not granises. It states so clearly in the contract. Even though there is a granis as well, the one the Game provides. So that's how it works, more or less."

The mercenary fell silent while I digested new information. So that meant that Gromana, by handing me ten granises in the Academy, must have marked me so that it would be easy to find me later! She had a trader's license! Blasted witch!

"You didn't say anything about local events," I reminded the distracted fighter.

"He wasn't supposed to anyway," Miltay appeared quietly and cut the whole conversation short. "What did you decide about the eye? Are you going to give it to me?"

"No." The theory as Rast told it was plausible, but it was useful to study it on my own first. It was possible that was just a sweet tale presented in hope that I would be gullible enough to give them all the granises right away so that I would not "shine". "After the Dungeon we'd see each other in the Sanctuary, so there we could discuss who owes what to whom."

"You don't trust me?" The mercenary grinned.

"You think I should?" I asked in surprise and, mocking Miltay, continued. "Look here, you play for a profit with minimum effort. Rating, reviews – it's all nonsense when we are talking about hundred of kilograms of gold. If it were really so bad as you are saying, players would get rid of granises at the first opportunity. But no – everyone is trying to get them. Right?"

"Right, wrong, quit acting like a parrot," grumbled Miltay. "Did you pay for the Dungeon or for free lessons? I don't recall being hired as your nanny. You could have thanked for us for shedding some light into your stupid head. Anyway, I'll just add one thing: one granis will always be attracted to another. Later you'll find out for yourself how things work. Here, look, the passage stops after the second cave. That critter was sitting under the ground and waiting for us. I take it Tomcat flushed it out, so it rushed forward. So then, look here, it's simpler to shoot ourselves right here. Or shall we go fight some more? Think, commander."

"What's to think about?" I was not sure what the catch was. "Let's go on."

"Good, fine. So, how are you going to get out from under that pile? I don't have no lifting jack with me."

The stone that pressed down on me would not budge no matter how much I jerked my leg. Both mercenaries tried to roll it aside, but failed. I was really pinned in place.

"Look here, that's what I'm talking about – what do we do? We can't pull you out; if we leave you here, we breach the contract. Want to go on – I'll have to cut your leg off. But I'll just have to cut if off as it is – I have no painkillers. Afterwards we'll put the ointment on it."

"So cut!" I said angrily a minute later. There was no way we could move the stone – it would not budge no matter what we did. Even a lever made of pieces of chitin cracked, failing to move my trap even an iota.

I didn't have to ask Miltay twice. He pulled out a huge machete and aimed at my thing with competence. Looking at his face I felt queasy. Hell, who did I make a deal with?!

"So, look here, no offense – you asked for it yourself. I hope your armor is simple enough. Yari, has it been a long time since you got some booty?"

"What? What boo..." I did not get the question, then screamed "AAAAA!" and, thanks to my still dim consciousness, blacked out again. The armor was quite strong, and, despite all his ardor, Miltay wasn't able to cut my leg completely with one blow. He cut about half way through. I did not remember what happened next.

"Want it for a souvenir?" I regained consciousness, covered in cold sweat. Even though there was no pain, its phantom still loomed close, making me shudder in horror. Grinning Miltay threw the remnants of my leg extracted from under the stone at me. "You pull Burst, Rast and I go first.

Forward!"

Crawling along I did not lag too far behind the mercenaries. I had to work with my hands and teeth, grabbing onto everything that happened along. In addition, I managed to pull Burst along on sort of a rope sled, using my stumps, and listened to the quiet conversation of the two walking ahead.

"Here!" The lead of the mercenaries turned around, lay on his back, extracted a jackhammer from his inventory and started working on the ceiling of the passage. Rast helped by removing the dust and crushed stone using an industrial vacuum cleaner. Once the hole was big enough that he could stand, Miltay rose and took out a radar.

"Here they are, our dears! The whole cave troop gathered near the breach. Yari, pull Burst over here!"

As soon as the ear-shattering noise from the jackhammer and vacuum cleaner stopped, we could clearly hear the staccato of hundreds of "hammers" right above our heads. The crabs could easily hear us and were impatiently awaiting our visit. Deciding that the mercenaries knew what they were doing, I did not ask them any questions. Even our invalid smiled, knowing full well where we were dragging him. After several testy jokes he uncomplainingly took the wires that were extended to him in his teeth and then Rast performed, basically, a miracle. A huge warhead appeared from the personal inventory of our player responsible for the force dome! Those guys were just maniacs!

"Look here, that's a mini beauty," Miltay said lovingly. "Almost a kiloton. Come on, dear, don't let us down."

The warhead was placed vertically and Rast started tying Burst to it. After finishing that, he attached to the bomb the wires extending from the cripple's mouth. Cold shivers ran down my spine and my instincts nearly forced me to rush back into the first cave: Burst had become a living detonator. While he clenched his teeth together, we would stay alive, but as soon as he opened his mouth, the mini-beauty would evaporate everything within twenty meters.

"Don't you worry, we are afraid ourselves," Miltay grinned, seeing my reaction. He extracted a large bag from his inventory and pulled out of it a huge mess of plastic explosive and detonators. "Catch that! Attach those to the ceiling. We need to close this hole."

I was starting to like this. The mercenaries had found out that getting to the crabs directly was impossible, and decided to do it in a different way: simply obliterate them. Well, that way would not provide any loot, but we'd pass through the second cave and be able to see the Dungeon boss. One should not discount the experience, either: I expected there would be enough for at least a couple of levels. Turning over onto my back with a grunt, I followed orders, starting to turn the passage into a hanging minefield.

"...you'll get a second, no more." As I finished with the charges and returned to the group, I heard the end of Rast's instruction. "If you blow it up yourself, you get the experience, if you croak from the explosions, you get nothing. And, if you open your stupid mouth too early – I'll personally stuff your balls into it. Got that?"

"Mmm," Burst responded, settling more comfortably in his ropes.

"Excellent. Retreat!"

Using wounded fighters as living detonators was one of Miltay's favorite tactics. A nuclear charge would detonate practically in ninety percent of all Dungeons; it was getting the signal to it that was the problem. Differences in the physical processes in different worlds, blockage by debris or interference from some jamming force fields... every time something non-standard happened that required immediate action from an actual live player. Miltay did not like risks, so practically all of his fighters had been through this act of ritual suicide. Twenty meters of stone debris that was supposed to form once we activated the explosives we placed in the passage were supposed to reduce the shock wave to a tolerable level. The rest would be absorbed by the force dome. Due to the hole we had made in the ceiling, the main impact would be directed upwards, turning crabs into crab spread on the walls and, if we were lucky, it would also damage the final boss pretty well. The mercenaries ignored minor side effects such as radiation sickness: elves' ointment would help us survive the first few moments after the explosion even if we were to be falling into pieces on our feet; then, after respawn, we would come back to normal anyway.

We retreated to the point where we entered the Dungeon: the cave that was furthest from the epicenter.

" I hate y'all," having activating the protection dome, with his hand over the detonator, glum Rast exploded with emotions that seemed to boil up out of nowhere. "You freaks!"

"Granis, Rast. Blasted basic granis!" Miltay cheered him up, and this conversation was over my head again. "Plus the experience. If it all works like it's supposed to, we'll show up in Lertance with a new level. You know what that will give us."

"Fuck you.," Miltay calmly ignored his subordinate's insults. "You won't be the one spitting blood, you bitch... I hate you!"

That was followed with a flood of curses so foul and elaborate that I thought even the long-dead Sintsov would have died again – of envy this time. It seemed even conjunctions were cursewords. That was pure talent. I gave Miltay a questioning look, hoping for an explanation.

"Rast is a shang by race." The mercenary didn't bother to put on airs. — "They look just like people, but their insides are different. From radiation they croak right off, even at low doses. Elves' ointment will keep him alive, but after the explosion that shang will cough all his guts out. The longest he ever lasted was two hours; but we don't really need more now. So he'll stuff it and go next."

"To hell with all of this!" The flow of cursing stopped and at that moment the mercenary, highlighted with the green color of new knowledge, pushed the detonator button. The Dungeon shook with a series of powerful explosions; no matter how much I prepared myself, the ground shifted and vanished from under my body and I rolled on the ground once Burst activated the bomb. The Dungeon did not just shake – it stood on its head.

The shock wave failed to tear our protection as we crouched under the impenetrable dome. While I was trying to get into a more or less vertical position, Miltay was already pouring the healing potion down Rast's throat. Information on receiving experience and new levels flashed before me: the explosion propelled me up to level 24, adding ten levels. Rast swallowed the elixir and was now coughing horrendously, spraying the stones with blood and shreds of flesh. A minute later the mercenary was on his feet though. His head was concealed with an elaborate helmet: Rast did not want us to see his face, so he made it opaque.

"Look here what we've done here," Miltay drawled as soon as the force dome was down. Personal protection immediately beeped in alarm and my Energy bar started edging down. The temperature in the Dungeon was such as to make normal organic life impossible. I was waste deep in melted stone, so, in order to not burn up I had to take an elixir right away, bringing up my Energy level. The class armor, even though it was damaged, still functioned well enough to ensure a comfortable temperature and sufficient air circulation. I was glad that I had been able to replace the standard set with this improved armor.

Pulling me out of the magma trap, Miltay put me across his shoulders, nodded to Rast, and we trundled forward, knee-deep in lava. The shock wave obliterated all the rubble, clearing the path for us. I poured the next elixir down my throat and sighed heavily. At this rate all my stocks would last an hour at most.

"Rast," Miltay called, and the dead silence of the Dungeon was shattered with AK shots. Several ricochets followed by explosions of my "Templar's Blows" and the players leveled up with a little more experience.

"Those blasted monsters are hard to kill though!" It seemed Miltay never lost his optimism. Throwing me over the other shoulder he bent down to pick something up from the ground, and I saw the other cave with crab apocalypse. There was a lake of molten stone in the middle of the huge cave. Lava poured into it from all the side passages, filling up the explosion epicenter. At the edge here and there crab remains were melted into the walls: even the incredible temperatures and shock wave were unable to fully obliterate the monsters with tenfold enhancement. Miltay seemed to be particularly glad to see that some crabs still moved. Without claws or eyes, with only half a body remaining, they still were striving to survive, and Rast hastened to finish off the monster closest to us.

"Look here!" The head of the mercenaries drawled his favorite saying as he gladly threw the loot into the inventory: the already familiar chitin, black mucus and meat. "There's a real virgin land here! Rast, you go left, I go right. Yari, just lie here for a while. You have enough elixirs? So, just stay here and drink them. Come on, quick, we don't have much time!"

I wanted to believe that Miltay dumped me into the hot lava with at least some care and concern; otherwise I really would have to file a claim against him. The experience scale started climbing pleasantly: the mercenaries worked fast, leaving no chance for the surviving crabs.

"It's your turn." Twenty-two Energy elixirs later Miltay yanked me out of lava that was not even thinking of cooling and put me over his shoulders again. "Just be quick. See any secret cashes?"

I heard Rast choking in another fir of coughing on the right; he was already unsteady on his feet, but hung on with the last of his strength.

"Nothing," I quickly checked out the walls, but there were no familiar red highlights. "Even if there had been something, it must have all burnt to hell,"

"Look here – the data on the loot; let's keep moving." An information message quacked, showing me the list of loot. I whistled with pleasure: there were seven crab eyes among the other stuff. Seven enhancement gems with tenfold level! Who was that person laughing at my double luck?!

"Rast, can you walk?"

The mercenary barely nodded and, holding on to the wall, moved towards the passage to the third cave; his gait was unsteady. According to the Dungeon map, we were in for the meeting with the final boss of the level.

If there had been any traps between the caves, the shock wave and heat swept them out mercilessly from our path. The walk towards the final crab was just like a pleasure stroll. Miltay, who was completely unharmed, had to carry the legless me; Rast, who was coughing up blood and dragging his feet, was trying to keep up with us. However, as soon as we entered the third cave, all traces of joy vanished. In the middle of disfigured and melted hall there was a stone pedestal, occupied by slightly singed Dungeon boss. What joy can there be when a ten-foot monster is staring at you – the one who had just easily survived a nuclear explosion? Miltay sighed heavily and cursed. I already knew that he did not have a second bomb. The current license of "Zeltan" team allowed them to carry only one "argument of last resort".

We came closer and the customary green highlight around the gigantic crab dissipated. The wall behind the monster glowed blue, and I gladly informed my companions of that right away. Apparently, the pedestal and the crab had protected it from the shock wave.

"There's not much to rejoice about: look here, how this bastard regenerates." Miltay nodded at the crab's chitin, on which the cracks were growing smaller. "What could we do?"

"Since we can't kill it, you need to distract it till I get to the cache," I shared my bright idea and encountered a contemptuous stare.

"Would a second be enough for you, speedster? That's how much this freak would take with Rast and myself. Never mind that it's big – this critter is faster than both you and me, even if you still had your crunchers. Look here, just the front paws are..."

Miltay was describing the abilities of the boss' physiology, making me more and more depressed: the situation looked really bleak. Regeneration, extreme speed, powerful protective shield that enabled it to survive the explosion – everything was stacked against us. Rast leaned his back against the wall, stuck his hands into virtual space and a couple of moments later a big metal backpack clanged onto the floor. Lifting his head Rast wheezed something unintelligible, but Miltay understood him and perked up.

"Look here, he can barely breathe but his head's still cool! That could work! Yari, the situation is shit, but we are clever!"

The mercenary meaningfully nodded at the backpack

"And serendipitous. This is a Garlad Tactical Backpack," Miltay started clarifying the idea. "Today you have already walked and crawled, so now you get to fly. Don't you worry, the speed this thing gets is really good – you should be able to slip by the monster. Well, in case you don't we are going to lengthen you a bit. If it grabs you, it would just get something that was gotten before already."

With those words Miltay took out two machine guns and attached them where my legs had been, tying all this contraption together with the cloaks extracted from his own and Rast's inventory. I was looking on, silent, as all of this was sinking in. Meanwhile Miltay continued:

"Look here, once you pass the boss, Rast and I start shooting at it with whatever we've got left to distract it from you. The crab gets excited and comes over here. This is just a moment or two, no more, even with the protection we've got. And after that it depends on your luck. You'll have three or four seconds. I'll point you in the right direction – your task is not to croak as you hit the wall. Just grab the cache right away. Got that?"

"So I don't need to control it?" Silent Rast was already attaching the backpack to my armor.

"That skill takes many years to learn," Miltay admitted. "Look here: frankly speaking, I don't think it'll work. We've tried this twice. Failed both times. But with your luck... the Game can play any trick. There's nothing else we can try anyway. Look here, this is the switch: once you hit the wall, push 'off'. It's simple – look here. Got that?"

"I got it, I got it already!" I reassured him.

I was gently lifted and then I floated in midair. I did not know the principle of operation of the backpack, but I did not notice any flame jets, air jets, or any other kind of jets. It felt like the thing worked using magnetic fields. I would need to find one like that at the auction for myself and learn how to use it.

"Three is the number I shall count." Miltay adjusted the direction of my future flight, holding me lightly by the head, and then performed another miracle: a Kord appeared from his personal inventory. A heavy machine gun – its characteristics made it more like a small cannon rather than simply a machine gun.

"Of course," he grinned, seeing my admiring look. "We still have something to surprise the monsters. Rast: ready? Yari: activate your shields, push on the switch and drink the elves' shit. Like, right away. Better stick it into your mouth. Here, I'll help you. Look here, don't swallow it yet. So come on, dear! One! Two! Go!"

My stomach seemed to lodge in my throat, trying to leave my body completely: the flying backpack was set to maximum initial speed available. I did not even have time to feel anything: Miltay had placed my hand right over the "off" button, and inertia was what helped me: the backpack turned off a moment after the launch. But that split second was enough for the boss to flicker by somewhere off to the right and then the massive wall gladly slammed my long-suffering body. An astounding crash on it crushed everything that was still left of my body. The class armor held, so I did not just splat into the wall; however, it did not help against inertia. Had it not been for Miltay's advice, I would have been thrown out of the Dungeon that very moment: the stone under me turned red instantly. However, the healing and painkilling potion flowed straight down my throat from the broken vial despite my jaw being totally shattered. The pain faded so I was able to avoid pain shock even though I felt like I did not have a single whole bone left in my body. For some reason I could not see out of my right eye, but the left one was fixed on the bright blue point on the wall. Miltay's calculations had been correct, and my goal was literally just about under my hand. The problem was that my hand refused to move.

Boom-Boom-Boom!

Phphpht! Phphpht! Phphpht!

The Kord's shots and ricochets filled the cave. Cheering myself on by screams I turned my shoulder and dropped my numb hand onto the cache. My loot fell into my palm: the hexagon so coveted by all players. Twisting, I fell onto the ground, managing to do two important things at once: stick the stone into personal inventory and turn towards the center of the hall. The boss was just finishing with Miltay, tearing him in half with its claws. Rast was already gone from the Dungeon.

Knowing that our adventure was over, I pulled all the ammunition I had prepared from the personal inventory. The shells that fell into the magma started melting but were immediately covered with a new bunch and thus did not fully burn up. They were followed by scrolls rolled up into tight packs: my personal bombs. I had made so many of those that I had even attained the status of junior craftsman's apprentice in draftsmanship. That meant 400,000 successfully created items! Now I was looking at a huge pile of scrolls that caught fire immediately – it was amazing how they had even fit in the inventory. I did not see any point in keeping them: no one would need such low level work at the auction. My attack capability was too low. It was funny: I had been preparing for the Dungeon for so long and lost all my materials in such a stupid way. I decided to go out with a bang, and activated the detonator. In five seconds the Dungeon would see another nuclear explosion, this time a local one. The "Templar's Blow" impact area was a mere five meters.

The crab appeared suddenly. From the right.

With a precise move it grabbed me by my body and the imitation legs. I noticed only now that the machine guns had been cut in half: apparently, during my flight the crab actually had managed to reach me. Had my limbs still been intact, I would have crushed into the wall screaming and basically unconscious. I was lucky, there was no arguing about that.

There was a crash and I was thrown upwards like on a roller coaster: the crab tore me in half. One claw clutched my body, the other – the machine guns. The claw that was holding me started closing as if to crush me, when the Dungeon perceptibly shook. The claw opened, and I fell, bruising all my insides on the stones yet again. Only after I automatically downed a blue elixir and a red one, which granted me a few extra minutes of life, I saw that this time it was not the stones that assaulted me. The unwelcome impact came from the internal surface of the boss' chitin. I was lying inside a ten-foot crab; one half of it was simply missing. There was no claw, no legs and no eye. The meat had fallen into the lava and hissed and smoked in the most disgusting way; however, the armor filters prevented me from smelling roasted crab. Everything jolted again, so I had to grab onto some sharp edge which started growing slowly even as I was holding it. The boss was regenerating. I did not know if crabs were not prone to screaming or I just happened across a mute one, but at least the boss twisted in agony without making a sound.

The chitin grew another few inches and it

became hard to hold onto the crab. The Book of Knowledge immediately produced a projection, indicating that the boss would return to its original state in two and a half minutes. Angry at my inability to do anything, I pulled out a piece of still-soft chitin and threw it at the boss' insides. Die, blasted freak!

The crab could not care less; it kept moving in circles and actively regenerating. Tracing the flight of the chitin with my eyes I basically despaired of getting out of this whole thing alive, when I noticed that something inside the boss was pulsing oddly. The artifact pinpointed the phenomenon and highlighted it in green: yes, something was beating inside the boss. The AK I had put away at the very beginning of the Dungeon raid jumped into my hands and I put the entire clip into the crab's insides. I was shaking so badly that there was no way I could aim precisely. And I only had one clip – all the rest I had thrown into the lava a few moments ago. The crab jerked sharply yet again and I hit my head on the chitin. The last thing I saw before I fainted was a system message:

You have completed Dungeon "Alveona"

CHAPTER FOUR

THE MEETING

MY HEAD RANG as if a hundred drummers were giving a concert there. I opened my eyes reluctantly and tried to look around. Compete darkness was slightly diluted by the glowing semi-transparent energy dome that encompassed me on all sides, protecting from the hellish inferno of the sizzling Dungeon. The dome was small; there were just a few inches of free space, beyond which I saw the white and red insides of the crab. The boss was dead, but its body kept regenerating; it sealed me completely within its insides. I tried to sit up, but hit my head on something and fell back.

Drip! Pshhhh!

The force shell protected me from pressure and temperature extremes; however, as it turned out, it did not help against dripping ichor. Another drop fell precisely on my neck and rolled down disgustingly. My neck started itching badly, and I turned my head every which way to ease my suffering. Bending my head forward to the extent my "coffin" would allow I noticed the way my armor looked. The armor that once used to shine even covered in mud now seemed to be covered with stains and an elaborate lacing of scratches. Another drop fell through my dome and splashed muddy red on my armor, covering the last clean bits. Worried for my expensive armor, I opened the properties screen and rejoiced at what I saw. My protection had acquired additional attributes.

From now on my class armor blocked 10% of damage from lightning, and overall physical protection had increased by 5%. The "scratches" that had scared me were actually a spell – "Level 3 Energy Shield" – which did not require Energy usage and automatically activated in case of a sudden blow. Now it would be hard to take me by surprise or knock me out unexpectedly. Those advantages were worth the deteriorated appearance of the armor.

Would you like to collect your winnings?

Once I closed the properties screen, the Game offered me the chance to collect my "hard-earned gains" I acquired in the Dungeon. A virtual window appeared again; this time the interface was a rolling drum with the possible options of final loot. I got used to the rotation speed and read the words on the sections: "Gem", "Artifact Enhancer", "Attribute

Stone", "Engraving Pattern". "Gem" again, and the other options rolled through. All in all there were about fifty sections. There were only two that did not repeat on the drum; they were located opposite each other: "Game Set Enhancement" and "Double Game Set Enhancement". Oh yes, I wanted that. I wanted that very much.

Where is my double Luck? Hoping that there is fortune and luck in the Game that would help me, I closed my eyes: this way I would not see it if my luck were to float away right from under my nose. Then it would be easier to accept whatever super prize I received and not torment myself with the thoughts of what could have been.

Your prize is determined. Would you like to collect it?

YEEESSSSS! Lady Luck, if you were a person, I would have kissed you heartily! There was a reason I was so excited: the arrow of the virtual drum stopped right in the middle of "Double Game Set Enhancement". Come here, my Precious!

Daro Set cannot be received automatically; request for Viceroy generated
Received: 10 granises
Grandeur +10
Do you wish to leave Dungeon "Alveona"?

That seemed unfortunate. Now I would have to wait till the Viceroy deemed it acceptable to give me the set. Well, fine, at least that was clear. But where did the ten granises come from?! Miltay's words echoed through my head. This amount of granises would make me even more attractive to head hunters. My imagination readily painted a couple of scenes with evil seekers of easy money who would send me for respawn time after time until they killed me for good. I swallowed and asked for help.

"I need information on the current reward!" I screamed into the darkness. "I cannot accept it. This way I will just become prey sought by everyone! I must understand what threats I will be facing, or else I demand an equivalent exchange to the amount of the prize!"

Another information message appeared almost immediately:

Request is granted.
Access to Temple of Knowledge is provided.

"Welcome to the Temple of Knowledge, young Paladin." The keeper of knowledge spread his arms in a welcoming gesture. "Your request was deemed justified and your teachers will be subjected to well-deserved punishment for their negligence in training you. In this scroll you will find the information you have requested."
The old man fell silent, letting me stretch my shoulders and legs with a great deal of pleasure. It was great to feel my lower limbs again! I had been transported to the Temple of Knowledge in a completely healthy state.

Granis: official monetary unit of the Game used for settlements among players. Granises received directly from the Game are considered basic; they increase player's "Basic granis" scale.

Grandeur: dynamic parameter; determines player's achievements/punishments. Cannot be negative. Each Grandeur unit equals 10 virtual levels (cannot exceed 20 times player's current level); removes constraints on visiting Game worlds, using abilities, spell activation and other actions linked to player's level.

Daro set: second strongest set in the Game. Cannot be purchased. Issued by Viceroy for Game achievements. Set properties depend on player's class.

If the difference between all granises available to player and parameter "Basic granis" is from 3-10, player acquires a temporary attribute "Failure".

If the difference between all granises available to player and parameter "Basic granis" exceeds 10, "Terror" is initiated. A player with attribute "Terror" acquires specific aura enabling traders to significantly overstate prices of their goods; it also aides headhunters to locate and kill the victim.

Exchange rate: 1 granis = 100 Game gold coins = 200 kilograms gold.

Your current level of "Grandeur": 10.

Difference between granises available and parameter "Basic granis": +14. 2 quests are initiated for your permanent respawn. Quests accepted by: 1447 headhunters.

"Did all the mercenaries receive ten granises

each?" I asked once I finished reading. The old man frowned in concern, and I started pushing bluntly: "You can't tell me that it is not relevant to my inquiry! I received ten granises and I need to know if I have to give them away or no. It will determine the difference between available and basic granises, so it directly relates to my inquiry."

"Well, you are right," the keeper agreed reluctantly and scratched his beard. "I need to provide a clarification. Ten-fold enhancement of the Dungeon affected only the reward of the owner. Instead of the guaranteed one basic granis he received ten. Everyone else received one."

"Three granises that will be paid to Miltay for helping in completing the Dungeon: what type are they?"

"Once received, they have nothing to do with the Game. Your mercenaries are quite young; they've only been working for twenty years. That's why they accept all orders: they need to accumulate the initial capital of basic granises; doing so in the Dungeons is simplest for novices. The group was lucky with you. Because of the Luck they received Grandeur having completed a 10-fold Dungeon. This will enable them to register for hire in a different world."

"Judges." I hastened to start on the next topic of interest to me before the old guy would decide that he had had enough questions for the day. "It does not say anything here about Judges and granises that they receive. What should I be concerned about?"

"Judges don't receive granises, they receive a virtual reward for headhunters. That activates neither

'Indignation', nor 'Terror'. The hunter, or whatever being executes the sentence, will receive granises from the Judge, not from the Game. The 'Basic granis' level in this case will not increase." Apparently, the keeper was tired of my curiosity. "Enough, you have already received all the information you needed."

So that would have to do. The space around me shifted, returning me to the innards of the giant crab. Finally I understood the universal interest in the Dungeons and reasons why barter was so popular. Everyone wants granises, but large amounts of them are dangerous.

I poked listlessly at the crab's insides, hoping to reach the organ that had pulsed in the middle, but realized it was futile. I was not able to advance a single inch. Deciding that I'd had enough Luck for one day, I hastened to agree to the Game's suggestion to finish the Dungeon and return my legs. Miltay cheerfully greeted me in the Sanctuary.

There were no problems with sharing the loot. While I was away, the mercenary prepared the final list, separated my share, added a bit on top and presented all that to me in a red bag with a blue bow. I really wanted to make a joke about it, but decided against it, to Miltay's extreme disappointment. Apparently, that was the team's thing, with a well-prepared response. On my part I presented to them the attribute stone I had collected, and my parting with "Zeltan" team was quite friendly, as we were pleased with each other. I was assured that in case I needed them they would be happy to assist, this time with the two nukes their new license allowed.

"Hello! What an unexpected meeting!" A familiar female voice called to me as I was leaving the building with the Dungeon portals. I stopped and looked at Helen. I had expected an encounter with the Doll, but not so fast. The Game's creation was waving its hand at me with a friendly air from the other side of the street. In a couple moments Helen was standing next to me, and I let myself drown in her baby-blue eyes.

"I wanted to take a stroll around the city and got lost – can you imagine?" Passers-by were looking warmly at us. The NPCs felt that my Doll and I were ideally suited to each other, and were glad to see a really beautiful couple. "It's just that no one speaks Russian here, and my German... is quite limited. At least the navigator in my phone works really well. Listen, would it be too forward of me to bring you to a café? I would be so glad to hear someone speak my language! What do you say to that?"

The girl extended her hand to me and I surrendered, accepting her invitation with a smile. To me Helen was first of all a pretty girl with a sweet smile and charming dimples on her cheeks, and only then a Doll. After all, I had not had sex for a very long time!

"Paladin Yaropolk, come with us. The Viceroy is ready to meet you." We made barely ten paces when a crowd of players appeared out of nowhere and encircled us. A druid elf stepped forward and made a gesture, inviting me to step into a portal that opened right beside us, but I disagreed with that approach. I noticed that some of those in the escort had a tattoo covering their entire shoulder: hissing snakes entwined around a shining stone. The Book of Knowledge told me that it was the emblem of the Viceroy, and I recalled looking at it during the speech his highness had made before we were all sent off to the Academy.

"Guys, but who are you, actually? And why am I supposed to follow your orders?"

Helen shied away, frightened, then hid behind my back and pressed herself against me, seeking protection. Maybe I did not want to follow the unexpected escort stupidly as a sheep on a rope; maybe I was just trying to show off in front of the girl. They say that you can tell what the master is like by his servants or followers; following that logic the Viceroy was quite something. I had expected that an invitation would be handed to me festively, that it would highlight my grandeur and my unique achievements. Or something like that. But definitely not an armed escort. Now what, would they pull out shackles to prevent me from biting his blue-skinned highness accidentally?

"Paladin Yaropolk, we are wasting time! You don't have enough brainpower to make a guess?"

"Well, let's be clear: you are wasting time exclusively due to your stupidity." I underscored the "you" part. "And I have enough brainpower not to jump into portals with everyone who sports the Viceroy's tattoo."

"You, dog meat, you don't get it – you are supposed to be delivered to the ceremony in one piece, but afterwards there's nothing that prevents us from making you pay for the insults," the druid exploded indignantly. He did contain himself, but his flaring nostrils indicated that he was ready to burst. Apparently, in his worldview I was already supposed to be rushing for the portal so fast that I would overtake my own shadow.

"Is this a threat?" Fatigue was taking its toll, and I was becoming angry as well.

"It's a warning!" barked the elven-descended arrogant upstart in response. "If you don't voluntarily get in gear and run towards this portal, I'll just toss you in there like a sack. And even the Sanctuary will not stop me! Like I'm supposed to bow and scrape in front of every random half-wit!"

I did not respond to the lout. It became crystal clear to me that those guys were from the caste of "tough guys that no one wants to mess with", imagining that they were an important part of the universe machinery, and it would be pointless to try arguing with them.

"Vorta, get the net ready," the druid signaled to the player standing behind me, and actually turned away, considering the incident over. We'll just haul him like a pig."

I was nearly gnashing my teeth in anger. Servants who confused themselves with masters would have to answer for that "pig".

Case initiated: Insulting a Player (Slots available for: 8 more cases)
Description: You consider that Viceroy's servants, namely <list of players>, insulted you.

**You wish to defend your honor and dignity.
Task: Investigate this case and deliver a verdict.
Case investigation: Not applicable; the case was
initiated by the Judge himself
Period of limitation of action: None**

"For demonstrating disrespect and insulting a player I sentence the Viceroy's servants listed in the case 'Insulting a Player' to pay a fine to the Game in the amount of ten granises. This sentence is final and not subject to appeal!"

Following Redel's advice, I stated the sentence silently to myself. The Game recorded the verdict and I calmly awaited its confirmation by the Emperor. I sincerely believed that my decision was just, and so decided to hit them at what they valued most: granises and Grandeur. A few moments seemed to drag forever, but finally the message I needed appeared, and I exhaled with relief. It was not the way of the Game to allow insults to go unpunished:

**Verdict is confirmed
Verdict is deemed harsh
Case "Insulting a Player" is closed. Sentence has
been executed by the Game
Award for correct verdict: basic Energy level
increased by 100**

Immediately in the top of my field of vision a scale with an arrow appeared, like what I had already seen in the Academy. Now it indicated that I was 10 percent closer to the next level from the initial one. I studied this phenomenon in dead silence. The Viceroy's servants did not say a word as they let the events sink in. Of course; just now I had dropped their "Grandeur" level by ten points at once.

"Shall we attempt a dialogue, or shall I continue?" I asked the druid in a deliberately nonchalant way.

"We didn't...," the druid lost all his arrogance like a tree loses its leaves in the fall; his inability to speak coherently only underscored that. I was kind enough to help:

"You are trying to apologize?" The elf hesitated, but then nodded. "And are inviting me to follow you to the Viceroy?" The elf nodded again.

I looked at Helen, thinking what to do about her. She was still clinging to me, frightened.

"I need to run off again." She was so defenseless and attractive that I could not resist and stroked the girl's head. Helen's cheeks turned pink, and in response to my simple caress she clung to me tighter, but this time not in fear. The Doll felt that the danger had passed, and that it could now perform its intended function. Which was bringing me pleasure.

"You can take her along. There is a place in the garden where players may leave their things for safekeeping." The druid's voice changed again. No, there was no respect in it; neither was there fear. I could not identify the change, so decided to be extra cautious:

"Fine; you will bring the Game to witness that the portal leads to the Viceroy and not to any other place. You will also confirm that no issues will arise if

I arrive at the court with my Doll. Once we receive the confirmation we can go."

"I agree." The druid regained his composure, and white light washed all over him as soon as he uttered the oath. "Please follow me – the ceremony is about to start."

Helen did not ask anything; she just followed me unquestioningly, even though she halted at the portal. I wanted to cheer her up and reassure her that there was nothing to fear, but from her admiring look I realized that I had been wrong. She smiled as a child as she looked at her hand in the bright glow coming from the portal. Then she shut her eyes tightly and stepped into the unknown first, pulling me after herself. A moment later we arrived at our destination. I suppose at that moment I did not look any better than my Doll. We were both like children in a magic dreamland. Huge green trees, elaborate plant sculptures and immaculate lawns were next to urbanistic structures of silver metal and glass. A shimmering waterfall rushed down from the top of the nearest building and created a rainbow amazing in shape and richness of color. Funny animals dashed everywhere, chasing each other playfully through teleports; giant flower beds were covered in fantastic blooms. My elation gradually diminished and then I was able to calmly observe the ideal state of my surroundings. Helen kept twirling around, periodically exclaiming to show her excitement and admiration; she was squeezing my hand harder and harder. Even though it was amazing – how could such a small hand be so strong?

"Welcome to the residence of the Viceroy of Biological Life-Forms Sector," a semi-transparent hologram of the local master of ceremonies, similar to a ball lightning, appeared in front of me. He was obviously not a biological life-form. "I will accompany you there. We must hurry – the award ceremony is about to start any minute now. Please leave your property here. Don't worry; it will be taken care of."

I'll be back soon," I promised Helen, and after several jumps through portals I found myself in front of a crystal gazebo in a green garden. Another miracle of the local landscape.

"Paladin Yaropolk!" the master of ceremonies announced, and the eyes of those present converged on me. There were ten beings: two elves, an orc, a catorian, a smallish black dragon who immediately fully captured my attention; I was unable to determine the race of another three right away – they were covered by water domes. The last one was human. Even though I had not noticed too many human features in Dolgunata during our acquaintance.

Finished with looking at the rest of the guests I looked at the dragon again.

"You did complete the Dungeon, after all," Dolgunata smiled, handing to me a glass of clear liquid and finally distracting me from the dragon. The latter, apparently, could not care less about the attention: all the while that I was staring at him he did not even bother to open his eyes. I sipped from the glass and was barely able to restrain myself from gulping the whole thing down at once. I had never tried such delicious wine – and it was not just the matter of its taste – even though the taste was impeccable as well. My body filled with strength, my mind cleared and my ability to perceive the world around me improved by an order of magnitude. Green glows appeared here and there, and disappeared at once. My video recorder was working non-stop. "Congratulations! I did not expect such prowess of you."

"You, though, have way too much," I smiled broadly in response; now I began to figure out what was going on. The ceremony was for players who had been deemed worthy of the enhanced set. Since the druid was here that meant she had also received +2 enhancement for her armor. That could mean only one thing: 10-fold Dungeon enhancement and greatly elevated Luck. I could not call her a successful explorer, so...: "Did Archibald present you with the attribute stones?"

"You are far too smart for a player who did not know a week ago that the Game even existed." Dolgunata was being her nasty self. "Did you get a brain as loot?"

"His Highness the Viceroy of Biological Life-Forms Sector!" The master of ceremonies' booming voice resounded in the gazebo interrupting our word parrying with the druid. We were told to stand in a semi-circle, and one of the four Masters of the Game strolled in leisurely. The other players kneeled, and so did I.

"Greetings, brothers and sisters!" The Viceroy spread his arms in a welcoming gesture, and a light breeze wafted through the gazebo. "Those who have gathered here today are the select few who have proven by their play that they are worthy of receiving a reward from our hands. Daro sets and even an Imperial one will from now on speak to your enemies of your strength and of our magnanimity! Our congratulations to you! Now receive our reward! Xenobiologist Xarkan!"

One of the water beings floated over to the Viceroy; solemn music filled the gazebo.

"Five hundred and twenty three years in the Game; level two hundred and seventy; seventy two years as the Head of Class for xenobiologists of the game world Artey." The Viceroy listed the water guy's regalia. "We consider that there is no being in the Game more worthy to receive an Imperial set! Wear it honorably!"

The armor glared bright gold in the Viceroy's hands and disappeared into the dome of water concealing the strange being. He bubbled something from the water to express his gratitude, and hastily returned to his place.

The blue-skinned ruler continued with the ceremony.

"Shaman Mahan!"

Wow! It turned out that the Shaman was the dragon; he smoothly moved towards the Viceroy.

His name definitely sounded familiar to me! The thoughts twirled in my head, I could not catch it... for a while I lost awareness of my surroundings. Was that not the Mahan about whom I had read a whole saga? I was sure it had been about him. There was something there about dragons, shamanism and beautiful women who could be good as well as evil. But those were just books... Or not?

Hm. Could it be that not all sci-fi was just a figment of the imagination of writers, graphomaniacs, and – let's be frank – schizophrenics? Or maybe there is no fiction at all, and what there is represents documentary descriptions of some game worlds? The universe is infinite, so it could have truly odd things in it!

Thinking about the degree of realism of the worlds depicted in the sci-fi I had read in my previous life, and the probability that I would run into my favorite characters within the Game, I missed the award proceedings for practically all the players. I was only yanked back by the sound of my own name:

"Paladin Yaropolk!"

I came towards the Viceroy like the players before me.

"Has been in the Game but for a short time – level thirty five; yet you have enough arrogance for about a dozen of those servants of ours that cannot serve us any more because of your doings." The Viceroy looked me up and down and extracted a silver set of armor out of his virtual reality. "We doubt that your young age and your character deserve such a high reward. However, the rules are the same for everybody. Time will tell if we were right. Try to be worthy, and wear the Daro set with honor!"

Achievement attained: "Daro Set: "Grandeur increased by 5 units

Pleased that Viceroy was not going to punish me for curtailing his servants, I enjoyed my fresh achievement. It was nice to know that they existed in the Game. Even though I did think it was strange that it was not granted for completing a 10-fold Dungeon, yet receiving a set of armor from the hands of a Viceroy improved "Grandeur" quite a bit.. I would have to look into this matter in detail.

Dolgunata was the last to receive her highly pleasurable set of armor; after that the Viceroy quickly concluded the ceremony and strolled regally out of the gazebo. Seeing that other players were stripping naked quite unabashed and putting on the new sets just presented to them, I turned towards to Dolgunata, who hesitated, and took my old armor off with a smile. I did not feel shy: one would have to be bonkers not to use this safe location to change one's armor. Dolgunata snorted demonstratively, and a moment later was regaling us all with a set of lace underwear one would not call modest under any circumstances. Unfortunately, there was not much time to enjoy the view: she dressed much faster than I did.

Sighing with frustration, I put on the last element of the armor. As soon as it clicked in place a whole sheet of system messages appeared before me. At least I had had no time to make the helmet transparent, and those around me did not see my mouth open wide as I was reading the properties of my new outfit. I swallowed with joy. It was completely incredible to receive, after barely a week of playing, 30% percent of blocking of impacts at any level and a permanent energy shield that blocked hits at 100 times the basic Energy. Who said the Game had no tanks? Yeah, right! From now on I was a tank! Besides everything else, the set enabled me to dive to 3000 meters without having to bother about the pressure; it could offset an ambient temperature of 1200 degrees – I could easily sit on top of a lava lake without spending any Energy; it had a built-in generator of water, amino acids and oxygen, so I did not have to bother with such trifles as food and drink. The Daro set was truly a one-player Game fortress.

We decided not to overstay our welcome at the Viceroy's place; everyone left the gazebo using the same stationary teleports, accompanied by ball lightning beings. I came back to the beautiful garden where my Doll was waiting.

"Yaropolk!" Helen rushed towards me without concealing her joy. "Look, just take a look at this little creature!" A strange furry animal appeared in the girl's hands. It was slowly chewing on a purple berry which had smudged Helen's face, "It's like a fairy tale here! Everything is so wonderful and magical!"

I approached Helen with a smile and cleaned her cheek with my finger. I had already forgotten ever seeing anything so full of sincere joy.

"I once had a sweet little doll, dears." Dolgunata's voice sounded behind my back, slowly reciting a nursery rhyme. I was so bloody tired of her. I turned around slowly to see that Dolgunata was staring steadily at Helen, screwing up one eye. "But I lost my poor little doll, dears, as I played on the heath one day."

"What are you doing? I asked, frowning.

"Studying your Doll," Dolgunata responded contemptuously. "Or did the brain you receive go completely to your other head that you cannot see obvious things?"

"Have you looked enough? Your portal is waiting," I nodded in the direction of the glimmering spot behind the girl's back. "If you are so interested in dolls, find yourself one in the Sanctuary and stare at it till your eyes leak out."

"Yari, are you really an idiot, or are you just pretending? Have you seen men and women in the streets strolling alongside sex toys?! Do you not understand that people hide their Dolls in the same way they hide the fact that they visit brothels?"

"She is not a toy to hide her so!"

"Oh really?! But she has no choice! She is like a prostitute that has already received her payment; so she cannot do anything else other than strike a proper pose and tell you how handsome and smart you are because she has to work for her money! This sweet little doll has no choice!"

"Yaropolk, is everything all right?" The Doll asked with concern; she did not understand the point of my argument with Dolgunata. The Game protected the Doll's mind most thoroughly.

"Don't you worry, sweetie!" Dolgunata answered for me. "Everything is just fine!"

"Why don't you go visit your own 'toy' – maybe that will mellow you," I growled. "It's good for a woman's health."

"I don't need surrogates," the druid snorted.

Now it was my turn to laugh out loud:

"Judging by your character, the Game didn't have the wherewithal to satisfy your requirements. What, did your doll come out defective?"

Dolgunata fell silent for a few moments, and I decided I would not hear a response from her.

"Those who have the real ideal thing don't need artificial substitutes," the girl finally said without a trace of irony as she kept staring at Helen. Then she shifted her gaze at me, grinned and continued: "Fine; I am not going to distract you. Don't forget to dress your property up, and make sure you start with the underwear. I can recommend 'Victoria's miracle'. I noticed your appreciation."

The druid batted her eyelashes theatrically and disappeared into the portal.

"Who was this?" Helen's voice was trembling. She did not enjoy the scene, but she worried about me first of all. "Are you sure you won't get in trouble?"

"I am sure. Forget about it; none of this matters." I sighed and grabbed the girl into a hug. Was she a thing? Probably. But she was my thing, and I was not going to allow her to be harassed. "Here! We cannot take local animals with us, but instead I have this little wonder. Now he's yours. You'll take care of him and boast his achievements to me. All clear?"

"Rrgra?" My pet tumbled out from his virtual shelter and sat on the ground. The half-meter tall furry wonder scratched behind its ear in a funny manner; this delighted Helen to no end. She wriggled out of my arms immediately and settled next to the pet.

"Rgra, rgra," I answered, just in case, and nodded at the motionless Doll. From now on you will obey her. Her orders are my orders. Get that?"

The young Neanderthal scratched his butt as if indicating what he thought of my orders.

"You don't need to order him," Helen's voice softened – mothers talk to their children that way. "You need to ask him: right, little one? Come, I'll rock you in my arms."

"Gra! Gra!" the furry beast murmured, and quickly climbed into Helen's arms. He shuffled his bum, settling more comfortably, and embraced her neck with his long arms. After that, looking into her eyes the creature said affectionately, to the extent his throat allowed: "Mm-ma-ma-a-a!"

I watched this cute bonding scene in amazement, realizing that I would have totally failed to find a way to establish contact with the pet. There was no question about that!

"Yaropolk, what's his name?"

"Rragr; he is a delvian. He was given to me as a present, but I was never told what to do with him. I think you'll find a way. He definitely likes you better than he does me."

"Thank you, Yaropolk!" Helen exclaimed happily, and in a fit of gratitude reached to kiss me.

"Paladin Yaropolk," a ball lightning interrupted us, and the kiss had to be postponed. "This type of physical contact with Dolls is supposed to be private. His Highness will be insulted by such behavior in his castle, particularly given the recent incident."

"You mean the punishment?" I guessed.

"Yes. Two of the players you punished lost the ability to serve His Highness. Their level makes it impossible to be on this planet without escort. Please leave the Viceroy's residence."

Granting that the Viceroy had reasons to be displeased, I decided to continue the evening over the promised cup of coffee. I grabbed Helen by the hand and jumped into the portal; however, my hopes were to be dashed again. As soon as we ordered some coffee, Gromana plopped down at our table without too much ceremony.

"Showed up, didn't you?!" The witch asked from the start, took Helen's coffee away and downed it in one gulp. I raised an eyebrow, puzzled.

"Actually, you are the one who showed up! Even more so – crashed in when no one was expecting you!" Despite the sarcasm I demonstrated, I was actually glad to see Gromana. I needed a source of information, and I also needed to meet that mysterious being."

"Like hell I need your jokes! Why did you take so long?" Gromana was as straightforward as a rock falling on your head.

"I was busy. But your timing was good. I was about to try and find you anyway." I was not lying in the least. Well, not much, anyway. I had been planning to visit Gromana immediately after several pleasant hours with Helen.

"I hope this is not the reason why you were so busy." The witch nodded dismissively in the direction of my Doll.

"Yaropolk, should I leave?" Helen started worrying again.

"Shut up." The witch grimaced in displeasure and waved her hand, sending the Doll into a trance.

"Another one. What did she do to you? You know, sometimes I think that you simply use your 'curse of truth' as an excuse for your natural rudeness and tactlessness," I grinned. "No, you missed your guess; here's the reason."

With those words I thrusted my chest forward, showing off my new armor. Why not? I had a good reason to boast. Let the weak ones be modest.

"I had already noticed. My congratulations!" The witch bowed mockingly, and I responded in kind by flinging up my hands:

"Oh, thank you very much! It's so nice when people appreciate your abilities as they should!"

"Yeah, right: boast your abilities to me – go on! For what kind of feat did the Viceroy present you with the armor? Maybe you don't even need to see Bernard anymore? Eh, Paladin?" Gromana was staring at me suspiciously.

"You should not be the one complaining, witch. I was not the one who graced a poor Paladin with ten granises so that you and a thousand hunters could see his every move. Right, Gromana?"

"You found out already." The witch grew quiet for a moment, but then flared up again. "Had you come to me in time, that would not have been a problem. Anyway, Yari! Forget about that! What was the reward for?"

I snorted disdainfully indicating that the witch

was not getting an answer.

"Whatever. It's time to go, Bernard is waiting. He'll be the one to appreciate your abilities as they deserve to be appreciated for sure." The witch rose from the table, indicating that the conversation was over. She cast a glance at Helen and added:

"Leave the doll here, she'll find you later. You understand: that's not a place for things like that."

I let the last statement go, knowing this was not a good place or time to argue.

The witch turned away and activated a local green portal with her hand. I was already familiar with the distinctions: green ones were local, enabling you to jump a couple of kilometers, the blue ones were global – they extended further, sometimes to different worlds; as for the red ones: I knew nothing about them yet.

"Gromana, you don't think that I'll go anywhere without an oath, right?" I asked the witch calmly. "I have no idea where this portal leads. Come on, my caring dear, call the Game to witness that you are not plotting anything evil against me and that if I chose to do so I would be able to return to the Sanctuary unhindered after talking to Bernard.

"That's reasonable." The witch hesitated, yet complied with my condition. I waited till the white light washed over her, then left the tip and ordered Helen, who was still sitting like a statue, to go home. I cast another glance at the Doll, with whom I was frustratingly unable to advance, and followed Gromana.

The local portal was set to the maximum

distance possible outside of the Sanctuary. The moment I appeared in the normal world, all hell broke loose around me. Someone quickly pushed me down under the force dome, yet six lightning bolts still hit on the armor. The Daro set worked without a glitch: it absorbed all of them.

"All clear!" During the moment while I was rising to my feet it was all over. The dome was gone and I found myself surrounded by armed fighters, carefully scanning the surroundings with their eyes and in every other way available. A necromancer, a rogue, a couple of warriors; hunters and some from classes unknown to me – this motley crew seemed to have just about everybody. Like the Viceroy's servants, they were wearing an emblem on their right shoulders: three thick spirals originating from the same point at an angle of 120 degrees to each other. The Book of Knowledge told me the name for this symbol: triskelion.

"I have removed the markers. Let's go, we're getting visitors real soon!"

Carefully to the extent that was possible at all in this melee, they took me by my arms and brought me to the next portal. Then another. And another. After each leg of the journey the escort team scanned the area, waited for about ten seconds, then made the next leap.

"We made it just in time!" One of the fighters turned his helmet transparent, and it turned out to be Gromana. Her armor class easily transformed from a silk dress into a full chainmail outfit. "We barely grabbed you from the hands of Volt and his cutthroats. Just a little longer and you would have been sitting in the Citadel until your own people would sell you out. Yari – give me back the ten granises. We need to take the 'terror' off you."

I did not want to part with such a huge amount of money, and the witch noticed it:

"You will receive a huge amount of knowledge that you would not be able to buy with those ten granises. Yari, enough of this silliness! We have just a couple of minutes before they find you, and then we'll have to start that race all over again!"

Common sense overcame greed and I became ten granises poorer, to Gromana's relief:

"Shal, open the portal home. He doesn't stand out any more."

"Home" turned out to be a huge private residence; some castles would pale in comparison. The architecture inspired awe, and clearly indicated the social distance between the owner of this miracle and a commoner such as myself. Hiding under the mask of indifference so as not to look like a country bumpkin allowed for the first time into a "big house", my eyes glided over the aerial fish dancing intricately in the air; I calmly glanced at the unbelievable beauty of an incredible living hedge that moved freely within its area... Oh Great Game, it really WAS alive! Say, one day you will be tired from the rat race of life and decide to take a break in the peace and quiet of nature... and you would sit and look at the hedge... and the hedge would look back at you... with the millions of its curious eyes on every leaf. Or, say, you have a private tryst with a lady... Brrrr! To hell with that!

"Ladies and gentlemen, please follow me." The torture, with its miracles borne of someone's sick imagination, was finally over, and a butler came towards us. "The master is ready to meet with you."

Agreed, a common butler would not be good enough for a place like that; however, a vampire with a dark cloud over his head instead of a parasol was just the ticket! A dream of millions of NPC girls in my old world: handsome, tall, dark-haired, white-skinned and with fangs. As far as I cared, the most important thing was that he was polite.

"Earth has had many interesting Game plots," Gromana said, noticing my interest in the vampire. "For example, in 2007 there was a local quest held here; vampires won the contest. As winners, they chose a curious reward. Garbital, the head of the vampires, decided to make the race more popular. To make them more prestigious, so to speak. Books, films and thorough brain-washing created a whole generation of brainless morons whose only desire was to become vampires. A generation of blighted idiots. On the other hand, what else could you expect of NPCs?"

"That's funny," I smirked, recalling the vampire sagas that were a fad at some point. "Wait, but as far as I remember that vampire hysteria lasted only a couple of years. Then it was replaced by dystopia – all those 'chosen against the system' etc, etc. Before that Tolkien fans were all the rage."

"It's possible. Different events are initiated throughout the Game just about every month, so it's hard to follow everything. So there is no surprise that they are forgotten as soon as someone else wins the next quest. Someone has to be ahead." Gromana shrugged.

"Over here, please." It was not the custom in Bernard's residence to use teleports, so we ended up walking up to the huge massive building. Having made sure that we followed him, the vampire added: "If you don't mind, I could clarify. You are right – our race did not start this popularization of ideas. This method of altering popular perceptions is widely used. Those whom you called Tolkien fans were aiming to extol elves and gnomes, while showing people and orcs as weak and dim. We had to share the fame with shape-shifters, who were our allies in the quest you mentioned. Dystopia, as you call it, became popular after the victory of the gyrdannes. The thing is that there were mass revolts at the time in their clan against the ruling elite; so that's the origin of all those slogans: 'Down with Social Inequality!' 'Power to the People' 'Destroy the System! But they are fading into oblivion now as well: preparation is underway for a new local event planned for next year. We are going to see an invasion."

"Oh! Now it's clear that my presence here is not accidental!" Gromana stopped, struck by the news. "Soluna must have known what was coming, so that's why she selected Earth! Who are going to be in it?"

"The choice will be held on January first. The options are already known though: either nernians or vances".

"Space aliens or zombies." Gromana was

contemplating. "Whatever – that's even more interesting.

The vampire nodded and stopped in front of the entrance to a gazebo, which was our destination. I grinned to myself – I wonder when I will reach a point at which I am seen at least in the entrance hall of the house? Or maybe they hold all meetings in gazebos here to prevent their silver cutlery from disappearing?

The owner of the residence was standing in the gazebo with his back to us, enjoying the view of the garden in bloom. Hearing our steps, he turned around, and we had a chance to look at him. Human. He looked about fifty, but it could be that the grey beard made him look older. His loose clothes hid his class, but not his good physical shape. Smooth movements, the grasping stare of brown eyes. Bernard gave the impression of a respectable and distinguished man.

"Welcome, Yaropolk!" Bernard said. He had a pleasant low voice that resonated throughout the gazebo. "A pleasure to meet you. Have a seat. We have some things to talk about."

The vampire extracted three soft armchairs and a small table out of the air. A moment later servants were fussing around us setting the table. The host sat down first, nodding to Gromana and myself at the other chairs:

"As host, I would like to introduce myself first. Coordinator for sector 446, nobleman by birth, Bernard Kalran at your service.

"It sounds very impressive!" I responded, but my curiosity egged me on, and I decided not to hold it back. "But I would be even more impressed and would very much appreciate it if you could tell me what those sectors are and what their coordinators do. Is this a title that indicates how cool its owner is, or is it the same as calling a janitor a 'cleaning manager'? Believe me, I don't want to offend you; it's just that I have certain gaps in my knowledge. I really like Gromana's curse in this respect. Why hide behind fancy words things that can be asked directly?"

"Well, your frankness is quite engaging, and your age accounts for a lot." Bernard smiled in a fatherly way. "Besides, if one were to choose between hypocrisy and harsh truth, I'd choose the latter. The Game space is divided into sectors; the coordinator is in charge of developing his sector, and of relations with neighboring ones. To make it easier for you, it's like President of the Earth and another three game worlds. Is this impressive enough for you?"

"Impressive does not even begin to cover it," I answered honestly, noting that this time I was way over my head.

"You don't seem to be too pleased," Bernard said pursing his lips; apparently that was not the reaction he expected.

"Well, you know, when a fresh graduate of the Academy is invited by a sector coordinator to talk, it makes you think about what's in store for you. 'Beware of masters, they will cause you trouble any day'." Once again I was not trying to cover myself with pleasantries.

"Well, your concern is understandable." The velvet and care faded from Bernard's voice, and he instantly turned from a kind uncle into someone accustomed to giving orders. "Everything will depend on you. You give me the Diary and tell me everything you know about restart. Lying or hiding something would not make sense, I would feel that. Afterwards, if I have no questions, Gromana will see you to the Sanctuary, and I will make sure that everyone forgets about you. Otherwise you have to understand that your life will be very short once you return. At this stage only my interest in you has protected you from headhunters and prevented them from sending you into respawn cycle till final death. Someone else would find the Diary later. So, do you agree?"

I did not have any real choice; just like any other creature, I wanted to live. If not long, then at least happily. It was beyond my power to stop restart anyway:

"I agree."

"Smart boy. Diary," Bernard stretched out his hand.

The ubiquitous butler appeared next to me, and extended his hand to take the Diary. Perhaps handing anything over directly was prohibited, so I did not bother to argue or protest. Realizing that I would never see the Diary again, I held onto it for a moment. Maybe it was for the better: this was the price of my safety, so I was prepared to pay it.

A fraction of a second later, the butler placed the Diary in his master's hand. Before Bernard was even able to close his fingers around it, his eyes rolled and his body arched. I grabbed the arms of the chair tighter, not sure what was going on. Straightening up sharply, the coordinator for sector 446 was staring at me, his hair ruffled, his eyes turning as red as an albino's. I felt uneasy.

"YOOOOUUUU!!! I GOOOOOOT IIIIT!! I WAAAAITED FOR SOOOOOO LOOOONG!!!!" Bernard's voice had also changed so that it became practically unrecognizable. He hissed and spat. I pushed myself deeper back into the armchair.

"I CAME BACK TO GO AWAY, AGAIN AND AGAIN AND AGAIN!!!!! DEATH!!! DEATH IS SALVATION!!!" the host kept raving. Gromana jumped as if something had bitten her and began quickly rummaging through her bag, saying quietly:

"Wait, wait, wait..."

Bernard turned around and stretched a hand to her in a jerky movement:

"FREAK! YOU WILL DIE!!! NOW!!!" He was screaming at Gromana now.

Finally the witch grabbed some small object out of her bag and threw it precisely at Bernard:

"We will all die some day, but not now, not today. Bernard, come back!"

The white thing turned out to be a small animal that climbed up the man's body and sank its teeth into his neck. A shudder ran through the coordinator's body, and he slumped like a broken doll. His arms dropped listlessly and the Diary fell out of his hands onto the floor with a loud thump. A moment passed in tense waiting, and finally Bernard drew air heavily and opened his eyes. I did not know what that little white thing did, but it returned the Bernard I had already met to the gazebo. In his right mind and sane. He stared at Gromana angrily, making her cringe, and I perked up my ears, hoping to figure out what all that was about.

"What took you so long?"

Gromana was embarrassed; she dropped her head. Meanwhile the white animal returned to the witch and disappeared into her bag:

"Forgive me, Bernard; it was my fault. You have had no fits for so long that I had relaxed. Now I will always be on guard."

The man did not respond; his eyes traveled to the book lying nearby:

"Yaropolk, pick up the Diary!"

I was surprised, and decided that now was a good time to say something:

"Why me? I thought our agreement was different."

"The deal is off. I changed my mind." Our host said with finality, without batting an eye. "You will leave the premises as my underling, or you won't leave at all. This is not a threat; I am just stating the facts."

I stared at Gromana inquisitively; she just shrugged her shoulders, as if to say that her word carried no weight here and her oath to me had nothing to do with it. My internal voice still refused to call my situation desperate. There were reasons for that. Redel had clearly indicated that Judges without protectors in the Game are under clear and present threat of death. While previously I had considered approaching Gerhard or Iven, everything else paled before my option with the sector coordinator. With a protector like him I would be able to breathe easy. I never signed up to be a hero. But! Before promising anything I needed to consult a specialist.

"I need all information on vassalage in the Game. Obligations and duties of both parties. First and foremost: the possibility of revoking the vassal oath. I will have to make a choice that will change my fate."

An instant later a system message on admission to the Temple of Knowledge appeared in front of me.

"Congratulations, young Judge." The keeper of knowledge greeted me as if I were family. "Your Luck keeps working for you. Bernard Kalran is a powerful and fair protector."

Now I felt like the main character in "The Truman Show".

"I wish I knew what I was getting into," I hemmed. "And that's my question to you."

"The answer to it is in this scroll. Study it."

As I supposed, vassalage did not bring anything irrevocable. First of all the liege lord, suzerain or, as Bernard preferred to call himself, "protector", is obligated to arm, feed, keep and pay his vassals, who served him as company or as bodyguards. Actually, there was no threat of the latter happening to me. Bodyguards in the Game were a special cohort of NPCs or players, and I definitely had nothing to do with it. The unpleasant part was that I would be in Bernard's full service. In addition to the normal requirements like "do not kill" and "do not betray" I would be obligated, at my suzerain's whim, to serve him at table, follow him everywhere, and in case there was some skirmish I would be the first to go to respawn or die, protecting my boss with my life. The relations between us would be sealed with a voluntary oath; it would assign me to my protector's "house"; there would also be an emblem on my armor letting everyone know who was backing me. In case I decided to leave Bernard, I would need to hand him, in person, a thirty-day written "notice". It obviously implied that my main task during those remaining days would be survival, but that did not concern me now. The good part was that I was not obligated to open my pockets to him, nor tell him all my secrets. A vassal retained a certain degree of personal freedom, which was definitely an advantage.

I finished the scroll and was thinking, since the old guy was in no hurry to throw me out. From the standpoint of survival, no matter how you looked at it, Bernard was the best option I could possibly find on Earth. Now I needed to understand what was the meaning of the scene I had witnessed in the gazebo, and how to extract some additional benefit from it; also, I had to figure out the situation with the actual Diary.

"I agree, but I would like to receive answers to my questions. Also, I will need you to provide me with an opportunity to level up my artifact, preferably using books." I tried to at least say it with calm dignity, as if something actually depended on me.

"You will certainly receive answers to some of your questions. I will help with the leveling up, fine. Now let's get to business; repeat after me: 'I swear to serve...'," Bernard responded calmly.

The oath of loyalty to the suzerain was completely identical to the text I had seen in the Temple of Knowledge, so there were no problems in that for me. Bernard stated his part of the oath, and lightning flickered between us. The butler appeared next to me and completed the ceremony: my suzerain's emblem appeared on my left shoulder. The triskelion.

"What do you know about restart? Just make it brief." Bernard leaned back in the armchair, breathing heavily. Even though simple, the ceremony had taken practically all his strength. And mine as well. My Energy dropped all the way down to one. "And do me a favor, pick up this book already."

I did not protest, and the Diary was in my hand again. While I was doing that, Bernard drank some wine leisurely, and immediately looked noticeably better. Before answering, I also took a sip from the glass presented by the servants, and my Energy started creeping up.

"I know that there have been several of them. It takes three participants, not two as some mistakenly believe. All of them are people. Two men and one woman," Saying all this aloud drove home the thought that I did not know that much, after all. "Well, actually, that was the brief version. May I ask my questions now?"

The man nodded:

"But don't expect me to answer all of them. Go on: surprise me, young Paladin."

"Why did you return the Diary to me? Why do you need the Game to restart? Why do so few know about the third participant in the restart? Why me?"

"The first and last questions are essentially the same. Levard made a mistake by leaving you in the cage. You repeated his actions and activated your copy of the Diary; by doing so you became the Guide. Not the Keymaster, as Archibald thinks. Is there something you know?" the suzerain noticed my smile.

"I know who could be the Keymaster. I don't know the rest of the terminology. Does that mean I am not Merlin? What does it mean: the Guide and the Keymaster?"

"Believe me, you are not Merlin," Bernard's eyes warmed up a lot; apparently he had expected some heavy duty conversation and pressure. It was nice to know that I had ruined his plans. "As for the Keymaster... If you know that, I definitely do as well. It's Dolgunata, Archibald's student. They have been training her for this role for the last thirty years, naively supposing that I knew nothing about it."

"I feel like a first grader talking to the professor about quantum physics theory," I honestly confessed."That makes my question even more important. Why me?"

"Because of this," Bernard pointed at Madonna's Diary. "By initiating the restart you became the Guide. It's a being who is supposed to take all three to the restart point. This role cannot be taken away from you any more, unless you are completely wiped out. In that case the activated Diary would disappear and the restart would stop. That's why you are so valuable to me now, and so inconvenient for my enemies. Accepting you as my vassal makes it easier for me to ensure your safety. I am not going to lock you up in a cell or keep you tied up here. The Game is open to you."

"So I am not going to die?" I asked with joy; however, Bernard's reaction told me that I had said something stupid.

"The second question: the third player. Gromana, leave us." The witch immediately rose, made a polite bow and left the gazebo, accompanied by the vampire. "The flaw of my protégé is too great to allow her hear too much. Unfortunately, I have not figured out how to remove the curse; Soluna is a strong witch. The reason no one knows about the third player lies in his own self. He carefully and thoroughly removes any mention of himself from all the sources. I found out about his existence only thirty years ago, even though I had been working on the issue of restart for over four centuries. I still know little. It is a man – human – Madonna's lover. His name and class are unknown. One thing I know for sure: he and Madonna always find each other. It's an axiom."

"Why?" I could not restrain myself, but Bernard ignored my question.

"The third question was why I need restart. Now, that's more complicated. You have just witnessed a rather unpleasant scene, right? My other self. My personal curse. My echo. Every time a player reaches a hundredfold level of "Grandeur", the Game gets a glitch. It creates the player's echo, his complete copy both externally and internally, only with a defect: the echo knows nothing about the Game. It's not an

NPC, nor is it a player; rather, it resembles a Doll in some way: it's an unusual something that craves to find its progenitor. But while Dolls are created for love, an echo is created for death. It has the same strength as the creature for whom it was generated. Oh, and there is an important point: the number of echoes is determined by the level of "Grandeur". At one hundred there is one, at two hundred there would be two... I had four. Three were destroyed at once – the laws of the Game are ruthless to them. The fourth, however, was quicker and got to me. You have seen what came of it. I was able to survive because I dared a full merge. So this body houses two beings, which are continuously fighting. Myself and my echo. Occasionally it comes to the surface, scaring everyone around. Until today I thought I had things under control. But, apparently the energy of the activated Diary affected my mental control. You have seen the result. That's why I want a restart: it will help me get rid of this curse. Nothing else can undo a merge."

"Why did Gromana throw that animal at you?" I decided to clarify that point for myself as well, while my host was being so cooperative.

"It's a manushka. They are very fast and have a particular venom. Gromana told me about those animals and suggested I could use one. Their bite puts the echo into a coma, thus enabling me to restore my mental shields. Before that I used other methods which were less effective. With the use of a manushka the fits became rarer and rarer, and I had allowed myself to relax."

Bernard fell silent for a moment, recalling the

unpleasant events again. Then he continued:

"I know where to find Merlin. Archibald knows where to find Madonna. You need to convince the catorian to share information; you can tell him about everything you have seen here, except my other "self". No one should learn that I have swallowed an echo. Malturion will see you to the library; however, you should know: already tomorrow you must set out on your class quest. You should not quarrel with Iven; I have certain plans for that Paladin."

Bernard demonstrated how formidably well-informed he was about all my affairs.

"I answered all of your questions, Yaropolk."

"Not quite," I resisted, remembering that Madonna and the third restart participant always find each other.

"Right. And I will leave you this question to explore on your own. You are an explorer? Right? Your Doll will help you in that." With those words Bernard broke into laughter. And I was stunned. What did my Doll have to do with it? "My advice is: don't reject her. There is nothing bad about sensuality."

Thoughts were flashing through my head at lightning speed. Really... That would be just incredible. I was staring at the man with my mouth open, contrary to all good manners. He smiled playfully, and praised me:

"Good boy. We'll find a way to work together. "He rose from the table, indicating that the meeting was over. "Complete your quests and talk to Iven. This is your task for next week. Then we'll see."

"Please follow me." The butler appeared nearby. "Gromana mentioned that you cannot use Light books; that somewhat limits the list of what's available, so we can begin with…"

The butler was explaining the logistics, but I was distracted. I could not get over a fascinating thought to which Bernard had led me.

Madonna – or the third participant of the restart – was a Doll who had become a player.

CHAPTER FIVE

LADY LECLEUR'S ESTATE

BERNARD'S LIBRARY, unlike his material wealth, inspired envy and amazed with a practically infinite number of books, scrolls and fragments of documents in various languages. Most of the scripts looked to me like "nonsense" or "some scribbles". That was frustrating. My eyes kept catching artifacts from previous eras; the oldest one was a collection of poems written three restarts prior to ours. I stopped near the beautiful holographic crystal floating in the air, regretting that modern technology was unable to read it. Even though who knows? – maybe there were nothing but some silly love sonnets there.

"That's always sought after." Malturion reminded me he was still there, as he noticed my interest in the crystal. "As of now we know of about fifteen hundred quests generated to destroy this object. The Game does not like rare objects from the past and tries to destroy them. Uninvited visitors show up steadily, about once a week."

"I suppose it would be naïve to imagine you offer each one some tea?" I asked with a smile. "A person like Bernard should easily be able to protect his property from assaults, even within the Sanctuary."

"Well, actually, any guest is welcome to appreciate my master's hospitality over a cup of tea with a chimera or Cyclops several worlds away from here." The butler returned a wry smile and clarified politely: "Portals. Any careless touch would take a guest on an unexpected safari."

I nodded understandingly, and silently praised myself for my reserve towards the crystal. A few moments ago I had really wanted to touch it, but now the urge vanished completely.

"I wonder to what extent the worlds before our restart were more technologically advanced?"

"I would not be able to tell you. I belong to the current one. Perhaps Gromana could help you with this question. I dare to remind you that time is short. In the morning I am supposed to send you off to Lady Lecleur's estate. Until then the library is fully at your disposal. Don't worry about the portals; until morning you have authorized access. Unless you need something else, I'll leave you to your studies."

Admitting the butler was right, I took the nearest book off the shelf. A moment later the green light on the open pages faded: my personal video recorder scanned and analyzed the text, then the Book stored it in its virtual compartments. My scale of artifact experience increased by one hundredth of a percent, and I immediately turned the page without reading the text. My task for the moment was to load information; I would sort it out later, when I had a calm environment of private eternity. The knowledge, facts and terminology started flowing into me like a river.

Installing update

"Greetings!" A hoarse voice suddenly whispered, and a small transparent image of an old man appeared before me; it looked precisely like the Keeper from the Temple of Knowledge. *"Protocol 250-201 is available; assistant has been activated. Estimated time required for initial analysis and processing information in the Book of Knowledge is three hours seventeen minutes and thirty one seconds. During analysis the assistant's functions will be limited. Initialization initiated.*

Staring at the image in bewilderment, I realized that I had been scanning information for several hours on autopilot, without noticing anything around. It turned out that my "Neuronal Network" properties had attained 30 units, and I had received a virtual assistant as a bonus. Its appearance was quite welcome: no matter how I squeezed and rubbed my eyes, the fatigue was noticeable. Unlike in an eternity pocket, it was hard to do in the real world without sleep, particularly when it was five o'clock in the morning and Energy-wise I was riding on fumes.

"Display information on customizing assistant." For a few seconds I hesitated between the urge to just keep on the autopilot and scan everything that came to hand, and my reluctance to miss the slightest chance to use the remaining hours with maximum efficiency. In the end the scales tilted towards the potential usefulness of the assistant, and I decided to allocate some of my precious time to him.

"Inquiry is accepted. The information you need is in this scroll. Study it." The imitation was so perfect that even the manner of speech was exactly like the prototype. Damn, I would go barking mad after five or six "your inquiry is accepted – study this scroll"s! I'd rather make him mute than listen to that impersonal navigator voice!

Fortunately, I was able to customize the assistant's appearance, even though the choice of interfaces was not great: the old man from the Temple of Knowledge, average male or female characters of the same race as the player, the player himself, and his Doll. Without much ado I chose the guy. A new face would be interesting, and I would not have a woman as an advisor: this was a sure way to turn into a hen-pecked pansy. As for the rest, the options were not much fun: it was possible to turn the assistant on or off, or adjust its transparency and location. That's it! Suppressing a disappointed sigh, I kept scanning, hoping that something interesting would turn up after the Book analyzed that.

"Based on a current analysis of the uploaded data, the desire of the subject to maximize artifact level and time remaining on the current location in the amount of two hours forty-two minutes and twelve seconds I have to inform you that the current book, with 80% probability, will not provide additional data value," half an hour later my "new friend" suddenly piped up, reacting to the book I was about to scan into my artifact; with this official statement he was trying to help me. I turned the book in my hand: it was a thick one; it would take about fifteen minutes to scan.

"Analysis of the nearest books that could provide maximum leveling up." I decided to trust the new function and put the rejected book aside. One of the books close to me was suddenly highlighted in blue. The assistant scanned the cover and supposed that the information within would be most useful for me. A few moments later the blue glow changed to green. The scanning volume was determined.

"Analysis complete. Potentially useful books are selected and highlighted in blue."

"Could you talk in... a less impersonal manner?" I was very pleased to find out that it was possible to talk to the assistant in my mind, without having to scare those around me with suspicions of acute schizophrenia. The appearance of my navigator was that of a simple-minded fellow with an open and friendly face. When this face said: "based on current analysis..." and the rest of it, it completely threw me. Something had to be done about that.

"Protocol 250-201 implies installing a standard assistant module without personality matrix. Development of a personality matrix occurs in the process of assistant performing its functions and close integration with the mind of its subject. Typical time required for development of a personality matrix and adjustment to subject is two years."

"Personal time or Game time?" I was curious.

"Personal."

"Great! I this case, I name you Steve." The name suited the virtual guy like no other. "Work on the Book of Knowledge, and I'll keep scanning."

"Renaming and specified task accepted. Personality matrix 'Steve' initiated."

By the time the butler appeared, I could boast, besides a humming head, level 10 of "Context Search" and 33 of "Neuronal Network". Because of the "Explorer's Book" presented by the Chancellor of the Academy, those parameters were enhanced by 10%, which made me a very happy player.

"It's time," Malturion's appearance interrupted me; he was standing expectantly at the portal, not allowing me to finish the book I was holding. "You will have many more opportunities to use the library. The master is offering to change your anchor point to this residence. He considers that would be safer; however, he has left the choice to you."

"I agree." The vassal oath turned out to be much better protection than assurances from Archibald and Sharda, so I did not hesitate for a moment.

"Follow me," the vampire said briefly, and

stepped into the portal. "Let's finish with all the formalities."

Two hours later I stepped outside and sighed with pleasure. After the registration hall I was taken to the armory. A strange silent creature wrapped from head to toe in a black cloth, who turned out to be the local metalworker, listened to the vampire's requirements and worked on my armor by making a few quick gestures. This enhanced the protection that was already incredibly strong; then the creature installed the gems that I had acquired. Even though I did not receive any additional armor attributes such as antigravity devices or inertia neutralizers, yet the enhancements were magnificent. Lastly, Malturion handed me defense and attack amulets, inventory expanders, about a hundred vials of Energy elixirs and the scroll with the portal to Lady Lecleur's estate.

"Only the emblem will save you from heavy duty players," the vampire explained Bernard's generosity. "But lesser opponents will break their teeth. You understand, not all players would actually care about the emblem. Master ordered your Doll to be delivered here. I will open the portal to the Sanctuary as soon as you are ready."

Helen was sitting in the garden playing with the pet, oblivious to the outside world. Noticeably grown Rragr was jumping over a stick and babbling something. Having noticed me, the girl waved her hand in greeting.

"Three hairs in the seventh lock of her hair on the right do not belong to the Doll." My assistant woke up. *"The artifacts are highlighted."*

A strand of Helen's hair flashed red.

"Master took care to have a portable tracking device installed on your Doll." The vampire saw concern on my face and hastened to explain. "For the first several years players tend to be very worried for the safety and current location of their property. Master does not want you to be distracted with such trifles. I will help you set up the communication device."

A few minutes later I approached the playing pair. Rragr reacted with a warning growl, but received a slight slap on the butt for it from his "mom". Responding with a puzzled stare he sniffled, offended, but completely refused to leave her arms.

"Observed: psychological attachment of the pet to the Doll." Steve continued working: *"The process of pet transfer has been initiated and within several days will become complete and irreversible. To preserve attachment to you it is necessary to immediately remove the pet and reset its mind."*

"No, thanks, you are enough of a pet for me," I grinned silently to myself. I had no time to work with the pet now, and hiding it in its virtual shelter long-term was not too good of an option either. Helen was the ideal girl for me, and the best solution for the pet or rather for leveling the pet up. However, I decided to clarify with my resident know-it-all: "If I were to reject the Doll, and the Game erased her, what would happen to the pet?"

"It would revert to the initial owner at its then current level of development." I heard the answer that satisfied me.

"Hi!" I smiled at Helen and she immediately demonstrated impressive skills of controlling the pet, deactivating it with a wave of her hand. "I think now is just the right time for us to repeat our attempt and have some coffee."

The next day I finally spent resting in the Sanctuary, allowing myself to relax both my body and mind. Helen really was ideal for me in every way. I supposed that this was what a person would feel when he met his other half. As if a puzzle fit together. We enjoyed every second of each other's company. In the evening I decided to leave the hotel for a bit, take a stroll around the city and talk to Helen. I was pleasantly surprised, realizing she was able to maintain any conversation on culture, fashion, films, and other things that I was used to while I was still an NPC. It was true – I missed Moscow and all those things that had been part of my life. We even talked about the Game. Some things the Doll knew from the point she was created; some things I had to clarify. Actually, those things were rather few: the Game took care to ensure the Doll would bring its player only pleasure and not trouble. Spending time with Helen was easy and pleasant. Watching her I was still an explorer. It was lucky that I was thus able to explore myself, as the Doll was the mirror of my needs as a man. And sex was not the point there. It's hard to understand what you expect of a woman in a relationship. For example, my sensitivity to praise was a revelation to me. Yet I practically purred when Helen subtly admired me in one way or another, or praised me for even the most ordinary things.

Apparently, this is very inspiring.

Despite all the pleasures of the relationship I had discovered, I decided against bringing Helen to the estate with me. It would be better if she settled in our apartment in Moscow and worked on making it a better place. Handing her the keys and some money for a start, and instructing her to develop Rragr, I was leaving Helen feeling completely satisfied. Both physically and spiritually. Practically before activating the portal to the estate I recalled the Judge's task. It would not be right to leave the Sanctuary without closing all my cases.

Case received: "Stolen Pendant" (Slots available for: 8 more cases). Description: Sophie Lecleur, granddaughter of Lady Marie Lecleur, filed a complaint because the "Pendant of Joy" was stolen from the family safe. Suspects: None. Clues: None. Task: Investigate the case and deliver your verdict on it
Case investigation: 0%
Period of limitation of action: 1 month

My spark of enthusiasm at playing a detective fizzled. Malturion had warned me that the quest to find the pendant had been issued to all players graduating from the Academy in the last ten batches. On top of that there was this far from unique task from the Judge and the fact that I was still supposed to be sent to respawn for making a mistake in judgment. All that would result in quite a royal pain in my armored backside. Right now the Lecleur estate would most likely be hell on Earth. It would be stupid to hope that under those circumstances the triskelion emblem on my shoulder would stop anyone.

For an instant the portal turned the space around me into a kaleidoscope, only to reassemble it into a glum gray medieval castle, surrounded by a multicolored lively tent city. The players were so numerous that there was not enough space for everyone. A long winding line of those willing to try their luck at locating the lost jewelry stretched towards the main gate.

"You a new one?" A plump member of the local servants jumped out in front of me like a jack-in-the-box. He stared at his tablet, then said: "You need to register. Your number is 1,321. Approximate waiting time is seven days."

I sighed in indignation. I was rather fed up with all those registrations. What week?! I was busy up to my gills! Finally the NPC tore his eyes from the tablet and looked at me disinterestedly, waiting for me to answer. As soon as his glance reached Bernard's emblem, the servant immediately stood to attention to the extent his belly would allow.

"Sorry, Milord! Pardon my natural inattentiveness, Milord! I will immediately see you to the estate, Milord! Please follow me!"

I liked the reaction to my suzerain's emblem. I was calmly walking towards the entrance, passing by the queue and not in the least insulted by the nasty monikers hurled at my back. Shame on those who envy!

"Where you think you're going? Get in line like

everyone else!" About twenty yards before the gate a huge red-skinned orc blocked my way. "It's not right honor getting ahead of everyone!"

"*Paladin, Zharkee set armor, three visible amulets, two gems, one engraving, no suzerain's emblem, chosen artifact is a sword; presumable place of origin – game world Zagransh; in case of conflict caution is advised,*" Steve immediately provided me with all the background of the obstacle that had appeared so suddenly. Great, another champion of justice and knight of the Light.

"Brother, step aside," I responded calmly to the Paladin. "I am here on the personal directive of Milord Iven."

I was not running much of a risk using such a lofty name as cover. It would be impossible to accuse me of lying: Iven really did send me off out of sight.

"Who?" The orc did not move an inch; his question confirmed Steve's supposition that he was from afar. For the local Paladins Iven was too important a person to not know of him. Quickly assessing the situation and the frowning orc, I realized that unless I made this champion of justice shut up somehow right away I would risk a respawn before I even had a chance to start my search. The players would be happy to cut me into ribbons as a crowd so that I would not try to cut the line. No armor would help against that. Weighing my prospects, I sighed and said solemnly:

"Paladin from Earth, Yaropolk, is glad to greet a brave Paladin from Zagransh on Earth. It's a special pleasure for me to meet Logir's compatriot here.

Valiant Paladin, did you happen to know this highly honorable femorc?"

"Sure, she's Grygz's daughter," the orc was taken aback by hearing a familiar name. His pose became less tense, which I interpreted as a good sign. Apparently, the old teacher was well respected on Zagransh. "How you know her?"

"Oh, I was lucky to go through the Academy shoulder to shoulder with her and see her valiance and courage first hand. It's such a pity that the mages and the Game took the most worthy. She always extended a helping hand in time of need." The orc's face fell and he hung his head sadly. I even felt sympathy for him. Of course, I would not play poker with him – his emotions were immediately obvious – yet I found that cute and attractive. There were few players within the Game who were so open, yet unafraid to put their head on the line to fight for justice regardless of consequences and the strength of their opponent. "What is your name, brother? And how long have you been waiting here?"

"Alard. Waiting for five days. By evening should be in. Will buy myself a room, get some sleep and start looking in the morning. Three days should be enough. Have a tracker!" He grinned meaningfully, causing protesting noises among the players standing nearby. Steve immediately commented:

"*A device for finding treasures and hidden objects. A scanner; an advanced version was used by the mercenaries in the Dungeon. Rare object; unavailable for purchase at open auction.*"

"That's impressive! But why only three days?" I

was surprised.

"Everyone is only allowed for three days; if you fail – get out."

"In that case there is no time to lose," I liked the orc's pride for his device so much that it made me feel like helping my brother in class. I nodded at the Paladin, introducing him to my escort: "This one is with me. Alard, you are ok with accompanying me, right?"

"Have to wait in line," the orc frowned immediately. "All wait, we have to wait. That's fair!"

"Is it fair, however, to make poor Madame Lecleur worry about the thing she lost?" I would not give up. To some extent I was doing it just for the fun of it. Would I be able to convince the orc to yield his principles or no? "A true Paladin must help a weak being in time of need using every opportunity to do so! Or do you believe differently? Tell me now! I am sure, Logir would support me in this."

The orc's face betrayed his confusion. The Paladin's lips moved as if he were arguing with his inner voice concerning this situation; finally, he made his decision:

"Brother Yaropolk, you are right! Let's hasten to help!"

At the entrance to the castle our escort whispered something to the guards, pointing at my emblem, and one of them immediately dashed into the booth visible beyond the gate.

"Just a moment," the fat servant mumbled obsequiously. A well-dressed man with a funny pointed nose strolled out of the booth. The feathers on the wide-brimmed hat were supposed to conceal their owner's defect, but they were not really doing the job. Casting an owner's glance over the castle's inner courtyard, the man approached us in a dignified manner.

"Milord." He bowed his head slightly. "Herald Sleevan, a minion of the Lecleur family, at your service. How shall I announce you to Lady Sophie?"

"Paladin Yaropolk, vassal of Lord Bernard, with a friend." Since the title of my suzerain impressed everyone so much, that would probably be the best way to introduce myself.

The herald turned towards the players and announced in the voice enhanced with magic:

"The visitation is over for today!"

The queue exploded in indignant rumbles, and I felt with my very skin the waves of hatred emanating from the crows towards me. Of course, one would have to be a total idiot to fail to identify the culprit of all the trouble here. I did not feel any pangs of conscience, though. Perhaps my allegiance to Darkness was affecting my character.

"What do you mean – over?" The hunter who was first in line expressed his indignation more loudly than the rest. "You just started a little while ago!"

"It's over because I said it's over! There are no free rooms!" Sleevan was adamant. "Come tomorrow!"

"You are bloody mad!" The unlucky hunter kept screaming. The guards were slowly pushing everyone outside the gate, and this made the player even angrier. "Blasted Paladin, I've been sitting here for three days! I'll have to lose another day because of you! Don't touch me! Get your paws off me!"

"Hunter, initial set of armor, no visible amulets, no emblem, chosen artifact is a bow; no danger in case of conflict."

"That's what I was saying too. That's wrong. No honor in that," Alard wanted to back off, but that was not part of my plan. The guards already had taken all the players out except the raging hunter. I attracted the herald's attention and nodded at the player:

"Let him go. No need to raise a ruckus."

"Is he also with you?" I was surprised to hear irony in Sleevan's voice.

"With me, with me." There was nothing I could do other than agree to that. I thought to myself in a sort of pun: "Seems as though I am becoming too soft. That's a sign I am in for some hard times."

"Unfortunately, Milord, we really do have only one guest room available. It is a double room. You will have to stay there together. All three of you."

Once more I noted to myself that the herald was strange. He behaved in a manner too assertive for a servant. He did not try to ingratiate upon seeing my emblem, did not apologize for the inconvenience which would be expected. He simply stated a fact.

"Hunter, did you hear that?" I shouted to the now quiet player, who was listening to our conversation as best he could. "Either you go with us today but sleep on the floor, or you get out and wait for comfortable accommodations tomorrow."

"Let go of me already," the hunter jerked, getting out of the tight hold of the guards. "I heard! I agree to wait on the floor today until I get a more comfortable room tomorrow. It's better to sleep with you rather than take part in one more deadly orgy with those morons."

"What do you mean?" I did not understand any of that.

"The tent city," Alard came to the aid of our newly acquired partner. "In the evening a crowd of mummers come. Trash and burn everything. Kill the players. Call up the dead. Teacher says it's normal. That it's not too bad. That one has to endure. But argh!" The orc even stomped his foot with feeling. "That's wrong! No honor! Especially when no one can fight back! I tried; it didn't work. And they don't beat on everyone – bastards! Those who have protection they don't touch. But the rest... argh!"

"How many times were you killed?" I frowned. The orc's reaction was telling.

"Five. Three times the first night. Wanted to fight, ran straight here after spawning, but no use."

"I would like to point out, Milord, that the Lecleur family has nothing to do with this incident, and totally condemns it," Sleevan clarified, just in case. "The violators have been blacklisted and are not allowed within the estate."

"Fine. We'll see in the evening what kind of mummers wander around here. I do hope that Madame Sophie will not limit me and my companions to three days of stay?"

"I am sure that you will be allowed to stay as long as you need. Please follow me. Your arrival has already been announced."

The inner courtyard of the castle was

decorated, in great contrast to its grey stone walls. Actually, the decoration was in line with what a common average person would normally expect of a feudal medieval castle: the most important thing in the décor would be that it should look rich and expensive; therefore there were plenty of elaborate marble columns, snow-white ancient sculptures, fountains finished in gold, as well as players, out of place and moving everywhere. The estate was full of life and colors. I was ready to see the hosts in yet another gazebo so I was infinitely surprised to find myself next to the main building of the ensemble. Imperturbable and well-trained guards threw open the massive doors, so that a moment later we could join the players in the minor reception hall.

"Paladin Yaropolk with companions!" The herald's enhanced voice boomed across the hall, riveting everyone's attention to us. Mizardine – that was the hunter's name – and Alard stepped back, leaving me at the head of our group.

"I am glad to welcome you to Mother's home, monsieur Yaropolk!" The crowd parted and we were honored by the Lady of the Castle personally. Lady Lecleur was a luscious woman slightly over forty. The "slightly" part could equally well have been one year or fifty, since game mechanics could do really strange things with NPCs. Madame Sophie was not a player. "Our family is always happy to see people of Master Bernard. How do you like our estate?"

"It's very impressive," I replied politely, introducing my companions to Sophie and adding: "One thing is a little uncomfortable though: the huge crowd."

Oh, Monsieur Yaropolk!" The red-haired hostess waived her hands in the air. "I am already regretting asking for help! So what is the big deal if a pendant is lost! But no: Maman is so upset it makes me feel bad in front of the neighbors. There was so much ado – as if it were the last piece of jewelry in our family. And so many players showed up; the only way to have any privacy is in one's personal rooms!"

The hostess was not so simple. If the NPC were aware that everything around it was the Game, I would have to suppose that she was a minion. Would be nice to also understand the class.

"I was forced to cut the duration of stay for these guests to three days. But you, of course, don't have to worry about that! The estate is at your service. I hope this nightmare will be over soon." As she was sighing with concern, Sophie fluttered off to greet the next group.

"Where shall we start?" I did not waste any time, turned to my companions and sighed heavily. Right behind them my personal Game curse was standing, and waving her hand in welcome. Dolgunata.

"With the introductions, of course," the druid smirked, and raked my companions with an assessing stare. Seeing nothing of interest for herself, she quickly switched to me. "Even though – no, don't bother. I think these ones won't hang around you too long either. Every time I run into you I see new faces. You are simply amazingly fickle. Men! What else could one expect from them!"

"Druid, Daro set, ten visible amulets, twelve gems, three enhancing engravings, emblem on the left shoulder indicates vassalage to Gerhard van Brast, chosen artifact is breastplate. Extremely dangerous opponent."

"Good day to you, too, oh most steady of players," I smiled so hard my lips started hurting. It was by now impossible to imagine us meeting without parrying words. "I need to introduce you to everyone, not least out of mercy to those poor creatures who could, due to their lack of knowledge, decide to have any dealings with you. So please meet druid Dolgunata: headhunter, student of Archibald, vassal of Gerhard van Brast and generally the kindest soul, as you have just had a chance to see. Alard. Mizardine. So what ill wind blew you here? Your inner woman awakened and decided she wanted a pendant?"

I projected friendliness and joy as if I had actually come across an old friend; this noticeably puzzled the druid.

"Don't overact. My quest is to send you to respawn." Finally, the cat got tired of playing with the mouse and decided to astonish it. Me, that is. But the druid really overestimated herself, or, most likely, underestimated me. Our expressive meeting was starting to attract attention of others, which displeased Dolgunata. I, however, used the opportunity to tease her.

"Oh, I knew you would not miss this chance to meet me. You've been looking for excuses. Admit it, you just don't know how to confess your feelings toward me – that's why you stalk me." I pulled together all my acting skills so as not to laugh, looking at the druid. "Let's end this once and for all! Tonight it will be my pleasure to give you a chance to let your dream come true. Do you agree?"

Dolgunata rushed forward so fast that I thought she was going to fight me right then and there. However, she came up very close and, looking into my face, barely able to contain her feelings, said:

"I agree! Tonight! You and me! Dreams do come true! Do you confirm?"

The last phrase made me tense. But it was too late:

"I confirm. Your place or mine? I warn you, I'll have witnesses," I egged the druid on.

"Great! Witnesses don't scare me."

"Aren't you kinky!" I grinned, and the crowd laughed after me.

"Of course," Dolgunata joined the general mirth. "The more the merrier. It would create... such an atmosphere! As for the place... Let's say at the entrance to the estate would be just right!"

"Just right for what?" I stopped smiling.

"To fulfill my dreams, you silly," the druid sang in a sweet voice. "I've been dreaming of kicking your ass for some time! So don't be late, we'll meet at eight at the gate. One on one! Or have you changed your mind?"

"You are offering me a fight?" I knew the clarification was redundant and must have looked like an attempt to buy some time, but a fight with Dolgunata was really not what I needed. Even though it did not frighten me.

"I am kindly proposing to you a duel! Appreciate how noble I am and remember that! See how many are witnessing it. You have a couple of minutes to decide what you will be betting."

"In accordance with the dueling code each party must state the reward for winning or losing the fight. The rewards must not be identical. If the opponents are satisfied with the rewards, offered by the other party, the duel is then considered official. A special feature of such a fight is that the Game monitors the players fighting properly and follow through with their promises afterwards."

"So be it – a duel then. If I lose I give you two level 10 enhancement gems," I considered there would be nothing untoward in fighting the druid. The only constraint that I imposed on myself was that that I would risk only things that I had earned myself, and not ones I received from Bernard. Two gems would be quite a worthy reward if I were to lose. "As for the prize for winning, we will go back to where we started. If I win, you fulfill all my sexual desires for this night."

The crowd buzzed. They liked the demand I voiced. Meanwhile I bent to the druid's ear and added for her ears only:

"Not like I am particularly attracted to you. But your constant barbs aimed at my Doll make me think that this is what you are really missing. I am willing to help you."

"Fine!" the girl's reaction to me was suspiciously good-natured; the crowd roared, excited even more. "I accept your demands. If I lose, you will receive an attribute stone. If I win, you will give me that Diary that you dragged out of the Academy. Duel?"

Dolgunata extended her hand, offering to seal the deal. I lingered, as I had not expected such a reaction to those demands. I had not known that the catorian wanted to take the Diary. Before, he had not made such attempts... Or was it not him? Maybe the Keymaster wanted to play her own game?"

"Analysis of Dolgunata's fight records leads to an estimate of your chances of winning as 26%." Steve was firm. *"It is recommended that you give up the duel and pay the fine: two gems identified as the reward."*

"Two stones," the assistant's forecast was bleak, and I stood still. The druid was already drawing a chestful of air to accuse me of cowardice. "Two gems from my side, and from yours, two stones. That would be fair."

"Fine!" Nata's determination was alarming. "Shall we duel?"

"We shall!" We sealed our agreement with a handshake. The girl, not bothering to hide the joy on her face, turned around and quickly went outside.

"Granis on the druid!" The crowd immediately came up with a new entertainment.

"Counter bet! Granis on the Paladin!"

"Two gems of level 3 enhancement! On the druid winning!"

"Amulet +10 to defense! On the Pal!"

Herald Sleevan was acting as an auctioneer, taking bets with such Olympic calm that it seemed he had been doing it all his life.

"Serious opponent," Alard looked after the retreating Dolgunata. "A victory over one like that is a great honor."

"Pointless and silly, though." I was dissatisfied with the results of yet another encounter with the druid. What honor was there in that? Dolgunata knew very well why she needed that duel. It would be hard to invent a more sure way to grab the Diary. So then I need to do everything possible to make sure she does not get it.

"Honor cannot be pointless or silly," Alard disagreed. "It's either there or it is not. I believe in your victory, brother."

"Dolgunata is half Paladin," I grinned. "Gerhard van Brast, her suzerain, is the Head of the Paladins of Earth. Her teacher, Archibald, is also a Paladin. So she is a druid only by birth. Technically, she is our sister."

"In this case there is nothing dishonorable in betting on a contest between a brother and sister!" Alard rejoiced. "I believe in you, brother!"

Orc took off, taking the silent hunter with him. I had no idea about what to do with Mizardine. I had no intention to involve him in looking for the pendant.

"Sleevan!" Because of my strategic location next to the entrance, I was able to call the herald, who was in a hurry to get somewhere. "I need to talk to you about the pendant. Now!"

I added the last sentence, since the herald was not even thinking of stopping.

"As you wish, Milord," Sleevan slowed down reluctantly, and, without hiding his displeasure, approached me. He was quite an odd herald. "What did you want to know?"

"Herald Sleevan is not violating Game rules or laws. Guests have no right to direct or order the servants of their hosts," Steve hastened to clarify the situation quickly to prevent the possibility of me initiating a case. By the way, I did not view the behavior of NPCs as a Judge anymore.

"I need information about the pendant." I ignored Sleevan's displeasure. "What it looks like, where it was stored, who saw it last, and generally everything that has to do with this case. Right now.

"As you prefer," herald bowed respectfully. "I will immediately make arrangements for all the necessary information to be provided to..."

"Sleevan!" A loud tipsy roar boomed through the monotonous humming of the people in the hall. The herald paled but stayed in place. He lifted his head and slowly turned towards the man, who was as enormous as a mountain. Sleevan looked like a convict dragging his feet to mount the scaffold. The huge thug was making way directly towards us across the hall. His glassy stare clearly indicated that more than one bottle of strong spirits was already sloshing around in that ample belly.

"Where's my brandy?" He roared like an angry bear at Sleevan. "Why are you still here?!

"Forgive me, Milord, it's my fault," Sleevan was answering quietly, without lifting his eyes so as not to provoke the drunk. "I will do everything imme..."

"Silence!" "Milord" roared again, sending the herald flying with one flick of his hand. Knocking down the players, he flew across several yards and crashed into the wall. My host was unbelievably strong. "Ten lashes will teach you to respect your master! Guards! Flog him!"

"Darling! Not in front of the guests!" Sophie latched herself to the man's arm. He was her husband?!

"Get lost!" He jerked his arm away and growled, staring at the gathering guests: "I tolerate this riff-raff in my house, but I shall not have disobedience from my servants! Ten lashes! Now!"

"Sleevan was delayed because of me," I interjected. The information that the herald could provide was more valuable than good relations with the owner.

"Like I care!" His bloodshot eyes shifted to me. "Guards! Some lashes for this twit as well!"

"Darling, he is Bernard's subject," Sophie whispered, hanging on her husband's arm again.

"Hellnard's!" the drunk raged. "I am so sick of those blasted 'subjects'! Next time he'll know better than to meddle in our family affairs! It's my house and I am within my rights here! Guards! Why has he not been punished yet?!"

Just a few seconds and the guards neatly grabbed me, twisted my arms behind my back and handcuffed me. Without trying to protest, I was thinking of my advanced protection with disappointment. As it turned out, I had nothing that could oppose raw physical strength. Only my own strength, or rather whatever I had instead of it. The only advantage was the force shield which would make it impossible to touch my body directly. Actually, the handcuffs were restraining me, but did not touch my wrists. Deciding, reasonably, to not exacerbate the situation by resisting, I let Sophie resolve this conflict. Later, I would demand preferences from the hostess as the injured party.

"Throw them into the basement!" The thug apparently changed his mind, as the sight of the beaten Sleevan and my restrained self calmed him somewhat. "Let them sit there till tomorrow and think about life. Bring me more brandy!"

Without much ceremony I was quickly dragged off into a damp and dark room. I remembered the way easily: my head seemed to have counted every door and frame on which my guards kept "carelessly" hitting me. A shower of stars from my eyes reinforced my decision once again: as soon as I had a chance I needed to install an inertia neutralizer on my armor: I was fed up counting the stars already! In the basement, the handcuffs were replaced with shackles solidly attached to the wall. I pulled on them a couple of times to make sure, but realized that I was chained good and strong.

"Thank you, Milord!" I heard Sleevan's voice from the right. I turned towards the voice and saw that my "comrade in need" was calmly adjusting his shackles so that they would not rub his wrists too much. He was not protected by a force shield against such trouble. "Shackles are better than lashes, don't you find?"

"It's a dubious advantage, in my view," I disagreed. "I would have rather avoided this choice altogether."

"You are right. However, don't worry. It will barely take an hour, and we'll be free. Lady Sophie will take care of everything."

"Madame Sophie? I doubt that she is able to make any decisions here. Or else we would not be sitting here now."

"It is not quite so," Sleevan defended her. "The head of the Lecleur family is Lady Elizabeth, Milady's mother; however, after the pendant disappeared she does not receive guests. Lady Sophie began caring for the estate. But she is just a woman. And now she is acting as a wife. You have to admit that this would not be the best moment to argue with Milord Ervan. He suffers from an unpleasant phobia: he is afraid of groups of people. An influx of guests has unsettled him, so the master has started to drink. As soon as the pendant is found, everything will be back to normal."

"Are you trying to trying to make the consequences of my stay here easier on your mistress?"

The herald shrugged his shoulders noncommittally, as if to say you can take it in whatever way you want.

"Why does Elizabeth not receive anyone? Has the loss of some bauble undermined her health so much? "

"Milady does not feel well. As to whether this is related to the pendant or not is outside of my competence." The herald pursed his lips.

"Come on! 'Outside of your competence!' You

could share the information out of gratitude – I saved you from a lashing!"

"For fairness' sake it is useful to note that had it not been for you, the master would have received his brandy promptly, and we would not have been sitting here," Sleevan quipped.

"You are right, I smiled placatingly, but the herald showed no desire to talk any more. I tried to bring this up from a different angle. "But still, why is the pendant so dear to Lady Elizabeth?"

"Because the pendant is part of a set received as a gift from a person close to her. Milady wore it all the time and never came out without it," the herald explained dryly.

"And?" I prompted him.

"And that's it. You would do better to review the report on its loss, like the other players." Sleevan was being stubborn. I was losing my patience. It was bad enough that I was stuck in the basement for who knows how long, but now this bullhead refuses to share information.

"Sleevan, I wanted to have a talk in a nice way – not officially. But I could do it another way."

"Whatever way Milord prefers," snorted the herald.

"In the name of justice I demand that you speak the truth and nothing but the truth! You are summoned as a witness in the case 'Stolen Pendant'. For the duration of your testimony you are released from all physical, moral, mental and emotional binds." Sleevan's eyes became round when the information message appeared in front of him. He was not an NPC, so he did not turn glassy-eyed; yet he was not a player. A minion. He was forced to answer with the truth and only the truth, otherwise the Game would turn him into dust.

"Let's start over. Tell me the history of the pendant."

"It was received as part of a set from the person whose minion Lady Elizabeth was for a long time. The set includes the pendant, earrings and a ring. The earrings have been lost for thirty years; the ring is stored in the safe of the estate."

Now that was better.

"Did Elizabeth become a player?"

"Yes. Lady Sophie, Milord Ervan, chief doctor of the estate, and I are her minions."

"Fine, this is clear. Under what circumstances did it disappear? Which residents of the estate were already questioned as witnesses, and who visited the estate?"

"It was stolen a week ago. All the personnel at the estate, including myself, as well as Milord and Milady, were checked at once, and confirmed that they were not involved. During the last month four players visited the estate, and only one of them was here when the item disappeared. That was an old friend of our family: Mister Devir. But he also passed the test administered by the Game. Four weeks before that there were his Excellency Milord Sirtal, a priest; his Excellency Milord Iven, a Paladin, and his Excellency Milord Dorian, a cleric. All three players are Lady Elizabeth's spiritual advisors."

"*A spiritual advisor is an experienced player*

who voluntarily assumes the functions of advisor to another player due to the final death of this player's initial teacher." Steve was prompt as always.

"Is that not too many spiritual advisors for one player?" I asked in surprise. What player class does Lady Elizabeth belong to?"

"Lady Elizabeth is the same class as her first teacher. She is a Paladin. She has twelve spiritual advisors."

I was surprised by so large a number of spiritual advisors, but I decided to concentrate on the pendant for now:

"Why do you consider that the pendant is still at the estate?" If Devir were actually involved in this he would definitely not have hidden it here.

"If the pendant had left the estate, Lady Elizabeth would already have been dead."

"But she is a player." I did not really understand what the herald meant. "She would have just respawned, would she not?"

"Lady Elizabeth is not an initiated player. She has not completed the Academy, yet she was acknowledged by the Game."

"How is that possible?" I immediately asked my virtual bud. Steve thought for several seconds before shaking his head negatively.

"There is no information. If one assumes that what Sleevan is saying is true, the maximum level Lady Elizabeth could have is three. The experience she receives would increase her global level without upgrading the current one; theoretically, over a thousand years, the mistress of the estate could have

accumulated a nearly infinite number of experience points. Several respawns would make her die the final death, as it would be impossible for her to attain a new level. But that does not explain the connection with the pendant, nor the need for the pendant to remain within the estate."

Summing up my subsequent questioning of the herald I came to the following conclusions.

Elizabeth turned out to be a level zero player; her life was tied to the pendant and its location. In effect it was a spirit, a non-material entity locked in a physical shell. How it had been possible to convince the Game not to kill off the old lady, Sleevan did not know. Therefore it was possible to assume as a given that Elizabeth was sort of dead on her feet – forever tied to her estate. There was also an answer concerning the number of Elizabeth's spiritual advisors. Twelve spiritual advisors renewed the energy of the pendant monthly, each during their assigned month. Sort of high-born Twelve Months Brothers taking care of a non-initiated player voluntarily. The Lecleur family did not pay them anything. The position was considered prestigious, and many players waited for a chance to attain it for several dozens or sometimes even hundreds of years. But even with the "witness" status I was not able to find out who was Elizabeth's first teacher. Sleevan managed somehow to resist the Game.

Moving Elizabeth from one room to another would not make sense. Even if the pendant were just an arm's length away from the old lady, she would not be able to take the vitally important item herself.

Without the pendant Elizabeth lost her mind. That's why the players could not find out the circumstances of theft from the owner herself; Ervan, who had taken to drinking what had previously been forbidden to him, was actively taking advantage of that. That's a fine how'd-ye-do. He started a veritable campaign to rule the estate, which would have been impossible while the old lady was in her sound mind. He actively interfered with the search, threw players out and introduced a three-day limit. However, as Sleevan stated, those were just the subjective thoughts of one individual herald, which could not serve as records for the case. The spiritual advisor working this month had personally checked the owners and all the hosts for connections to the theft. None were involved. The estate had a high level of protection; intrusion by an outside thief was quite unlikely. Therefore it was someone who had freedom of movement within the estate. But who? That was completely unclear. The estate was equipped with surveillance cameras that operated both in normal and magical range, but footage from them showed no sign of the theft whatsoever. For understandable reasons Elizabeth's actual room was not in the camera circuit, but during the night the thing disappeared no one came into or left the room. It was practically impossible to enter the estate via a portal – that required special permission. There were only twelve of those issued – to the spiritual advisors – however, they could be crossed off the list of suspects right away.

During the two weeks that had passed since the time of disappearance, the players were practically no closer to solving this mystery. First of all, there was little information; second: Ervan was relentless. He hosted major parties, getting the players dead drunk, then throwing them out three days later. As for the teetotalers, he found what to do with those as well. For example, he threw them into the basement for a day until Sophie released the poor creatures. In other words, he was an active and devious guy!

I finished the examination with a demand to provide a picture of the pendant. Sleevan immediately withdrew, perhaps upset that he had shared with me his own thoughts concerning Ervan. Oh well, he'd just have to get over that.

"There is information!" As soon as I looked at the picture, Steve yelled with joy, or at least so it seemed to me. *"This is the very pendant that is shown in the picture of the warrior lady in the main hall of the Citadel!"*

A series of video records flashed in front of me. The Citadel. Minutes before departure to the Sanctuary. Langirs dragging me towards the portal, eager to finish with his orders, while I look around trying to see my surroundings for at least a few moments. My video recorder records. The frame stopped and zoomed in on one of the walls of the hall. Painting. A woman in Paladin armor, with bright golden hair and gray eyes, raising a bloody sword. In the Citadel I only saw the top part of the painting, so it was not clear what kind of monster she had pierced. So there was the detail of interest to me: the pendant that I had already seen was hanging around the warrior's neck. Feeling what I would like, Steve zoomed in some more. The image drifted, turning soft, but I was able to see the earrings and the ring. They were in the same style as the pendant. So then Elizabeth's teacher was a female Paladin? And the portrait was hanging in the hall among other Paladins' portraits. Surely they did not all end up in there for the cuteness factor, right? Paladins must know their heroes!

My communications device did not offer a lot of Paladins' numbers. In fact, there were very few. Gromana and Bernard were unlikely to be able to help me. I ruled out Dolgunata right away.

"You chose a bad time, as always! Is this something urgent? Or are you calling to tell on Dolgunata?" — Archibald picked up at once, but I could clearly hear sounds of battle in the background, and he sounded like he was short of breath at times. But that did not prevent my teacher from his usual mockery. "I won't tell you how to beat her – I bet on her. So don't let me down."

"In the Citadel, next to the main hall, there is a Paladins' portrait gallery." I ignored the catorian's testy comments. "One of the portraits shows a woman in golden armor wielding a sword. Who is she?"

"Is this related to the pendant?" Archibald asked. I had to admit that it was. "You are barking up the wrong tree, Yari. The pendant is still in the Lecleur estate. Search there. We'll talk about the painting later. It's not so important, and I, as you understand, am a little busy here!"

"Archibald, for once, can you simply answer a question? Who is in that painting?! Was she

Elizabeth's first teacher?"

"Good bye!"

Upset, I stared at the silent device. What happened had not been unexpected, but it had been worth a try We could leave this question for now. Time was passing and Sophie was not in a hurry to release us.

"Steve, what will happen if I miss the duel?" I decided to find out more about the rules, just in case.

"The duel was to take place in a couple of hours. There is still time," the assistant reassured me, but immediately added: *"If we stay here, the reason for not appearing at the duel will be justified, and it will be postponed by five days. If you fail to appear again you will be considered the loser regardless of the gravity of the reason."*

At least there was one piece of good news. Dolgunata, of course would not fail to humiliate me and accuse of cowardice. But by now I had developed an immunity to her vitriol. The timer counted minutes till the duel, and I suffered from idleness and boredom. I tried the "Templar's Blow" on the chain a couple of times but the recoil hit me pretty hard even through the armor, so I abandoned my attempts to unshackle myself. Sleevan went quiet in his corner, so there was nothing else left for me to do than to try to use the remaining time in the basement with maximum utility – that is, have some sleep.

"Monsieur Yaropolk!" Sophie's concerned voice broke through the sweet drowsiness. "Monsieur Yaropolk, wake up! Please! Believe me, I am so sorry!"

The servant who accompanied me quickly

released me from the shackles. I looked at my watch: it was nine o'clock at night. An hour since I had missed the duel. Despite her assurances, the madam did not look regretful in the least. Quite the opposite – her pleased stare was fixed on me, while a sly smile danced on her lips.

"Your room is ready; your companions have already checked in." Sophie moved closer, took my hands and said confidingly, lowering her voice: "Monsieur Yaropolk, do assure me that this small misunderstanding will stay between us. And us alone. On behalf of all the Lecleur family, please accept my sincere apologies! But on the other hand, Monsieur Yaropolk, where else would you spend time to such advantage?"

"So am I supposed to be actually grateful to you on top of all this?" I raised an eyebrow ironically.

"Well, not to go so far as gratitude... But think for yourself, monsieur: I am certain that you were able to have a fruitful conversation with our herald." The hostess underscored the "certain", and I silently wished that the ears in the local walls would ring for a long time or, even better, go deaf completely. Meanwhile, Lady Sophie kept going. "You rested well here. Believe me, the guest rooms are so crowded right now, it would have been problematic there. And as far as I know... Lady Dolgunata is aware that the duel was rescheduled for a good reason. Please do not consider that I am meddling. I am just a silly woman and don't understand all these games, but there were plenty of witnesses to see that she imposed that duel on you..."

"Really? Straight benefits every way I look." I picked up that "torch" and even smiled at the lady. Her attempt to force me to owe her angered me. "Please do not consider me too forward, but it's by no merit of yours that I was able to have a useful conversation with your herald. Then, I prefer to choose myself where to rest. As for the duel... Are you trying to hint that I am weak or cowardly?"

The smile ran off Sophie's face, and she rattled on, frightened:

"No, not at all monsieur. That could not have been further from my mind. Please, I understand that you were insulted by my husband's actions, but I do hope for your mercy. Of course, I owe you. May I request that you do not report this to Sir Bernard?"

Wringing her hands, Sophie took just one careless step towards me, stumbled on the chain and nearly fell, but I was there in time to help her.

"Thank you." The lady dropped her eyes, adjusted her dress, and turning towards the entrance.

Purely out of reflex, I was being helpful, and placed my hand on the lady's back in order to be able to support her in case she took another careless step. Silence fell over the cell, and I fell the lady's back tense even through the heavy dress.

"With respect to nobility this gesture indicates that you are willing to share a bed with lady Sophie," Steve noted calmly.

I jerked my hand away, but it was too late: Sophie blushed and stopped. The servant carefully looked elsewhere, pretending that none of this was any of his business.

"I will be prepared to discuss your demands in one hour," Sophie said breathlessly. "Sleevan will accompany you to your rooms."

Great Game! Could she really think that this was my way of requesting retribution for the insult and my silence? Sophie left the cell quickly. The servant followed her, and I was left standing still, with my mouth open. Sleevan, who had also been released by then, showed some signs of life:

"Please follow me." The herald cast me a glance of pure hatred as he was passing by me.

"I am noting a deterioration in the herald's attitude towards you to the level of personal hatred. Potential reason: your desire to share a bed with lady Sophie. Probability of herald having certain feelings towards Milady: 70 %," Steve supposed constructively.

We walked to the room assigned to me in silence. Despite the lateness of the hour, players were still wandering to and fro around the estate.

Mizardine was waiting in excitement for me in the room. The hunter was pacing, and as soon as I opened the door, he rushed to report to me:

"They grabbed Alard! Today at midnight under the walls! They said that you should come... Alard resisted, but they..."

"Quiet!" I barked, and he froze. The hunter was so eager to convey all the information quickly that he swallowed words.

"They who?" I tried to find out more about the situation.

"I don't know. Mages." The hunter had not yet not recovered, so he answered briefly, but to the point.

"When and how was Alard captured?"

"Three hours ago. We went outside the walls; the orc just wanted to say a few words to someone he knew. Then seven mages grabbed him there – the eighth one was directing them. He gave me this for you." Mizardine handed me a sheet of paper.

"Yaropolk! We shall be waiting for you at midnight at the main gate, on the outside, for a conversation. If you come, I promise not to touch the orc. Otherwise – no offense, but... Ahean."

I knew the name without Steve having to remind me. Ahean was Devir's other student. There would be no visit to Sophie then.

CHAPTER SIX

MUMMERS

"WHAT ARE WE going to do?" Mizardine was nervous and probably regretted not having spent an extra day in line.

"You will do nothing. While I will go talk to people," I looked at the hunter in contemplation. Having him as partner was of questionable value: he had no experience, and his nerves were shot to boot. The only thing he was good at was hysteria. It was hard to believe that a player like that had completed the Academy. "Where are you from?"

"From Delgard," Mizardine replied. "You've probably never heard of it."

I nodded to indicate he was right.

"It's a small game world," the hunter

continued. "People are not well respected there. We are considered inferior goods. Too fragile and capable only of being servants."

"Were you a servant?"

"Yes. One player needed a servant, so he hired my great-grandfather. Then my grandfather served him, then my father, myself and my son. A couple of years ago this player reached the hundredth level of Grandeur and an echo appeared. I was nearby and was able to hold it up for a few seconds. My master ran off and brought help. To reward me, he made me a minion. After the Academy he sent me to Earth to gain experience. In Delgard a human player would be a pariah."

"I see," I said slowly. There were as many stories as there were players. I had thought, naïvely, that only outstanding individuals became players, such as I, who had completed the harsh trials of the Academy, or, at least, after some time in the school of hard knocks as minions. What a pain; it was simply a game of chance! And it did not matter that accidents were not accidental. "Wait here – I need to prepare for the meeting."

Just before leaving I remembered that I had never received the standard report on the disappearance of the pendant. I borrowed it from Mizardine and went to look for the herald.

I found Sleevan in his cottage. He was preparing to make his nightly round of the estate, and was not glad to see me. Without hiding his feelings, he asked ironically if I had been lost, wandering around at such a late hour.

"I need a portal to the Sanctuary, to the headquarters of the Paladins. Who would be the person responsible for this on the estate?

"Monsieur Ervan, Madame Sophie and myself." The great level of access Sleevan enjoyed on the estate was still a mystery to me. I could not help but ask:

"What did you do to deserve such an honor, Sleevan?"

The herald gave me a venomous look and said through his teeth:

"If Milord's wish is to exhibit curiosity, the best way to find out would be to hold another interrogation!"

"Sleevan, I wanted to talk in a nice way at first," I said apologetically. I did not want to aggravate the drunk or explain myself to Sophie, so I had to negotiate with Sleevan. "I need the portals right away. Do I have to talk to the owners, or are you in a position to resolve this yourself?"

"No reason to bother the masters with such minor things. Two scrolls will cost you one-tenth of a granis.

"Portal scrolls in this game world cost from one-tenth of a granis to five granises, depending on the distance and the precision needed for destination coordinates." Steve piped up in time to explain Sleevan's actions, because I was going to protest such a huge price. *"For your information: players are prohibited from rising above the surface of the world more than eight thousand eight hundred and forty eight meters."*

"Why?" I asked aloud, without even thinking

whom I was asking.

Herald was the first one to respond:

"The Lecleur estate does not set mark-ups for scrolls intended for friends of the family, monsieur Yaropolk. Madame Sophie has accepted you as a friend. That's why for you the scrolls cost just one-tenth of a granis, and not half of one as it would be for everybody else."

Steve provided clarification on his part:

"*Conventionally a player who has left the current game location without permission to transition to another one (in this case the 'Solar System') is treated as a violator and is destroyed by the Game. The upper boundary of the game location 'Earth' is the peak of Mount Everest, and the lower one is the bottom of the Marianas Trench. Below it is the 'Underworld' location.*"

Finally a lot of things became clear. In fact, in the beginning I could not figure out why, in order to get to the Games in Brazil, it was necessary to buy a portal rather than fly on a plane, which would have been much cheaper. I paid, Sleevan made the scroll using the local anchor point, and an instant later I was standing in front of the Paladins' headquarters, just as planned. Old Grizdan obviously suffered from insomnia, as he was sitting at his work desk at that late hour.

"Are you done with your quest?" he said, by the way of greeting.

"No: I need to complete some training in order to do so." I decided to not waste time with politeness either. "Who would be a Paladin who could help me?"

"Training?" Grizdan frowned in surprise. "That's an Archibald question. He is your teacher."

"He is not available right now, and I cannot wait," I almost did not lie without batting an eye. What I needed to do was get a normal teacher, whereas Archibald had long ago disgraced himself in that respect.

"Is that so?" Grizdan scratched his head. "Unavailable, eh? In that case you need the teachers of your teacher. Milord Iven or our Head, Milord Gerhard van Brast. These are the only teachers you can have among the Paladins. The rules allow no others."

"Maybe Sharda?" I reminded him of the gnome.

"No, Shardaganbat works only on the training of new recruits, without exception!"

"How do I arrange to see Milords Iven or Gerhard?" I was not going to give up.

"What, are you just going to show up as you are?! Kind sirs, would you please train this young one for the sake of Light?!" the old man straightened, and even though he had just one eye, that did not prevent him from looking at me as if I were a retard. "Are you in so much hot water, or has Mister Bernard's mark made you so forward?"

"Not Light." I felt somewhat embarrassed. "I am a Dark one, after all. So how do I see the Milords?

"Both at once? Or do you need to see them individually?" a mocking voice inquired from right behind me. I did not even bother to turn around, trying to delay the moment when I would have to stare into the insolent catface, and I kept looking at his tail swishing at my feet. Even the catorian's tail showed how pleased he was with himself for catching me as I was trying to go over his head. When it became completely impolite to keep turning my back to him, I turned around sharply:

"Archibald! I am so glad that you happened to be here by chance!" We both knew how much he left to "chance". "I need one of you to train me!"

Apparently my acting abilities left the catorian so unimpressed that he said calmly:

"Craving knowledge? How commendable! It's music to the ears of a teacher who is so tired of talentless knuckleheads." Archibald was addressing Grizdan, who just shrugged his shoulders.

"The triskelion becomes you." Archibald looked me over from head to toe and his glance stopped for a moment at Bernard's emblem. "And the Daro set as well. So, you have decided to prepare to meet Ahean?"

Just a couple of sentences, and here I was again in the role of Truman. Steve started commenting on what was already obvious:

"*With a 70% probability there is not only a tracking device on you that shows your current location, but also a magical transmitter which relays sound and a video recording.. Archibald can see and hear the same things as you. Recommended action: Update your protection.*"

"Right. Kill the jerks, save the planet," I agreed. At this point I was ready to agree with the catorian on just about anything, so as to obtain what I was looking for. "So how about training?"

"Attack, defense, support?" Amazing, but

Archibald was not beating about the bush and cut right to the chase. "We are not in the Academy; a player can receive only one ability per week. Choose what you need right now."

"Attack." I was more than happy with what I had for defense right now. "What is there available for a level 50 player?"

"Do you need something for individual or mass attack?" the catorian continued indifferently. "Instantaneous or time-delayed? Costly and strong or a little weaker but less energy-intensive? I could go on like this forever. Stop mincing like a wallflower! What is it that you want?"

A little earlier I had discussed with Steve all the acceptable options, and so I was ready with the answer to that question:

"I need 'Leguria'."

The catorian's eyes turned into two narrow furry slits.

"Great Madonna...," Grizdan exclaimed at the back of the room, but Archibald silenced him with a harsh gesture.

"Your suzerain keeps interesting books in his library," the catorian said slowly. The tip of his tail twitched, betraying his puzzlement. "I cannot teach you for 'Leguria', as I am a Light one. You need Gerhard van Brast. He is the only one who would be able to help you. I have no right to deny you training, so I will arrange for you to see the Head. As to whether he will agree to train you is not my problem. Grizdan, a portal to the Citadel."

I lingered, getting cold feet about my seemingly

simple and interesting choice.

"Come!" The catorian entered the building and pulled me after himself to the second floor. "How's your interest in art? Still there?"

"As if you don't know," I grumbled, but, fearing to break my teacher's good mood, continued to the facts. "The problem is the name of the person in the painting. I only know that she was Elizabeth's teacher."

"That amount of knowledge will not take you far. What you have, though, is such a surfeit of attitude that it is as if you had the pendant already in your pocket," my teacher said testily. "You don't know anything – right? A mockery of an explorer!"

"It's because I don't have anyone to help poor lonely me. Even my teacher turned his... tail from training me," I quipped insolently. "I have to do everything myself, working hard day and night. Slowly, maybe, but surely I will reach my goal."

Archibald said nothing. We quickly reached the room with the anchor ball; a thin ray from it created a portal for us. Once we were in the Citadel, the teacher dragged me straight to the room with the painting.

"Look," A beautiful fair-haired lady was looking regally from the canvas, her foot placed triumphantly on the slain monster. The monster was horrifying, with a body seemingly made of fog, without a clear outline, but with a huge number of tentacles. The painting was titled "Great Warrior", and rightly so. "This monster actually is 'Leguria'. You still want to learn that skill?"

I shuddered. Before I visited Bernard's library, I

had supposed that all skills were universal and didn't depend in the "coloration" of the player; however, a book I had come across while scanning literature, titled "The Dark Talent", dispelled those notions. Dark ones had a whole cornucopia of unique spells that varied greatly in terms of impact. The most horrendous ones were able to destroy entire worlds in a matter of seconds; weaker ones were localized, destroying all life only within a certain area. "Leguria" was one of the latter, and was not limited to any specific class. In effect, all the Dark player needed to do was to call up the actual Leguria. It was impossible to control the creature. It immobilized everything alive within a radius of 30 yards from the location to which it was called, and then methodically destroyed them all by sucking up their Energy. Within 50 yards all living beings felt ill and tried to get away as fast as possible, while the weakest ones despondently followed Leguria's call and died in great suffering. Half of all the Energy it obtained Leguria kindly transferred to the accumulating device of the owner, who was off limits to it. Sort of a localized Armageddon for Energy production. In order to generate the maximum amount of Energy, the victims died in horrible agony: the monster plunged them into primal fear. The more fear was experienced, the sweeter the deaths were for the monster. UN representatives would have definitely vetoed the ritual of calling the monster had they known about the existence of the Game.

I was never sadistic, but at this stage there was nothing else I could use to fight against the mages and Dolgunata.

"I know what Leguria is." It was hard, but I held Archibald's stare. "I am not going to try and find excuses for myself, because I am at war, where all is fair. Who is she?" I nodded at the lady warrior.

"Anna, the only student of Madonna. Perished several centuries ago."

"Was she Elizabeth's teacher?"

"Where did you come up with that?" The catorian's eyebrow flew up quizzically. "No, Anna never was Elizabeth's teacher."

"But what about the pendant?" I pointed at the warrior's neck. "That's the lost jewelry of Lady Lecleur. I discovered that the pendant was a gift to Elizabeth from a person very close to her, and that her life is tied to that thing. That's why there is such a hullabaloo about its disappearance. If we suppose that Anna was Elizabeth's teacher, that would explain twelve spiritual advisors for the mistress of the estate. She is the third after Madonna."

"Cool theory. It explains a lot. I am even almost ready to praise you. However, as always, you are wrong. Let's go: we need to see Gerhard."

That was it! Archibald glumly ignored any attempts to continue the conversation, in a hurry to bring me to his teacher. We quickly passed through one hall after another until we reached the anteroom of the Head of the Order, where we encountered the puzzled stare of another visitor. Milord Iven was waiting to be received.

"Wait here," Archibald said curtly, and disappeared behind the inner door.

"What is this supposed to mean?" Iven looked with displeasure after the catorian who had cut in line, and decided to take it out on me. "Why are you here? I ordered you to look for the pendant!"

"That's exactly what I am doing, Milord." I overcame a sudden desire to kiss the ground.

"Here?!" The tone in which Iven asked me that question demonstrated quite eloquently the golden one's opinion of my intelligence.

"Among other places." I responded evasively. "May I ask you a question?"

"If it's relevant to these matters." Iven obviously had not expected me to be so forward.

"Of course it is. I can't put this puzzle together. Lady Lecleur has twelve spiritual advisors who give their own Energy without compensation in order to charge the pendant. Right?" I waited for Iven to nod, then continued. "There is also a line of those waiting to replace any of those twelve as soon as they so much as sneeze. So, Elizabeth is a pretty important person in our game world. However, neither you nor Archibald seem too worried about the theft of the pendant. Moreover, you send unskilled newbies to look for it. And this search is more like a farce, don't you agree? So, my question is: why are you not at the estate? It is the Order's task, since Elizabeth is a Paladin!"

"Because the pendant will be destroyed if even one spiritual advisor shows up at the estate. Or another high-level player. The list is attached. Come on, Gerhard is ready to see you. Come with us, Shiny" Archibald looked at Iven. He was sitting silently, letting Archibald answer my questions. "I want to see your face when Gerhard approves this."

"What list?" I heard new information and clung to it.

"The list of players forbidden from entering the Lecleur estate; it was kindly provided by monsieur the thief. How can that be more clear?" Archibald regained his former gaiety. "Actually, that's why small fish are working on the case. At least, that's the official version. In fact, maybe you are right. Maybe the value of Lady Lecleur to the Order is much overestimated... What do you think, Iven? Maybe one of us should teleport to the estate and be done with this search we are all so fed up with?"

"Bastard!" Iven jumped to his feet instantly, and loomed over Archibald. The huge two-meter gold killing machine was ready to stomp the furry upstart in silver into the ground. Only the catorian was not fazed in the least. He was amused by events. "If you only dare ..."

"I will, if I need to! But it's too early. Relax. Two of my best students for the last thousand years are working in the estate. I would even say two and a half," Archibald looked at me with sarcasm. "So they'll find your pendant, it's not going to get away. I swear by the whiskers –Yari's whiskers." Archibald slapped Iven on the shoulder unceremoniously.

"Get your furry paws away from me!" Iven angrily threw off the catorian's limb.

"Don't get so worked up! You armor will keep shining! I stopped shedding last week, and I licked my paws clean barely a couple of hours ago. Honestly!" I could bet that someone was going to catch one in his insolent furry kisser. I'd cheer for Iven, just out of spite. I've never seen Archibald in battle, but still hoped that his most skillful part was his mouth.

"Don't forget to thank Gerhard once again for protecting you. His request is the only thing that's stopping me." The head Earth Paladin Fighter regained his composure and stepped away from the pleased catorian. That explained the cat's insolence. "But you will still answer to me for the Knights Templar!"

"Always at your service!" The headhunter bared his teeth. "You also ought to remember from time to time what I promised to do to you for the St. Bartholomew's Day massacre."

Realizing that there was not going to be a fight, I felt extremely uncomfortable. It was like witnessing a quarrel between husband and wife: a dubious advantage. Both husband and wife would be likely to blacklist such witnesses afterwards. Not as though I craved love from those like Iven or Archibald; but getting a "ban" from them in the Game was not something I wanted either.

"So, are you coming?" Archibald was tired of staring daggers with Iven. "We shouldn't make the Head wait. My protégé wants to lay his hands on Leguria."

"What else could be expected of your students?" Iven continued to argue with his opponent in words, but actually moved towards the door. "I think the Head should prohibit you from taking students. You are just multiplying your ilk and compromising the reputation of our Order!"

We entered the hallway and the door shut. The space around us filled with light blue fog. I was zapped with electricity seven times quite substantially. Each jolt was accompanied by a high-pitched pig squeal, as if the antivirus system had discovered a Trojan and was happily destroying it.

"You have really stopped taking care of yourself," Iven grumbled once the system informed us that Archibald had caught a marker somewhere as well, while the Head of fighters was without reproach on this.

"I must be getting old." The cat shrugged his shoulders indifferently, while all I could do was to watch in amazement how quickly the interaction between the Paladins changed. Just a moment ago they were ready to tear at each other's throats, and now they were talking like two old buds. That was an impressive level of emotional control!

"What's wrong with the Knights Templar? Why are you supposed to answer for them?" I asked Archibald in a whisper: until the fog dispelled, we were stuck in the hallway.

"One of the accusations brought by the Inquisition against them was that those poor souls worshipped a cat who sometimes appeared to them in their meetings. That's nonsense! I only attended three times!" The cat did not bother to lower his voice, not in the least concerned about Iven's reaction.

"That was enough to rule my Order discredited, and provide the Inquisition an opportunity avenge Black Tuesday!" Iven did not hold back, and hissed his comment. "Get your student to a library. You must be ashamed for his ignorance! What kind of teacher are you, when your student is a total advertisement against our class?! Because of those like him there are rumors that Paladins have degenerated!"

The fog dissipated, opening an ample and well-lit library to us. Book shelves lined the walls all the way to the high ceiling. And I started drooling in my mind, like Pavlov's dog. I even closed my eyes: the richness of the place touched me to the core!

The head of class was sitting in a comfortable armchair, his legs covered with a cozy blanket. A stack of papers was in front of him on the massive desk, and Gerhard was sorting it in two. As we appeared, the owner of the study lifted his head and nodded affably to Iven; then his fatherly stare shifted to me. I lowered my head by way of greeting and as an indication of my respect.

"Greetings, young brother. I have reviewed your request. But before responding I need to make sure that you understand the consequences and are ready to go through with the tests."

I must have looked bewildered at that moment because I have not known of any consequences or, even worse, any tests. But I decided quickly that it was better to look stupid now than be dead in a few minutes, so I confessed:

"I must admit, while I know quite well what Leguria is, I know nothing about the consequences and tests." Even my back felt my teacher's facepalm. I didn't care! He should have been more diligent in teaching me.

"Hm. I cannot say I am surprised. Thoroughness is a trait that comes with experience, so it is characteristic of old age or maturity, while curiosity and haste are normal for youth. And that's the way it should be. It's impossible to be experienced from birth. Right?" Gerhard spoke unhurriedly, making pauses, as if thinking of something extraneous. "Never mind an old man's grumbles... You see, those tests are not really tests as such. They are just test activations of your skills. Yes... Only that... And the consequences... You see, not everyone can be transported into the body of a murderous monster and then calmly return back without damage to their psyche, if you know what I mean. 'Leguria' is not just a useful skill for fighting your enemies, but is also a burden that you assume voluntarily. I will give you a few minutes to think of all of this."

The Head of the Paladins, having provided me with time and food for thought, nodded, inviting Iven and Archibald in for a private conversation. Their conversation would have to be called private rather tentatively: even though they spoke in lowered voices, I still heard snippets of phrases, and it was not difficult to interpret the whole line of conversation correctly. The time Gerhard had allocated for revisiting my request I used for eavesdropping without any qualms. Once I had made my decision about Leguria, I did not see any point in doubting.

"Brother Iven, you wished to see me. I hope you come bearing good news."

I did not hear Iven's response, but caught a

testy barb from Archibald:

"Everyone is pretty sick and tired of your moaning about 'Poor Liza'! Nothing will happen to her! We are not providing any excuses for the thieves. I would still recommend that you not make haste, and let my students work in peace. I am sure they will produce results."

And again Iven's words faded before I could hear them, no matter how much I strained my ears. However, Gerhard's response to him was quite interesting:

"I share your feelings, brother Iven. But let's trust Archibald. You are not impartial on this issue."

I could not say that I learned something new on the case of the stolen pendant – and that's what Gerhard was discussing with the Paladins. But there were a few pointers that have moved the focus of my investigation towards the Head of the fighters. In order to move forward I needed to understand the connection between Iven and "Poor Liza". A common teacher would not worry so much about her well-being if she were simply a student.

"So what is your decision, my young brother?" Gerhard was addressing me again. "Or maybe my student? Are you ready for the tests?"

"I have thought about your words as thoroughly as I can, and I am ready to take the tests." I tried to speak confidently so as to convince the Head that my intentions were serious. I was going to figure out what the deal was with this skill in the process.

"We shall see. Take the accumulator." A brilliant diamond appeared on the desk. "It is yours for the duration of the testing."

Gerhard waved his hand, opening a portal. That made me envious: I also would like to open portals or materialize objects with a gesture of one hand. Steve only shook his head. I followed the Paladins, and for a moment bright sunshine blinded me. It took the light filters on my armor just a few moments to adjust to the new environment. The blazing son of some southern country washed over the armor harmlessly, and went on to bother some locals hustling around nearby and a crowd of tourists.

"We are currently either in Southern Turkey or in Northern Syria." Steve had industriously found a map and estimated our current location.

"The way the test works is simple." Gerhard turned towards me and handed me a scroll. "You need to activate it. Leave us." The last phrase was addressed to Archibald and Iven. The Paladins headed off to the side without a word, cutting through the crowd.

"That's it?" I verified, as I still could not understand what the catch was. "Just activate the scroll? No shaman's dances? And then what?"

Gerhard nodded, looking around at the people.

"No dances. The strongest one grants the right to call the creature. What's next? But you know the point of this ability. You know what will happen to these people."

"Yes – they will die." I looked around as well. "But they are just NPCs; there are no players among them.

"A month ago you were one of them," Gerhard

reminded me. Activate the scroll. Or have you changed your mind? It's not too late still."

"Em... No, I have not changed my mind. Leguria will kill everyone within a radius of 30 yards. Including you." This really was the only consideration that stopped me from activating it.

"Your concern about me is commendable, but unnecessary," the Head smiled. "You should be wary of the monsters within, not without. Go ahead."

I nodded as if I had actually understood what monsters within he meant, and found the key phrase of the scroll. I drew a lungful of air and clearly shouted in Latin: "Non sum qualis eram, Leguria sum ego!"

The asphalt around us cracked and buckled; then it started melting rapidly, turning into hot lava. NPCs, terrified, were becoming stuck in it like moths in a spider web. Everything around turned dark and quiet. The city noise died, and I could not even hear the cries of the people. It felt like I was watching a silent horror movie. Just my own pulse thundered in my ears. The more dead was the silence, the more horrifying it was to hear a sudden peal of thunder in it and see a meteor tumble from the skies, cutting through the twilight and immediately turning into the creature whose assistance I was hoping to engage.

The monster found me unerringly among its future victims and stared at me, acknowledging me as its master. From that point on I could not feel my body any more. I realized that I was a person, a Paladin; so there were no changes to my personality. All that changed was my outer shell, and I felt a surge of childish delight in freedom. As if together with the old body I had shed some numbing shackles. That was so fantastic! To be everywhere. My body was in all the different locations. I squeezed by the people who turned still, I could weave around their feet or I could fly high up for a bird's-eye view of the square. What could be greater than flight? I somersaulted in the overheated air. That was so wonderful! I was free!

The thirst caught up with me while I still was in the air. All-encompassing, making me forget everything. I did not want to fly any more, I just wanted to make the thirst subside. Or to die, just to make it all end. But it disagreed with me: it did not want death. It promised to show me how to quench the thirst. To do this, it moved my consciousness aside and came into play. It knew what to do. I just needed to trust it, and I would feel better. The thirst pounded with pain in my whole body, my head was burning, as if on fire. From then on I acted on pure instinct.

Having cast a look at my victims from above, I unerringly saw the tastiest piece – delight. There it was, large and tasty! It should be enough to allay my thirst. A lunge, and my body flattened against the invisible wall that guarded the head of the Paladins from my advances. It was hopeless! His delight, so tasty and desirable, was out of reach. What a pity. So I had to make do with smaller morsels.

It whispered calming words to me, promising that we would get even with him later; then it taught me how to make the surrounding vessels of food tastier. I did not resist, and we cried out together, sending horrible visions to all those fumbling creatures and bringing their worst phobias from the depths of their minds. Yes: that was the way! The vessels screamed, drowning in their own terror. That made things so much tastier and sweeter! That way generated more Energy, and my thirst gradually subsided. I found myself next to a bearded man. His scream was tasteless, so I tore out his tongue and with pleasure stuck my tentacles in his ears to reach the brain. The pain center was there, and I influenced it directly to receive even more sweets!

Leaving a part of me to work on the first vessel, I rushed to the second one. My time was limited, and the thirst was still torturing me. I had not a second to lose! The next vessel was small, soft, and yielding, but contained so much Energy that it took me a little longer than the first one. He was followed by the third, fourth, fifth... then I was engulfed by darkness.

I came to lying on my back on the ground. I opened my eyes slowly, and reflexively covered them with my hand to protect against the blazing sun. Awareness of my human body returned before the memories of what I had done. I was even able to stand up and look around. I was surrounded by piles of the bloody remains of NPCs and I only wanted one thing: to die, so as to remove the picture of that bloody massacre from my head. Recent events flashed through my mind as a series of bright cartoon drawings, and I bent down, retching shamelessly.

"You passed the first test." That was Gerhard's comment on the events. I was jerked to my feet. I turned my head towards whoever had saved me, but encountered a hateful state from Iven. That was the way the gold-armored Paladin sometimes allowed himself to look at Archibald; the only difference was that there would be no protection from Gerhard for me if Iven were to decide to kill me.

"Thirty two dead, one hundred and four injured," Archibald joined us. "Pretty good catch for a Dark one. Judging by how much they all wriggled, I would suppose that the crystal filled to one hundredth of a percent. Am I right?"

"To one thousandth," Gerhard corrected. "There were too few NPCs within the impact radius. Yaropolk was too slow with activation and several groups left the area; they were just in the fear zone. People will call this event the 'Suruç bombing'. The second test is awaiting, let's go."

Another portal appeared and I was shoved into it like a limp doll.

"Second test." Gerhard gave me the next scroll. He ordered the others: "Leave us." "Activate it!"

I took the offered item from the Head, my hands numb, and looked around, feeling cornered. While previously we had been in a relatively deserted location, now the calling point for Leguria was a huge mall.

"*Al Hamra Tower.*" Steve saw a sign somewhere. "*Shopping mall and office center.*"

"It's rush hour now, conveniently," Gerhard added to my assistant's words. "So the crystal charge could increase by another one tenth of a percent."

"Does Leguria affect two dimensions on a plane, or is it three-dimensional?" I began to understand why the Head had made this choice. Even though I thought I knew the answer, I wanted to hear it from Gerhard. But he just gave me a patronizing grin and pointed at the scroll.

"I would like to inform you that the 'Darkness' scale has reached its limit value. Current level of Allegiance to Darkness: 2 units." Steve added to the general confusion distracting me from the scroll as I concentrated on the scale. It became brighter and more vivid than it had been the last time. As soon as I concentrated on it, the assistant came up with a whole sheet of text describing this thing; however, I had no right to take the time for it now.

"Mommy, let's go to the movies!" A high-pitched childish voice cut through my concentration. "Come, come now! I want caramel popcorn and a toy!"

A family of German burghers passed by us. A stolid dignified dad with a huge beer belly dragged along three ankle-biters and his long-legged wife, whose face hinted at past beauty. It seemed that the look on the face of this respectable frau was broadcast to the whole world: I have a rich husband, three healthy children, a good job and sex every day, and what do you have to show for yourself? The family quickly passed by, pushing us aside.

"Yaropolk?" Gerhard politely reminded me he was still waiting.

"I cannot." I sighed deeply and handed the scroll back to the Head. It was a hard decision. Not only was I not ready to feel again the delight brought by the sweetness of the pain and suffering of other creatures, I was not ready to kill a thousand innocent

NPCs. My whole being protested that, and had I activated the scroll, I would have had to initiate a case against myself. There is no place in the Game for such a beast!

"You understand that by refusing to activate the scroll you forfeit this ability?" Gerhard clarified, so all I could do was nod. "Please explain your choice."

I told him the whole truth without hesitation. There was no point in concealing the obvious from a being who could open portals with a flick of his finger and resist Leguria.

"We are going back." The head created a portal, and in an instant we were standing in his office.

Amazing, but Archibald greeted me with a disappointed stare. Apparently, the headhunter was bored doing nothing for so long:

"So where is the sea of blood, my hapless student? Or were you not consistent enough even in your allegiance to Darkness?"

"Your student was a consistent Judge, and that is enough, Archibald! The second test is complete." Gerhard settled down in his armchair and immediately the blanket slid onto his lap, making him look like a homely old man rather than the Head of class. I could not restrain myself from looking under the desk: the Paladin's feet now sported comfortable slippers sinking into the thick carpet. "Yaropolk, you are right. There is no place in the Game for players with maniac inclinations – Dark and Light alike. Had you activated the scroll after what you had felt during the first activation, I would have had to kill you. Even Bernard would not have interfered. Take this; by my

right of the strongest Dark I grant you Leguria."
Gerhard gave me the metal hexagon with the three-
eyed skull. The message on acquiring a new ability
flashed before me. Iven, who had been standing with
his back towards us through all this, turned around
sharply and addressed the Head:

"With all due respect, Milord, I consider it a
mistake to allow access to Leguria to a young and
inexperienced Dark one! You know to what it may
lead!"

"I know, Iven, but I would like to remind you
that I am also a Dark one who has Leguria. And that
presumption of innocence applies regardless of Light
or Darkness," Gerhard responded and sighed. "Iven:
it's not really that important what killed Anna or what
color her murderer was. Your grief makes you view
each Dark one as a potential murderer; that affects
the entire Order negatively. Think about it."

"Yes, Milord." Iven bowed his head humbly. "I
suppose you are right."

"Yaropolk, I hope that your new ability will be
used only for good endeavors worthy of the name of
Paladins. From time to time I will monitor your use of
Leguria. Remember that, and that the consequences
of your actions will always catch up with you!"

"Thank you, Milord!"

"It's always a pleasure to help young Paladins!
Archibald will take you to the Sanctuary."

The Head returned to his papers, and I
gratefully made a farewell bow. And froze still.
Perhaps I would never have another chance. So it
would be stupid to let this one get away:

"I apologize, Milord Gerhard, but may I ask for some more help?" The catorian, floating behind my back like a shadow, kicked me in the knee from behind and hissed into my ear:

"You are not so dumb as to bother the Head with questions?"

Instead of answering him I was trying to elicit some pity in Gerhard, who was taken aback by my forwardness:

"I understand that this is not in line with the Code, but you just said that it was a pleasure to help... I am sure you did not say that just out of politeness. I need some information regarding the disappearance of the pendant. The success of my investigation hangs on it. The order is interested in having this case resolved as soon as possible, if my understanding is correct?"

"Your understanding is correct. And since you are posing the question in this way, I am ready to hear you." A brief smile curved Gerhard's lips.

"Please tell me – what is the connection between the great warrior Anna and Elizabeth?" I started with my main question.

"That's it?" The Head look disappointed; he asked Archibald: "Aren't you supposed to provide this kind of information as his teacher?"

"Milord, I have been saying for a long time that Archibald should be prohibited from taking students! He shirks his duties, and only cripples the young ones! Their ignorance is a shame to the Order!" In his righteous anger Iven decided to remind everyone he was still there.

"Brother Archibald, there is truth in brother Iven's words. What can you say to explain yourself? The Order of Paladins is going through a hard period right now; each new player is a bonus to us!" Gerhard pursed his lips and looked at the catorian with displeasure.

"I cannot agree with you, Milord. I am not a nanny. Yaropolk is an explorer, and information is his weapon. He will be able to appreciate its value only if he has to get it with blood and sweat. I don't agree with the statement that I shirk my teaching duties either. My students demonstrated a high level of skills. They have been trained in battle and have demonstrated better academic achievements then others. Well, and Yaropolk cannot be considered truly uneducated. He is just very young and... inexperienced." The last word sounded rather like "he is an untrainable moron, this Yaropolk – what could you want from him?"

"I have to agree with brother Archibald. Everyone has their own training and teaching methods. Let's hope that they will yield the right kind of fruit," Gerhard noted philosophically and finally deigned to answer. "Elizabeth is the only daughter of Anna, who was Madonna's student. Anything else?"

Archibald sighed with disappointment, and hastened to reproach me:

"Yaropolk, this was obvious! I rejected your version about teaching! Where is your deductive skill?"

"It was not obvious!" I replied angrily, becoming more and more irritated with the cat. This furry ass managed to wiggle himself out of being guilty in front of Gerhard and made me look like an idiot. Some experienced teacher, right!

I did not hide my disappointment, so the Head of the Paladins decided to cheer me up:

"Brother Yaropolk, do share your thoughts with us. I am sure that your exploring abilities will help brothers Iven and Archibald take a fresh look at the disappearance of the pendant."

Encouraged by Gerhard, I continued:

"I consider that the pendant was stolen by one of the spiritual advisors."

"That's out of the question!" It was the first time Iven deigned to address me directly; however, doing so he copied the condescending intonations of my teacher. It seemed to be that rare case when two opponents were siding together. "I checked each one personally! None of them were involved in the theft!"

"And Milord Gerhard checked you?" I asked, and immediately regretted it. Iven turned to stone and shifted his eyes to the catorian:

"Shut your half-brain up! Or else you will have to answer for his cretinism!"

Archibald grinned, came up to me and patted me on the shoulder good-naturedly.

"You see, my practically dead student, Iven simply could not do that. Anyone could, but not he."

"Since I am practically dead anyway, perhaps you would now care to explain the whole thing to me?" It seemed I had nothing to lose at that point. I was so grateful to Bernard for suggesting that I change anchor point. If it came to that, I should be able to hide in his residence.

"I think it would be better if brothers Archibald and Iven wait for you in the anteroom, particularly since they need to coordinate their further work on this case. Meanwhile we'll have a short talk." The Head took pity on me, realizing that if those two were to stay, the talk would not likely stay short.

Iven walked to the door quickly, and opened it for the catorian. The latter just shrugged his shoulders and continued mocking the irritated fighter:

"You want me to open my back to you of my own will?!

Iven turned purple and roared:

"Are you hinting that I am capable of ..." He was lost for words in his indignation.

"I am not hinting at anything at all! The moment one hints at anything in your presence you run tattling to the Head!"

"Out!" the library owner ran out of patience, and both Paladins retreated quickly.

Looking after them I noted:

"Are you sure they won't reduce your anteroom to rubble while they coordinate their actions?"

"Well, some friendly venting won't hurt them," the Head grinned.

I grimaced skeptically.

"With such friends..." I sensibly did not finish the phrase, as Gerhard's eyes turned icy.

"Yaropolk, you need to learn to think before you speak! Frequently your youth cannot serve to justify insults!" Puzzled, I quietly waited for him to continue. What was so insulting in what I had just said?

"Just a moment ago you cast aspersions on my ability to rule my advisors and therefore, the Order! You put in doubt the foundations of our clan: all the Paladins are brothers, not enemies!"

Ow, that really had not come out well... I felt ashamed before Gerhard.

"I am sorry! I did not mean it! I just wasn't thinking..." I hung my head in repentance.

Gerhard softened a little:

"I hope this will serve as a good lesson to you. Now about Iven. Anna, Elizabeth's mother, was his other half. She was killed by Leguria. And Elizabeth is their only daughter, so this excludes brother Iven from the list of suspects."

Tension hung in the air. I realized how deep I had gotten myself into it! Steve noted something that was already obvious anyway: the other half was a doll who had become a player. It used to be allowed. Therefore, Iven just physically could not... Wait! Madonna took a doll for a student? Or, rather, a player who used to be a doll? Why would she do that? What if she did it out of solidarity and memory of her own past? A Doll took another doll as a student. That's quite logical. And when Anna died, then, using the right of the teacher ... Oh really?!

"Was Elizabeth a minion of Madonna's?" I asked in astonishment, and received a glance of respect from Gerhard. It was nice to prove that I was not hopeless.

"You could not have found that out in the estate," the Head noted.

"I received some information from Bernard; the rest is my conclusion."

"Commendable. I hope you don't have any new requests?" It was obvious that the conversation had tired Gerhard out, and I hastened with the last one, not hoping for success.

"Would it be too presumptuous of me to ask for access to the Library of the Citadel? I would like to learn more about the Lecleur family."

Gerhard sighed tiredly:

"Access to the Library is granted only after six months. Let's not break the rules. Particularly since the information you need is in a restricted section. It's time for you to go. It will be better if you leave for the Sanctuary straight from here."

Actually, I was glad to get away from the company of Iven and Archibald; they were too oppressive with their continuous self-importance and vitriol.

Inhaling the cool air of freedom, I checked to see that there was not that much time till I had to see Ahean, and decided to do one last thing that would bring me at least somewhat closer to solving the mystery of the pendant. I addressed the Game itself:

"In order to complete the quest "Stolen Pendant" and deliver an objective verdict for the case "Stolen Pendant" I need architectural plan drawings of the Lecleur estate, including all secret passages, niches and other concealed elements where the pendant could have been hidden. I am not requesting information regarding protection of the estate nor about all the traps that are abundant in those passages, since that is private information of the Lecleur family; however, without knowledge of what secret passages that exist within the estate and their configuration, it is impossible to compete the quest."

"The request is denied. Information on secret passages of the Lecleur estate has been made unavailable based on the decision of the head of the family. To obtain said information, permission from the head of the family is required."

"In order to complete the quest...," I was not going to give up, and repeated the long rationale once again. "I need information as to when the head of the family made the information on secret passages unavailable?

"The request is denied. Information on secret passages of the Lecleur estate, including the date of concealing the information, has been made unavailable based on the decision of the head of the family. To obtain the said information, permission from the head of the family is required."

"Please generate a request to the head of the Lecleur family to provide me the necessary information." I resorted to extreme measures. If Sophie was fulfilling the responsibilities of the mistress of the estate, it was reasonable to suppose that she was the one designated as the head of the family. I did not think that in view of recent events she would deny me that small service.

"Your request has been sent... Response is received – request to grant information on the Lecleur estate to Paladin Yaropolk is denied. You have received three negative responses within 24 hours. Next request

for accessing the Temple of Knowledge will be available tomorrow. Have a nice game!"

Could it be that during the time I had been absent from the estate something had happened to Sophie? But what if I had been wrong, and the head of the family was, for example, Ervan? Well, no. His level was not high enough. However, it would be quite possible for Iven to be that person. So then the denial to provide access to Paladin Yaropolk would make sense: not the right background, not the right teacher, did not breathe the right way, and on top of all that did not demonstrate the right level of respect. Get out of here, stupid kid! Smart adults will figure it out without you around.

"Response to your request came from the head of the Lecleur family too quickly. There is up to a 90 % probability that the head of the Lecleur family is Milord Iven. Possible reason for denying request is personal antipathy due to the insult you inflicted, your allegiance to Darkness and availability of Leguria. However, if one takes into account the level of interest of your suzerain in the chief fighter, one should review the motives for which your request was denied more carefully. It is possible that the initial assessment is flawed."

Thanks, captain Steve the Obvious! Immediately after I arrived at the estate I would try to work through Sophie until other options become available. With those thoughts I jumped into timelessness in order to prepare for the meeting with the mages. I needed scrolls, and the more the better.

"So what do you think – why does Archibald still

have only a Daro set? He is a creature from the previous era and known outside of the Earth game world, but the Viceroy has not issued Imperial armor to him. Why?" After I had spent a month outside of time, Steve's personality matrix became more or less independent of my consciousness, and the assistant started coming up with his own hypotheses. In actuality they were my own thoughts. Only hidden deep in the subconscious; Steve extracted them into the light, but it was much more pleasant to discuss them with a smart and educated person. Me, that is. I just had to take care not to catch narcissism from that!

Why so much interest in my teacher all of a sudden?" I asked in surprise. The assistant, however, was right – it was odd that Archibald was not shining in gold just like Iven.

"No reason," Steve spread his arms. *"I just noticed a strange thing and reported it."*

"So how frequently are you now noticing these strange things?"

"One of the latest was your energy accumulator. It was never taken back from you."

I put my hand on my thigh mechanically, where the crystal was installed. My old one, the one Gromana had given me way back, was sitting in the inventory while Gerhard's present worked without fail and sucked in the emotions from the world around like a good old vacuum cleaner.

"The crystal is 22.6632%, full, which makes it possible to use the Energy for a whole year without fear of depletion to zero. I suggest that you set up an

automatic transfer of Energy right away."

I reviewed my video of the events in Gerhard's office once again. What is accidental or deliberate?

"Do you have any ideas as to why he would have done that?"

"I think that the most appropriate answer would be 'accidental deliberation'. Players like Gerhard van Brast have a predilection for multimove combinations." I hated hearing this obvious response so much that I grimaced. You can't deceive the subconscious.

"There seem to be too many of those with a liking for multi-move games. Levard, who is temporarily out of play. The mages who killed immune Monstrichello. Incomprehensible and therefore strange Archibald and Sharda. Dolgunata who wants to play her own game. Gerhard who demands nothing at all. The gold-clad head of the Lecleur family with his entire brood. Dualistic Bernard with truthful Gromana, and finally, me. Eight different groups of beings interested in the pendant or restart! And me by my lonesome self! And nobody loves me!

"You are not alone – there are two of us," the assistant reassured me.

"Just stop right there!" I warned Steve. "Let's keep to respect and no corny stuff! Since there are two of us – any ideas about how to look for the pendant?"

"You need to offer Sophie an exchange: sex for access to secret passages," Steve suggested. *"We'll rescue Alard and use his tracker to look for the pendant. We'll use Mizardine as bait for the traps. We don't care about him and he needs to work for the*

service we provided. The search should be started from Elizabeth's room; there must definitely be a secret passage there."

"Is there a chance to beat Dolgunata without Leguria?"

"Still the same 26%. That's the probability I assign to the chance of a meteorite falling on her head during the year that Dolgunata will need to destroy your protection based on the new crystal. There is a 100 chance that Archibald will let his student know about Leguria and the new crystal, so she will be prepared, and I do not see any other way to win."

"You sure know how to cheer people up," I sighed. "Let's go back, I have to find out what the mages need.

Our return to the Lecleur estate was uneventful. The portal brought me to within a few yards of the entrance to the castle, and I was thrown, as they say, "off the boat and into the party". And what a party it was! There was no line of players any more, but the tent city was bustling with activity; besides, it was literally on fire. Everything was flying about: ricocheting lightning bolts, icicles, some black shadows; several tents were burning, someone was cursing someone else, amidst cries for help there were sounds of hysterical laughter, screeching and screams of pain. Normal working atmosphere of looting and lawlessness. Deciding that the mages were not going anywhere, I decided to go down to the frantic players. I wanted to see who started it all and punish someone already.

"Group one – extinguish the fire! Group two –

don't let the enemy approach! Group three – attack!"

What had seemed at first glance a chaotic frenzy among the players was an illusion. While at first I had thought that the mages have gone wild and I would need to punish some, now I saw them in a completely different light: they were trying to help common players. Ahean was standing on a cart and commanded the players quite skillfully; they, in turn, followed his commands without objection. Another thing that helped the mage in managing the groups is that each of them was headed by a member of his dark-robed class. About half of the players from the tent city were participating in the local event, the others were standing a short distance away and watching all this as if it were a show in the theatre. The main evildoers were necromancers and an army of zombies and skeletons they had called up.

"Yaropolk, over here!" Ahean waved his hand on seeing me approach. I was pushed several times by running players, but I did not protest – they looked concentrated on the enemy. A new wave of the undead was coming down from the nearest hill while the tent city dwellers were still fighting the previous set. "Group one, aid with attack! Reserve, get ready, they are coming! Second, attack! Third group, defense! Come on guys, today we'll do it!"

"What have you got here?" I made way towards Ahean and climbed up onto the cart next to him.

"We are, like, having fun, can't you see?" The mage scowled, sending a fireball towards the zombies. The mage made sure to attack even as he was directing the defensive action. "Yesterday we spanked the mummers, now they, like, came for revenge. Even dragged their teacher along. There he is, standing on the hill, like, commanding and all. Looking how his brats are trying to retrieve their inglorious defeat. Dumbshit muttonheads."

"It seems as though you aren't doing too well fighting them back." Another tent was toppled by the zombies and immediately caught fire. The wave of the undead flowing down from the hill came up against the protective domes of the players and they started pushing to crush them, slowly but surely. They were beating the live players by sheer numbers. "Should you perhaps ask for help?"

"Like, we are little lambs who can't protect ourselves? Like, come save our asses from bites of old skull bones?"

"Never mind – that was a dumb thing to say. Where's Alard?"

"Running around in group one. There, see, he's just about to attack." "Ahean pointed out a Paladin in shining armor. The orc was slashing about with his sword wildly, chopping off the oncoming zombies' heads. "You are, like, here for a show, or, like, want to help?"

"So, conversation later?" I asked the mage. That was not the reception I expected. Ahean nodded:

"Like, sure."

"So then. You get experience from killing the undead?" The decision came instantly.

"Sure you do! Let's talk later; join group one – they are hit the hardest. Here, catch the invite."

I saw a huge sheet of frames in front of me.

Green bars of protective domes were creeping down, and with scary regularity the players' frames turned gray. Even the mighty flow of incoming experience could not make up for the fact that players were dying like flies. There were just about eighty defenders left from the original hundred and fifty. I quickly attached my artifact to my hand and rushed into the thick of the battle.

"For Tores!" Alard's battle cry dampened even the noise of the battle for a moment.

"Rago rat kol!" Other players responded, and in that instant the Energy scale of all the fighters filled to 100%. The countdown timer to the next battle cry appeared: 10 minutes.

"Yaropolk! Come on over here!" Alard was glad to see me. A few strokes with the sword, and a free space appeared around the orc. Zombies, even after they were cut in half, still tried to inflict at least some harm by scratching at the fighters' shins, but the front line had the players who were wearing armor; even when their shields ran out of Energy they were protected to some extent.

I rushed over to the orc and hit the nearest enemy square on the head. The spikes on my artifact pulverized the skull of the skeleton to smithereens, but that did not stop the monster. The headless creature did not seem to notice the disappearance of a vital part, kept stretching its bony paws towards me. They scraped on my shield helplessly, but the monster would not give up, continuing to draw down my Energy bit by bit. I was not concerned about this anymore, but for the majority of players this tactic of the skeletons was deadly.

"You have to crush them totally!" Alard twisted his sword and hit the skeleton flat on, toppling it to the ground and breaking it in two halves. They kept twitching but were not really dangerous any more. "I am glad to see you here, brother! It will be a hot night tonight!"

There was no time for us to talk. The enemies were charging as a solid crowd, ignoring losses among them. From time to time here and there cries of the players were heard. Players ran out of Energy and fell prey to zombies. I pulled out a stack of scrolls with the "Templar's Blow" and threw it at the oncoming undead, making sure to spread the sheets over a wide area. Five seconds, and for a little while the pressure of the attackers was reduced. The explosion took out at least a third of the oncoming enemies, and there was not enough time for the next wave to reach us yet.

"Great!" Alard grabbed an elixir out of his inventory and downed it in one gulp, replenishing his Energy. "We'll live another minute! Prepare the next bomb!"

"Second group to defense! Reserve, forward! New wave! Incoming!"

Even though the scrolls were very effective, the results of using them were not too impressive. I was able to clear out a space only in front of the orc and myself, while the battle in the other parts of our line was just as fierce as before. I threw some more scrolls, now trying to throw them not just forward, but as far to the side as possible in order to help my neighbors. Activation, and a couple of seconds of rest again. However, this time one of our own was caught by friendly fire: a scroll was thrown at him by a blast of wind. The hapless guy's protection crumbled and he was sent to respawn; meanwhile my Darkness bar jumped by an entire percent. The Game considered that I had done it from malicious intent. It was hard to stand, our feet slipping in the remains of zombies and skeletons; we had to take a few steps back. Several more tents went up in flames, burning brightly. Ahean immediately sent some players to put them out. The Energy that the fire stripped from the players' shields was much needed elsewhere.

I threw the scrolls back into inventory and returned to battle. Once I started using the "Templar's Blow", it made things easier: even a light touch of the spikes with the ability activated tore the opponent into shreds, showering us either with bits of quivering flesh or bones. The new wave literally crushed the remnants of the previous one and attacked us with the force of a tsunami.

"First group, retreat! Second, defense! Third, attack! Reserve, retreat! Replenish resources!"

Ahean was not going to surrender to the mercy of the outnumbering forces; he continued commanding his troops and sending fireballs at the enemy. I took in the situation: only about twenty players were still alive. Only Alard and I were still standing from the first group, everyone else was taking a break, to be printed again in an hour by the 3D printers of the Game.

"Retreat!" I ordered the orc as I crushed yet

another zombie to shreds. On top of the hill they were preparing to send the next wave at us, and that was guaranteed to sweep us over. Unless we crushed those preparations in the bud, which is what I was planning to do.

"I will not abandon a brother!" The mind of a true Paladin could not grasp the idea of abandoning a comrade alone in the battlefield. With a swing of his sword the orc devastated a few more skulls, stomping on the nearest one for good measure. "Retreat, I'll cover you!"

"Do whatever you want!" I growled, and rushed forward. A crowd of hungry undead bowled me over at once, toppling me to the ground.

"I'll help!" Alard shouted. He dashed after me and his frame turned grey. The orc departed for Zagransh. I was not going to cry about my partner – Alard was not a level one player; besides, during the battle he must have gained at least three more, so he'd come out of this better off than before in any case. Bones and crooked fingers scraped on my protective shell, vainly trying to piece it, so I was relatively safe. However, the crowd did the most important thing: they pushed me down with their sheer mass, preventing me from moving forward. I did not have time to lie around contemplating the meaning of life, so I extracted some scrolls and activated them. A shower of bones and rotten flesh covered the ground, removing the weight from me, so I rushed forward, only to be buried under the next wave of the undead. Scrolls, raining bones, dash, and the next wave of those craving my life. Scrolls, raining bones...

It took me twenty dashes to come through the attacking wave. No one bothered to turn back to catch me: a new army was about to rise on top of the hill. The necromancers must have decided that one player would not do much harm, sending their puppets on to crush whoever still resisted. Seven players, including Ahean. Not too many! Jumping to my feet I ran up the hill and literally ran headfirst into the protective dome of the necromancers, defending them from uninvited visitors. I heard extremely nasty laughter, as if they were mocking me, on top of everything else! The ground bubbled like boiling water, and the new army started climbing out from under it. That was what was supposed to completely bury the entire tent city with all of its inhabitants. I had no time to try and overcome their shields, so I inhaled deeply and did what I had to do.

I started a counter-attack.

My consciousness faded in Leguria. I looked around and flicked my tongue rapaciously: from the castle I could smell such tasty fear and desperation that I floated in that direction, but stopped hard against a wall. I was just a couple of dozen steps short of catching the trembling food and enjoying its emotions. Roaring bitterly – that actually made the emotions tastier – I rushed back. The sounds of my indignation made the sweet fear bloom there too. I needed to check it out.

There was something stumbling under my tentacles – moving, but totally unattractive. It tried to stop me, grabbed the tentacles it was even biting, so I was a little delayed tearing that something to pieces. Totally tasteless, as though it was not even alive. I let out another long roar and cheered up: the aroma of fear blossomed right under my nose. I reached for it, but encountered another obstacle. One more wall? I was so unlucky! My belly started rumbling and my thirst became unbearable. Unless I drink someone pretty soon, a horrible thing will happen. I will die! Upset, I pushed on the wall with all my might, trying to crush it and get to the tasty fear. Blow, and another, and another...

"Noooooo!" the food screeched, once I plopped right on top of it. The wall disappeared and I fell right into the thick of the sweet smells. Letting out another scream, I licked my chops again: five of the beings present emanated the tasty emotions of fear. Sticking my tentacles into the ears of the first dish, reaching the brain and causing the maximum amount of pain possible, I reached for the others. My thirst will be quenched!

I was not able to satiate myself. What is five puny bodies? I shouted once again, trying to see if there was any more tasty food in the vicinity, when I came up on an unfamiliar note. Tart, a little bitter with a slight nuance of disgust. Memory brought forth the name of this dish: "indifference". Someone could not care less about my presence, making me grimace. The taste of that emotion was quite unpleasant. Not wanting to lose time, I scanned the area I could cover, but did not find anything else other than the unattractive moving mass. Crushing it just out of spite so that it would not get underfoot, I stopped in place. There was nothing more to eat. My mission was complete.

My consciousness returned, and the memory of five necromancers appeared in front of my eyes. I bent over, retching, but then straightened out again. I had taken that step knowing what I was in for, so no need to demonstrate my weakness.

"Dark one." A hoarse voice broke the silence surrounding me. The words sounded forced, as if it was hard for the creature to speak. I turned around and in the center of the chaos that I had wreaked saw a grey-haired skinny necromancer. It was definitely not a human being, even though I could not identify the race. The dry mummy somehow clutching on to this world could have belonged to anybody. I swallowed, and suppressing a new spasm, chased away the vision of Leguria and walked to the surviving opponent. Zombies and skeletons covered the ground in dead heaps, so during the next few minutes nothing was threatening the three remaining defenders of the tent city.

"Bernard's slave." The necromancer's eyes slid across the emblem and he rasped: "I see. We'll return tomorrow. Prepared. I had not expected Leguria. It's pretty."

"What is all that for?" I looked around and stepped out of the pile of remains of what used to be alive at some point. After I was Leguria such trifles as blobs of flesh on my boots did not bother me anymore; all I felt was a vague disgust.

"Training. Everyone needs training. Expect us tomorrow. I'll show the young ones how to hide emotions."

The necromancer waved his hand in the air and a portal appeared next to him. I hemmed – seems like whoever this creature was that visited us was not so simple. His strength level was comparable to that of Gerhard, the Head of Paladins.

"I killed your twits, so I deserve answers!" I shouted before the old man could disappear. He turned around:

"Death. That's all you deserve. We'll come back tomorrow. Expect us. The training must go on."

The portal shut with a clap and immediately all the conjured zombies and skeletons turned to ashes. The hill and tent city now looked like Pompeii after the eruption of Vesuvius. Ashes everywhere, ruins and fires; all that was missing was wailing mothers and marauders. Actually, I was wrong about the latter: the burnt tents were already being looted.

"So it goes every night," Ahean grinned, climbing down from the cart. The left side of his robe was torn and I could see bleeding wounds through the holes. I offered him an elves' ointment almost automatically. "Thanks, I got it. Seven levels, congratulations. I see you did quite well in the last thirty minutes. That beast – was that yours?"

"It was," I nodded without going into detail. "You wanted to talk. What about?"

"You want to talk about it right here?"

"Why not?" We dropped to the ground, leaning our backs against the cart. I could not say that I was exhausted – I was overflowing with Energy. But physically I was quite tired. The day had been too long, and it had ended too abruptly. I wanted to sleep. Punishing anyone was the furthest thing from my mind. I'd deal with the necromancers tomorrow.

"So here is fine too." Ahean rummaged through his inventory and extracted a small jewel box. "That's for you. A present from Devir for successful completion of the Academy and the incident afterwards."

"I like presents," I grinned, in no hurry to accept the gift. "Go ahead, open it."

"If he had wanted to kill you, he would have done it already. Quite a while ago, too." Ahean did not pretend to be frustrated. The mage put the box in his lap and lifted the lid. "Boom!"

The shout was so sudden that I staggered back, falling over. Ahean laughed out loud.

"Sorry, I just could not resist it. You had such a funny face as you were looking at... Anyway, doesn't matter. So, in here there's a pair of earrings and... And that's it, nothing more. Hm. That's a very strange present coming from my teacher. Is that some kind of a hint? Wait, let me check... No, just ordinary earrings."

Two earrings settled in my palm. Ahean created a small ball of light to look at them better, and then Steve started waving his hands desperately, trying to attract my attention. Even though there was no need: my memory of "The Great Warrior" painting was quite clear.

Devir's present to me was the lost earrings of the Lecleurs.

CHAPTER SEVEN

"SHAZAL" TREATISE

"MIZARDINE, YOUR TASK will be the most important one." I plopped a stack of scrolls with the "Templar's Blow" on the table. "You are the only one who can save us today. Do you know how to dig?"

The hunter looked from the scrolls to me in bewilderment, not understanding my drift.

"The Necromancers will return in the evening in force, and mad to boot. I have found out that they always appear on the hill. Yesterday the big guys scattered everybody, and only after that did they let loose their dead troops. Most likely the same thing will happen today. From the hill it's the simplest path to send the undead to the tent city. So let's prepare a "Tsar Bomba" for them.

Now Alard, who had come back at dawn, stared at me questioningly as well. Finding out about the inglorious demise of the necromancers, the orc had cheered up considerably, and was helping me in every way to plan the destruction of the enemy. Even though I found it difficult to consider propositions along the lines of "let's meet the enemies head on and kill them honorably", phrased in various ways, to be help.

In a few words I described the explosion of the most powerful bomb in the entire history of humanity. Alard misunderstood my idea, furrowed his brow and objected:

"This explosion will destroy everything. The necromancers, us and the estate. There is no honor in such victory."

"I agree! The victory that is won easily is not worth much," I grinned. "And that's why we'll do something completely different. So, Mizardine, do you know how to dig?"

The hunter nodded reluctantly.

"Great! Take this shovel, take the scrolls and get yourself to the hill. Bury the scrolls, all of them, near the area where the necromancers appear, within a meter of each other, and conceal the trap. The whole hill must be covered in these little presents! Thinking about returning, blasted boneheads... Now do you understand?"

The hunter beamed, grabbed his work tools and rushed to fulfill my directive.

"So he did turn out to be useful after all." I looked after Mizardine and turned to Alard. "Wait for me here, and set up your tracker. We'll start the search today."

"Did you find something?" The orc drew himself up.

"I don't know yet," I said contemplatively, went out into the hallway and caught a servant who was running by.

"Take me to Madame Sophie. I have an appointment."

In a couple of minutes I was standing in the reception hall, where yet another party was in full swing. Ervan was true to himself, having brought in the players in the morning. Sophie was appearing here and there among the guests, settling minor troubles and preventing catastrophes.

"Monsieur Yaropolk, I am not..." the hostess started fearfully as soon as she saw me next to her.

"Here you are, you blackguard!" Enraged, Ervan jumped out of nowhere instantly between Sophie and me like a jack-in-a-box. He did not even let his wife finish the sentence. Pointing his finger at me, he came so close that I could feel the stench of his breath. An eerie silence fell over the hall. "Paladin! You have dared to tarnish my wife's honor!"

His small bovine eyes betrayed an irresistible urge to tear me into small pieces and throw them out the door of the estate. I had a feeling that Sleevan had had a hand in all this. I would not be surprised to discover that this was his expression of "gratitude" for the incident in the basement.

"Ervan, I beg you!" Sophie continually hung on the thug's arm, trying to slow him down. Seeing that she was failing, she left her futile attempts and cried out: "Monsieur Yaropolk, I beg you! Run!"

I hesitated just for a moment or two. I was not afraid of having to battle Ervan openly. A common minion would not be able to inflict any harm on a "charged" player with a limitless supply of Energy. One "Templar's Blow" from me would kill Ervan quite dead, while I would have a chance to see for myself that the castle was very reliably protected and that it dutifully defended its residents against aggressive guests. This was not a suitable turn of events for me.

Nodding to trembling Sophie, I activated invisibility, which I had been neglecting. Of course, it sucked Energy like a vacuum cleaner, but with my crystal I could afford to be a little profligate.

"Where is he?!" Ervan blinked in surprise, staring at the place where I had been standing just a moment before.

"I hasten to inform you that invisibility will not save you from the video surveillance cameras, which operate in the magical range as well." Steve reminded me that not everything in this world was as fine and dandy as I would like to have it.

"A granis to whoever drags Yaropolk to me!" Ervan was really going apeshit.

I scowled. These pissants didn't need to bother dreaming of getting a granis for nothing! To see a player under invisibility one had to have experience and a high level like Zangar. I doubted there was anyone here who qualified. Dolgunata did not count: too petty for her. Nata preferred to make her own mischief, without being told what to do.

Stepping quietly, I retreated behind the nearest column near the wall to wait out the ensuing ruckus. Some of the players, in a drunken frenzy, rushed off right away to try and catch me in the hallways and rooms. Some smarter ones suggested fishing nets, and having gathered some followers, ran off to look for the wherewithal. The rest avidly searched for me under the tables, behind curtains and even in the servant girls' cleavages. Ervan, sporting yet another glass of wine, swayed in the center of the hall awaiting some results.

Making sure I could move around the hall without fear of running into someone in the crowd, I sneaked up on Sophie. The poor girl was wailing like a banshee in the nearest chair.

I caught a pause between her sobs and whispered right into her ear, "We need to talk, alone."

Frightened, the lady hiccupped loudly and quite unfashionably.

"Just to talk – nothing else."

Her unexpected faux pas brought Lady Lecleur to her senses, and she stopped crying. Covering her mouth with a handkerchief she looked around slowly. To an observer it may have seemed that the lady just wanted to make sure that her slip had gone unnoticed, but in fact Lady Lecleur was scanning the players still in the hall. Noting the most sober ones, Sophie cried out loudly, attracting attention to herself, and waved her hand towards the passage furthest away from us:

"Quick, I have seen the scoundrel! Ervan, he ran towards the greenhouse!" The lady turned to her spouse: "You must catch him!"

"Freeze!" Ervan roared, and rushed in the indicated direction. "I'll tear him up and throw him out! Everyone follow me!"

A crowd of players rushed after the thug as one man. Lust for money was working.

"I feel ill. I'll go check on my mother," Sophie said to distract chance observers, rose from the armchair and started in the direction opposite from where the crowd had rushed. Trying to make as little noise as possible, I followed her, close on her heels. We passed through several hallways and stopped at a door.

"Lecleur family heir to see Lady Elizabeth," Sophie said seemingly to no one.

Suddenly the statue to the right of the door came to life and said:

"Right to visit by heir is confirmed! Access authorized for one person!"

"Lecleur family heir with a guest," Sophie hastily corrected her inquiry, embarrassed. "Paladin Yaropolk is under my protection and should be near me!"

The statue kept silent for a few moments, then confirmed the corrected inquiry:

"Access authorized for two persons!" The internal door mechanism came into motion, smoothly opening the door panels.

"I hope you have something to say," the lady sighed, and entered the room. I followed her.

Elizabeth's private rooms did not bear even a hint of ostentatious luxury. There was a simple double bed with an old lady sleeping securely in it, a couple of old armchairs, an armoire and a bedside table. Nothing extra.

Except for Sleevan.

When we appeared, the artful herald was sitting peacefully by the bedside and holding lady Elizabeth's hand. As soon as Sophie saw him, the gates opened for a new waterfall of tears and moans. Sleevan rushed to the lady at once:

"Sophie, what happened? It's too early for your shift. Why are you in such a state?" The herald worried sincerely about the scion of the Lecleur family. His ministrations made Sophie cry so hard she could not say a word. Watching this scene made me feel uncomfortable and out of place. Yet I was not going to stay invisible. Dropping the concealment, I coughed a couple of times, attracting attention. Sleevan turned to me harshly and his face contorted in an evil grimace:

"What are you doing here?! Sophie's honor was not enough for you? In addition you forced her to bring you here? The guards will throw you out of the estate and even Bernard won't help you!" Sleevan rushed towards the door but Sophie stopped him.

"No, Sleevan. He didn't make me! I did it myself! Ervan..." another bout of weeping cut short her explanations at the most interesting point, and I said loudly, wanting to clarify the misunderstanding as quickly as possible:

"Lady Sophie, please accept my apologies for a careless gesture. I did not know of its meaning, and I was not in any way planning, nor do I plan in the future, to cast any aspersions on your honor. I simply wanted to protect you from the fall. May the Game be my witness!"

Snow-white light washed over me, head to toe, and while the herald's reaction was to be expected, Sophie's response was rather off the wall, as far as I could tell. Her hysterics reached a crescendo. I was not the only one bewildered by that reaction. Sleevan brought Sophie to a chair, sat her down and carefully presented a glass of water, trying to find out in a whisper what the problem was. In response I heard disjointed fragments like "I had hoped so much", "It could have worked", "You know what grandfather is like." At last the herald seemed to have worked it out for himself and exclaimed reproachfully:

"Sophie, are you really capable of such a thing?!" The lady only wept harder.

At this point my self-restraint snapped with a bang, and I barked:

"Quiet, both of you!" Sophie was so startled she jumped in her chair and, thank the Game, stopped wailing. But my joy was premature. I must have scared the lady so much, she started hiccupping. I let her be, and addressed Sleevan, calmly this time:

"Now please explain what happened! Of course, I am flattered by Lady Sophie's reaction, but really, I am not so handsome that she should cry her eyes out over this!"

The herald paused, but Sophie, who was still hiccupping, pulled on his sleeve to attract his attention, and nodded.

"Sophie applied to Mr. Bernard for a divorce

without the knowledge of the Head of the family. Now her petition is being reviewed, but if Iven were to find out about it, he would rescind it as the Head of the family. He has forbidden Sophie from divorcing. She was hoping for your help. And... was glad when you showed an interest in her."

What a surprise. Even though the poor woman's motives were not hard to understand. I mean her desire to divorce, not her intent to use to use me to achieve her goals. Even though that was also fairly clear. A mutually beneficial relationship. It was strange that Sleevan talked about it so calmly. I was thinking of the ways I could use this new information. Sophie kept hiccupping, which irritated my already high-strung nerves. I had always hated women's hysterics.

"Sleevan, please give Lady Sophie some more water already!"

The Herald grinned and sighed.

"It won't help. Sonia always hiccups when she is scared. She'll calm down presently, and will be able to cast a spell. That's the only thing that can stop the hiccups. She's been like that ever since she was a child. We were playing with her in the attic when I decided to scare her by saying there were ghosts living in our mother's old chest. She could not talk for three days after that and just hiccupped. Mother spanked me very hard that time." Sleevan smiled at his memories, and looked at Lady Elizabeth with affection.

Mother?!

"Mother?" I repeated aloud, astonished. "But

you are not a Lecleur?!"

The Herald shrugged:

"Sometimes this happens. I don't know my actual father. Monsieur Lecleur was kind to me, and kept me on the estate close to my mom. But, of course, no one knew about that. To everyone else Madame Lecleur was caring for a little orphan."

The Herald turned to Sophie:

"Are you all right now?"

Sophie nodded and said:

"Hiccup, hiccup, go away, go to Cora for a day; then to Iven far away, then to Raven and there stay!"

The little familiar nursery rhyme dispelled the tension. Sophie stopped hiccupping, and Sleevan even clarified it to me:

"Cora was our nanny. She was really mean. Been dead about ten years by now. So for the next half an hour our grandfather will be fighting the hiccups to no avail."

I laughed and said:

"Would do him good, too. And who is Raven and what has he done?"

Sleevan shrugged:

"No one knows that except Sophie." He turned towards his sister, whose cheeks immediately flushed.

I said placatingly:

"Whoever he is, if he is on that scary list I am sure he deserves it."

Sophie smiled gratefully:

"Monsieur Yaropolk, I apologize for the recent scene – please understand me! Since the pendant was stolen, so much has been weighing me down. The burden must have been too heavy. I am incredibly tired of the guests and of Ervan's antics, and I am tired of pretending. Ervan was never sweet of character, but mom ruled him with an iron fist. Only when we were alone did he show his true self. Our children have long grown, I don't owe him anything and I certainly do not wish for him to order me around here. Ours was an arranged marriage, and his family was not nearly as rich as ours. I think I have paid my dues to my family, and now can live the rest of my life for myself. My grandfather did not support me in this; moreover, he expressly forbade me to even think about it. But Sleevan convinced me to try my luck with monsieur Bernard. My brother and I were hoping to relocate to a different world after the divorce."

Lady Lecleur fell silent, and I was in no hurry to answer. I was contemplating whether I would be able to convince Bernard to grant Sophie's petition despite Iven's wishes. Everything depended on my suzerain's plans. Probably he would want to hide Sophie and her brother on some world, and then, when a proper opportunity presented itself, sell this information to the fighter for a pretty penny of some sort. It was worth a try:

"I will do everything I can to convince my suzerain to help you! However, I cannot guarantee a positive result. I am just a vassal." I spread my hands, "You must understand this."

Sophie and Sleevan nodded, and I continued:

"In exchange, I would like to have your complete cooperation in the case of the stolen

---

pendant. You are interested in making sure your mother stays in good health for as long as possible?"

Again, a joint nod of agreement, even though not a very enthusiastic one.

"Unfortunately, monsieur Yaropolk, we cannot help much. The pendant simply disappeared. Both the players and we have searched the estate from the cellar to the roof.

"You looked in the secret passages as well?" I was trying to fish for information, almost holding my breath.

"The estate has no secret passages." Sleevan spoke with certainty. "It's a classic structure, the walls are not more than a meter thick, and the non-load-bearing walls are even thinner. There is no space for secret passages there."

"Sophie?" I continued obstinately, still blindly hoping for some luck. "Have you confirmed that the estate does not have any secret passages or something similar? Bear in mind that a lot hangs on your answer."

If the family heir also were to confirm that there were no passages or space pockets in the estate, all that would be left for me would be to pack and get out of here. But Iven's strange denial indicated differently. He wasn't just doing that to be mean to me, right?

"We have already told you that..."

"Be quiet, brother." Sophie sighed heavily and, closing her eyes, announced: "Promise you will do everything you can! And keep Sleevan's secret!"

"I call the Game to witness that I will appeal to my suzerain for the success of your petition for divorce and relocation to a different world, secretly from Sir Iven, and that I shall not disclose the secret of Sleevan's origin!"

There was another flash of white light around me, and then Sophie continued:

"This secret is only known to the acknowledged heirs. Grandfather expressly prohibited us from disclosing it, even on pain of death. The estate actually does not have secret passages," Sophie was speaking slowly, as if she had still not fully decided whether to risk it or not. Finally, courage gained the upper hand: "The Lecleur estate has the Reverse."

Steve was only able to spread his hands helplessly. We were not familiar with this term.

"How do I enter it?" I decided against betraying my ignorance.

"Monsieur Yaropolk, I rely only on your honesty and decency. Do not let this information leave this room. The entrance to the Reverse is located in the treasury." Having made her final decision, Sophie did not withhold information. "The head of the family has the key to the treasury."

"He is the only one? How do you access it then?" I asked in surprise.

"We don't. There is no need. Milord Iven provides the funds to run the estate. His steward runs all the money matters. We are far from being poor, as you noticed. Mother does not want much. Several times she asked to be allowed into the treasury, but every time her requests were denied. And I don't need it. Even the guards at the treasury are his."

"Guards?!" That caught my attention at once.

"Yes, there is a fighting unit of three Paladins. You know that my grandfather is the Head of the Battle Wing, so he uses this for training his fighters. At this stage there are skirmishes with the guests several times every day. There is always someone who wants to get into the hosts' treasury. So he sent his Paladins here to have some fun."

"Why does the report I received not mention anything about guards?"

"But why should it? It was definitely not the Paladins that stole the pendant. They appeared at the estate after it disappeared. That's number one. Number two is that they are not allowed to leave their posts or talk to the guests or household members. They even have their own food they bring."

"Fine, so Paladins could not have stolen the pendant, but how do we know it's not in the treasury? It seems as though no one looked there!" I was thinking up a very neat version of events now.

"That's impossible! Grandfather looked everywhere before bringing in the guards. Nor is it possible to bribe or switch the Paladins. The guards change once every day and come to the estate via a portal which is in grandfather's private office." Sleevan joined the conversation.

Like hell Iven doesn't know who stole the pendant! With all these facts fitting into a single picture, not a single Judge would dare accuse me of being partial to Milord Iven. Now I needed to check the reaction of the Lecleur heir to the idea.

"Sophie, I feel very awkward telling you about this." I paused, watching her expression carefully."I apologize in advance should I offend your feelings for the family. Have you thought that your grandfather may be involved in the theft? I am not stating that he did it himself, but perhaps he abetted it?"

Sophie did not look surprised. The thoughts I was trying to instill in her flickered across her pretty face. It was apparent that the heir did not have any warm feelings towards her grandfather, and her doubts caught on.

"Monsieur, I am just a woman. Men's games are not for a woman's mind. Forgive me, but I cannot confirm or refute your suppositions." I silently bowed my head to Sophie's acknowledgement of her right to stay out of it.

"Lady Sophie, I would like to explore the Reverse and check my suppositions. May I count on your help?"

"I have told you so much, monsieur, that it does not make any sense to deny you your request. Here. Take this." Sophie took from her neck a pendant with a golden key and handed it to me. As soon as the key touched my hand, the countdown timer appeared in front of me. Twelve hours till the key must return to the head of the family. "It will open the way for you; without it it's impossible to enter the Reverse or continue to be there. But I have to warn you! Only four sentient beings can be present within the Reverse concurrently, and one is already there. I don't know who that is."

"Sophie, you astonish me!" Sleevan whispered in amazement. "You never... you never even hinted..."

"Sorry. It's all our grandfather's doing!" Sophie

explained. "The key has to be linked to a living soul, it cannot be taken from the estate or hidden in a cache, or else the Reverse will collide with this plane. It used to be linked to mom. Immediately after the theft occurred, grandfather rushed to my room, handed me the key, explained its meaning in a couple of sentences and told me to keep quiet. Said that if a single soul finds out about it, he would personally make sure that I never left the Earth. Monsieur Yaropolk, I have told you everything I know about the Reverse and the key!"

I was looking in contemplation at the dozing old lady, my thoughts far from the room. So it would seem that if the pendant actually were in the Reverse, then Iven must have stolen it himself, rendering his daughter incapable. What for?

"The set includes three pieces. The pendant, the ring and the earrings. What would happen if all were gathered together?" I decided I would do well to clarify that while I had a chance, but Sophie disappointed me.

"Nobody knows. Mother never wore the whole set. The ring was always in the treasury. The earrings would come and go at times. Right now they are gone again.

"So in order to enter the Reverse one has to enter the treasury?" I asked the last question thinking of a plan that was emerging in my head.

"Yes. But that does not mean that once you beat the Paladins you would be able to freely enter the treasury." The herald confirmed once again that it would not be easy. "It's impossible to break down the door. In order for the security system to let you through, you need the access code. There is only one. How you get that from our grandfather, we do not need to know. This is all we can do to help you."

"Last question: I need to have free passage to and from the estate. Can this be arranged? I will have to leave the estate now and then; therefore, Lady Lecleur, it would make sense for you to keep the key for now."

Sophie took the key and replaced it in its location.

"Call me." Sleevan told me his comm number. "I will meet you and bring you in. The only condition is, you will have to wear your invisibility. I'll take care of the security cameras."

"Thank you! I need a teleport scroll to the Sanctuary and a map of the estate. Could you mark on it where the treasury is located?"

While we were having a productive conversation in Elizabeth's room, Ervan had completely forgotten about his wife's tarnished honor and the promised granis. Having reached his daily limit for alcohol consumption, the aspiring estate owner was snuffling peacefully, his head on the table next to a plate of broccoli. Of course, it's quite a perversion to use that disgusting stuff as an appetizer, but there is no accounting for taste. Meanwhile all players, having tried their hands at searching for the lost necklace, switched to a more available target: a free granis for catching me. While I was walking, under the cover of invisibility, towards the treasury, I encountered several drunken groups, and each one sported a captured "Paladin Yaropolk". Some denied it and were ignored. Some thumped themselves on the chest and yelled for all to hear that they were the very same escaped "Don Juan". Some were simply tied up and gagged to prevent them from spoiling the moment of triumph. False Yaropolks were springing up everywhere like mushrooms in the fall.

Having reached the treasury enabled me to verify that it did in fact exist, and to evaluate the guards. Everything was the way Sophie had described with one minor detail: the three Paladins were wearing Daro armor. The Paladins perked up as soon as I turned the corner. Even despite the invisibility the fighters felt that they were not alone. My suspicion that the treasury did in fact hold something important intensified: it was guarded at too high a level to be accounted for simply by a caution in case some newbies were to rush it. I stepped back and quietly took off for my room. I needed to work on the orc in preparation for the task we had to perform.

But as soon as I turned into the hallway, I ran straight into Dolgunata.

"Nice sight, isn't it? I would even say, telling!" Dolgunata was standing not too far from my door studying a tapestry adorned with a scene of a jester being executed by some nobles. Whatever their quibble with him was, hell knows. But the hint was clear.

Five players ran by us, and I whispered:

"Let's step aside." As I had supposed, my invisibility was child's play for the druid. "It's crowded here."

"Who do you think I am?!" Dolgunata responded in an indignant whisper. "I don't take any side trips anywhere with men! Only to my room! Come!"

We passed unhindered through all the havoc wreaked by the guests of the estate all the way to Nata's room, which was in another wing. The girl closed the door, activated a crystal, and a force field dome opened around us.

"Go on."The druid settled on a chair. "And take off that stupid masquerade of yours. In infrared vision you look like a sack of rutabagas with feet. That's fine, it suits you, but if I have to listen to a talking sack it's not going to be conducive to a productive dialogue."

"Nata, do you happen to know that insults are a resort of the weak?" I pretended to parry her new barb. She raised an eyebrow in an exaggerated gesture and hemmed skeptically. "I agree. It's not very original. But right now I am wittily daft. Call Archibald. I do have something to tell him."

It was a rare occasion when I was able to render Archibald silent so that he would not put in snide remarks, but today I succeeded. They listened to me in silence without interrupting once. The current situation seemed so incredible that I decided not to hold anything back, telling them about the Reverse, about Iven, about the treasury guards and even about the strange attack from the necromancers. Well, actually, I did hold back one thing: I did not tell them about Devir's present. That was personal.

"What is going on in this estate?" Archibald

was trying to assimilate the new information.

"You may be proud of your student, teacher. The whole estate is in an uproar – all because of him. The owner promised a granis for Yari's hide," Dolgunata smirked. "All because Yari seduced his wife and found out all the estate's secrets. I'd take offense too."

"You would do well to work harder rather than taking offense! Yari has a result to show – that's what you should think about, not about his moral character." Did I really just hear him praise me?! I had always thought that from Archibald it would sound like: "He is a stupid but kind Paladin!"

Having scolded his negligent student, Archibald switched to me:

"So then, there is a grain of sense in your suggestion. Send me an invitation to do the work and I will do you a favor and help you. Without me you'd either mess this up beyond all recognition or it would take you forever to figure anything out. And don't you dare say later, Yari, that I never helped!" Archibald was so forceful that it became clear why he was all oh so generous all of a sudden.

"Actually, I have not proposed anything," I said, slowly but clearly. "I just shared some information. And supposed that in order to complete the case it would be necessary to find the key granting access to the treasury, which is kept by Milord Iven. However, I do not know how to do that. I don't have the slightest clue: may the Game be my witness!"

For a better effect I even made my eyes bug out. Like: what do you want from me? I am dumb. I was not going to play Archibald's own games with him. It was obvious that he was looking for a client who would order the operation. So as to pass on all the responsibility to him if something were to go awry. It's one thing when you try to hack the estate of the chief fighter Paladin on your own accord; if you are just a contractor it's quite a different matter.

"You think you are smart, eh?" I did not even need to see the catorian's face to imagine him grimacing. "Dolgunata, call your brother. We'll make him the customer."

"Just a moment." Since she had been talking to Archibald using her own comm, the druid stepped out from under the dome and took out a simple cell phone. I shook my head, displeased: for some reason this small trick had not occurred to me. Cell phones were only guaranteed to work in our game world; their use in other worlds was not known; so everyone used the special Game comms. However, Helen, for example, did not have one and was unlikely to ever obtain one, but why should this prevent me from talking to her? It would be stupid and naïve to consider that. I needed to obtain a cell phone as soon as possible.

"Sakhray will be here in a couple of minutes." Dolgunata returned just a moment later. "What are we doing?"

"I provide Gerhard's seal so that the Paladins would not dare delay you and would let you into the treasury," Archibald started his instructions. "I cannot go into the estate myself, Gerhard would not allow me to risk myself in this manner. Follow plan D, paragraph three. Go in, the three of you, but I rely mostly on you in this. Try not to fail with the monster of the Reverse. I will give you the access key in the Sanctuary in two hours; ensure you have the portals."

"Will Sakhray be the third?" Dolgunata asked for clarification.

"No. I will need him." Archibald fell to thinking. "Yari, you had an orc. He will do. It's too late to look for anyone else. What did the necromancer look like? Emblem, any distinctive markings, race? I need to know who is training his fighters on the newbies.

"The emblem was a diamond with oddly uneven edges. There was a sun or a ball in the center, it was not clear. Race – human; no distinctive features except for a hoarse voice, as if it were hard for him to talk." Steve helped me with the main features of the necromancers' teacher.

"Don Fabio with his bunch," Archibald nearly spat. "His Game world is Altair. He is an exceptional bastard, with just one redeeming quality: he is a high level experienced necromancer. He trains exclusively teachers. And even that strictly to dispel his boredom. That's why the newbies were unable to beat his undead. Too high a level. He is such a strong mentalist that he can ignore the new players' immunity against mental control. He can think up something of his own and no less nasty. Fine: that's it for the necromancer! Now Fabio is not your problem anymore. All that's required of you: keep out of his sight. There will be worthy opponents for him without you, snotty-nosed kids. Is everything clear?"

Archibald spoke more for Dolgunata's sake, so

when she nodded I ignored the question. Amazing how much he was worried about her well-being.

Suddenly my comm started vibrating. Gromana.

"Not now, I'll call you back..." I started answering, but she cut me off:

"What?! I'll see you at the gate of the estate! You have two minutes!" Gromana was obviously lacking such important things as calmness and patience. The witch was out of sorts.

The comm switched off and I stared at Dolgunata, puzzled.

"Go: this may be important." Amazing, but the druid quit her mockery. "I'll see you in a couple of hours here. Archibald?"

"Say hi to Gromana." The catorian indicated that he was not going to hold me back. I activated invisibility, the druid opened the door and let me out into the crowd of greedy players looking to profit. The search had not stopped for a second. I went down to the courtyard and out of the estate gates. The guards glanced at me, indicating that they did notice me, but they took no action. I was not listed as a violator of some kind despite Ervan's ire; I was not planning to come back into the castle secretly, and as for leaving in such a manner... oh well, players are pretty weird folks anyway.

Gromana was standing near the entrance, and was nearly stomping the ground with impatience.

"Hi!" I appeared a couple of steps away from the witch. "Why so mad?"

"Yari, are you completely bonkers? What

possessed you to use Leguria against players? Fine, you were trained on NPCs, and your superiors even got backdated permission for having done that. But against players?! How did that even occur to you?!"

I had not expected such an outburst of emotion, so I was taken aback a little.

"Bernard was called in by the Viceroy, who demanded explanations for the use of Leguria on Earth against players." Gromana kept raging, attracting the attention of those around us. Some were already pointing at me, recognizing the target of the local search. "Several projects were terminated in which I was a participant, among others. This game world lost several points of "Light"; we dropped even further in the world rating, and all this because of you!"

"And you are in favor of the 'Light allegiance' of this world, Dark one? Since when?" My initial astonishment faded, and I attacked back. "You should thank me that there are at least some crumbs of emotions that can be gathered without having to beg some deity. As for Leguria – what kind of a maniac allows a strong necromancer to train his students on newbies, given that each student is a full-fledged player? I never signed up to be a sacrificial lamb and die just so!"

"Lie ahead, but take it easy! At that estate you drank yourself into seeing necromancers in a Light world?" Gromana tried to regain her edge, but I would not let her:

"I dare you to keep me company over a glass of wine in the evening, and together we'll enjoy the sight of Don Fabio from Altair." The witch's rounded eyes indicated that the name was more than just vaguely familiar to her. "Yesterday he was standing on that hill over there and directing the attack. Once I used Leguria to kill his students, he promised to come back today having taught them how to protect themselves. So you take it easy, witch!"

"Don Fabio... That's a heavyweight. We need to warn Bernard that someone issued him permission to visit our world and went around the Coordinator." Gromana's tone changed instantly, as if she had not been scolding me vehemently just a moment ago. And no apologies whatsoever. Then, without any transition, she handed me a small package. "He sent something to you. Are you going to open it?"

I turned the parcel in my hands, in no hurry to unwrap it. The witch was clicking her fingers impatiently. She obviously resented the role of a courier, but one does not argue with the suzerain. Gromana must have decided that since Bernard chose her to send a present for me there must be something important and interesting inside.

"Why did we have to meet outside the castle?" I was holding a theatrical pause as a matter of some small revenge against the mean witch for her recent scene.

"The thief threatened to destroy the pendant and kill Elizabeth with it. Paladins have asked for help, so that's why Bernard gave me those instructions. I am on the list... Blast you, little morons! Have you no respect for your elders?!"

Gromana threw some kind of a protection over

me, and dark force ripples started spreading in a circle from her, turning everything living into ashes: grass, bugs, and about a dozen players who had been preparing to attack me and ignored Gromana. Which was extremely short-sighted on their part.

"Have they gone completely mad that they can't see who you are talking to?"

"They can," I objected, "but not very clearly. They are drunk. You are an experienced witch – you ought to know that the deeper the bottle, the crazier the deeds. What they are seeing now is not a high level witch; they see a broad chatting with a granis."

"What does that mean?" The witch was astonished.

""What you think it means! The one who catches me and brings to the host of the estate will receive a granis."

"A granis for catching Bernard's vassal?! What kind of a game world is this? What did you do – steal all their table silver?" Gromana kept expressing her surprise, meanwhile, by the way, blowing off those attempting to get to my body. "Where the hell do you think you are going?! What do they teach them in those academies?!"

Using a controlled blob of dark matter Gromana grabbed a player who was trying to shoot me from a distance, peeled his armor off together with his skin and left him hanging in the air as a lesson to all those trying to get a granis for nothing. The stuck player was squealing like a stuck pig, but the witch just glanced at him, noting with a grimace that pedagogy was not her forte after all. There were no more around trying to get to me. Gromana thought for a moment, and activated some crystal on her armor. An energy dome appeared around us, separating us from the rest of the players.

"What's in the parcel – a thousand curses on your reckless head?!"

Gromana had reached a point when lingering further would be a really dangerous thing to do. So I opened Bernard's present and stared in bewilderment at a black brochure the size of my hand, and probably barely ten pages thick. But the witch's reaction was quite telling – she swallowed and whispered reverently:

"The Dark Book of Lumpen. Merlin take me!!! How did Bernard do it..."

"The library that he has..." I shrugged.

"The library," Gromana repeated mockingly. "It's a sacrilege to keep such things in a library! Everybody thinks this book has been lost ever since the previous era. Hide it right away!"

I sensibly followed Gromana's instructions, and threw the book into my personal inventory. I'd deal with it later in a quiet place.

"It's more than just a book! Actually, all it has of a book is appearance," Gromana clarified, and looked around. "Invisibility curtain, thank Night. No one could have seen it. This is an artifact of Darkness! If you activate the book, Darkness will forever become your ally, but you will have to give your whole being to it as well, fully! It's like a vow to your betrothed that you will stay with her forever."

"So much pathos. Let's go over it again in a

more down to earth manner; keep it simple. I never grokked poetry. And why are you looking around again? Will I be beaten if I flash it around?" If those around me would be brief and to the point, it would make it so much simpler for me to get on with the Game. Had there been an option somewhere to "turn off pathos and windbaggery" – it would have been a truly priceless one.

Gromana sighed, remembering whom she had to work with, and proceeded to specifics:

"If you were to activate it, you would have the mark of Darkness on you all the way till the end of the Game. It would be impossible to change sides after that and become neutral or Light. If you ran into high-level Light fanatics, yes, they would definitely beat you. Small fish Light ones would dislike being near you. Your presence would annoy them."

"It's not like they were really fond of me before. In the Academy I was told that the choice of allegiance is made once and for all and cannot be changed." What I had heard before was different from what Gromana was telling me now.

"That's right. It cannot be changed by standard means. But the Viceroy, the Emperor's Councilor, or the Emperor himself may ignore the rule if you found the right approach to them. But even they would be powerless to change the allegiance of a player who has this book."

"That's a dubious advantage the way I see it. Is there something more unequivocal?" I still could not understand why Bernard would make me such a gift.

"There is. While the Light ones would

subconsciously feel aggression towards you, the Dark ones would do the opposite: they would consider it an honor and pleasure to help you. Your level of Darkness would reach 100 and stay there forever, never dropping even if the book owner were to worship some gods or become an ascetic. Besides, the force of dark spells would reach simply fantastic levels. Your Leguria enhanced with absolute Darkness would be a hefty argument against that Don Fabio. Now, silly head, do you understand that this is more than just a gift? Just think; Lumpen's creation in such hands... Under other circumstances I would..." Gromana did not finish, shaking her head indignantly.

"Under other circumstances I would still think long and hard before activating it. We are in the world of Light ones, Gromana! As soon as I activated the book, it would serve as a command to attack for everybody, and I would become a constant target. While the Dark ones are so few and far between here that you could count them on one hand. I doubt that their friendliness would outweigh the hatred of the Light ones."

"Then give it to me," Gromana laughed gratingly, bowing and scraping her foot in jest. "In exchange you will have my gratitude, granises and generally everything I can give you."

I responded in kind with a forced grin:

"That's a great joke! I am sure Bernard would like that." I had to visit the Temple of Knowledge. As soon as I understand the core essence of the book, I will figure out how it could help me. I looked at the witch and it confirmed that there was a grain of joke in every joke. "If you wish, we can discuss your offer at a later time."

The witch mumbled, upset, that it was worth a try, and nodded. Taking advantage of her willingness, I asked:

"Do you know anything about the pendant or its thief?"

"What is there to know? It's all so boring." Gromana waved me off, still upset. "Some local twit decided to bump off an old decrepit lady, but miscalculated his strength. Who is this Elizabeth, after all? Small fish – there are millions like her."

"And if I were to tell you that she is Anna's daughter?"

"Then I will tell you that you have not impressed me!" Gromana was working herself up now. "If you have something to tell me, then go ahead. No need to play charades here. My plate is so full it's flowing over, and here I am playing courier to some pipsqueak. What is it then about this Anna-Elizabeth?"

I need you to pass on information to Bernard, since you can't help me." I steered the conversation back to business. "Not only was Anna the mother of the victim, but she was also the only student of some Madonna. While the victim, Elizabeth, was Madonna's only minion."

"What a complicated story..." Gromana was looking quite despondent now. Apparently, Bernard had never told her about any of that.

"In addition, Sophie is Elizabeth's daughter and

a granddaughter of Iven, toward whom Milord Bernard had exhibited some interest. She has filed a petition for divorce and transfer to another world secretly from her grandfather. But there has been no response so far. If Milord Bernard were to grant this petition, he would have one loyal Lecleur bound to him by gratitude till the end of her life. And through whom it would be possible to get to Iven himself. Please convey this to him as food for thought."

"This information is useful but I am sure that Milord Bernard is well aware of all that. Since he is taking no action, no action is necessary. Did you promise anything to her?"

"Only that I would put in a word for her, nothing more. I have fulfilled my part of the deal, so my conscience is clear!"

"What a good boy. Now you, with your clear conscience get yourself off to look for the pendant, while I with my clear conscience will deal with my own business. I am removing the dome... I am tired as hell of this shit of yours!"

Another dark wave rippled from the witch, reducing nearby players to dust. Gromana activated a portal, paying no attention to the already gurgling player still hanging in the air, and disappeared. The hapless guy dropped to the ground and died. Soon the body predictably glimmered and disappeared, to reemerge at the respawn point an hour later.

Before the other players had a chance to figure out that the danger Gromana represented was no longer there, I activated invisibility and Sleevan helped me return to the estate. Having made sure that Dolgunata invited Alard for the walk I hid in the herald's house, and without further ado, started examining Bernard's gift.

As soon as I tried to open the book the Game inquired if I was ready to accept the Darkness and let it into myself? Naturally I refused, and received a message indicating that those who had not passed the above-mentioned initiation were denied access to this manual. For a few moments I contemplated whether I should dedicate some time to try and find some information regarding the book in the Sanctuary library or other sources available to me, but then followed the familiar path, and requested access to the Temple of Knowledge straight away.

"In order to make a decision on using the artifact of Darkness from Lumpen I need information regarding the consequences of activating it within the game world 'Earth' for a player with allegiance to Darkness." I tried to make my inquiry as detailed as possible.

"Welcome to the Temple of Knowledge, Dark one." The Keeper responded at once. The old man pointed affably at the chair that appeared out of thin air, and settled on the one that materialized next to it. The furniture and absence of the habitual coffee table with the scroll on it puzzled me.

"Have a seat – we ought to talk." The old man was suspiciously friendly and pleasant. It seemed that someone had at least heard me silently bewailing the lack of an option for turning off pathos and windbaggery: the Keeper cut straight to the point. "The Temple of Knowledge is offering you an exchange. You give us the artifact, and we will allow you to ask two questions unrelated to the main query whenever you visit the Temple of Knowledge."

"Are we talking about the book of Lumpen now?" I was taken aback. The Keeper nodded.

"What is so valuable about it that you are extending such a generous offer? Or is the catch in the fact that I will be allowed to ask the question but will not be guaranteed the answers?" I decided to clarify just in case.

The Keeper smiled patronizingly in response:

"Let's try. You ask a question and assess the completeness of the answer. Some topics fall outside the scope of the agreement. You will be warned about that and you will have the right to ask a different question."

"Why do you need it?" I came back to the matter of the book.

"To destroy it. Artifacts of previous eras, when they move about freely in the game world, upset the balance, which is already fragile. They can cause catastrophes by their mere presence. Frequently, as a player activates them, he has not the slightest clue of hidden danger. This book, as so many other similar things, has nothing to do with what it appears to be. You did the right thing by coming to the Temple of Knowledge for help. Unfortunately, frequently curiosity is stronger than reason. In your case, by acknowledging the Darkness as your ally and master, in addition you would have received yet another master. Quite a material one, unlike the Darkness. You would have voluntarily accepted the mark of a slave."

I frowned, unable to understand his point:

"A slave?" Bernard's gesture of good will did not look so good any more.

"Yes. Lumpen was a great player of his era. One of those who made his own rules rather than following someone else's. He created powerful artifacts similar to this book. They provided strength to his allies and killed his opponents. But Lumpen never was a philanthropist. Each copy of the book like this one made its carrier a slave, a channel for Lumpen's will No one could gainsay their master. However, having lost a part of themselves, those who carried the book received power and Darkness."

"Did Lumpen survive the restart?"

"His power was tremendous, but he was not all-powerful. He was not among those who survived to enter the new era. Lumpen died unconquered."

"If he is dead, what's the danger in his books?" I steered the train of the old guy's thoughts to the track I needed.

"Lumpen's books have started to look for new owners, and this is very dangerous. This plague of his may spread throughout the world yet again at the speed of light! The previous era was the era of the heyday of pain and suffering. The point of life was to 'kill another or die yourself'. At first players joined forces and fought as clans, but having killed all their enemies the allies started killing each other. The entire Game was plunged into Darkness, and Lumpen put quite a fair effort into that. The ones who were left forgot that there used to be Light, so the Emperor returned sense to the incarnations of Madonna and Merlin, and the Game itself initiated the transition to the new era. Now the equilibrium has become fragile again, and any disturbance would lead to an imbalance."

"Did you say Madonna and Merlin? But what about the third participant of the restart? Did he die as the eras were changing?" I hung on this topic which interested me like a pit bull.

"Unfortunately he did not. The founders of the Game made a mistake by granting all five participants of the change of the eras free will and the right to choose. You are already aware of four restarts, as you call them, and in only one case did all three fully complete their mission. In the other cases the third participant survived.

"Which automatically triggered the next change of era." I looked at the old guy pensively. "Because the world turned out not to be the way it was initially designed. How much time passed between the changes? The Game has been in existence for 75 thousand years in total. How much time passed before it restarted the first time?"

"Sixty one thousand years." The old guy delayed his answer to the last. "Five thousand before the second. Four till the third. Three till the fourth."

"And there will be two till the fifth which is the next. It takes less and less time with every new one for the Game to degrade into chaos. Why is it so?"

"A mistake of the founders. Free will and freedom of choice for the restart participants. The resources of the Game are not infinite, and during the change of the eras a lot is ceded to the discretion of the chosen five. They are the ones to decide what the next world will be like."

"Why? Why does such an honor befall some random players?"

"None of those involved in the change are random. Only the Keymaster can open the path to the heart of the Game. Only the Guide can bring everyone together and guide them there. Only the seed of the Nameless can conceive the new world. He has to give himself totally in order for the world to be wholesome. Only the womb of Madonna can bear the world. She also has to give all of herself in order to produce a wholesome world. Only Merlin can deliver it and breathe life into the world. Again, he should not spare himself in order for the world to be harmonious. None of those participating in this process were ever random. Everything is predetermined, except for one thing: free will and freedom of choice. The Nameless has not given himself fully for three restarts already."

"And the Nameless is..." I repeated after the Keeper, but had no time to continue.

"This is classified information." The Keeper indifferently curbed my curiosity. "Are you satisfied with the completeness of the answers?"

Justly considering that I had received a lot more than I could have counted on, I nodded to the old man.

"Why are you entering into this deal? If these brochures are so dangerous you could simply impound them."

"That would be against the rules. A player

could lose potential benefits. Do you agree to voluntarily turn in the book of Lumpen, and in exchange receive the right to ask two additional questions during each visit? For an explorer it's quite a worthy reward."

"Well, that might me true," I mumbled. "But I am afraid that would not be enough to compensate me for the advantages I would have received from using the artifact. Moreover, that could be potentially problematic for me."

"Even so?" The old man pursed his lips. "Please clarify that."

"How would I explain to my suzerain that I gave away his present to you? He could be... offended. That's one. Second, the book would turn me into a true Dark one, increasing my Darkness level to one hundred, which is extremely important to me at this stage. Knowledge, of course, can be a deadly power, but not against the opponents I am facing."

"Worried about your suzerain's feelings? Commendable. But what about the slave's mark that was his present to you?" The Keeper smirked.

Bastard, he did get the last word, after all. But I decided to bargain to the end:

"The vassalage oath already makes me his slave quite legitimately, so I don't see anything particularly awful about that. So, if you want to get the book – offer me something more substantial."

"Fool," the old man noted dryly, and added after a brief silence: "We are extending the same offer of two extra questions and adding to it a treatise 'Shazal' that was written already in this era.

Activating the said treatise and including it in your Book of Knowledge will bring up your Darkness level to the 100 you so desire. You will become a true Dark one without the slave's mark, while Bernard would think that you had used his gift. We would be able to breathe easy. Everyone wins. Almost everyone, but that will be our small secret."

"Now that's an enticing offer," I smiled, and decided to make sure: "Gromana really wanted to receive this book, despite all those scary things you were saying about loss of one's will."

"Don't compare yourself to Gromana, Dark one." A smile appeared on the old man's face. "Gromana lived during Lumpen's time. She was part of his army. She enjoyed and worshipped the time of the Dark ones. Only her weakness and lack of a sufficient Dark force became the deciding factor in including her on the list of players in this new era. It was important to keep a balance. She wants the book not in order to activate it, but it is dear to her as a memory. As a symbol. We repeat our question – do you agree to the exchange?"

"I agree." Pleased with myself, I extracted the book and offered it to the old man. He did not move, but the book shimmered and disappeared straight from my hand.

"Shazal treatise." The familiar coffee table appeared next to me; on it there was a hefty dark volume. A far cry from some flimsy brochure. "Study and activate it. You will become a true Dark one. We are ready to answer two of your questions."

"Who are the incarnations of Merlin and

Madonna?" Not as though I really believed it would work, but I did have to try. I was not losing anything by doing it.

"Unfortunately, this is also classified information. The Creator has specified that it is forbidden to disclose it. And, as I anticipate your next question, the name of the Creator is classified information as well."

"Even of those two who are not involved any more?" I grinned, demonstrating my knowledge.

"Even for them," the worker of the Temple of Knowledge smiled back. "The names of the erstwhile Creators will tell you nothing. You have not heard them, either in your current life or in your previous one."

"Does the Creator transition from one era to another in the same way as the rest of the players? Or is there some kind of special procedure for them?" I would not give up trying to find a gap in their defenses.

"No special procedures. He acted in the same way as everybody else. The rules of the Game are the same for everyone, even for its creator."

"In that case I would like to receive the list of all players who transitioned from one era to the next. All transitions. All players."

"There is no restriction on that information." The old man was thinking hard, scratching his beard. "Each list contains up to several million records. Are you sure that you want to spend time on this?"

"Absolutely!" The longer the old man stalled, the more certain I became that my inquiry was the right one. "My first question is the list of all players who transitioned from one era to another, with a breakdown by eras."

"There is a limit on the quantity of information...," the Keeper started, but I cut him off:

"We are not discussing a standard inquiry! We reached an agreement – it's too late to backpedal. Or do the workers of the Temple of Knowledge not follow the rules of the Game?"

"The information you are seeking is in those volumes." My interlocutor started as soon as I brought up the question of following the rules; so, there were no more delays. "Study them. Given the specifics of the situation, the level of your artifact will not increase. For you the information from these volumes will remain just information and nothing else."

Four weighty volumes materialized on the coffee table.

"It is not allowed to take them outside of the Temple of Knowledge. However, there is no limit on the time you spend here. Study, compare, draw conclusions. We shall be waiting for your second question."

"We'll do it!" Steve, who was gradually developing a distinctive personality, assured me. *"Bring it on! I will analyze it! Don't worry about the experience points, we'll level up on the analysis later!"*

Boring lists of names, race and game worlds made me want to yawn, and inspired no enthusiasm whatsoever. In Bernard's library books had figures, diagrams and the text made sense, while here nothing caught my eye. Page after page of names were flowing into my artifact, and soon the list felt like just a jumble of letters. I attempted to keep count of the most common names just to keep myself entertained, but that stopped working fairly soon as well. My brain refused to assimilate vast volumes of monotonous information no matter how much I tried to force it. Steve was my only hope.

Once I turned the last page of the last volume it felt as though I had been through punishment for all the lessons in school I'd skipped. The dumb work was now done.

"Complete analysis will take me a couple of days," Steve was working for two, processing the information he had received. *"Preliminary results will be ready in a few hours."*

"You may still ask another question," the worker of the Temple of Knowledge reminded me.

"Sure, just a moment," I squeezed my eyes hard several times, fighting the drowsiness that was washing over me."What would happen if I were to bring together the entire set of jewelry which includes the pendant of the Lecleurs? That's the object temporarily borrowed by Iven, the head of the family."

"Do you mean the 'Joy' set?" The old man clarified, and I had to risk agreeing with that name. Until now no one ever named the set this way.

"The set was created by the last incarnation of Madonna for her only student – Anna the Great. When all components are collected, it surrounds the carrier with a permanent shield which blocks thirty percent of any damage."

"Is that it?" I asked again, discouraged, as I had never expected such a simple answer. "It has no additional properties, nothing else?"

"Initially that was the only property of the full set. It was not a strong artifact so much as a token of care and attention," the old man confirmed.

"Does the word 'initially' means that the properties were changed later?"

"That's question number three. We clarified to make sure which set you had in mind." The old man shrugged. "The set used to be called 'Joy' and had a certain set of properties. Now it has a different name and different properties. We have answered your questions in full. It's time for you to go back."

The space around me shifted, returning me to the herald's dwelling. Angry at myself for the slip with the name, I peeked out the window and snorted. The same players with the net that I had seen before were running around the inner courtyard of the estate.

"This is my house!" Sleevan was shouting indignantly, but in vain. Someone insolent and booming commanded loudly from the porch:

"Shut your kisser before you catch one in it, and get out of the way! Surround the house, the marker shows he's in there! Get lost, I tell you!"

I hid behind the curtains so that it would be impossible to notice me from the outside, and I saw Sleevan thrown from the porch in a cloud of dust. The herald's face looked badly bruised. He tried to get up, but fell back, cradling his unnaturally twisted right hand.

"Ready! Door! Four at the entrance, the rest go

in! The granis will be ours!"

Invisibility concealed me before a dozen or so players rushed into the room. The door was shut at once, blocking the way out for me, and four of the intruders rushed into the next room. One of those remaining took out a large bag and looked around mockingly. He could not see me, but the information on his PDA clearly indicated that I was close. Apparently someone had managed to tag me with a tracer!

"What, Paladin, you decided that you are immortal now?" The player shoved his hand into the bag, thrust it out and shook in front of himself, spreading white powder in the air. Flour! "Never fear! We'll show you right at once where you're wrong."

I was standing near the wall watching the white cloud approach and vainly trying to think of something to counteract such a simple solution. Not waiting for the flour to settle on my armor, revealing my location for all to see, I cast a glance in the direction of Sleevan, who still was not able to get up, and three scrolls with the "Templar's Blow" were deploying towards the enemy in order to destroy everything living and moving within the room five seconds later. My protection took a hefty blow; I heard it squeak from a fast drop in Energy, but the main purpose was reached: out of the six players who had been in the room, only the ringleader survived as he fumbled at the door and therefore avoided the blast. My artifact settled in my hand with a familiar feel. I activated the spikes. A momentary confusion sent the leader for respawn: I was not going to wait for him to react to my impressive approach, jumped on him and drove the spikes straight into his face, shredding his protection. Gems and enhancements rule!

"What's up?" The remaining four emerged from the next room only to follow their pals a moment later. "The Templar's Blow" ignored the initial level defense, and as soon as I touched their body they exploded in a rain of bloody giblets across the room. As for the last player, I did not kill him at once, as I recognized he had been the one beating Sleevan. I toppled him onto the floor, sat on top of him and shattered his kneecaps with one hard blow. I felt no pity for my opponent: once you go hunting you should be prepared for the possibility that you might turn into a quarry yourself. I set up the crystal for receiving emotions and drove the spikes into the shoulder of the guy, whose eyes rolled in pain and shock. I twisted the spikes in the wound. The player's endurance was not so great: he was ready to swoon like a girl on her first date. I pulled the spikes out of his shoulder and patted him on the cheeks mildly. As soon as consciousness appeared in his eyes, together with terror, I drove the spikes in again. In a Light word a Dark player needs to learn to take care of himself, his life and his Energy replenishment. I am far from being a Santa Claus, bringing joy and happiness to those who behaved well. I am a Paladin bringing pain and suffering to morons who behaved badly and threaten the NPCs with whom I have my own business. Sleevan could not do anything against the players, and this wriggling scum knew that. I, however, could.

The player squealed and wriggled, but could not throw me off. Deciding that his other limb was too much of a distraction for me, I pierced his other shoulder as well. It was odd, but my victim's emotions were not flowing to me like a river; I was just getting meager crumbs. Energy was leaking out into space and I could not understand why. I simply did not have enough knowledge and experience. Right!

I grabbed the "Shazal" treatise with my free hand and several times agreed with various system warnings to the effect that I should know, accept and assume full responsibility for whatever I will do in the future. Having plowed through a multitude of informational messages and agreements I made it to the final "OK", and, now without hesitation, accepted the gift of the Temple of Knowledge. Enough! It was time to make up my mind once and for all in this game!

You have reached the Darkness allegiance cutoff value

Another second went by as I read the information on this long-awaited event; then I found myself once again within Sleevan's house. At first I had to screw my eyes, getting used to the new appearance of the game world. But even then I was quickly able to identify the source of my discomfort. All objects acquired an additional green bar, notifying me of Energy available for acquisition, as well as ownership by their protector. All the space around me was in the possession of a player named Jesus.

Returning to my victim I noticed a similar bar and indicator of ownership. However, unlike inanimate objects, the player had an additional scale: "Faith limit". Its value was wobbling like a cocktail in a bartender's shaker and every time it dropped below a certain threshold, I received a crumb or two of Energy. The spikes pierced the shoulder again and I, following my intuition, reinforced the process with words:

"So your god is not helping you. Have you forgotten that there are no gods in the Game? There are only high level players, but they are far away now and nobody can hear you. You are mine alone! And your soul is mine as well! I will drink it whole and you won't even get a respawn! You will become my slave!"

Compassion and benevolence were things of the past; now all I had in front of me was not a sentient player, but a vessel with Energy; I needed to learn how to extract it.

"What are you doing?" I heard a stunned question from behind me, and another several players tumbled into the room, attracted by the bloodcurdling screams.

"Eating!" I informed the intruders, looking them over pragmatically. "And I can see that a few more dishes have come in on their own."

I resumed work on the first victim, who was now cooperating: the top line of his "Faith limit" dropped significantly. So that's why Dark ones need a Light world! In order to survive without hundreds of thousands of Energy vials. All that was needed was to make the victim forget about his god by torturing him while showing that his faith and god will neither save him from pain, nor render any aid. Steve helpfully pulled up the video of Gromana ruthlessly skinning the player while keeping him conscious with the help of her magic. As I was standing next to her at that time a thought flashed through my mind about her sadistic inclinations, that she was doing it just for fun. But now that I understood the specifics I figured out why the witch did not kill him. She needed pain and emotions! She needed Energy!

I noticed with my peripheral vision that the guests were dangerously close. One quick dash, and the only one left alive out of the four was the player with the lowest "Faith limit". Dropping him on the ground as first one died I continued my experiments. I needed to finally understand all the subtleties of the rules for Energy replenishment.

"There he is, surround him!" I was greeted by a shout from some random player as I emerged from Sleevan's house fifteen minutes later. Asking after the health of the herald who was taken away by caring servants and already given some elves' ointment, I headed towards Dolgunata without even attempting to conceal myself. The players were at first rejoicing at my appearance and rushed forward to earn their granis, but their fervor faltered as the distance between us diminished.

"A Dark one!" The first victim of the dark aura rushed at me from the crowd of puzzled players. With a fanatical shine in his eyes and animal-like growls the player bared his weapon against me, hoping to perform a great feat in the name of Light. Out of control, the guy completely was not thinking about protecting himself. Of course I used that to my advantage, and met him with a simple blow to the face. The spikes went easily into his eyes and as easily went out the back of the fanatic's skull; blood poured over his face and body. The other players were in no hurry to react to this execution. At least a minute passed, during which I threw off the body and covered about fifty steps, when another young defender of Light went bonkers. Another blow to the face and thirty more steps towards the castle With each killing the number of steps dropped; during the last few yards I ended up having to kill noobs practically at every step. It was easy.

There were about a dozen in all, I thought. Actually, I lost count a couple of times. Twelve low level players who lost control over their emotions and went wild from the present of one with the hundredth level of Darkness. May that be a lesson to them. I hoped that at the respawn point they would think of protective artifacts against players such as I. Or spend some time in the timeless zone to learn to control their emotions. In any case, I made it to the main gate and all that bothered me was: do I extract Energy properly? I need to check with Gromana as soon as possible.

"I have some interesting information." Steve could not care less about these events; he was working on his own thing. *"The final analysis of all the data is far from being complete, but I can say already now that there are not that many potential Creators. About a hundred beings by my estimate. That's how*

many of those born in the first era were in the lists for the last one."

"Is this the information you wanted to share with me?" I stopped, and the players nearest to me froze in place, not knowing what to expect of me, and fearing to provoke aggression on my part.

"*Not only that,*" Steve smiled, indicating that he was already developing an independent personality. "*The main thing is the last. I checked out one of our acquaintances, and was simply amazed by the results.*"

"Come on already! What did you find?"

"*He was born during the first era. Went through all the restarts. And lives in a second-rate world called 'Earth'. Guess who it is!*"

"Enough!" I flared up. "I'll just reformat you! Name!"

The crowd scattered in all directions, just in case. The players felt so uncomfortable near me that they immediately recalled all the things they had to do urgently, just to get away as far as possible.

Even Steve kept quiet – he had not expected such a reaction out of me. However, after sighing a couple of times, just for show to make me feel guilty, he did go ahead and announced with pathos:

"*Paladin Archibald, catorian, game world 'Earth'.*"

CHAPTER EIGHT

THE LECLEURS' TREASURY

THE DARK AURA worked without a glitch. I tentatively divided all players into two categories: cowards and idiots. The first one ran off as I approached, the second one attacked without warning or preparation, led by his overwhelming desire to erase the scary Dark one off the face of the Earth. The stupid ones were so numerous that as we were going to the room I was able to gain an extra level.

"Great Light! What happened?!" Alard whispered, astounded, as soon as I entered the room.

"You know, Yari, while before I wanted to

strangle you quietly, now I am looking for a reason not to tear you into pieces right here," stated Dolgunata, sitting in my chair.

"Risk your old bones, sure," I nodded to Sakhray who was standing by the window. All Archibald's students were there. "What's with the key?"

"Nothing yet. Archibald has not..." Dolgunata started replying, then jumped up in one fluid motion and shoved back her brother, who had tried to jump at me. He hit his head on the wall and slumped. The druid turned around and growled angrily: "Yari, do something about your aura! Or else it will drive everyone mad!"

"Alard is doing well and so are you. As for the rest – it's their problem," I said with some disdain, looking at Archibald's second best student. Sakhray came to quickly, and was now looking glumly at me, trying to understand what had just happened. Why had he just rushed to attack me and why did he want to do it yet again?

"I have a hard time keeping calm, brother," the orc admitted, taking a few steps back. "Only the understanding that it's dishonorable to attack a brother is holding me back. Honor above all!"

"So far as it's holding you, that's fine. While Archibald is not here I'd like to take a stroll through the estate, stretch my legs. Nata, are you coming?"

"To watch you torture the kids? "The druid snorted. "Spare me the sight."

I turned around silently and left the room. Even though I was showing off, the uncontrolled aggression coming from everyone around was starting to bother me. This unexpected problem required a quick solution. It would not do to go into the treasury with the Light ones and continuously worry that their self-control will fail. I covered myself under invisibility in an isolated spot and dialed Gromana. If there was anyone who could help, it would be she. The witch was not inclined to be long-winded; moreover, she was not too eager to talk to me generally:

"I can't get rid of you, eh! If you don't like attention from the Light ones, turn off the artifact! Big deal! Enough, I don't have time!" Gromana wanted to drop the call, but I stopped her.

"Wait! I don't want to turn it off, I just want to dim the aura. How can I do it quickly?"

"What is it about you – 'I want this'; 'I don't want that!' You want to eat your cake and have it too! It doesn't work that way! I told you in common Game language: the fastest and simplest way to resolve your problem is to deactivate the book."

I fell silent, thinking. Was I ready to give up this enhancement? If the witch says it's the simplest way, then so it is. It's a pity I am so short on time.

Meanwhile Gromana, mistaking my silence for agreement, continued:

"Open the character settings. If you follow the path: Darkness-Settings-Deactivate, you should have acquired an icon with a dark octopus. Have you found it?"

Still thinking, I followed the path:

"Yes, I have."

"Well, since you have, click on it!" Gromana

responded, calming down.

Thinking sensibly that once I know where to find it I will always have time to click on it later, I decided to verify in conclusion:

"So what are the ways that are not quick nor simple?"

"Have you clicked it?" The witch ignored my question and repeated her own.

"No."

"Then click the blasted button already, damn you!" Gromana suddenly exploded, giving me a thought.

"Once I push it, will something irrevocable or irredeemable happen to me? Will I not lose the book?"

After a short silence the evil witch deigned to answer:

"You won't lose it!" Gromana sighed heavily. "Once you deactivate the book, you can generate it again, but you won't be able to activate it any more. But you will be able to transfer it to another player. Me, for example. And you won't get any dark aura!"

By this time Steve analyzed all the current settings and shook his head negatively.

"Looks like it's true. So, it looks like it's impossible to conceal the aura using settings?"

"No," the witch was obviously contemplating whether to respond to me or hang up. She chose the former. "You have made your choice, and this aura will stay with you till deactivation or death. It's possible to conceal it with an external influence, but it takes time. And you said it was urgent."

I grinned at the witch's attempt to justify

herself.

"Not so urgent as to forfeit an advantage. Is there some amulet for this?"

"No. You need a powerful Light source."

"A Light source will simply kill me," I objected, but Gromana waved that off.

"I am alive and all the Dark ones are alive as well. Why should it not work for you? Can you jump to the Sanctuary now? I'll explain it all to you. It's inconvenient over the comm."

"Is there a threat to me?" I asked habitually. Gromana's reaction was quite adequate:

"Why did I have to teach you for my own trouble. No, there are no threats to you, no tricks or other bad things. I promise! At least, until you deactivate the book," the witch laughed, and I could easily see that this joke was no joke at all.

"Then wait for me; I'll be right there. Where should I look for you?" I needed to do something about my aura before Archibald showed up.

"Let's meet at the auction in five minutes. It's the only place I know where one can buy everything we'll need."

Scolding myself for only having bought a few return trip scrolls to the Sanctuary from Sleevan, I activated the last one. Had I known that I would be jumping all over Europe like a crazy grasshopper, I would have bought a dozen portals. Then I would not have to think where to find the herald all the time. Once I was in the Sanctuary, I decided against visiting the Paladins' headquarters so as not to test Grizdan's nerves with my Darkness at 100. Worried stares from passers-by were quite enough as they noticed me appearing in Zurich and scattered every which way in a hurry. So this way I made it to the auction, followed by curious stares; one time I even noticed an eye on a long stem peering from the sewage manhole – an inhabitant of Zurich below. Everyone wanted to know what kind of Dark wonder had shown up in the Sanctuary.

"Oh well," Gromana drawled, as she met me at the door of the auction. Inhaling contentedly, she even closed her eyes with pleasure. "I am not even going to ask how you made it here alive. The cloud around you is so dense it is as if I were at home again before respawn. I can imagine how you freaked them out... Anyway, now to business. Go to the auction and buy a looped anti-grav. It looks approximately like this." Gromana took a cylinder made of glass and metal off her belt. A piece of wood was weightlessly floating inside.

"This is a Light source from my old world," the witch explained, pointing at the piece of wood. "Its force is comparable to my level of Darkness and completely cancels the aura. To everyone else it looks like I am neutral."

"Does it work only on the aura or on the force as well?" I was examining the cylinder carefully. It would be interesting to know what was keeping the piece of wood weightless in there. Magic or something else?

"It affects the force a little, but primarily the aura.. The cylinder completely blocks the effects of the source of Light. While it's intact. If it were to be damaged even slightly, the source would touch a wall, and I would go to respawn. Well, first I would be dragged through all the circles of hell the way Christians imagine them."

"Has that happened to you often? I was looking at the device skeptically.

"A couple of times for sure," Gromana smirked. "What, are you scared?"

"Is this really the only way to turn off the aura without losing the book?"

"Yes – the only one I know. As to why it is so complicated: where have you seen a Dark one who has reached the maximum level of Darkness and would voluntarily give up the aura that suppresses the Light ones? It's like buying a flying carpet and then walking everywhere because you don't want to get it dirty. Stupid and pointless."

"But we don't really have a choice," I grinned. Gromana hooked the cylinder back onto her belt and snorted:

"Like hell. The moment you take the anti-grav off you become a dark blot on the reputation of this blighted world."

There was nothing to say to Gromana's reasonable comment.

"I get it. So I buy an anti-grav, and then what?"

"You'll buy a looped anti-grav," the witch corrected me. "Then you will be facing another problem. You will have to take an interesting trip to one of the local Force points and steal their source of Light. Given that the latter would have to be of maximum strength, small in size and available for stealing, there are not many options in this game world.

"Any suggestions?"

"Not a single one. You were born in this world, so you should know. I hope that I am not even here for very long and Bernard will allow me to move to Centauri. So you'll have to deal with the issue of the source on your own. I can only help you with the anti-grav; not every random one is suitable for your purpose."

Twenty minutes later Gromana left me to deal with my new acquisition – a small metal cylinder we bought from a nameless dealer for the three entire granises. Craftsmen in the Game have a gilded life it seems! You find a niche for yourself, fill it with your goods of different price categories, and that's it! The world is your oyster! My draftsmanship was not going to take me very far here.

Settling down in the nearest internet café I delved into studying available sources of Light. Even though our world was rich in terms of various relics, there was no reason to rejoice. I had to immediately rule out almost everything: various holy icons, remains of saints, the Black Stone of the Kaaba, the Spear of Destiny that had pierced the side of Jesus, and many other objects that would just physically not fit into my cylinder. And when I found mention of something useful, like the hair of the prophet Muhammad, it turned out that it had been lost. Christianity, Judaism, Hinduism, Islam... I went through just about everything, but did not find anything, Despairing, I finally selected the only thing that seemed acceptable: the Buddha's tooth.

"Look who's calling an old mercenary!" The joy in Miltay's voice was so sincere that I also smiled. Apparently he was looking forward to a lucrative order. "Are you calling for business, or just, like, been missing me?"

"I've been missing you, so I have some business for you. How about earning a couple of granises?

"Look here, make something! And a couple of granises to boot! Why so generous? Where do we have to run? Who do we have to bury?"

"Game world Earth, the city of Kandy, Sri Lanka, Temple of the Tooth. I need to have a relic stolen."

"Look here, how about some more detail – what is it you want stolen, like?" Miltay grumbled, as he hadn't caught it the first time. So I had to clarify:

"A Light source with the code name 'The Tooth of the Buddha'. I would like to temporarily borrow it forever for personal use. Is that better? Since a thing like that is likely to be guarded, and guarded well, I'll need supporting fire."

"Messing with the monks, eh?" Enthusiasm vanished from the mercenary's voice, and his joy clearly faded. "Yari, you are a cool guy, but here you are knocking on the wrong door. If you needed to complete a dungeon, or shake up some NPCs, like, that's something we'll always do gladly. But against players... Our little fart-guns won't be any good for that. You must recall how long it took us to destroy the crabs, and players are bound to have much stronger protection. They won't let us even come in from the cold. They'll drown us like kittens straight at the door."

"I heard you," I replied in a voice devoid of emotion. "Do you know a good contact though?"

"Look here, seems like you know one yourself, judging by the markers on you. Archibald and Devir. Those two are the best on Earth. Only, as far as I recall, you aren't so rich as to hire them. So then, look, there are some players who won't be asking so sky high: Tselmet, Sherzal and Valir. Actually, I wouldn't recommend the last one: he's unreliable. One could call up some from other worlds, too. All you need is granises. That old Khalisad, say, from Zhardin. In our sector, he'd be the cleverest trickster when it comes to borrow 'n forget. But he's an expensive little bastard. Won't work for less than ten granises an hour. But still, like, cheaper than Archibald or Devir will cost ya."

I thanked him and after a little more light conversation, I ended my talk with Miltay. The mercenary was right: any more or less significant relic would be guarded, and a common player like myself would not even be able to come close to it. They'd be killed before they even have a chance to approach.

The option of hiring a trickster would not work either. There would be no guarantees, even beside the fact that I did not have so many granises. Thinking of all the pros and cons once again, I concluded that I could only do one thing:

"Greetings, Yaropolk. Did you have questions for milord?" Malturion responded, even though I had thought that I was calling Bernard's personal comm.

"Greetings, Malturion. Not questions as such, but problems that have to do with Milord Bernard's present. Can I talk to him?" I really did want to talk to Bernard.

"Milord is busy right now. You can describe the problem to me. Perhaps I would be able to help you without bothering him," the butler insisted, and I gave in.

"Gromana passed on to me the present from Milord. After I activated the book my dark aura became so strong that it oppresses the Light ones around me too much and scares the NPCs. I am not complaining – not at all. But with an aura like this I won't last long in the Light world. Gromana suggested a way to conceal my aura, but for that I would need an extremely powerful but small Light source. I can't obtain one on my own; I don't have either connections, nor granises, nor opportunities. So it seems I would have to deactivate the book in order to resolve the problem. But I would not want to offend my suzerain by doing this."

"It's highly commendable for the vassal to care about his master's feelings. I wish everyone would respect their master so much," I heard a grin in Bernard's voice as he came on the line. Open irony in his words grated on my self-esteem.

"Good afternoon, Milord Bernard! I am very grateful to you for the present, and apologize for bothering you. I wanted to steal a source of Light on my own, but the only team of mercenaries that I know would not agree to the order, since no one wants to quarrel with the monks."

I specifically did not state directly there was a connection between Bernard's present and the activated book. For all the game world to see I had an active book of Lumpen and nothing else. Bernard's tone made it clear to me that was in my best interest to mislead my suzerain as long as I could.

"Of course. So what drew the eye of my vassal?" Bernard clarified, and laughed on hearing my answer.

"The tooth of the Buddha was never kept in the Temple of the Tooth. A pretty legend that it is hidden in seven gold caskets is just that – a legend. What is kept in the temple is but a copy; the relic itself, as it should be, is located in the well-protected treasury that belongs to the monks. One would have to be an idiot to consider that an artifact so strong would be exposed for everyone to see. It receives its force not because it is seen, but because it is known. For this purpose the temple is more than sufficient. This would not work."

"I see." Actually, I was discouraged by the open contempt in Bernard's voice. The hope that he would help was fading fast. "In that case, I would have to follow Gromana's other piece of advice."

"And that would be?" The Coordinator asked curtly.

"Gromana said that the simplest way is to deactivate the book."

"Don't even think of deactivating the book. That's an order." It was stated in a manner that made it clear: it was the Coordinator of three game worlds speaking. The man whose middle name was Power, no less. "Wait in the Lecleur estate – in ten minutes the source of Light will be delivered to you."

Bernard hung up and my dismay vanished without a trace. However, my mood was in no hurry to bubble up to sheer joy either. Rather I was visited by worry threatening to bloom into paranoia. That's it? The masks are off? Good uncle suzerain is a thing of the past? Bernard believes that I have activated the book of Lumpen, therefore to him I am no more than a puppet. Really, had I been simply a vassal, I would have had some freedom of choice with respect to following my suzerain's orders. So suppose I disagreed with my lord, so it would be possible to argue against his orders. Naturally, Bernard and the Game would be within their rights to punish me for it. And, in order to prevent possible insubordination, Bernard would be playing a good master. But after the activation of such a convenient gift the vassal instantly turned into a puppet able only to act in accordance with its master's will without asking any unnecessary questions. Then there would be no need to play the role of being good. How convenient. The question was: what was the point of such drastic measures?

I had no specific answer, nor did I have time for contemplation. The most obvious answer was: Bernard would need a puppet during the restart. Setting this question aside till a better time, I hastened to return to the estate. Regular nightly battles with the necromancers did not weaken in the least the players' desire to get into the estate and complete their quest. The long line was still snaking all the way to the gate. Trying to maintain some distance from the players, I was quickly moving towards the entrance. However, it did not go entirely without casualties. My estimate of distance was good, and the "impact" zone of my aura caught players one by one; they also attacked one by one, which was convenient for me. Without unneeded emotions I sent them to respawn, then made a step forward and used my dark aura to check the next player. Who is he – a "trembling creature" or "has the right"? I would have never thought that there would be a time in my life suitable for quotes from the immortal "Crime and Punishment" by Dostoevsky.

"C-c-come in." The guard at the door held up despite the beads of sweat that appeared on his forehead. His sense of duty overcame his fear. "You are on the l-l-list."

I looked back – the line of those wanting to come into the estate had become noticeably thinner, but was still numerous. Those players who had been able to control themselves used the opportunity to become considerably closer to the coveted gate. Nothing new, just natural selection at work.

I decided against going deeper into the estate, so as not to provoke the players and local NPCs. I settled near the entrance and tried to hide from everyone, to quietly wait for the parcel from my suzerain.

"Yaropolk, come out of the estate, take out your anti-grav and hold it in your right hand." Malturion called precisely at the time Bernard had specified. As I followed his instruction, the butler appeared next to me. All I was able to do was to nod in greeting, when something bent me and pressed me to the ground. My heart was banging in my throat, my ears rang like huge bells, the world darkened in front of me. I could not breathe; I could not move. It felt like a huge stone pressing me to the ground, threatening to crush me flat. Steve was shouting something, and I could even hear him clearly, but my brain refused to function and the meaning of the sounds escaped me.

"If you decide to leave this game world," Malturion's voice miraculously made its way through the weight of the stone and removed it, "you will have to return the Light source. That is the master's order. Also, I would like to give you some advice: learn how to control yourself, even in situations like this one. Now you are rolling in the dust and bringing shame on your master."

I was lifted off the ground effortlessly and set on my feet. Making sure that I was not going to fall over again, Malturion activated a portal and disappeared without another word. Still, I was grateful. I opened my right hand and saw a clump of hair within the anti-grav. Judging by the thickness it was definitely not human. Not as though it mattered; for all I cared it could be a yeti's – the important thing was that it worked!"

"That was funny! You, with your hand outstretched, at a vampire's feet!" I heard the cutting voice of Dolgunata as she was approaching the estate. "Let's go! I can see you got your alms already, so now it's time to work. Everything is ready. We need to get into the treasury before Iven notices that the key is missing."

"You are such a bitch after all, Nata. I used this alms, as you called it, to dampen the aura so that you would feel better," I grumbled as I joined Dolgunata. In response she only snorted like a cat, showing me where I could stuff all my care. Without hiding we went straight to Sophie for the key to the Reverse.

We found the lady in the small reception hall with Ervan, who was dead drunk. Even though she detested her husband, Sophie stayed close to him so that no one would try to bring him out of his Dionysian stupor too early, so the estate would have some respite. Exchanging quick glances with us, she nodded lightly towards the gallery that led to the treasury, then said to the nearby servant:

"I feel a little ill. I will go lie down. Make sure you keep a eye on my husband."

We waited for a couple minutes, then followed her; we caught up with Sophie as she was turning towards her rooms.

"Monsieur Yaropolk, mademoiselle Dolgunata." The temporary mistress of the estate nodded, welcoming us and looking us over. "Here, I hope this helps to find mother's pendant and put an end to all this chaos."

The key to the Reverse was in my hands again, and the system started its countdown. Twelve hours till Iven would be notified of his granddaughter's betrayal. Sophie's shoulders drooped and she disappeared into her room. "The die is cast", as Julius Caesar said during the hard times.

Further preparations did not take us much time. We picked up Alard and gave Mizardine detailed instructions and a detonator in case we were delayed; then we hurried towards the entrance to the treasury. The three Paladins were not glad to see us.

"This place is off limits!" A bearded gnome stood in our way. He was about as wide as he was tall. "Turn around now!"

"Who is the head of the guards?" Dolgunata came up to the halfling, unabashed, and looked him over from top to bottom the way only she could.

"An' who you be, lass, fer me to answer to ye? I said, it's off limits! But..." the gnome looked back at Dolgunata with a measuring look, bottom to top, and stopped just above his eye level, which happened to be at the druid's chest, "...if ye have something to offer nicely to a tired Paladin, don't be shy, show me what ye 'ave."

"What I can offer you nicely is only to step aside and not keep myself and my companions from entering the treasury. And I am only extending this offer on the principle of not crippling those who are already crippled by nature. Here, take a look." Dolgunata handed the Paladin a scroll. It was a pity that at this moment I was the only one capable of appreciating her politeness and restraint. She was actually capable of moderating her rudeness when needed for common success.

The gnome took the scroll and read it carefully and unhurriedly. After that, in the same unhurried way, he rolled it up and offered it back. Dolgunata jerked her head, puzzled, in no hurry to take the scroll back. Seconds ticked by, but Nata still waited for a different response. Finally the gnome frowned in irritation and lowered his hand with the scrolls, stepped to the side a little and took out his comm.

Even we heard the signal as he called, but whoever the gnome was calling did not pick up. The gnome's eyebrows furrowed: he was puzzled. He made another call, also to no avail, then turned to Dolgunata again:

"Sorry, lass, but there's nothing good I can tell you. Gerhard van Brast might be a big laird here, but he's not the one who hired us an' he's not the one to order us."

"Is that so?" Dolgunata's eyebrows flew up so high they were about to collide with her hairline. "Are you an idiot or have you lost your mind? That's an order from the Head of the class of Paladins of the Earth game world!"

"I'm mighty impressed and a' that! But I tell ye again, as your mind's too dim – I 've a contract! Get that? And your Gerhard will ne'er shower me with granises for breaching it!"

Dolgunata jerked in the direction of the tense Paladins, but was pushed back softly by the force field. The druid slipped back a couple of yards, but kept her balance.

"You shouldn't be like that, lass. We might take offense at tha'. Naw' one's allowed to enter," the other gnome clarified mildly. We were pushed further away by the expanding field, and Gerhard's scroll flew after us. "You try tha' agin, we'll send ye for respawn without talkin'much."

Dolgunata joined us and we turned a corner.

"Yari: your conclusions?" The druid stopped

and pulled on a lock of her hair impatiently. "Any suggestions? Damn. We are wasting time so stupidly!"

"Who could have supposed they were not from Earth?" All that my conclusions could bring about was desperation. The druid chose the simplest solution: she took out her comm:

"Teacher, we have a problem!"

"Nata, solve it yourself!" The catorian barked so loudly that the girl jerked the comm away from her sensitive cat's ear. The teacher's voice was so tense that the druid did not dare argue with him. "Bye!"

A long pause was interrupted by the orc:

"Why our bearded friends are behaving so dishonorably?" Alard was extremely frustrated with the gnomes' behavior. Apparently, he alone drew no conclusions from that. "There is no honor in such behavior."

"They are strangers here – that's why they behave like that." I responded, sighing heavily. My seemingly ideal plan for searching for the pendant was about to disintegrate; we would not be able to get by those Paladins. Neither by force, nor by tricks, nor by any other method known to me. Well, actually... Leguria with 100 Darkness would probably help, but then most of the estate would be hit as well. Was I ready to feel all the joys of torturing a hundred players and NPCs? Frankly speaking, right now – not ready at all. The Paladins were from somewhere else. Iven hired them specially to guard the treasury. A little odd that he did not entrust his own fighters with that task. Wanted to keep them from talking? Could be. And it is logical that the outsiders would not let us through without notifying their employer of an off-nominal situation. Wait! But how come the gnome did not know that Gerhard van Brast was the head of all local Paladins?

"Alard, when you were preparing to travel to our world, did you need any paperwork?" I recalled my conversation with Gromana that something provided the necromancer access to our world past Bernard, as well as Steve's mention that if a player were to travel to another world without permission, he would be eliminated. What if Iven had dragged the gnomes here illegally? Brought them in by portal directly and then sent them back the same way? They would not need to know who was the head of the Paladins in this game world. By the way, Bernard's interest in Iven could easily be due to this – as a channel for people smuggling. I needed to check my guesswork.

"Not myself, no." The orc frowned, clearly not understanding the reason for my interest. "There was permission granted to all the Paladins of my world, it was prepared by our Head. All I have is an excerpt from our orders."

"Show me, would you?" I asked tentatively. The orc hesitated, then pulled out his tablet and showed the picture of the order. In it, his name was mentioned, among other Paladins; the order was signed by the Coordinator of sector 446, Bernard Kalran. Gerhard was also mentioned as the responsible party from the hosts' class. What a tangled web indeed!

"Yari, look here. I haven't changed my mind."

Miltay was mistakenly considering that I was going to offer him that same job again. "We aren't going to fight against players."

"Forget about the monks, I have already solved that problem." The orc and the druid stared at me in a way that practically ordered me to tell them everything in detail. Well, tough luck! "I have a different question. Your group can work on Earth, even though you are definitely not from this game world. Did you have to obtain a permit?"

"Of course I did." The mercenary's voice expressed genuine surprise. That was obviously not a question he expected. "In order to work in any world you need a permit. The level of my team made it possible for us to work only in sectors 446, 282 and 1077; after completing the Dungeon with you we were granted access to a couple more. I'd thought I told you about it. Did I not?"

"That's what I was I calling you about – thanks!" I hung up without going into detail, and could not contain the joy that showed on my face. Even though it was premature. We still had to take one last step to checkmate Milord Iven, if I was correct in my analysis of the positions of the pieces on the board.

"Yaropolk, you have problems again?" Malturion picked up at once.

"Rather, some questions," I clarified. "Within the Lecleur estate there are three fighter Paladin gnomes who are obviously not from the Earth game location. I don't know their names, just the description of their appearance. According to reliable information Iven, the head of the family, is responsible for the presence of those bearded creatures within the estate. The question is, did Bernard issue a permit to gnomes to be in our game world, or did Iven act by going around him?"

"This is a grave accusation." The vampire looked alert. "Can you send me pictures of the gnomes?"

"I will try." My Context Search was already leveled to 15; that enabled me to download pictures and video to other players. Steve was a little slow doing it for the first time, but just in a few moments the comm was connected to the Book of Knowledge and the vampire received a video clip of the gnomes.

"I will check on it. Wait." Malturion hung up, and then Dolgunata sharply turned me towards her.

"You knew that from the start?!" The druid was enraged, since I had not discussed it with her.

"Are you completely bonkers?" I was somewhat taken aback by her attack on me."I have never even seen gnomes until now. It's just that they are from a different world, and that gave me certain ideas... Now, Malturion will check all this out and it will become clear whether I was right or not. Come on, we have not a moment to waste. If I am right we'll have just a few seconds to enter the treasury."

We settled right around the corner to keep out of the Paladins' sight. I did not want to aggravate the eager guards any further, so periodically I would check out the situation under my invisibility cover. The gnomes were calmly guarding, not trying to call anyone on their comms any more. I held mine in hand, but Malturion was in no hurry to provide any updates.

The portal opened next to the gnomes right at the moment when I was yet again staring at my comm screen. I hid around the corner quickly, peeking out just enough to have a good view, and made a sign for the druid and the orc to keep still. Despite the harsh demand of the thief that those on the list were prohibited from appearing within the estate, the chief Paladin fighter appeared from the portal in no hurry, and in all his shining shamelessness. Could anyone say still that Iven had nothing to do with the theft of the pendant?

"Follow me – your relief will be here shortly!" He ordered the gnomes; after that Gerhard's right-hand man turned sharply towards us. I barely had time to hide, and held my breath. Dolgunata dropped silence cover on us just in time. In a few seconds I heard Iven's voice, tense and not very close:

"Did anything happen while you were on duty that I should know about?" Presumably the fighter sensed our presence but was in too much of a hurry to stop and investigate the area.

"Aye, m'lord. I called ya aff-hand. A druid Paladin came he' with scrolls o' Gerhard van Brast. Wanted me to let her an' two more Paladins in the treasury. We told 'em to bolt 'way."

"And they just left?" Iven asked, surprised.

"Aye, m'lord. Right 'way." The response came immediately.

"Amazing." The fighter snorted skeptically and urged the gnomes. "Hurry up, get into the portal, quick. You'll report later."

Soon the ruckus died down. I decided to wait a little longer and heard the loud voice of the golden Paladin:

"I know that you are here. Scuttling in the corners like rats. What else could be expected of Archibald's brownnosers? You should be afraid to put your noses out, because I will be back, and it will happen very soon." His voice was calm, but oppressive. It sent shivers down my spine, making me want to hide in some obscure corner or other safe hiding place. Even Dolgunata and the orc cringed, as if Iven was using some ability to beat on our group's morale. "Neither Gerhard nor Bernard will save you. If you have any brains at all, use them to make sure to keep out of my sight! I have warned you! I hope you heard me, scum."

And only now I heard the pop indicating that the portal had shut, taking Iven and the gnomes with it. I shook my head, fighting the desire to rush away, find a safe and quiet place and huddle there, hiding from Iven the Great and Powerful. It was prohibited to exert mental influence over recent graduates of the Academy, but there is no proscription on scaring them or forcing them to submit using charisma.

"Come: Iven will send the new guards soon!" I took several deep breaths to get some oxygen in my blood and dashed forward, pulling Alard with me. Unlike Dolgunata, the orc was hit by the golden Paladin's grandeur, and now was kind of "stuck", staring off into space. So I had to bring him around and practically drag him along. Iven's words had no effect on the druid whatsoever; she did not bat an eyelash hearing threats hurled at her. Her restraint and self-control were truly admirable despite her tongue being so sharp she could slice one to ribbons with it.

"Yari, this is the point of no return. Are you really sure that you want to acquire such an enemy?" Right at the door to the treasury Nata paused, turning towards me. "Don't even think that Iven will forget this."

"If he is guilty of the disappearance of the pendant, that Paladin has no honor." I answered in the way Alard would. "Gerhard will get rid of him as soon as things start heating up. All we would have to do would be to throw some oil on the fire to see his golden ass fried. After that Iven would be too far up shit creek to bother with us. Open it."

The druid simply shrugged, and took out a long metal rod suitable for a Chubb lock. The lock got stuck, but Nata was still able to turn the key. There was a sharp click and the huge metal door slid aside smoothly. Actually, I did expect to see mounds of gold, precious stones and other nice things a treasury was supposed to be full of right away, at least in my understanding. However, all we saw was thick grey fog in the door. It was soft, cool and slightly resilient to the touch. My intuition screamed that we were unlikely to encounter anything nice in there.

"Guys: prepare all the ammunition we have." Nata was showing she was ready to fight, and expressed what all of us were thinking. "I can't say I like this fog a whole lot. Although if it had been a normal treasury with the pendant on a pedestal, I would have been disappointed in Iven."

"I would have been fine with that." I poked the fog and cringed from the cold. It was impossible to see anything beyond the door. "Who's on first?"

"What does it matter? I'll just do a quick foray to find out the lay of the land. Don't get lost." Nata breathed deeply, turned into a panther, flashed her eyes in parting and sank into the fog. "Boys tend to cover their cowardice with fake gallantry as they let girls go first. But we get all the glory!"

"True Paladin knows no fear!" Alard practically roared, and rushed straight after Nata as if he wasn't the one I had just had to drag along the hallway. I did not hurry. I waited for a few seconds, watching my companions' frames. Seeing that they had not turned grey, I looked at the empty hallway and took a step into the unknown, shutting the door behind me. From now on the only way lay forward.

My whole body was shivering. I was not in pain, but it was unpleasant. It felt like I stepped out of a warm apartment into a damp and windy November. I had to move slowly, like a blind kitten, trying to distinguish things around me. But the further I advanced, the more apathetic and listless I became. I lost my sense of time. It could have been half an hour or a couple of minutes when I realized that I had forgotten why I was here and how I had arrived in this place. I was overcome by panic. I was lost! This damned fog was everywhere. It grabbed at the skin and seeped into the brain! Like a dog endlessly chasing its tail I circled in place, trying to find a way out. I shouted and called for help, but all around was silence, grayness and cold. My thoughts were confused, my heart was pumping blood boiling with adrenaline... An eternity later my consciousness mercifully faded. We were caught in a trap after all...

"Doctor, will he live?" A voice came through the darkness, an unfamiliar and well-modulated voice.

"Yes, there is no more need to worry about that. His condition is now grave, but stable. The crisis has passed. It is truly an amazing case, general, sir. The soldier lost a lot of blood. In medical practice we call such cases miraculous. His thirst for life is amazing! We were even able to reattach one arm..."

"Leave those details for the relatives! What I am interested in is when he is going to wake up." It was obvious that the general's preferred mode of communication was issuing commands.

Were they talking about me? Was I the one in grave condition? I was frantically trying to remember what had happened and why I was in the hospital. So, I ended up in the army. That I remembered. What happened next? Then we went on a scheduled patrol assignment with lieutenant Sintsov. Yes, that was right. And then my entire body shuddered from the flood of memories: "Issue live ammo!" "It blew Vas up!" "All the way!" Hell, arms!!! My arms!!! Where in hell did that bastard with super-abilities spring up from? Apparently, I became too excited, since the sensors nearby trilled a whole sequence of alarms. The doctor reacted immediately, and I felt the prick of a needle. He stayed by my side and answered the general impatiently:

"Today, maybe tomorrow. But I do insist on letting him rest for a couple of days before you question him. Consider that I am the commander-in-chief here. And I will be the one to decide when you start your attack, general! For the private it will exacerbate psychological trauma, and may have additional negative effects! He's facing a long road to recovery."

Retreating steps were all the doctor got in response to his warning; meanwhile I was sure that had I opened my eyes, the "local commander-in-chief" would have to stuff it.

The general needed to know what had happened to the Lieutenant Sintsov's platoon. And I was the only one who could shed some light on that. Everyone else had been killed by the superman. I wonder, would they shut me in a nuthatch once I described all this to the general? I imagined their expressions once I told them that a mage had killed the group. It made me laugh. As I was falling asleep from the shot of sedative, I recalled that the name of the mage was Devir, or so I thought. Strange, how would I know that?

I was having a strange dream. Someone said that my world did not exist any more. That all there was was the Game in which I was playing the Dark Paladin. But first the mage called Devir had killed me with a fireball. He tore my arms off, and while I was writhing on the ground in pain, came up to me and said: "My name is Devir, mage Devir! And what's your name?" Then I saw an oversized cat who was trying to lick himself through the armor he was wearing. When he failed, he faded into the air; only a nasty smile was left in his place; it kept sneering: "You are a system error. Can true Paladins be Dark?" "Idiot!" A red-skinned orc answered him. Something to the effect of "True Paladins are only Paladins of Light. There is no honor in Darkness!" A black panther rubbed itself at his feet. She had mesmerizing eyes and hissed instead of roaring "Closer, Bandar-log, come closer..." I rubbed my eyes, pinched myself and shook my head in order to wake up faster. There was a status bar in front of me and a hologram of Steve. I knew he was part of my subconscious. Well, that must be a symptom of a split personality, but there, within the Game, he was my friend. He shouted, but I could not hear a word through the cacophony. They drifted more quietly, then became louder again. Sometimes it seemed to me that it I was on the verge of hearing him. The noise around grew, and new freakish faces appeared: evil elves, a man with a wolf's head, a blue-eyed doll Helen who bent down to me, blinked her eyes and said "ma-ma". I knew all of them. They pinched, talked, asked something, pulled on me, distracting me from Steve. All my attempts to hear him were in vain. Meanwhile, he looked me straight in the eye and kept shouting. I sweated with the effort; then there was a moment of silence pierced with a scream: "Yaropolk, wake up!" My subconscious was able to get through to me. I opened my eyes sharply and inhaled, as if coming up from under water after a long dive.

It was a dream, just a bad dream. There were blinding white walls and ceiling. And no strange beings or Steve. No one besides the people dearest to my heart. My mother and my sister. Dear. Alive.

"Sonny!" My mother wept, seeing that I had opened my eyes. "My baby!"

"Mom, he woke up!" Sveta cried out and threw herself on my chest. It was hard to breathe, but I welcomed the feeling. The sensation from the touch of people closest to me was priceless. The flood of feelings caused tears to flow down my cheeks. It was so good that all that had been a dream, and now I was with my family again. The doctor rushed in to shatter the idyllic picture.

"Get down, now! He just had surgery! Patient, can you hear me? Nod if you do!"

"Y-yes." It hurt to talk, my throat was bone dry, but I wanted to hear myself speak. To feel that I was alive. "I can. Did anyone else survive?"

"All the questions later," the doctor cut me off. "First we need to stabilize you. Your relatives need to leave the room."

"N-nno, don't!" I was alarmed. It must have sounded pitiful, but I did not care. I was scared that they would abandon me to myself. Apparently, the stress had affected my emotional state pretty badly. The doctor made a show of grumbling some, but then gave my mother some instructions and ran off to tend to other patients.

"We are here, baby. Don't you worry." My mother patted me on the hand reassuringly. She squeezed my pinky finger three times, like she used to in my childhood when she wished me good night. This half-forgotten gesture had a calming effect. At that point the door to the room opened and someone else came in. My mother sighed with relief: "Thank God they let you in! Helen, dear, he just woke up!"

I frowned, not understanding why "Auntie Helen", our neighbor, would be here. Our families were not so close as to visit each other in the hospital. However, as soon as the guest came closer, the world stood on its ears again.

Helen was standing next to my mother and smiling. It was the doll from my dream.

"Hello, darling!" my ideal girl said tensely, and smiled through her tears. I returned a weak smile and looked at my mother with a question.

"Dear Nellie called me right away when this happened. Your phone had so many calls to her that Nellie was notified first. So that's how we met. They didn't want to let her in when they found out you were not officially married." My mother started her tangled explanation, and was unable to restrain herself from reproaching me. "And you never told me anything about her when you called…"

I lost any understanding of what was happening, and was looking carefully at Helen, remembering in detail the first time we met. In the Game. Along with our walk around the city and the best night in the hotel in the Sanctuary. I knew this girl only as my Doll. But it was complete nonsense!

I swallowed and rasped:

"S-s-sorry, but I just don't know what to say. W-water…"

Helen rushed to fulfill my request, trying to conceal her embarrassment at my words. Bringing a glass to my lips, she asked timidly:

"How can that be? You cannot remember who I am?" She tensely clutched the glass so tightly her fingers turned white.

The water was really the water of life for me. Speaking became much easier now, and I answered carefully:

"I can remember... but not very well."

Helen sighed with relief and chattered quickly:

"My love, I was so scared that something was wrong with your memory. The doctor said you had real bad shell-shock and it was possible. He said it was such a miracle that you survived at all. I called your mom right away. It's a pity we had to meet under such circumstances, but it doesn't matter. We still wanted to have me meet her during your vacation. Right?" Apparently, my memory had gotten lost somewhere together with my other arm. Because I could not remember any of the things presented by the girl. But she babbled on so happily and with such certainty that I did not doubt her words. She would tell me everything and I would surely remember it all. Otherwise, how could I possibly explain Helen's presence here in a rational way?

"Frankly speaking, I can't remember much," I admitted.

My mother immediately rushed to reassure me:

"No problem, sonny. Once you get better, it will all come back to you. Nellie will tell you everything, right now she can. Start now, that is. We'll go with Sveta, bring you some nice broth. You need to eat well, you do, get your strength back. And you talk here, little doves. It will all get better, it will."

My mother grabbed the resisting Sveta by the arm and quickly pushed her out the door; then she left as well. Helen settled down lightly on the edge of the bed and stroked my cheek:

"You can't remember anything at all?"

Her touch made me feel warm, and I said:

"I do, but it's kind of weird. Everything is topsy-turvy in my head."

Helen smiled again, looking into my eyes, and then brushed my hair back behind my ear with an all-too-familiar gesture:

"I will remind you of everything. We met a couple of months ago when I came to visit my father's military base. You fell asleep right on the bench in front of the barracks, and I was going by in the morning and offered you coffee. You were so scared that I would tell my dad, you ran away almost immediately. Do you remember that?"

Apparently, my shell-shocked mind had changed that scene somewhat. But on the whole one could say that I did remember, so my conscience was clear. I nodded and dared to add a note:

"I think you were wearing a huge baggy sweater."

Helen laughed, happily and openly now, while I lay there and enjoyed the sound of her laughter:

"Right! You kept calling it a sack until you found out it was my dad's favorite sweater. The mornings were brisk at the base. So you see! Everything will be fine, and together we'll remember it all. Together. And now you should rest. I will sit with you."

I closed my eyes with relief. This conversation exhausted me. This time as I was falling asleep I felt calm. I had the sensation that I was falling, but it did not scare me. Suddenly a harsh shout yanked me out of my drowsiness:

"Yaropolk, wake up!"

My eyes opened at once. Helen was still sitting next to me, and frowned, concerned, as she looked at my face:

"What? Did you have a nightmare? It's to be expected, after all of this..."

"It seemed that you were calling me," I whispered.

"No, no, of course not. I was not going to bother you. You just fell asleep," the girl reassured me.

I tried to relax again and fall asleep, but different thoughts crowded my mind. If Helen's father had served at my base she would know what happened to the others.

"Helen, did anyone else survive?"

She shook her head.

"No. There was one soldier whose body was not even found. He had a funny name."

I raised an eyebrow to indicate a question without opening my eyes.

"Monstrichello," I heard her answer almost immediately. "It's a funny name so it stuck in my mind."

It was a funny one for sure. I mumbled something in response as a way of agreement. I did see it all happen as I looked, yet hope refused to die.

But what if? We fell silent and Helen was sniffling quietly; I was remembering the guys. Monstrichello, but that was... And then again I heard quite clearly: "Yaropolk, wake up!" The shout derailed my train of thought. I froze, then asked Helen:

"Did you hear anything?"

"No..." the girl said, puzzled. "Was I supposed to?"

"It seemed to me again that someone was shouting 'Yaropolk, wake up!' Could it be that I have audio hallucinations?"

"Don't worry, Yaropolk. This must be consequences as well..." I did not hear the end of Helen's sentence when that same "Yaropolk, wake up!" exploded in my brain.

Yaropolk! Helen called me Yaropolk also! Not the name I was given at birth!

The doctor stormed into the room:

"You have to leave at once! He's getting worse!"

It was my pulse that alarmed the doctor: it had risen to 200 beats per minute. The physician supposed that the conversation was what had stressed me and made Helen leave, leaving me alone. But he was wrong about the reason. It was not from talking. I remembered everything that had happened to me after I died on Earth. And I realized that I was within the Game. Because in my past life there was no Yaropolk, and no Monstrichello. There were Sergey Lemeshev and lance-corporal Fagov. But the Doll could not know that. The Game took great care to erase all the player's memories of the past! Had I not been an explorer, I would have forgotten about my past as well.

"Welcome back!" A projection of a homely guy wearing a plaid shirt appeared in front of me. Steve, my semi-transparent assistant, waved his hand in a friendly greeting.

"Hello, Steve!" Together with the visual image of the assistant I regained the skill of silently talking to him. "What's up?"

"Finally you are back!" The emotions caused my subconscious to call me " you". *"Yari, we need to return at once! The longer you stay in the mental trap, the harder it will be to get out!"*

"Got it. How do I do that?" It seemed superfluous to talk about anything else at this time.

"First you need to destroy your mental anchor, then kill yourself." Steve was straightforward to the point of being brutal. *"That's the only way to have your brain get back to the Game from the mental trap. You will die within your mind. It will not send you to respawn. If you tarry, you will stay in the mental trap until the treasury owner comes and gets you. Or until you die of exhaustion, but that's unlikely. The crystal will keep supplying you with Energy for another hundred years or so."*

"That sucks. What so you mean by destroying the anchor?" I asked skeptically.

"Now you are surrounded by things that caused strong emotions in the past. Think about it: your family, Devir's attack, the Doll, the absence of your arm. But the thing that holds you here most is your family..." Steve let the sentence trail off. It was clear, anyway.

To say that I was in shock would be a huge

understatement. Everything around me looked so real that I was confused – where was the true world and what was just a figment of my imagination. In addition, my blood-thirsty subconscious, which was more like a paranoiac maniac than an informed friend, added its own share of confusion.

"Now, that hurt." I got an immediate response from my apparently suicidal subconscious.

"Shut up. Stuff it and turn off your delicate emotions for now!" I barked in response. "Let's suppose you are right. I have two questions. Question number one, how do you know all this?"

"I read it somewhere. In one of the books we downloaded at Bernard's. I would like to note that the probability is quite high that you saw the books that your suzerain wanted to show you. He could foresee that you would need Leguria, and also that you would be caught in the mental trap. There are too many coincidences for that to be accidental."

I pursed my lips and reluctantly admitted:

"That's plausible... But that means Bernard can tell the future?" I asked with surprise, and then responded to myself: "Within the Game that would be cheating. It's impossible to predict the future, or the player would become invincible. If anyone were allowed to do such a thing it would have to be an NPC."

"Don't forget, Bernard is not a common being." Steve continued, unabashed. *"He has, within one body, two entities. Who can guarantee that the second being could not make predictions? Echo is not a player; it's generated by the Game itself."*

"Second question, smarty-pants," I cut off my invisible friend. "I can't move. How can I kill my family, Helen and myself? Come on: go for it! At this point I am ready to believe that I can do it by the power thought or by the force of me staring at them!"

"It's much simpler. I analyzed the possible scenarios and concluded that you need you use the Doll as a weapon." Steve's solution, once again, was anything but trivial.

As if she felt that I needed her, Helen looked back in the door as soon as the doctor left the room. Steve disappeared as if I had imagined him. I was looking at Helen and felt like an idiot. Now I had to tell the girl I loved that I wanted her to kill my family, then myself and in the end, herself as well.

"Helen, I need to talk to you. Everything you see here is not real. It's a trap! In order to escape it, we need to die. Don't be scared, I have thought it all through. You will turn off my life support system..."

"You must be crazy! No!" Helen shied away from the bed, terrified. Her eyes grew wide with amazement: "You are still in shock, to say such nonsense! This will pass! Don't you even dare to think of death. You can't imagine what we have gone through as we did not even know if you were alive or not! Mom aged twenty years in this time, she has had a heart attack, and you, ungrateful bastard, are asking me to do what?! Is that how you care about me and your family? I spent a day and a night at your bedside, not daring to sleep after your surgery, listening to you breathing!"

I swallowed nervously. Helen broke into tears

again, covering her face with her hands and making me feel like a right bastard indeed. They were waiting for me, they were trying to nurse me back to health and here I am demanding to be killed? Who am I after this?

The answer came instantly. I am Paladin Yaropolk! A 43rd level player with maximum allegiance to Darkness. And there is nothing but the Game! What I see in front of me is my property, and the whole purpose of its existence is to fulfill my orders and wishes!

"Helen, as your owner, I order you to call in my mother. I will ask her a question, and if she does not answer, or if she answers "Yaropolk" you will kill her and then my sister. After this you will lock the door, barricade it against the doctors and turn off the life support system. You will stop breathing at the same moment as I. When I die you will die as well. You are my Doll and you cannot resist a direct order. Do it!"

"Yes, master." The tears dried up in the girl's eyes instantly; now there was a robot in front of me. An obedient one, devoid of emotions and ready to fulfill its master's every whim. If the trap had extracted Helen from my mind as my ideal it could not fail to give it also the appropriate characteristics of the Doll.

Helen returned quickly to my mother.

"Dear, Nellie said you called me?"

"Mom, could you call me by name?" I asked and held my breath. More than anything in the world I wanted to hear the diminutive I had remembered since childhood. "Sergey-sunny-day".

My mother blinked several times, like a bird, and babbled:

"Sonny, what is this? Did you forget?"

"Mom, just tell me what my name is!"

Scared, the woman plopped down on a chair nearby and whispered:

"Yaropolk. sonny – Yaropolk."

I closed my eyes in order to distance myself from my surroundings, and nodded to Helen. I heard the crunch of bones and the sound of a body falling. Then the body was dragged aside. I supposed that Helen had just broken my mother's neck. The door opened and Helen called Sveta. A brief cry, and the same sequence of sounds. It was all over. I tried not to think about anything, pushing all thoughts away from me. Otherwise I would have gone crazy knowing that I just ordered my loved ones killed as I was right there.

The lock clicked and some furniture was moved to the door. I heard steps approaching; then finally the life support system went silent. I started choking – without pain or fear, as the painkillers and sedatives still worked. I almost drowned in the darkness when I heard the sound of another body falling. Thanks to the Game, it seemed as though we were done with that!

"Welcome back!" Steve did not conceal his joy as I returned into the grey fog. *"That's a clever trap. I am sure the owner has already been notified about the breach of the treasury."*

"Later, everything will wait. Where are the rest?" I did not feel cold any more, and the fog seemed quite ordinary as well.

"*I came back at the same time as you.*" Steve shrugged his shoulders. "*I expect they are nearby somewhere, trapped in their own visions. Shall we extract them?*"

"It's been barely two minutes." I checked the system time. "We can't leave them here. Let's find them."

I dropped to my knees and crawled around in a widening spiral, feeling the space around me. Even though I had defeated the trap, the fog showed no signs of dissipating. As I started the fifth circle, the search seemed pointless, but then my hand ran into something hard, and the familiar cold pierced my body. One rasping breath, and darkness swallowed my mind again.

This time I came to a lot more easily. Nothing hurt, and a brief look showed me that I was intact and battle-worthy. A bare plain stretched around me. Red plants were waving in a slight wind while leaden clouds churned in the sky, driven by a hurricane force wind. There was not a tree, not a stone, nor even a tiny hill all the way to the horizon. Only two beings decorated the blighted landscape. A beautiful femorc, and Alard kneeling before her. His head hung down despondently, and his cheeks were wet with tears.

"Who is this, Alard?" My appearance frightened the femorc, and she stepped to the side so that the orc was now standing between us. He turned his head and looked at me listlessly.

"A Paladin," Alard concluded, then immediately lost any interest in me and turned away. "Don't worry, Alune. A Paladin would not tarnish himself with unwarranted evil. There is no honor in that."

So the orc remembered this, even though he did not remember who I was. I kept my memory in someone else's mental trap, which was a definite plus. I could see Steve, the game panel and properties of the object I was looking at. Why was she an object? Because the femorc's description had a huge red note: "Alune, the Doll of the player Alard".

I had expected that my arrival would influence the orc's behavior. Since there was no honor in appearing weak to a stranger. But apparently, the emotional anchor was stronger than the concepts of honor drilled into him since childhood.

"Alard, I came for you." I was blunt. There was no point in procrastinating.

"For me?" the orc asked remotely, without taking his eyes off his "other half". "But you can see, brother, I am not done."

"I'll wait," I nodded without any understanding of what he was talking about. "But don't take too long."

"This I cannot promise." Despair was growing thicker in the orc's voice. "I am not a worthy Paladin; I cannot!"

"Alard, listen to me: listen carefully." The orc was already on edge. I could not guess what it was that he was unable to do, but I needed to help him immediately. The same way Steve helped me. "We are now in a mental trap of the treasury at Lecleur estate, and what you see around you is nothing but an illusion created by your fantasy. If you don't believe my words, take a look at this video. Give me an invite.

This is when we met; and this is us entering what turned out to be a trap. We are partners, and now you are going through one of the hardest moments in your life."

Thankfully, the orc did not resist, and extended me an invite for exchanging data. He closed his eyes, absorbed in looking through the materials prepared by Steve. First of all I needed to make sure Alard got his memory back; then we'd figure out how to get him out of here. A minute passed, then another. And another. The orc still would not open his eyes; tears kept rolling down his red face.

"Brother Yaropolk, I remember you," Alard's voice was barely audible, but at least I could hear reason in it. "I will not be able to do this again."

"Do what?"

"The orcs of Zagransh are a harsh people. There is no honor in being weak. When the Game grants player a Doll, he must send it into eternity. On his own. Not reject it, but kill it as his most shameful weakness. I remember this plain. This is where I sent to eternity my Alune. My life. And you know, brother, I don't believe it when my people welcomed it as the cleansing. I do not! Light should protect the weak...not kill them! There cannot be honor in that! But I did it. That was my duty before my father, my family and my chief. So then why are they forcing me again? I ... I cannot. If I don't do it, no one will know. Right, brother? You won't tell, right?"

Alard was staring at me expectantly. Alune put her hand on his shoulder and was staring too. The tears kept pouring silently onto the orc's red chest; I knew now that those were the rare tears of someone who was one of the bravest people. That's where they got their desperate courage. If you are capable of rejecting the happiness that was presented to you, you would easily give up your life in battle. Honor is above all.

"No, Alard. I will not tell, but Alune still has to die." That was honest; since I represented Darkness, I was bound to be the harbinger of dark news. The orc screwed his eyes angrily at me on hearing those words. "In order to escape the mental trap you need to die together with Alune. She is your emotional anchor here. Once she dies you will be free. All that I can do for you is serve as a weapon. At this moment it does not matter at all if there is honor in that or no. My Doll killed me because I ordered her; and by my order she died together with me."

Considering rightfully that it's better to show once than explain a hundred times, I showed Alard the last moments of my trap's existence. The orc viewed the video and stood still, thinking over what he saw. Alune pulled on his shoulder:

"There is no greater happiness than dying in my beloved's arms. Just hold me tight, Alard. And look into my eyes till the very end, until I see eternity. I know that you will go with me and we'll see each other again the instant we part."

The orc rose heavily and took Alune into a strong embrace. She put her arms around his neck. They stood there, motionless, looking into each other's eyes.

"You may do it, brother. Just do it quickly."

I activated the spikes and came to the motionless couple. My own code of honor was against hitting from the back, so I stood to the side. A sharp blow with all my strength, and Alard's body slumped, supported by the strong femorc.

She turned towards me, and the grimace of displeasure distorted her pretty face.

"Moron, couldn't you kill us both at once? You spoiled such a scene! So now what, in order to die in his arms I am supposed to hold him?"

My jaw dropped, it was so unexpected. And that was Alard's ideal? To hell with that! On the other hand, thinking about Logir... maybe they were all like that. As they say, don't judge and you won't be judged.

So as not to upset the femorc further, I swung my fist again. This time there were no mistakes. I critically looked at the couple in their post-mortem embrace. I could say that I had fulfilled their last wish.

Now I had to get out of here myself. The scrolls would be ideal for that. A loud pop, and I came to in Alard's arms.

"Thank you brother! You saved my life!" I heard the orc's voice. "There is no honor in crying about the past. We need to live in the present for the future. Let me embrace you. It's impossible to see anything here. How did you find me?"

Time was too precious to waste it in explanations, so I just promised to tell him all about it later. I was certain that the castle security had notified Iven of an unauthorized entry into the treasury, and the only thing that kept him from dragging us out by the scruff of our necks was the fact that he had been summoned by Bernard. It was unclear how long my suzerain would delay the Paladin, so we needed to hurry. I told the orc what he was supposed to do and started feeling through the area trying to find the druid on one side while Alard was working on the other.

I was the lucky one again. This third time my mind took me to a small room that looked more like a hermit's cell. Dolgunata was sitting on a straw cot facing me and looking at a photograph. A collar lay next to her. And even though tears seemed to be a necessary attribute for the emotional anchors – it had been true both for Alard and myself – I still had not expected to see Dolgunata crying. I was all the more confused and surprised. I just never knew what to do with crying girls. And here it was not some damsel crying: it was Dolgunata, Archibald's strong and independent student. I would have to say the trap was excellent: it did not miss its marks.

Doubtful what would be the best way to show myself so as not to encounter open aggression, I coughed quietly a couple of times.

"I know that I am within a mental trap and in order to get out I need to destroy the anchor and then die myself." Dolgunata had lived up to what was expected of her. I felt relieved now that everything was simpler than I had feared. "The problem is that there is nobody here to kill me."

"Have you considered suicide?" I was approaching slowly in tiny steps, led by my curiosity about the photo. But Nata quickly turned it face down.

"I have, but it's prohibited for me." The druid was almost defiant now. "I can only kill myself if I am in lethal danger. Here nothing threatens me directly, so I have to stay alive."

"It's a strange prohibition. Do you sometimes doubt Archibald's sanity?" I kept staring at the back of the photo The mental trap dragged our strongest emotional anchors to the surface. What memories did the druid have so that it was visualized only as a photograph and a collar? She did not even have her Doll here. And I had hoped to see first-hand just how perverted her imagination was regarding men or women. But maybe her kink was that she was not aroused by living beings? Now my mind was definitely wandering in the wrong direction. The druid's personal predilections were her own business. I even shook my head, chasing away any surmises of the role of that collar in Dolgunata's life.

"Never!" Nata replied emphatically, and smiled. "My teacher is brilliant and there are few who can compare to him."

I nodded sagely.

"You know best. So what is so brilliant about restraining your ability to commit suicide? Or were there precedents?" This situation was getting curiouser and curiouser. So then, Nata was not lying when she snorted at my Doll saying she did not need surrogates.

"Think whatever you will. That is not brilliance, but simply caring. But you cannot understand this!"

Now the druid was looking like a real common woman as never before. I should remember this moment in case I began doubting it yet again.

"A caring catorian is something outside of my reality. And using collars as well. Just don't try to tell me it's a flea collar and that you are reciprocating Archibald's care." I had the last word in that after all.

Dolgunata was tired of trying to explain herself, so she changed the topic:

"Did you find the orc?"

"Yes, I did, he's already waiting for us. Are you ready?"

"Just a moment," Dolgunata picked up the photograph and tore it into little pieces. Still unhappy with the result the druid threw the bits into her inventory. Then she drew her sword and with inexplicable fury cut up the collar. Once she was finished with the emotional anchor objects, she straightened up and lifted her chin proudly."I am officially stating: you killing me now does not in any way affect the duel and its outcome. You are doing it because I asked you myself. Go ahead, strike now!"

"So that you would know the weak points of my strike? You have enough protection to rival a heavy tank!" I grinned, extracting a "Templar's Blow" scroll. "We'll do it differently. I think I don't have to tell you where to stuff this for maximum damage? You have five seconds."

Nata just flashed her eyes at me, grabbed the scroll and held it to her throat. I grinned: the druid was anything but stupid, and knew very well that I also needed to know her weak spots. Now she "showed" me her "unprotected" throat, so that was definitely NOT the area I should go for.

Nata disappeared instantly; I supposed she must have simply dropped all of the protection she had. I gave her only one scroll on purpose, wanting to see how it would affect her protection. I doubted very much that had it been active it would have any effect on the druid. Now that I was alone here, I took out one more scroll.

"Stop!" Steve shouted once I did it. *"Stop!"*

I stopped and waited for my assistant to explain himself.

"Pieces of the photograph!" Steve was pointing at the place where the druid had stood just a moment ago. *"You cannot take out of the trap things that were created by it!"*

I looked at the small pieces of paper without Steve's enthusiasm. Dolgunata had torn the photo up so thoroughly that the largest piece was hardly bigger than a small fingernail.

"Just turn them all face up." My subconscious kept insisting despite my sound skepticism, prodding me all the while: *"We have no more than a couple of minutes; after that the druid might start suspecting something. Two minutes can be explained by having to prepare the scroll and to brace oneself. Come on! Go for it! You do want to know who was there on that photo! I will be able to show you!"*

The assistant kept working on convincing me while I was already scanning the photo pieces. It was not easy, given how little time we had. About half of the fragments were scattered face down and I had to turn them over without scattering the rest even further. Had I not had help from my artifact, which highlighted the ones that were not yet scanned in red, I could not have hoped for success.

"Now! Time is up!" Steve ordered, rubbing his hands with pleasure. *"We can't stay here any longer! I processed 87 percent of all fragments. That's more than enough!"*

I activated the scroll, and found myself in the treasury once again.

"It took you quite some time." The druid frowned suspiciously.

"It's not every day that I have to kill myself." I gave her the reply I had thought about in there. The druid said nothing. Even if she did not like that explanation, in any case there was nothing she could say to object. We were glad to see that the fog had dissipated. All the prey had escaped from the trap, so it became inactive; now we could see a long hallway lit by electric lamps, with a metal door. Behind the door a loud argument could be heard regarding how to fulfill Iven's order and stop the intruders, if the door was locked. He had promised to be there any minute.

We turned away from the door and took in the space in front of us. It resembled the passage I had had to go through in the Academy to reach Madonna's diary. If so, the mental trap was far from being the only obstacle we would have to face.

"Yari, what are you standing here for? Dolgunata was standing next to me now. "You think that's a trap corridor?"

"I am practically sure." I nodded. "I've been

though one like that already. Besides, one fog trap would really not be enough, I think."

"I agree. But we don't have time. Either they will force the door open, or else Iven will show up. We'll have to risk it and..."

"Trust the orc." Alard finished her sentence with a grin. He proudly extracted a small box from his inventory by way of explanation. "Traps are a task for Snufflesnout."

"A tracker?!" The druid exclaimed without hiding her joy. Apparently she had not counted on such a boon from fate.

"Brother knows how to use it?" Alard handed the box to me. "Brother Paladin is an explorer. My teacher said good explorers are rare. And that if I meet one, I should hold on to him and listen. It's an honor with our people to be friends with explorer. You can see the right way. The tracker will help.

"Give me five seconds." Steve had rolled up his sleeves, and even put on a pair of glasses; he was rolling the box in his hands, thinking. *"Press here. This must be the ON button... Now, here, adjust the handle. No, not this one... Then... You know, let's ask the orc, shall we? It will save us time."*

"Thank you, Alard, but it would be faster if you show me first." I had to admit I was not up to using it. Alard quickly showed how to use the device. Steve nodded, looked busy and generally indicated he supposed that would be the right way. Even though I knew exactly what my subconscious was doing. People are such people. Until the device is still in one piece, we would never use the manual; only when it starts breaking and smoking, we would start looking for the manual we had thrown out eons ago and leafing through the guidelines in contemplation of the developers' stupidity. Because we would have done it so much better!

"There are dynamic rays here." A minute later I was standing in the corridor and exploring the space around me. Steve showed the first obstacle, which was some laser rays that were moving chaotically, or so it seemed at first glance. Back, forth, sideways... even after a minute of analysis there was no discernible pattern to the movement. "Even if I were to pass through that, I wouldn't be able to guide you through."

Then there must be a switch somewhere," Nata stated. "I can't really imagine Iven jumping here to avoid the rays.

"The rays may be just nothing." The orc shrugged. "I am going in."

Before I had a chance to stop him, Alard rushed down the hallway.

"You can go now," he shouted from the other side. We could not evaluate the damage he sustained from the rays – the orc had no external symptoms. He did, however, drink an elves' ointment while he was waiting for us to join him. I checked the hallway with the tracker once again: the rays had disappeared as if they had never been there.

"Valiant, but stupid," Dolgunata mumbled. "Right in the spirit of the Paladin orcs. You, at least, activate your protection! The last thing I want is to have to keep going alone."

"Are you alive?" I asked once we reached the orc. But my concern was groundless: the orc's face had just turned pink, as if he had spent too much time in the sun.

"I am fine!" Alard hissed through his teeth. "Orcs are resilient! We need to move in that direction."

The orc pointed at the spiral staircase, which went straight down. Without waiting, Alard kept playing the spearhead and went down first.

"Come on down!" we heard him shout in a couple of minutes.

He did not have to ask us twice. We ran down hastily, and found ourselves in a huge space filled with neat rows of shelving. I was looking with some disappointment at a huge automated warehouse rather than a treasury. There were tags, numbers, mechanisms, rail tracks, points of acceptance and issue for the items stored on the shelves. Iven did not even need to come down here in person: computerized automatons would bring up anything requested on their own.

"The Lecleur's are obviously not begging," I drawled, looking at the shelves. Carefully arranged stacks of gold bullion towered up high to the ten-foot ceiling. There were transparent boxes with precious stones and jewelry, rolls of gold coins, rolled-up carpets, paintings in climate-controlled transparent containers... this storage had it all!

"How come they have accumulated such wealth?" Even Dolgunata was impressed with this picture. "Just the gold here is worth several thousand granises. I would have never imagined that the players who lived in the province could... Alard, are you sure you are OK?"

The orc was coughing madly, spitting clots of blood right there on the floor.

"Radiation," the orc rasped once he could talk. He sat on the floor exhausted but still managed to grin: "That was a lethal dose, the elves' ointment is not enough to overcome that. Go on without me. There is no honor in being a burden to you."

"Open your mouth!" Dolgunata ordered harshly and poured another portion of healing potion down the orc's throat. "Don't even think of dying here! Better if you run straight home then. You will go into the Reverse, hear me? Yari, what are you waiting for? Find the entrance and open it! The orc won't be able to hang on long!"

I had not expected such a reaction from the druid, and nearly missed the information provided by Steve that the Imperial set would protect Iven against the rays should he decide to visit the treasury personally. The shimmering entrance into the Reverse, visible only to me, was located a few yards away from the nearest shelf, but I was in no hurry to share my find. I had all my attention on the unit controlling the warehouse. I had never had to use a system like that, but as a child of the digital age I had a gut feeling that it was worth trying to figure out.

"Yari, come on! Look for the entrance!" Dolgunata repeated angrily, tearing herself away from the orc. Never before had the druid been known to exhibit such nonsense as love for orcs – love for humans was not her forte either – that made her actions look strange. Look out: Nata was going to become a saint and go praying with some priests. I chased away the persistent images of the druid in a nun's robe, and studied the control unit. The computer woke up from sleep mode, but was locked up. A small reader next to the monitor had a special slot which was exactly the same shape as the treasury key. Apparently I was in luck!

Dolgunata stared at me in surprise as soon as I asked for the key. She asked suspiciously if I were looking for the entrance before giving it to me. I unlocked the computer while assuring her that the search was the only thing on my mind. I was able to locate the search function pretty fast: at least whoever had developed the local software was familiar with the concept of a user friendly interface. I typed in the inquiry for "ring" and scanned the enormous list of things. I had to look at every line thoroughly. The druid could not wait any longer while I found my elusive "known unknown", yet she would not leave the orc.

"This is it! Send the robots!" Steve said enthusiastically, pointing at a line. I smiled. If the "Ring of Power" was not what I was looking for, then I must be a nun myself. So, the earrings I received through no effort of my own. The ring I stole like the damnedest... Well, whatever! One would be an idiot to miss such an opportunity. All that remained was to find the pendant in the Reverse. I hoped greatly that by collecting in one place the whole set that used to be called "Joy" and handing it to the owner would bring me just a step closer to Madonna.

The chance that the set worked as a compass of a sort was negligibly small, but I still could not afford to miss it!

CHAPTER NINE

THE REVERSE

"WHAT ARE YOU doing?" As soon as the system came into motion, Dolgunata realized that all that time I had been lying to her while pursuing my own objectives. A robotic arm rushed into the warehouse along the rails; very soon it returned with a small container.

"Get moving!" I ordered, stuffing the little box into my inventory and ignoring the druid. That's when the alarm went off. "Quick! We must make it!"

As I was running, I pulled out the key to the Reverse and rushed towards the glimmering doors that only I could see. Good thing we hurried – white foam that solidified instantly started pouring from the ceiling. Logically thinking, it was obvious that if we were caught in it, there would be no hope of escaping. The bulk of this nasty stuff accumulated near the exit, blocking it completely; a few rivulets trickled over the floor of the treasury. To avoid it we had to jump like grasshoppers from one shelf to another towards the entrance. That was the only way to move around the warehouse now. Nata grabbed the orc like a piece of fluff, and dashed after me, deftly avoiding the streams of dripping foam.

Actually, we were incredibly lucky. One stroke of luck was that the entrance to the Reverse was close to us but directly opposite the treasury entrance. Another was that as we approached, the door became visible to the others. Yet another was that Dolgunata was strong enough to throw in the huge orc and then jump into the passage that I had opened from three meters away. However, I doubted that the latter was simply a stroke of luck. It was quite likely that the druid was beside herself – barking mad because of what I had done in the treasury. In any case, the second leg of our quest was completed successfully. The moment I shut the door, cutting off the foam flows, the passage was plunged into complete darkness. I figured out where the druid was by her angry and therefore noisy huffs, and hastened to get out of her way, following the golden rule of drivers: "Keep back". It would be difficult to start the search for the pendant while being torn into a hundred little paladins.

The serendipitous druid, led by her desire to kill me here and now, lit a lamp right away.

"Are you a total moron?!" Nata hissed through

her teeth. Had she been a dragon, her flaring nostrils would definitely have breathed fire. "Do you understand you put us all at risk? Do you understand that because of you we nearly failed the quest? What did you take from the treasury? And don't you dare lie to me, you cretin!"

With each word the druid came closer and closer, making me retreat. I said nothing, just trying to drag out the time, so that she would blow off some steam without physical contact with me. It would hurt my feelings more than my body. If I were to be beaten by a girl, at least it would be better if it were to happen at the duel tomorrow; at least I would keep some semblance of dignity that way.

"Sister, there is no honor in...," Alard started rasping something to back me up, but the druid was not going to stand on ceremony with him.

"I am not talking to you!" The druid harshly turned towards the one she had just recently been protecting fiercely, transformed her right hand into a panther's paw, and easily cut off the red-skinned one's head. Her claws flashed in the dim light. Silence dropped over the Reverse. I used the pause to activate my defense. It would be silly to be sent to respawn because of a girl's moodiness, particularly now that we had reached our goal. I was in no hurry to take the first step, wary that I would provoke another fit of fury. To my relief, Dolgunata calmly withdrew her claws.

"Consider yourself lucky. Tomorrow, during the duel, your death will not be easy. I promise!" the druid smirked, and shrugged her shoulders in a very feminine way. Then she turned away and took care of the lamp, turning down the flame. I looked at my partner in bewilderment, completely taken aback by this turn of events. One moment she was protecting the orc like a mother, then the next moment she killed him casually in cold blood. Where was the logic in that? "I will ask you later about the thing you stole from the treasury. Now is not a good time."

I was able to see the logic a couple of minutes later once Nata took out her comm and called the teacher:

"Archibald, we are on location. We have gained access; the anchor works."

A portal opened next to us and the catorian came out of it purposefully, casting a measuring glance at the darkness around us.

"Amazing: it does exist!" Archibald drawled, obviously pleased. "Do you have the key to the Reverse?"

"No, Yari does. I have not had time to take it away from him yet," Dolgunata responded. That made me raise my defenses another notch. In the best tradition of game relationships they had already decided everything about me, not bothering to inform me. I noted dryly to myself that I had stopped having any feelings about that. Must be getting used to it.

"I see..." Archibald said slowly and shifted his measuring gaze to me, looking me over from head to toe. "That's yet another blunder, student," he said to Nata. "Before calling me, you should have made sure that you had all the necessary tools for staying in the Reverse. You have failed at that."

"I need one minute." Nata snorted. "It will be enough..."

"No it won't." My breath caught as Archibald beheaded Dolgunata with a quick flick of his sword. The druid's body crashed onto the floor while her head flew a couple of yards through the air and landed somewhere in the darkness. Seemed as though today was some kind of "Off with their heads!" day! But you could always tell a virtuoso – the druid was just a dabbler compared to him. I expect that would not be the last time the catorian would play the executioner to his student, and that Dolgunata, in her turn, would saw his furry ears off with a dull saw.

Archibald twitched his ears in displeasure, and kicked the leg of her headless body that was lying inconveniently across the hallway:

"I will have to continue with you, my hapless student. Don't bother wasting Energy trying to protect yourself. If I had decided to get rid of you, I would have done so by now. Although, whatever... An illusion of safety would do you good." The catorian waved his hand in the air, picked up the lantern and calmly started down the hallway. As he turned the corner I was left without the light, and Steve hastened to visualize the space around me, allowing me to get my bearings in the dark. I was in no hurry to catch up with the catorian. Quite the opposite – I stayed where I was, waiting for him to return, and preparing to bargain with all my might. I rightly considered that if Archibald needed me so much – and that had been demonstrated by the scene of getting rid of the unnecessary members of the team I had just witnessed – his furry highness would in fact stoop to explain, and then I would be able to demand a hefty piece of the loot. Otherwise I could just as well stick my spikes into my own neck and return to the respawn point. The key would then return to Madame Lecleur, I would be left without the pendant, while the catorian will not get his stroll through the Reverse. I was sure that this prospect would be about as pleasant as a kick in the balls for more than one party. So I simply waited for the negotiations, that promised to be pleasant in more ways than one.

"According to my information, only three players can be within the Reverse at the same time," the catorian purred straight into my ear. He actually managed to tickle me with his whiskers to boot. I jerked my head in the other direction – first in surprise and then in disgust. That was so like Archibald, to switch off the light and return silently in the dark, to set the stage just right for his victim. "There is a standard restriction for places like this. The number of visitors is set at the initial entry and cannot be changed. Had my dim student not dragged a live orc here, she would not have been able to invite me in. Now I have done the same thing. We have no information as to what kind of Keeper is lurking in wait for us here or what traps we could encounter along the way towards him. Therefore, I need a real helper, not a sorry sight of one who barely completed the training. So the choice was between you and Dolgunata. You won since you hold the key to the Reverse. It's quite simple. Are you satisfied, or do you want me to do a little song and dance for you in addition?"

The halo fell off the druid's head with a loud clang, and I could breathe a sigh of relief. There was a method to her madness. A logic that my male mind could follow. She treated the orc and cared for him in order to get the teacher in; then she killed him for the same purpose. Also, her killing now fit within my familiar perception of this world.

"A true helper? Let me guess. You are going to drag Devir here."

"Aren't you a smartie." The Paladin lowered his head and looked at me from under his eyebrows. "You can do it after all, when the respawn point is the only alternative."

"Now I did not get any of that."

"Maybe I was too hasty with praise." A comm call sounded in silence. "Devir, greetings! I have a great offer to you: a stroll through Marcus' Reverse together with me. Respawn without a chance to come back, torture, pain and hellish level-up are guaranteed. Are you in?"

"You have to ask?!" I could hear the mage's enthusiasm so clearly that I would not be surprised had Devir jumped out right from the comm's speaker. "Who's the third?"

"Does it matter?" Was I the only one immensely irritated by Archibald's habit of answering a question with another question?

"You don't do things that don't matter," the mage smirked. "The only living one I see is Yari, Dolgunata and Sakhray are out. So, then, I don't have to worry. You have cannon fodder available."

"You have a minute to decide, then I'll wipe out your tracker mark." The catorian cut him off and dropped the call.

"There's nothing to decide." The darkness around us faded from the blue portal and Devir joined us. "I said I was in."

Turning towards me, Devir joked about himself being right, and pointed out my mistakes:

"Yaropolk, you really ought to clean up other people's trackers on you, at least sometimes. You shine like Tokyo viewed from space! Archibald, he really is a shame to you. What will they think about you as a teacher?"

"There is a large room right around the corner." The catorian ignored the comment and started describing the task. "The two of us go. Yaropolk stands at the door and keeps out of it."

"We share loot fifty-fifty?" The mage clarified matter-of-factly.

"Forty-five each to us, ten to Yaropolk," Archibald corrected him magnanimously, and the hunters, pleased with themselves, started down the hallway. "I think the floor is out. Marcus likes to floor one with surprises. It would be better... Yaropolk, now what?"

The catorian was asking evenly, but without hiding his irritation. I quickly caught up with the player and launched into a list:

"First of all I want to know what I got myself into, and in detail. Second of all: ten percent? Oh really? Did I hear you right? I consider that I have rightfully earned already half of what is available here; you two are welcome to share the rest. Either you accept my conditions, or I leave for the Sanctuary and shut the Reverse. I have the key."

"Dearest child, the only way for you to leave the Reverse is feet first," Devir interjected. "Teleports don't open from here, and completing Marcus's reverse is as unrealistic as imagining Archibald a caring teacher. We are all doomed here."

"That's not a problem." I shrugged. "You will not even get a shot at passing through the Reverse; your losses will be far greater than mine. What is a level for me and for you? There's simply no comparison. And another thing: do I understand correctly that you don't care about the Lecleur pendant? So then why am I here? For your fun and potential ten percent?"

Silence hung over us. I really had nothing to lose, so I demonstratively activated my artifact and extended the spikes. As I knew, darkness was not a problem for those two.

"Do you know that the Reverse is not a natural phenomenon? When I was getting the key in the place that you know of," Archibald said finally, "I found out who was the maker of this Reverse. It was made by Marcus; he is a pedantic dorky gnome from the Center of the Game. He is known for his fondness for designing traps. However, he has a weakness: he likes to reward crafty players by building a lot of cool nice gifts into the Reverse. Even the client would not know what kind of Easter eggs his Reverse might be hiding and how to pass through it properly. But that makes it all the more interesting, no?"

Archibald paused, letting me think over the information he had presented and prepare for more. What a show-off!

"Naturally, Iven has a direct portal to the end point, which makes it unnecessary for him to pass through. If one were to evaluate his abilities in all fairness, he would not advance beyond the first room. I know what I am talking about. I have seen seven of those labyrinths with my own eyes; the highest personal record is completing the second room. Do you realize yet what you have gotten yourself into, or should I go into further detail about things that should be obvious even to an idiot?"

"What about the pendant and the share of loot?" By now I was already immune to the sarcasm in Archibald's voice, so it did not affect my business skills.

"There is nothing about the pendant. The problems of Iven and his offspring are just that: problems of Iven and his offspring. If he desires to restrict his daughter in her moves, no one can forbid this, except, perhaps, the Game itself, since it initiated a hundred quests. Once I get back to Gerhard and report my information to him, he'll interrogate Iven and everything will become clear. What's the point of wasting time on this? There are much more interesting things than that. For example, why in hell you think you are entitled to fifty percent of the loot? I got the key from the treasury, Dolgunata brought everyone here, not you. Devir and I will be doing the work, not you. Are you out of your mind, bringing up numbers like that?"

"Your information about my role is distorted. I found the information about the Reverse, I established trust with Sophie, and I was the one who obtained the key to the Reverse, as well. And there is another thing: had it not been for me, Dolgunata would still be wailing and drooling on the floor and would never have made it to the treasury! All she did was push the orc and herself into the Reverse once the alarms went off. But that was exclusively so that you and Devir could enter here!" I parried, trying not to betray my anger at being simply used to get to potential loot, when Archibald had no intentions to help with the pendant. "That's definitely more than ten percent. I suggest we split it even. One-third each."

"Listen, let's go already, shall we?" Devir snorted addressing the catorian. "I could understand Yaropolk; what do you do with a puppy like that? He'll fight for every granis. But what are you bargaining for? Should Yaropolk get a hundred granises, we'll just bump him off at the order of the Game, and no big deal. Why are you in such a huff?"

"Me, me, me... you are a loudspeaker." Archibald sighed. "You would do well to use your brain instead of your mouth. Later he'll shout at every corner that his teacher robbed him blind. So I have to take care of my reputation and in addition of the well-being of this twit, since he is unwilling to do it himself. Where else will I find such a knucklehead if they start hunting him? And stop your hooting!"

"There are only granises here? No objects?" I drawled with disappointment.

"Marcus is certainly brilliant, but he is not the Creator," Devir snorted. "How would he know what class player would decide to try his traps? And what specialty? What artifact would he have? What if a dark one were to receive a source of Light? Yaropolk, please stop playing dumb. We are losing time. As far as I know, Iven is already close. He ran off from Bernard's, saying his estate was compromised. Could there be a chance he has another key to the Reverse?"

"Another key would not help him," I explained briefly. "It would be a trifle difficult to reach the entrance. The treasury is blocked."

"What did you take?" Archibald reacted, and in his voice I clearly heard disappointment with himself: he had killed Dolgunata before she had reported the latest events. The catorian had believed we had entered the Reverse without extra glitches.

"Nothing." I cut him off. "My share is seven granises right away, all the objects if there are any to be found here, and ten percent that will be temporarily kept by Archibald."

Before voicing my new proposal I checked the balance: "Terror" would be about the last thing I needed now.

"We agree. Is that it, finally?" Archibald dropped impatiently.

There was no reason to drag it out and I agreed:

"One could say so."

The Paladin snorted into his whiskers, turned around and said as he was walking:

"Go on, I am listening! But I swear, if you buck

once again or get in our way I'll just lose it and send you for respawn myself!"

Suddenly a halo of white light flashed around Archibald, indicating that the Game accepted his oath. The catorian purred something very expressive, and Devir nodded with restraint. I was following them quietly, the way it becomes a student, the very picture of humility and diligence.

"I get it. Well, actually, I wanted to ask: why, of all the creatures in the Game, did you chose Devir? How about a thousand years of feud and relentless fighting? Another lie?"

"Why would that be? Personal disagreements are nothing compared to the opportunity to play with Marcus' Reverse," Devir clarified. "There are no opponents here, Yaropolk. Here we have a common goal: to go as far as possible and grab as much as possible. For such an endeavor any enmity can be put aside for a while so that it's ok to show your back to your ally. Until we respawn, of course. Afterwards it will be my pleasure to play some dirty trick on Archibald, and he will respond in kind. It's all a game, Yaropolk, and it's time that you learn how to be flexible, curb your pride and look for compromise."

"The hall is all criss-crossed with rays. I would bet that there are traps on the floor as well. We'll need hooks." Archibald did not even bother to answer, returning to discussing tactics.

"Marcus is unlikely to repeat himself." Devir lost all interest in me as well, indicating that all my whims were reviewed, accepted and no one was going to waste any more time on the newbie. "Did you find out what the nature of the rays was?"

The players started down the hall, discussing tactics for passing the upcoming trap. I kept quiet and followed them slowly. After a few turns that I negotiated by feel in the dark, finally I was able to see the entrance to a large well-lit room. The light stopped at the door, not reaching the hallway floor as it would in normal life. It was just hanging in the surrounding darkness, a regular rectangle that looked so alien it made you want either wipe it out or extend it. Archibald and Devir were standing right at the edge, studying the hall with advanced trackers. Steve was gradually becoming familiar with those gadgets.

I took out the device that I had borrowed temporarily from Alard and started exploring as well; that caused ironic comments aimed at me with the general deep thought along the lines of whatever the kid does is fine as long as he keeps silent and out from underfoot. I proudly adjusted the settings on the device they disdainfully called obsolete and rendered the dynamic rays visible. The only thing that could be said about them with certainty was that there was no obvious algorithm controlling their movement. Steve spent some time analyzing them, but his verdict only confirmed my observation. Another thing my assistant noted was that those were precisely the same rays we had encountered earlier in the hallway – the ones that had killed the orc.

"It's radiation." I shared my conclusion even though no one was asking me. I did not actually count on any response; I was just stating my observation about the nature of the rays to myself.

However, Devir did not let it go unnoticed, and asked why I thought so. I told him how we had made it to the main treasury and lost the orc in the process.

"Revol?" Devir addressed Archibald again."Seems very much like it."

"Most likely." The catorian nodded, and his tail twitched nervously. "I just hate it so much."

"You don't find it strange? The only race immune to these rays is catorians. Marcus is perfectly aware of you."

"As well as of my 'friendly' relationship with Iven." Archibald interrupted the mage, seeing where the latter was going. "But I agree, it's too easy for the first test."

"Would you let me look at the room through your tracker?" I barged into the conversation, angling for a more significant role than a silent and convenient piece of furniture.

"Archibald: tell me, for the sake of the days I spent as your student, are you losing your edge? Or is it that ignorance is not considered a flaw in your students any more?" Devir grinned without as much as looking in my direction. "To allow students to open their mouths without permission... I would have ended up parking at the respawn point in my time."

Even though his words were addressed to the catorian, it was obvious that they were aimed at shaming me. "Come to the Sanctuary; we shall talk; I am different from what they all think of me..." Twit in a gown! He still has to answer to me for Monstrichello!

"So maybe the teacher's attitude had to do purely with your abilities. You are a common mediocrity, which can be helped only by dumb drill exercise. While I am a talent that should not be constrained, or else there will not be enough space for me to develop," I parried, and grinned, seeing Devir's narrowed eyes. He was a dangerous enemy, no question about it, but at this time only Archibald has the right to mock me. And even so, I will make him pay for that later.

"I look at you and consider that maybe I should do you a favor and remove your tongue so that it does not hinder your talent from developing. Just to make sure that your entire head does not suffer from its wagging." The catorian was smiling openly. He liked my quip, and he handed me his instrument as a way of encouragement. "Iven, Devir. You don't waste time on small stuff?"

"You are forgetting yourself. Number one on my list." I studied the room through the prism of the new tracker. No change. Just the rays and nothing else.

"The floor," Steve piped up, showing an elaborate winding pattern. *"The dust in the room is distributed unevenly. A very long time ago someone passed along this path, and left a barely visible track after him. Squat down, I need to check it out from another angle."*

I returned the device to the catorian and strolled several times from one wall of the hallway to the other, allowing Steve to see the thickness of the dust layer from different angles. Apparently the teacher realized that I was circling the hallway for a reason, and made a meowing sound requiring that I share the information. Steve generated an image, and

I offered the exchange to the catorian.

"Look at the dust on the floor. In some locations the layer is thinner than in others. There are no drafts here, therefore, something pressed the dust down there. Most likely it was someone's feet; this gives us the path.

"You are trying to convince us that within a couple of minutes you were able to scan the room in detail and perform a comparative analysis of the thickness of the dust layer in different locations? Barely a week after the Academy?" Devir asked suspiciously.

"I told you I was talented! I said with a certain pride. The frowning face of Archibald as he was studying the path was my sweetest reward. I was able to prove that I was good as more than just cannon fodder. "I am an explorer. Perception is my tool, and information is my weapon."

"Come closer to the edge, I need to check something else," Steve asked me. *"Look, in some places the dust is compacted more than in others. As if someone was pressing down on it there with more effort. Were they jumping? But if so, they should have disturbed the dust a lot more at the point where they landed. And there is no sign of that. Therefore they did the opposite: they squatted. Look, those two rays are moving in a pattern different from the others. What if they are not 'revol', whatever that means?"*

I had no idea how my assistant was able to discern the microscopic differences in the thickness of dust layer from one location to the other, but I agreed with his conclusions. The two rays in fact did stop over the "squat points", deflecting by barely a dozen centimeters. I had to prepare the new map and inform my partners of the updated information.

"Now this room looks more like Marcus' creation." Amazingly, the catorian was actually more pleased with the new data. From an excess of positive emotions my teacher became more talkative: "The gnome loves triple tests. Revol, floor and two rays is a plausible trio that can grant us passage through the first room. Devir, you are responsible for Yari. Yaropolk, don't do anything stupid, I warn you! I need a minute to work on this.

Archibald settled on the floor in the lotus position, and stilled. The catorian's eyes remained open, which was misleading. In fact, while the Paladin's body stayed here, his mind had departed, and was now trying, again and again, to complete the first room in some kind of timeless training range. The seeming defenselessness of Archibald's body was an illusion as well. If one were to approach closer than a meter, a wall of protective field activated around him, going way up above. Only an imbecile with a death wish would try to test its strength.

"I want to give you some very useful advice, Yaropolk." Suddenly Devir addressed me in quite a friendly tone. "Tone down your airs. Archibald is not a creature to pay attention to formalities, so he dismissed that incident. At worst, he'll make a joke of it later. But not everyone in the Game is like that. Had you been careless enough to have a go at me like that in a different situation in front of others, I would have no choice other than to declare war on you, until

I totally wiped you out. Forget about Bernard and his protection. Only those who can stand up to their word at any time can afford to openly deride another player. Insolence indicates implied strength. I do not want to be your enemy. I like you, and I was even impressed by how you completed the Academy. If you decide to become a hunter, I would be glad to recommend you to a good teacher, or even take you on as my own student. You have signs indicating you would be a good hunter. A talented man is talented in everything, right? But that's only if you keep yourself on an even footing. I am not going to lose my reputation over a high-handed moron. If you want to be a dead man, you have every right."

It was said in such a way that I admitted the validity of the comment without hesitation, and nodded, indicating my understanding.

"Why did not a friend of the family return the earrings to one of the Lecleurs?" I wanted to clarify the issue that had been bothering me for a while.

"What a good question," Devir grinned. I will answer it after we complete the Reverse. Archibald will return from his testing range at any moment now; I would rather not talk about Paladins in the presence of the interested party. Secrets should remain secret."

So that's where the mind of the meditating Paladin was at the moment. There were so many things in the Game that I did not know; moreover, I had not the slightest inkling of their existence! Steve provided a brief clarification on that wonder. A virtual training range was intended to model conditions close to real ones; it enabled the owner to train on real battle tactics and working on obstacles, honing every move to perfection for years. The time you could spend in a virtual training range was extended compared to the general game time, even though it was not infinite as with normal timeless pockets. Archibald and Devir were the best, definitely, but now it became clear how they had become the best. Improvisation and sixth sense? Three ha-ha's! Exhaustive training sessions in the virtual range!

"Is it possible to buy a range like that somewhere, or is it a reward for some special feat?"

"You can buy it; it only costs two granises," Archibald answered as he returned and got to his feet. "They are made by Leonardo from Vinci world. Yes, that very Leonardo: a copy of his Gioconda is hanging in the Louvre. Actually, that's when we all bought our ranges – while he was here on Earth. It's a pity it's impossible to get a thing like that now."

"Why is it not possible to pay a visit to Leonardo at Vinci and buy a couple more?"I felt confused.

"Vinci is located in the center of the Game, thirteen sectors away from Earth. A sector is a cluster of game worlds governed by one Coordinator. Coordinators are the ones who control and concur with players' travel between sectors, and charge fees for that. For example, the passage from our sector to the neighboring one costs twenty basic granises and fifty Grandeur – it will be debited from your account as if it never existed. With each sector nearer to the center of the Game, the fees for transition become steeper. As I mentioned, there are thirteen sectors between us. That's number one. Now to number two: Vinci is not a normal world. It's a planet of masters who have dedicated themselves and their game to creating artifacts. There is no need to mention how tightly all the Viceroys and their advisors control the planet. Vinci even has its own auction that is separate from the main one. In effect, it's a local prison; once you are in it, it is practically impossible to leave. And I am too poor to visit good old Leonardo. But by itself, yes, the range costs two granises."

"Enough of that pap. As though poverty favors the young," I said, upset, as I had already developed a hope to obtain a personal training range, but then my hopes were cruelly dashed. "I was informed of the prices you and Devir charge for your services, so let's just pretend that I believed you. Since there is no honor for a teacher in misleading an inexperienced student!"

"I don't really like your tone, but I'll let you live for now. But we'll get back to that conversation, we definitely will. Here I go!"

The catorian dove into the hall, moving like a dancer trying to portray a raging flame. He flowed smoothly from one point to another without stopping for an instant. I held my breath without noticing it, looking at the movements of my teacher. A jump, leaning back at the verge of what is physically possible, jump, return and squat, and jump again. Not a single wasted movement. I watched with an overlay of the picture constructed by Steve, and noted with pleasure that his steps were absolutely precisely in line with the trajectory he had planned. It was art worthy of admiration.

"The first room is ours!" I heard the catorian's voice, and I started breathing again. Archibald shone with pure joy, without hiding behind his habitual mask of spite and sarcasm. The catorian was doing what he liked most, and now enjoyed every moment.

"How much?" Devir asked practically, carelessly striding towards Archibald directly across the room. I waited to make sure that the mage was not blasted to smithereens, and only then followed him.

"One hundred and twenty two granises," the Paladin responded, rubbing his paws with pleasure, his tail twitching in anticipation of further adventures. "The first one is the easiest, that's why it's so few. Here, there's your share."

You completed Hall One of the Reverse of Lecleur Estate. Grandeur +3

Subsequent movement resembled a snail race. Archibald and Devir literally crawled on all fours examining every crack of the blasted corridor, worried about stumbling into surprises from the maker of the Reverse. I checked the time and sighed heavily: in three hours the necromancers would show up and start their rampage, and I am stuck here. With each passing second the hope of collecting the entire set of the pendant, ring and earrings faded; the limitation on the loot did not make things look brighter either. I was hoping that at least Mizardine would do things as he was supposed to.

"Second hall," Archibald commented excitedly. Only having made sure that the corridors were relatively safe did the hunters move forward; after a few turns we reached the second goal. Neither my tracker nor the more advanced artifact of my companions found traces of any rays. Surprisingly, there was no dust either. The hall looked sterile like a freshly washed surgical room. Or clean as a cat's balls after he had licked them all day, since we had a catorian on our team.

"Any ideas?"

"The classic. Floor, gas, motion sensors." Devir hazarded a guess. "Instruments show nothing suspicious."

"Yari?"

"Nothing on mine either." I had to agree with the mage. "It feels like the hall was washed and preserved that way. No dust, no footprints. Is that actually possible?"

"Actually no – that's the thing." Archibald thought a little, then grinned and extended one fist towards Devir. "Rock-paper-scissors?"

"With you?!" The mage was clearly amused. "Not in this Game. You have a hundred aces up... each sleeve. Even when we play backgammon, you still manage to pull off something or other. So I'll just go straight in."

"I had to create an illusion of it being your own choice." Archibald shrugged. "Move, that way you have a chance to hang in there longer. Or maybe not. Go on!"

Before we figured it out, Archibald pushed

Devir out into the room and activated his tracker. The mage activated his defenses, stopped a step away from the entrance, and even bent his head down, not knowing what to expect of Marcus' creation. Nothing happened.

"Move!" Archibald ordered again, causally pointing his paw at the far side of the room. "Devir, you are disappointing me. Go, go on! We are losing time! I still can't see anything!"

"Strangely, neither do I!" Devir responded, nonplussed, and started moving in the direction specified. At first the mage was tense and very alert, but with every step confidence straightened his well-trained body, and by the time he reached the other side his steps were light and springy. Devir safely reached the exit from the hall, turned around and spread his hands, puzzled. Either the traps, for some reason, had not activated, or the mage's defense absorbed all the impact.

"This is impossible." Archibald was scratching behind his ear in a way totally incongruous to a player as experienced as he. But he could not understand what was going on. Tired of guessing, he crossed the room in a few giant leaps. But the hall remained indifferent to the catorian's appearance as well, making us all suppose that there were no traps altogether.

You completed Hall Two of the Reverse of Lecleur Estate. Grandeur +5

The headhunters greeted my approach with

sullen silence. There was no other loot besides Grandeur.

"Had it not been for the first hall, I would have supposed that someone had already passed through the Reverse." Devir pointed out the obvious conclusion. "But this is impossible. One could not have jumped straight to the second hall. Or else I am missing something."

"There is some 'Keeper' within the Reverse." I offered a reminder to Archibald. "What if it's he? Or Iven. You said yourself that he has a direct teleport to the Keeper."

"The second version seems more likely to me," Archibald said thoughtfully. "Could that golden ass have jumped ahead of us? And left the first hall intact as bait to drive away unwanted visitors?"

"I can't agree with you," Devir immediately started arguing. "I am in favor of the first theory. Suppose that the guard is not a player, but just an NPC; one could explain the absence of loot and the availability of Grandeur. He went through the Reverse first, but we are the first players who have entered this hall. Had it been Iven, he would have received the Grandeur."

"It's absurd!" In that case Reverses would be knee-deep in NPCs, while clever players would be skimming the cream." Archibald cut him off. "What difference does it make whether an NPC or a player passed through the hall? He would have collected the Grandeur, not we! Let's keep going!"

We rushed through the next corridor without bothering with such silliness as looking for traps.

Devir, without much ado, entered the next hall. Nothing. No explosions, no rays, no enormous rock dropping on his head to punish him for insolence. The traps were deactivated, if they had ever existed at all.

You completed Hall Three of the Reverse of Lecleur Estate. Grandeur +10

"That was rash." Archibald commented as soon as the next message flashed before my eyes. "I would rather not lose you so early on."

"Do you agree now that someone has gone through the Reverse? Besides, they were starting from there!" Devir pointed to the continuing corridor. "Who could go through the traps starting from the impossible and ending with a common one?"

"And this superhero was stopped by revol rays." I made a comment and instructed Steve to analyze the footprints in the dust one more time. "Look, these are the prints I found at the exit from the first room. And these are the prints Archibald followed to complete the first room. These are two different beings, even though both sets of prints are small."

"The prints inside the hall are really tiny," Devir said slowly, analyzing the new data. "It's, like, barely size 5. Could it be a child?"

"Or a gnome. Or a leprechaun. Or a lesser demon from the Underworld." Archibald was aggravated by the now inarguable fact that someone was more successful, so he vented all his irritation on those around him.

"Demons don't wear boots," I objected.

Devir pointed at the catorian with his eyes and whispered:

"Why not? Cats apparently have no problems at all with that." I glanced appraisingly at the catorian's steel boots, thinking that Earth folklore had not exaggerated much, after all.

"I think Marcus left his own footprints within the hall, and did it on purpose. Like a little hint. And the footprints at the exit belong to our mysterious Keeper. We'll see it at the next hall. If it's also empty, I'll eat my own tail, but I will make the acquaintance of this unique creature." Archibald did not as much as twitch his furry ear at the mage's barb.

A few minutes later, completely unharmed, Devir stood in the middle of the fourth room, looking sarcastically at the glum Archibald and the mad flicking of his equally glum tail. I started towards the mage, but the catorian stopped me with a gesture:

"Yaropolk, do you like presents? I have one for you. Here." An oblong object with a big red button in the middle appeared in the Paladin's hands. "Push it as soon as the message appears and imagine that you are in an anger room. Just make sure you don't go overboard. You will tell me about your impression later."

"What is this?" I was in no hurry to accept unexpected gifts.

"Absolute space blocker." Devir came back and nodded to the Paladin gratefully. "It blocks everything alive within a hundred yards for an hour. Except for the one who pushed the button. It cannot be used twice. Thank you. I missed that completely. And I will need help too."

"I will be holding this red rag in my hands." Archibald pulled out a piece of cloth. "Don't get confused."

"Could you share it?" The mage asked in all seriousness and, amazingly, the catorian obliged him. Both immediately stuffed their pieces into their pockets.

"How many of you will there be?" I asked, stunned, having figured out the nature of the request. After the next hall both Archibald and Devir will have received enough Grandeur to exceed another hundred, and the Game will happily generate their echoes. One for each hundred Grandeur.

"Enough to make it in an hour." Archibald cut me off. "One has to say everything aloud to you, so I will explain: if anyone were to find out how many echoes I have generated, we will quarrel bitterly, and the consequences for you will be quite unpleasant."

"I would say the same." The mage was not about to stand aside, and joined the threatening. "Our relationship is far from perfect anyway, so don't make it worse. Not a soul, Yaropolk!"

"Pfft! Like that's a great secret!" the catorian snorted. "Your Grandeur level is a secret everyone knows. There are forty-two fake Devirs, my lucky student. Forty-two times you get to kill this nincompoop in every way possible. And as for the forty-third you are welcome even to violate him in some violent way before killing. I will not be offended if only the two of us continue after that. The Moor has done his duty."

"For those especially talented, Yaropolk, this was a poor and dumb joke in the spirit of catorians." Devir flashed me a smile full of open menace. "I must see the Keeper who has passed practically through the entire Reverse and put Archibald himself into his proper place. This is going to be an interesting meeting."

"You are talking as if you have already decided everything for me and are just presenting the facts to me." I waited for the headhunters to finish talking and decided to fight for my rights. "I have a question: what am I going to get in return? Killing forty-two echoes who are as strong as Devir is no joke at all; I would have to work hard at it. As for Archibald, I just tremble, imagining the number of furries I'll have to drown in some bucket. PETA would eat me alive, if they found out about this. Moral satisfaction from the process is not really a sufficient reward. So I would like to receive some hefty bonus, since it did not work out with the granises. I know what happens when the echo touches its initiator, even through a sword. Are you really so sure of me that you entrust me with your lives? I am flattered, sure, but what if it will be more fun for me to do nothing at all, just stand there for an hour? And don't ask me what I want: surprise me!"

"Good relations is not enough for you?" the mage said testily, to which I parried:

"Good relations don't pay the rent, and that will not prevent you from killing me at the exit of the Reverse, so that I would not spread around your great secret."

"That's the feeling when your student justifies all the effort you poured into him, at least to some extent." The catorian's furry face suddenly beamed. "I promise you a reward for destroying the echoes, both mine and Devir's, but only after we leave the Reverse. And believe me, if you consider this not to be a great reward, I will give you my training range. Agreed?"

Not only did I stare at Archibald in amazement, but Devir did as well. The mage obviously did not expect that kind of "present" from the catorian, so he did not know how to react. However, the experience is something that stays with you for life, and a moment later the mage said, extracting a small box from his inventory:

"I'd be the last creature to owe Archibald. This is a level two inertia neutralizer, five hundred kilos per square centimeter. I hope I have surprised you?"

"Very much so." No matter how much I was striving to control myself, I had to swallow not to choke from salivating over the offer. Devir presented me with a much coveted award that I had not been able to find at the auction. The soft spot of the energy defense of the players was that it only blocked direct damage, not inertia. So, if some madman bonks you on the head with an ax, the energy shields will prevent the sharp blade from touching your body. However, the force of the blow will not dissipate and your head will still encounter the physics of the game and real worlds, turning the ax into a hefty club. No one supposes that brains would like to live outside the skull, so the player is guaranteed to suffer a respawn despite the coolest protection imaginable.

The level two inertia neutralizer would solve this problem. Steve knew very well how to activate the device, so a moment later the box was attached to my belt.

"You are within your right." Archibald shrugged, appreciating Devir's gift and turned to me again: "Are we agreed?"

"Yes," I confirmed, accepting the space blocker. "How long should I wait before activating it?"

"The echoes will appear immediately when we receive the system message. They will need two or three seconds to get their bearings and rush at us, and that's about the time we need to take the rags out of our pockets. Let's do it! I am tired of being stuck here."

You completed Hall Four of the Reverse of Lecleur Estate. Grandeur +20

"Archibald forgot to add that you receive experience for each echo you destroy," Steve's voice broke the silence that settled over the Reverse. The blocker worked as expected: within a hundred yards everyone turned into statues. Forty three Devirs and – I had a hard time believing it at first – one hundred and eighteen Archibalds. *"We will need to specify that experience is an extra bonus in addition to the future present, and is not a present in itself. Shall we begin?"*

"I am the Templar's blow!" I shouted, hitting the nearest fake Devir. The protection of the frozen figure worked in full and absorbed the blow. The first blow was followed by the second, third, and fourth.

Only at the fifth blow did the shield give out, allowing me to get to the robe. Which absorbed the hit, so I had to finish the mage off with the sixth. Even though the experience scale bumped up happily, I once more assessed the amount of work I was facing and sighed heavily. Six blows per Devir took about half a minute. Forty two mages would mean twenty minutes. Archibald would most definitely take longer and I would just physically not have enough time to finish them all off within the time allotted. I sighed once again, and started hitting the nearest fake Archibald. I had no choice!

What saved me was my proclivity to hoarding and the desire to have some cushion if times got tough. I replaced the six Templar's blows with the seven eponymous scrolls: thankfully, I had not given them all to Mizardine. That enable me to finish off all the mage's copies in ten minutes, of which most was taken up by installing the scrolls. Archibald took more work: the scrolls were enough to get rid of just over half of his echoes, and it took twelve blows to kill one fake catorian. I did not even feel any pleasure driving the spikes into yet another cat's face. I had to do everything quickly and precisely; there was no time at all to enjoy the result. I did not know what Archibald was thinking, embarking on such a risky enterprise and not providing me with some kind of powerful weapon. Devir, apparently, was basically just tagging along without ever thinking how I was going to destroy all the fake ones. Why was the catorian so certain? Practically throughout the entire hour I racked my head over what that was: an unfortunate turn of events for the catorian and therefore such a demonstration of implicit trust in my abilities, or an interactive performance for one actor and spectator accompanied by complete protection against all force-majeure events?

"Amazing: you made it!" Archibald's line indicated the end of my hour-long marathon of experience accumulation. I was so tired that I looked at my current level of 73 as if it was something minor and matter of fact.

"I hear genuine surprise in your voice," Devir frowned and even shifted his gaze back and forth between me and the cat. I was right: the mage had believed that Archibald was in control of the situation by entrusting me to destroy the echoes, and had no backup plan in case of failure. And Archibald immediately took advantage of that:

"Well, I have good reason for surprise!" His voice was dripping poison. "The player had barely left the Academy. He has no weapon, no experience, no levels! Nothing at all! He even has just one ability still: the initial one he got back in the Academy! And there you show up and pose him the task of killing forty-two of your precise copies within an hour! We all know your level, Devir; you are better protected than a small tank! Yari, how many blows did it take to kill one mage?"

"Six," I said angrily, seeing where Archibald was leading with this, and that I could have not hurried so and enjoyed the process instead. The catorian was in full control of the situation anyway. He had done it successfully one hundred and sixteen times before this.

"Six blows!" The Paladin even lifted up a claw, "Good thing you had the sense to deactivate your protection and take off the gems, so that your echoes appeared without all of that. Otherwise killing just one of you would have taken Yari forty minutes of working his arms non-stop! But he managed! A great talent, would you agree? I will not even mention my own precious self. I can't imagine where he found time for all that!"

"Bastard!" Devir flared, mad not so much with the catorian as with himself for showing himself to be a trusting idiot. "You wanted to set me up?!"

"Why wanted?" Archibald asked in genuine bewilderment. "I did set you up. Well, actually, no. I just made you share with a promising student of mine some useful thing that he would not have found anywhere else."

"Oh: I am a promising student now?" It was now my turn to be sarcastic. "Have I reached the same level as Dolgunata then?"

"Well... Not quite so promising." The catorian's smile was fit to freeze molten rock. "But you did catch up with Sakhray. Any more questions?"

"What was your backup?" The mage was able to control his emotions. "I admit, I acted foolishly."

"Do I finally hear the voice of reason?" Archibald laughed. "Devir, I would like to remind you that you were the one who gave up training with me, while I did not give up on you. So, in fact, you are still my student. I will always have time to kill you later, given enough reason, but the responsibilities that I assumed at one point will not allow me to overlook your carelessness. You were so worried of being indebted to me that you did not bother even attempting to think before trusting me implicitly! Why would you do that? What if he had suddenly become suicidal? Where is your sense of self-preservation and constant awareness of the situation? Don't even think of justifying it with the Reverse; you will tell these stories about compromise to Yaropolk! Am I supposed to cover your back till the end of the Game? Three thousand years down the drain; I poured so much effort into you, and you still believe every passerby conman, just like Yari! Cut that shit out!"

Devir looked, stunned, at the back of the catorian, who was assertively striding down the hallway towards the next room. Even though his tone had brimmed with righteous anger and indignation, Archibald's tail was swishing from side to side joyfully, betraying the Paladin's excitement. Of course! First Devir had thrown a barb questioning whether Archibald was tough enough to tackle the Reverse, and then Archibald was able to give a tongue-lashing for his naiveté to Devir for thinking himself a seasoned warrior, and in front of others, too. Now they were even.

We followed the teacher in silence. The catorian moved forward inexorably like a heavy tank crushing enemy lines. Nothing and no one could dampen his good mood. At least that's what everyone thought until we turned the next corner.

"Great Light!" Devir whispered , as we turned the corner and nearly crashed into the wide back of the catorian, frozen in place in full battle defense. The mage activated his at once, pinning me against the wall. I was trapped flat against it, unable to move, mad at Devir and the uncertain situation. For the last half an hour I had not even bothered by the darkness. I had become used to it, and now could see about a yard or two around me. But that was not enough to see who or what had caused such a reaction in my companions. If it was the Keeper, we were in for quite a welcome. As I was still trying to see something ahead, I heard barely audible cat's hissing that ordered me to freeze.

"Kitty!" A pleasant female voice came from the right. "What a big furry kitty! May I pet you, lovely precious?"

The stranger was talking languidly, with a funny drawl on the vowels.

"You are dead!" Devir mumbled. "I saw it myself! You were killed by Leguria!"

"Quiet, mage! I don't want to talk to you!" Shrill notes appeared in her voice along with open frustration. Suddenly Devir became straight as a rod. His eyes bulged out and then burst. The mage was clawing at his throat, gulping for air. A moment, and despite all his glorious protection Devir was crushed into a large ball. The robe was unable to absorb all the blood, and it pooled on the floor, forming a huge puddle. One of the best headhunters in the game world Earth was destroyed like a tiny insect underfoot. However, Devir did get his wish: he did meet the Keeper; and the greeting he received was rather extraordinary.

"Oh, hello, Anna!" Archibald immediately dropped his protection and spread his paws in welcome. "Long time no see!"

"A talking kitty!" There was a cry of admiration, and bright light flooded the corridor. As soon as my momentary blindness passed I was able to see the one who had scared us so thoroughly.

The Great Warrior, Iven's second half, the conqueror of Leguria, and Madonna's only student, turned out to be a miniature sweet woman who would hardly reach the chin of her image in the Hall of Fame. Her short stature did not prevent the lady from sitting regally in the armchair with legs crossed, rocking her foot. One hand was settled on the armrest as Anna was drumming one scarlet fingernail on the polished wood; the other held a glamour magazine. She was staring at the "kitty" with heavy unblinking eyes.

I glanced around the abode of the Keeper of the Reverse. A comfortable room with bookshelves lining the walls from floor to ceiling. There was a laptop, a TV set, a number of paintings and other pleasant and useful things that made it possible to stay in solitude for a long time without any detrimental effects to one's morale. A telling detail: fresh roses in a vase; there was also a man's silk robe, draped casually over the back of the other armchair, for guests. I could even guess who was the owner of this pretty robe with the colors similar to a royal mantle.

"A Paladin kitty. How cute! Why didn't anyone tell me that it's possible to get pets like that and assign them the same class as the master?" The warrior frowned in displeasure.

"Maybe because I don't have a master?" Archibald snorted and twirled around gracefully on the spot, waving his tail in the air like a banner Had it not been for his armor and weapons, the catorian could have easily passed for a feline. "But I have been dreaming of a mistress my whole life..."

"What a flatterer you are!" The hostess laughed with a tinkle, and beckoned the catorian towards her with her finger. I stirred, not sure whether to stay where I was or to follow my teacher; that attracted attention. "Is the second Paladin with you or with the mage?"

"With me." Archibald sighed, dropped softly on the carpet in front of Anna and purred, as she was unable to resist and scratched him behind the ear. I stayed standing, waiting for direct instructions; already dreading the consequences of observing the scene of my teacher's humiliation. Archibald would not forget it, and I was sure he would make me pay for this again and again. The delay of the execution for the Paladin, who "knew too much", that is, me, for an unspecified period of time was the only thing that allayed my worries somewhat; business was the first order of the day. "He's listed as my student, even though he is quite pitiful at that. He is astonishingly dim-witted. Not really capable of being anything other than a gopher: 'give me this bring me that, get out of my sight'. I keep him primarily out of pity. He is curious to the point of idiocy, keeps bothering everyone; no sense of self-preservation whatsoever: it's just so annoying. But you know, he'd just perish without me. Don't you get distracted – keep petting me!"

"You are full of surprises, my furry friend. Amazing: a Paladin servant to a Paladin cat without a master! Come in." With a graceful nod Anna indicated to the dimwit an empty armchair, without bothering to lift her hand from the fur, then fully concentrated on the catorian. "Iven used to bring me kitties some time ago, but they were so small and fragile that they didn't last long. Then I became bored with that: you just barely get used to one when it croaks on you, so I told him not to bring them any more. I hope you are strong, at least?"

"Oh, very much so." Archibald almost closed his eyes with pleasure, and purred even louder.

"May I say a word?" Archibald's hint, as he was distracting the woman and capturing most of her attention was loud and clear, so I was trying to carefully understand the lay of the land. Steve had already scanned the books on the shelves and concluded with 90% probability that they had nothing to do with the Game. The pendant was nowhere to be seen. Either Anna did not recognize Archibald, or was perfect at pretending she had amnesia. I was more inclined to believe the former. So the question was: what creature in the Game knows nothing at all about the Game, yet possesses astonishing strength? Crushing Devir into a ball without bothering to get out of the armchair commanded respect. Steve provided the answer at once, and there was plenty of food for thought. She was an echo!

"Here we go!" The teacher sighed, and rolled his

eyes so demonstratively that I really itched to upload an equivalent of "funny cats home video" to the local video hosting site. Regardless of the consequences. He was so good, the bastard, at making one seethe with just a flick of his tail. "A teacher's lot is so hard! Go ahead: my punishment; what help do you need from me this time?"

"No!" Anna interrupted him harshly. She even stopped stroking the cat, causing him to snort in disapproval. "I am not done talking to you! I forbid you to answer him!"

"Fine, fine, dear. As you say. I am all yours." Archibald rubbed against Anna's leg and purred harder, calming her down. "You can even answer him yourself, if you want. I'm telling you, he's a twit like no other. He'll never shut up otherwise. Even so, sometimes it's funny to listen to him."

"Why not. That might be interesting." The warrior's echo latched onto the idea. "Let's play teacher-and-student. Yaropolk! Today I will be your teacher. Go ahead, ask!"

Such extreme mood swings made me uneasy. I had never had any experience in interacting with beings so unstable.

"May I ask about anything at all?" I picked words carefully, feeling like I was on top of a powder keg.

"Right, you may ask anything. But I will only answer those questions I find interesting." Anna, now charm incarnate, smiled enticingly. "If my kitty and I become bored, I will punish you!"

Her charm was replaced by hysterical laughter.

"So then I would rather tell you about the craftiness of my teacher that he demonstrated as making his way through the traps to reach you." I was fishing for clues. Come on! If it was the little Anna who had deactivated the traps, she would find it interesting. "It was so... fascinating! The deadly rays passed through his shiny fir without doing him any harm, and his feet tapped out an enthralling dance!"

I even jumped up from the chair, waving my hands in the air and making my intonations as expressive as I could. Anna looked at me sharply and sank her sharp nails into the catorian's fur.

"So, you came by the 'Path of Trials?' I had thought Iven sent you to me for entertainment. But it's even better that way. Everyone he brought was boring. Iven would not let me play with them like with your mage." Anna laughed again and then fell silent. "I want to hear about this! How many stages have you completed?"

"Unfortunately, just one, my darling." The catorian meowed calmly, licking his paw in contemplation. Someone else completed the others before me. Whoever it was, he is worthy of admiration!"

"Yes, my little kitty! I am the one worthy of admiration – and you as well! Just imagine, there was only one remaining! Just one!" She shouted the last word, then talked loudly and heatedly. "You cannot imagine how many countless times I died! Again and again Iven told me to train, and it continued until I passed a stage. He admired me; he told me that I was the strongest, the unconquerable. And I tried so hard, and trained for hum, and at the end brought him granises as proof that I had completed one more hall..."

"What does she mean by 'died again and again?" I was so glad that I was the only one able to hear Steve. *"An echo cannot die multiple times!"*

"If she is the Keeper of the Reverse, then, apparently, she can. Like, maybe death in the Reverse does not count." I offered Steve a hypothesis.

"And why, did dear Iven not train himself?" Archibald snorted.

"I was the only one who could see the entrance to the path. Both for Iven and for those whom he brings the path is closed and invisible. But he is very courageous and valiant! He frequently regales me with stories of his heroic deeds!" Archibald's face was no longer concealing his attitude towards the "courage and valiance" of the chief fighter. "Come on, my furry friend, envy is not a worthy feeling. I am sure that you have lots of admirable features. I am already charmed by you. Tell me, how did you, beautiful cat, manage to complete the last stage?"

"Radiation. It does not affect cats." Archibald explained briefly, freely stretching on the carpet. "So we went through without a problem."

"So, you are not just a soft kitty; you are a useful kitty, too?!" False Anna concentrated on the catorian again, and contented purring once again reverberated in the Reverse. Archibald was flicking his tail and arching his back like a real cat.

"Oh, kitty, you must be hungry! I have milk and sour cream for you. Would you like a saucer, or do you prefer a cup? Yaropolk, are you OK?"

All this time I had sat quietly in the armchair and done my damnedest to stay calm and impassive. In order to do that I tried a number of methods – recalling poetry, thinking of trigonometry theorems, counting books on the shelves... Each method helped somewhat, but only up to the point when the treacherous thought of the video camera turned on in my head made its way to the forefront in my mind. And then I urgently had to come up with something else to calm down.

"Sure, I am fine. Could I have a cup of tea, if it is not a problem?"

Anna took out a remote control and the noise of a heating kettle could be heard from behind the nearest bookcase. That made me look at the space around me with new eyes. I had only heard about "intelligent buildings" systems, but had never seen one personally. It was amusing, encountering a "smart home" in the Reverse, used by the echo of a mighty Paladin of ancient days. Anna had perished about fifteen hundred years before; therefore the lady sitting in front of us was at least that old. So, did that mean that she had spent fifteen hundred years here, in the Reverse of the estate? In that case her behavior was not strange at all. She had simply gone mad from sitting forever in solitary confinement sometimes alleviated by guests.

"While the kettle is heating, tell me the latest news!" Anna demanded. "What happened to the mages? What was their punishment for the death of the Paladins? Is Katrina really as pretty as she looks in the pictures, or are they just airbrushed really well? Who will be selected next year for the team for the Games? How many…"

Anna was remarkably on top of events in the real world. Archibald was answering her questions casually, even lazily; swishing his tail softly, creating the atmosphere of relaxation and cozy comfort. I did not understand the logic behind the catorian's actions, and was about to break my silence when I saw that Steve was waving his hands at me quite actively.

"The aura!" He whispered as if someone else could hear him. *"Conversation with the false Anna creates an aura! Plus 50% to all attributes for a year!"*

I looked in surprise at the two Paladins engrossed in conversation, and for the first time noticed a gesture aimed at me personally. The catorian was showing me his fist, indicating that should I spoil anything, no one would ever find me again, no matter how long and hard they searched.

So then, the whole line-up for charging Elizabeth's pendant was just a front? Twelve high-born and super strong players of our game world came to the estate every month in order to talk to Anna and receive an aura for a year? And there would be no point insisting that Iven did it out of sheer altruism. In reality it was much more likely that Iven made a pretty penny on allowing the select few to come close to the echo of his beloved. But how did he manage to make her immortal? I was practically itching from my desire to look around and search for the pendant.

"I beg your pardon, fair lady, but would you allow me to wait on you and my teacher? I would be happy to serve tea and milk to you!"

Archibald used the opportunity to nudge the hostess, convincing her:

"I told you, as a Paladin he is only so-so. With his ignoble manners he'll always be a servant. He considers it a joy to serve others!"

"But of course, Yaropolk!" Anna even flung up her hands. "Iven had promised to bring me a robotic assistant, but he was having trouble arranging for permits to import one into our world. They keep telling him that Earth is too backward for artificial intelligence to be introduced here. Nonsense! This Bernard does not have a clue! And I already have one, anyway!"

"Will you show us?" Archibald asked, turning the other ear. "Yaropolk, why are we still waiting for our tea?"

"Yes, yes, I am running to make it!" I shouted as I did, in fact run. Despite her pretty appearance, Anna scared me. She scared me quite a lot. In her presence I felt so uncomfortable that even the astonishing aura could not offset it.

"It's not here." I heard Anna's sulky voice. "Iven took it for some sort of calibration. We were quarrelling and I accidentally burned out the controller. My robot turned out to have a very willful and nasty character! But you are so completely different! Stay with me. Iven and the others will like you!"

"Oh, I am sure of that!" Archibald grinned.

"The Pendant!" Steve shouted with joy, highlighting his find in red. Directly behind the bookcase there was a huge space that was used for everything: sleeping, walking, preparing food, and all sorts of other activities.. The space was divided with low 4-foot partitions; there were lots of portraits hung on them. So many that it would be enough for a few museums. To the right of me was a huge, amazing full scale portrait of Elizabeth. The thing we were looking for was sparkling with precious stones, hanging on the top of the frame. Iven had not even bothered to hide it, considering that just being within the Reverse guaranteed the protection of the pendant.

"What's keeping you?" I heard Archibald's shout, and it made me spring to action. A quick move of my hand and all three items from the "Joy" set were settled in the virtual shelf of my inventory. Done! Now we had to get to Elizabeth and present them to her.

"Your tea, please." I did not hide the joy in my voice, and Archibald cast a glance towards me; then grinned, as he understood the reason for my glee.

"At least some use from a slovenly student." Archibald took a sip and closed his eyes from pleasure. "I so enjoy Karla silverberry! It's such a pity it's so hard to come by! Anna, could you share just a pinch of that with me? Gerhard, Iven's boss, is an avid fan of this tea, I want to do something nice for him. I will say it's a present from Iven, too. Maybe he'll get some bonus in his service for that."

"Certainly!" Anna was quite happy with the idea. "Let your student take the whole bag, Iven will bring me more. My love would not deny me anything."

"No need to give away your whole stash." Archibald protested. "You don't know when Iven will come to visit you again, I would not dream of depriving you of such a pleasure."

"Oh, he comes to visit me every week." Anna waved off his concern. "So it's no big deal. And it will be a pleasure to help him in his service, so you may in fact take the whole thing.

Archibald lifted himself up on an elbow and with a nod pointed me towards the kitchen. The catorian's eyes were very eloquent: "Don't you even think stopping with a bag of tea!" I was in total agreement with that. Since I was given permission to use the kitchen it would be silly to confine myself to the small stuff. I should stuff my inventory to the brim, and there were two purposes to that: first: obtain some pleasant, and, as far as I was able to tell, rare items; second: inflict some financial damage on Iven. Hopefully, substantial damage.

While the catorian chatted with Anna, I was sweeping the shelves clean. I decided against touching the paintings on the partitions: I was not sure they were of any value to anyone other than Iven himself. As for the cabinets, I emptied them entirely, not even wasting the time to open boxes and bags.

"We ought to get going." As soon as I emerged from behind the bookcase, Archibald, with much flourish, started preparing to depart. "Should I convey anything to Iven?"

While the woman was contemplating, Archibald behind her back was making gestures indicating that we had to finish it up here. I was again in full agreement with that. The demonstration of her power against Devir was still quite fresh in my mind.

"Would you like to look at the paintings?" Anna behaved as if she had never heard Archibald's last sentences. "Iven always brings something. He says they're people he knows."

"We would love to, but unfortunately we have to..." Archibald was slowly retreating from Anna, making soft steps backwards."

"I have not dismissed you." Anna cut him off angrily. "Your student may leave – he is boring – but you will stay here. Let's go see the paintings!"

Anna stood up quickly, spread her hands and the bookcases flew to the sides, crashing to the floor and spilling their contents.

"This is so that you would not get into your head to kill yourself and escape." A small leash appeared in Anna's hands. Archibald froze in place, and the woman put the collar around his neck without a problem. "I'm your mistress now. And I am ordering you to go look at the paintings."

"Aren't you a smartie! The slave's collar is a high level submission artifact – just when I needed one!" The catorian said coldly, and tore off the collar in one fluid movement. The next moment it ended up around Anna's neck before she could even make a sound. The Paladin ordered her: "Freeze and answer questions. Are you an echo?"

"Yes, I am one of the echoes of the Great Warrior Anna." The creature spoke mechanically, standing in an unnatural posture as if stuck.

"Why were you not able to complete the last

hall?" Archibald wanted to know the answer to the question to which he was not able to find himself.

"I don't have radiation protection. Iven promised to bring it, but still has not received the permit to import it to Earth."

"Anna did not have an aura. How did you get it?" The catorian kept questioning.

"Nobody knows. The aura has been there since the time I was created; I can turn it off when Iven requests.

"Does he request that often?"

"Only when he comes alone. During the last three hundred years Iven brings guests and orders that I entertain them with the aura activated."

"How come you don't die?"

"I am tied to the Reverse. I exist while the Reverse exists. If I were to die, the Reverse would disappear as well.

"Did Iven create the anchor?"

"No. The Light Paladin does not have that kind of strength."

"Who?"

"I have no right to disclose the information."

"Yari: I will confirm just in case: you have definitely collected the pendant?" Archibald turned towards me and I nodded quickly. I had never seen the Paladin in this mode: the cold in his eyes could put the Arctic to shame.

"I order you to name the one who created the anchor!" The catorian resumed his interrogation. He did not care what would happen to the echo.

"Lumpen!" Anna said and the space around us

exploded with all the colors of the rainbow, and then turned to complete darkness. A moment, and the darkness dissipated as well, landing us in Elizabeth's bedroom. The Reverse did not exist anymore and neither did the crazy echo.

We showed up right in the middle of a family scandal. Wailing Sophie was kneeling by the bed; Iven was looming over her like a predator. The head of the house had failed to get into the treasury, and now was looking for a victim.

Our appearance did not go unnoticed, and the protective dome appeared immediately around the gold-clad Paladin. Baring his sword, Iven assumed a defensive stance; Archibald's reaction was immediate and predictable; his blade flashed in the light.

The pause lingered, but nothing was happening in the room. I was certain that the main battle between the two Paladins was now being held at levels inaccessible to vision, so I decided not to waste time, and to remind those gathered around what was the reason why of all of us were gathered here:

"For the theft of the pendant of Lady Elizabeth, for abusing power and authority, for lying to brethren in class, for misleading the entire game community of the game world Earth, I sentence Paladin Iven to ten respawns, reduction of grandeur by 200 units and to payment of a fine to the Game in the amount of five thousand granises!"

Three pairs of surprised eyes stared at me, as they had not expected such a turn of events.

"And go eat shit instead of an appeal, you gilded turkey!" I added to myself, proud of my actions.

Immediately a message flashed before my eyes:

Verdict is confirmed
Verdict is deemed optimal

Case "Stolen Pendant" is closed. The task is assigned to the nearest Headhunters
Award for correct verdict: basic Energy level increased by 300

Quest "Stolen Pendant" is completed. To receive your reward contact Paladin Iven

CHAPTER TEN

THE SECRET OF LECLEUR ESTATE

IT WAS SO SAD that the feeling of glee was so rarely available to me. Mostly that was the prerogative of Archibald and Dolgunata. Previously I had never been in a position to avail myself of all the pleasures that emotion offered. I was such a silly and naïve person! Looking at the distorted face of Iven, who was so astonished that he even lowered his sword, I felt incredible joy and elation. Darkness take them all – it was so nice to feel that I was worth something in this Game!

"You owe me a reward." I stretched out my hand and Archibald supported my claim with loud laughter and applause. That jerked Iven from his shock, and he realized how the pendant could have ended up in my hands. The Paladin's formerly noble face twisted in malice, and a deep purple flush replaced his aristocratic pallor. It only took a fraction of a second for the tip of his sword to fly up and stop within a hair of my throat.

"What happened to her?" His narrowed eyes zeroed in on me, searching for the slightest change of expression. I tried to keep my cool as best I could:

"My reward." After all, hanging close to the teacher and his other student did something for my character: I was enjoying my moment of triumph. "Or are you trying to take it for yourself"?

"What happened to her!?" The Head of the Battle Wing kept pushing, without moving the sword.

"That brings me to the conclusion that the reward cannot find its hero because of the greed and self-interest of the individual responsible for dispensing it." It seemed I caught a vibe and was riding with it. "I'll report it to the Emperor's Viceroy; let him sort this mess out; I wash my hands of it."

Just in case, I hastened to get as far as I could from menacing Iven and his equally menacing sword. I came up to Sophie, who had suddenly turned from the main character of a family drama into a spectator, and did not conceal her relief in that respect. I offered her my arm gallantly and helped her get up, thus demonstrating indifference to Iven's subsequent actions. Of course, I was just showing off, but on the other hand I was sure that in case of a direct attack Archibald would not allow me to be killed or maimed, if only because he would want to see this drama to the end.

"Before you demand your reward you need to complete your task! The pendant is still not in my hands." The right emphasis in my conversation with Iven produced the desired result, and he realized that the Reverse had given me not only the pendant, but also some valuable information unfavorable to him, which made the possibility of meeting the Viceroy an extremely undesirable prospect for Mr. Chief Fighter.

"It's not supposed to be in your hands. The pendant never belonged to you, and the quest was to find it. I did; I received the message from the Game on completion of the quest, you saw it yourself." I turned towards the bed of lady Lecleur. "And now I will return the pendant to its rightful owner.

With those words I grabbed the pendant from my inventory and put it in Elizabeth's hand. Two bolts of lightning flashed in the room: a gold and a silver one. Both Iven and Archibald rushed from where they were so fast that the eye could not follow their movement. A horrendous hit on my chest sent me flying to the opposite wall. The flight ended with an equally horrible crash. My protection squeaked and disappeared just at the first blow, so I was met by the wall in all its harshness. Accompanied by the inevitable stars and sparks. My consciousness was trying to prove its independence, so voices from the outside world were having a hard time filtering through. The catorian was doing most of the talking:

"...my student... only I have the right... golden-assed puffball..."

"We need to either find an armor-smith or head for respawn." I heard Steve's doleful voice as the outside world sounds faded again.

"What happened?" I asked with surprise.

"Watch." The sparks in my eyes faded, replaced by the video record of the instant just before I had found myself crashing into the wall. Iven and Archibald were like sprinters crossing the finish line together; Iven, however, had an advantage: he raised his sword in advance. Archibald twisted his arm, taking the blow and diving under the opponent's arm, but was unable to fully dampen the impact. Iven's sword went through my great energy protection as if it wasn't there. My Daro armor was next, parting as if was made of paper, but then Archibald came to my aid. He parried the blow of his brother in class, preventing him from completing the movement and cutting me in two. However, the blow was strong enough to send me flying. Steve showed me my breast plate with a huge hole torn through it. It was true: I would either have to find a smith or respawn. With a hole like that I was not worth much in battle.

"How dare you, in my house!" My consciousness fully returned as the actors on the scene changed once again. Iven was the only permanent fixture in this farce of a tragedy. Now our small group was augmented by the irate daughter of the golden Paladin. By all appearances she had inherited her character from her father, which made their reunion particularly colorful. The small bony old lady was standing on the bed, wrapping herself in a blanket and looking at Iven upwards, but threateningly. Her small height was not preventing her in the least from challenging her father's authority. Apparently I had not missed much, since Iven had not even sheathed his sword – either there was no time or he was too involved in arguing with his daughter. He was standing in the middle of the room, inhaling and exhaling heavily, trying to find arguments to defend himself. His sword moved in unison with his breathing. Sophie, totally exhausted from the stress, retreated into a far corner to get away from the quarrels of her relatives. And only Archibald, having made sure that Iven was not trying to threaten me any more, was enjoying the situation. The catorian sheathed his sword, sprawled in an armchair, and was leisurely eating grapes from a dish on the bedside table. He looked like a sophisticated US Academy member judging Oscar nominations.

"Go to your own place and issue orders there!" Elizabeth meanwhile continued. "This is my house! My rules! Don't forget that you are a guest here!"

"You forget yourself, daughter of mine!" Iven growled – not even through his teeth – through his nostrils. Even though that was physically impossible.

"You are the one who forgets himself, father!" The old lady was not lacking for certitude. Apparently relations between father and children were not ideal here, since there was a scandal underway rather than hearty family embraces. I was rooting for Elizabeth; it would be more appropriate to say that I was against Iven regardless of who his opponents were. The old lady commanded respect. One could feel a core of steel within her, that she wielded arguing with her father.

As the result of a long argument a strange equilibrium was reached when neither of the sides was able to achieve the desired result: Iven was unable to force his daughter to submit to him, and the rebel daughter was unable to throw out the overbearing dad, nor to inflict any revenge on him. I decided it was a great time to throw some oil on the fire.

"Lady Elizabeth," I said with reverence in my voice. All those in the room turned towards me as if they had not expected that anyone would stick his nose into their family affairs. The catorian even stopped chewing and his ear twitched towards me in surprise.

"I believe this belongs to you," I said, having made sure that I had become the center of attention of everyone within the room. This was my moment of triumph. The ring, that I providently extracted from the Lecleur estate, was sparkling in my open palm.

"You thieving scum!" Iven had once again demonstrated that he was not named the chief of Paladin fighters for nothing. Despite the distance between us, the bed and Elizabeth standing on top of it, he once again reached lightning speed trying to get to me, but instead froze like a wax figure in mid-jump. Most of all he resembled a fly in a force web. The web was made of blue force rays maintained by Elizabeth and the statues that were there, in fact, not only for decorative purposes, in each of the corners around the room. Archibald whistled, impressed by the old woman's reaction speed. If only men were so quick perhaps fewer bastards would be born in the world.

"Look who's talking, father!" Elizabeth shook her head in disapproval and turned towards me. "My young friend, you bring me infinite joy. I doubt we'll find anyone here willing to argue with me with respect to the ownership of this treasure! But they may try if they want to."

The last phrase Elizabeth addressed to Archibald, indicating for the first time that she was taking into consideration his presence and involvement in this affair. The catorian simply spread his paws as if to indicate that he was there only because of his love of theatre. Satisfied by the catorian, Elizabeth impatiently beckoned me with her hand.

"Don't you dare!" Iven croaked his order with the last of his strength. His eyes turned red and opened as wide as it was physically possible altogether; large beads of sweat appeared on his forehead from the effort exerted by the Paladin to fight the energy rays. But all was in vain. Elizabeth had the power of the estate on her side.

"Finally!" Elizabeth exhaled with relief, allowing me to be gallant and put the ring on her finger. While light enveloped the old lady, as in the classic games when you gained a new level. Involuntarily I took a couple of steps back, turning away from the bright light; when I regained my normal vision, I was truly astounded by the transformation of our cute "old lady". Just like that, in quotation marks. Because in front of me there was a perfection of female beauty with the appearance of a twenty-five-year-old girl. The ideal age, as far as I was concerned, since I believed it to be the peak of both beauty and intelligence.

It was enough to cast a single glance at Elizabeth to understand that she belonged to the category of those beautiful women looking at whom made you fully aware of the abyss between them and yourself. Next to them all your inferiority complexes become exaggerated, and no matter how much you try to lose weight, become smart and amass wealth, you will never be good enough for such as them. An encounter with such members of the fair sex is a good thing, since it provides a motivating kick, which is sometimes what you need in life. Then you start trying to develop all your abilities to the max, even the ones that always were rudimentary; but all of a sudden you are elated by the hope of "what if it makes sense" variety. The most important thing is not to turn this desire to "sleep with a queen" into an obsession, and not to drown in the abyss of regression after you realize how useless all your strivings have been.

"It is such a pleasure to become myself once again. I owe you, Paladin Yaropolk." The new Elizabeth smiled radiantly, adjusting her hair. The girl cast a glance at herself and said, embarrassed: "Please forgive me. I will leave you for a moment to freshen up."

The girl extended her arm demandingly, indicating that she needed help getting down. But while I lingered, Archibald was quicker; he helped Elizabeth, and lowered his furry head, bowing to her. Barely touching his paw, Elizabeth gracefully glided from the bed and nodded to Sophie, pointing at the armoire. The latest transformation of her old mother completely disoriented poor Sophie. It was clear that she had long abandoned all attempts to understand anything in the elaborate shenanigans of her relatives. Used to obeying her strong-willed mother and husband, Sophie submissively returned to her habitual role and approached the armoire, making a curtain out of a sheet. These simple actions not requiring any mental effort improved Sophie's condition at once. But it was so weird to observe that dysfunctional relations among the several generations within the Lecleur family were the rule rather than the exception. I considered that I believed that creatures who were unable to experience parental feelings should be forcibly deprived of the ability to have children; so that the share of the happy masses would increase significantly.

Without gracing her daughter with a word or gesture of thanks, Elizabeth went behind the curtain, leaving a rather wide gap. Totally unconcerned about that, she quickly discarded the shirt, dropping it right at her feet, and slowly, as if enjoying but still not quite able to believe it, stroked the beautiful curves of her body. The beauty was quite aware of how many pairs of eyes were on her at the moment, and it served to her as confirmation that she was still as beautiful as many game years ago. While we were unabashedly enjoying the sight of her body worthy of the most talented artists of all the worlds and races.

Donning an outfit presented to her by Sophie, Elizabeth grimaced in displeasure, cast a glance at the rest of the wardrobe, and sighed sadly. Dresses intended for a bony old lady's body certainly were not going to work for a shining beauty.

"It will have to do for now," she said, as if apologizing for her strange outfit: she obviously decided that if you can't resolve the problem it doesn't make sense wasting time on it. We all felt rather grateful for that attitude. "I have waited for fifteen hundred years, I can wait another hour."

"Iven kept you looking like that for fifteen hundred years?" I asked in surprise. "But what for?"

"I could ask that question of him." Elizabeth circled Iven, who was still striving to get out of the force protection grip, and stopped in front of him, looking her father in the eye. "But I am not going to do it directly. I am not strong enough yet. If I were to remove the binds, my father would end up in possession of the ring and the pendant again, and I would turn into an old shriveled prune once more. So for now, dear father, you will have to extend your visit. Don't worry, I hate this as much as you do!"

"So, then, forget him." Archibald proffered to Elizabeth a goblet of wine, which she gratefully accepted. "There are lots of methods to protect oneself against parental controls. For example, employ the services of a certain catorian who has something to match the Head of the Battle Wing of the Paladins. I promise, it will cost you a modest amount. In this case I will work for the sake of the idea."

"I would happily accept your proposal. Elizabeth cast such a carnal look at the catorian that I felt uncomfortable. Years of celibacy had taken their toll, and the young body demanded satisfaction. Even if it would be with the catorian.

"Don't worry though," Elizabeth added, having come to some conclusion in her mind. She impulsively placed her palm on the cat's paw, as if reassuring him, but Steve clearly identified the familiar gesture. Elizabeth was openly indicating her agreement to closely "cooperate" with Archibald. "I will not need permanent protection. At this time I will spare no effort to complete the work this sweet young man has started. And then I will also have something to match the Head of the Battle Wing of the Paladins. Right, daddy?"

"I hear you, and my offer of help remains standing." The catorian covered her hand with his other paw, accepting the lady's good favor. I shook my head. Apparently, I was not an advanced enough player to sleep with members of other races. "Do you need to find something?"

"Earrings," Elizabeth confirmed. "My strength is in them. My consciousness is tied to the pendant; my youth and beauty are in the ring. It is such a pity that the earrings disappeared again. I never had a chance to wear them together the pendant. And my father took the ring away fifteen hundred years ago. 'Youth and beauty are just extraneous for you, Lizzie. They are frequently accompanied by carelessness, and that would not be to your advantage! Mother would have approved.' He said that my excessive hot-headedness makes him ashamed both as a father and as a Paladin."

"Slut." Frozen Iven croaked.

"Youth and beauty are there to enjoy. Only a stupid man would leave a cake to rot on the table and live on bread and water!" His opponent jerked up her chin.

There was definitely some truth to Iven's words. Looking at Elizabeth made one admire Iven – one had to have superb skill to create a masterpiece like that, and sympathize with the poor sod: given her lineage the girl played her trumps to the max.

The catorian turned his face towards me, and quizzically moved the part that the cats have for eyebrows. Answering the teacher's silent question I could not help pretending I was thinking, and was immediately whapped on the leg with his tail. I stopped playing silly and nodded to Archibald, supporting his claim to be the clairvoyant of the day.

"My student has another present for you." Archibald steered Elizabeth towards me. "My offer of help is not just hot air."

Bastard! He found a way to share my triumph. I did not bother arguing; but my mental list of grievances against the catorian became even longer.

"Please allow me." I took out the earrings, and was enthralled by her happy shining eyes.. It was the feeling when you present a beauty with jewels, hoping they would be favorably received, and see the bits of very expensive metal and stone make her into the happiest of beings. Under other circumstances I would already have been receiving material expressions of her gratitude. Oh well!

"Are you going to fumble forever? Archibald spurred me into action. The catorian was impatient to see the result of the activation of the entire set, since one could only guess what its new properties were.

"Sure: just a moment." The only thing I was accustomed to closing and opening was female underwear; so it took me a long time fighting with the locks of the earrings and then finding the holes in the girl's ears, all the while pelted by the catorian's sarcastic comments. Finally I was done, and took a step back, looking at the result with a smile. Even when you have no hope for getting anything out of it, it's still nice to make a woman happy. Makes you feel magnanimous, that.

A harsh blow against a wall knocked all the self-congratulatory thoughts out of my head and knocked the air out of me. The blow was so forceful that even the inertia neutralizer could not fully absorb it. My mouth filled with saliva and blood, a disgusting trickle ran down my chin, finding its way below the collar of my armor. Did the set detonate so forcefully from being reunited? If so, that was a rather questionable joy from this "Joy" set. In hindsight I was now in agreement with Iven. It was a pity, though, that this good thought found its way into my head only when we were ass-deep in trouble.

Pinned against the wall like a bug, I was waiting for the new hit to throw me to the floor, expecting natural gravity to kick in; however, inertia's steadfast buddy was in no hurry. Instead I was now in the same boat as Iven had been recently, and strained against the wall, unable to move. The scariest part was the absolute darkness in the room, alleviated only slightly by my virtual interface and stunned

Steve, who was replaying the video in order to find the source of this suddenly emerging force. The replay confirmed that Elizabeth was the epicenter of the shock wave.

"Let there be Darkness!" a gravely whisper added tension to the atmosphere. It seemed like it sounded straight in my head, making some of my body parts successfully oppose gravity. My body responded by trembling unpleasantly, resonating to the voice of the unknown and therefore horrifying creature. One simple phrase made me want to run away from here as fast as my feet could carry me, as far as possible, hide in some inconspicuous hole and even breathe carefully, just in case.

"May the undying Light dispel the Darkness!" Archibald shouted loudly to the left of me, and finally a small yellow ball of light hanging over the catorian brightened the room somewhat. The strength of the Paladin's protection prevented visible harm; he was just thrown a couple of yards away from his original place, like myself. We were both incredibly glad of that. In the place of Elizabeth now stood a seven-foot monster remotely resembling a human figure. The creature was staring at its grey hands, clasping its long fingers, together and separately, as if it had never seen them or was trying to stretch the crooked unkempt fingers. It was cloaked in a black necromancer's robe; a deep hood partially concealed his face, but that did not prevent him from spreading around primal horror. Dense black fog crept from under the robe like octopus tentacles. It was gradually filling the room. Only when it started approaching the catorian, the fog swirled indignantly, circled around him, then resumed covering more territory. The necromancer made a sound that could be interpreted as a snicker, finished stretching its limbs and turned its hood towards the catorian. I could swear the shadow of the hood was concealing a huge grinning maw full of sharp teeth.

"Aa-achiba-a-a-ald!" it drawled with the same heavy and vibrating voice. Dark lightnings sprang from the tips of his fingers, leaving gashes on the wall where Archibald had been just an instant before. This round went to my quick-footed teacher, who had anticipated the attack.

"Lumpen, old friend! What wind brings you here?" The voice of the catorian, now at the opposite wall, did not sport any friendliness but plenty of tension. Another squall of black lightnings followed, and again the Paladin vanished to say something testy from another place.

"A flea-a-a. Still the sa-a-me nimble flea-a-a. Go-o-o on living for now, I need fo-o-od and slaves." The necromancer screeched with a heavy sigh and switched to Iven. Lumpen even turned his back on the catorian, demonstrating that he did not consider the former a serious adversary. In fact the long-tailed Paladin stopped jumping and froze, watching the necromancer, who was breathing heavily, as if gathering his strength circle around the immobilized Iven. Some dark threads sprang from the monster's fingers and enveloped the gold-clad Paladin in a cocoon of complete darkness. Hissing, the Darkness absorbed into him, and the shining of gold faded, replaced by matte black. At the same time the force threads that were holding the Paladin disappeared. Iven was released.

Iven banged himself on the chest, straightened, and stood to attention in front of the necromancer. The pupils and whites of his eyes turned black and unmoving, covered with a solid film of black. The former Paladin now regarded the world with dead unblinking eyes through the prism of the orders of his new lord.

"Not ba-a-ad." The necromancer praised himself, assessing the freshly produced slave. "Go sta-a-and in the corner."

Iven, walking like an automaton, went to the nearest corner and stopped there, standing still with his back to us. The necromancer proceeded to the next victim. I felt pity for Sophie and her dashed dream, but I pitied myself more. As I was next in line after the lady to be disposed of.

"Mi-i-inion. Fo-o-o-od.

I swallowed as Sophie was pulled away from the wall, guided by the light movements of the necromancer's hand and started burning as she was floating in the air. The monster had cleared the lady's mind from the stupor in which she was ever since the moment Archibald and I appeared in the room – so that the poor victim would be aware of what was going on. The room filled with screams of pain and suffering. The clothes on Sophie's body burned off almost immediately, showing her flesh, blackened and blistered, but the flames were not even close to going out. Her skin cracked, blood leaked out, but immediately the fire flared, encrusting it with horrible scabs. When what just recently had been Sophie Lecleur started disintegrating in the air, I was able to overcome my immobility and close my eyes. I did not know if I would ever be able to eat roasted meat again without shuddering; but at that moment I was definitely ready to join the vegans' camp. If I managed to survive of course.

Archibald, it seemed, was not in the least bothered by Sophie's painful death; he did not make the slightest attempt to relieve her suffering. I had a hope, however weak, that my teacher would show more concern about my fate. All I could do was wait to check my expectations against reality. There were just two thoughts torturing me: whose fate of the two would I share, and whether I could count on Archibald?

"Ne-e-ewbie." I heard the disappointed sigh. And I was immediately weighed, measured and found wanting, "Stu-u-upid. Just fo-o-od."

"Darkness take me, I don't want to burn alive! I don't want to die! I don't! Give me a chance and I will prove you wrong, you disgusting monster! Archibald, tell him something!" My thoughts were panicked, I was confused with terror, and when I heard Archibald's voice, I did not immediately realize that it was not a hallucination. I received a respite, however short it might be.

"How did you survive? I was personally checking the transition lists! You were not on them!" I calmed myself down somewhat by convincing myself to rely on the catorian, not to go mad waiting for the torture, and perked my ears.

Steve browsed through the lists quickly and nodded: Lumpen did not transition to this era. The workers of the Temple of Knowledge had confirmed that as well. However, apparently this monster could not care less about Archibald's checks or about the steadfast word of the Temple of Knowledge people!

"Interes-s-sted?" A sneer could be heard in the metallic voice of the monster. Even though that might have been an illusion: the Dark one was obviously limited in his emotions. In any case, Archibald's question made him more talkative, or maybe it was the result of having some "fo-o-od". "What can you of-f-fer me for th-th-that, Light one?"

"That's the wrong question." Archibald shook his head. "You owe me your freedom."

"Li-i-iar! Not you-u-u!" Lightning flew again in the direction of Archibald, but missed him again. The necromancer pointed at me without turning. "Him. I appreciate. He will serve as f-o-od for only an hour. Bargain, you flea-a-a!"

At that point I was totally lost. While it was understandable why Archibald would do it – he needed this information urgently, so he would bargain – but why would Lumpen want to lose such an advantage?

Delrand crystal full of Energy," Archibald offered and vanished again, appearing in a new place. The dust from the exploded wall was settling where he had been a moment ago. "You are weak now, and with the crystal you won't need food for a couple of months.

Instead of answering, Lumpen tried to hit the catorian once again.

"Does this mean no? Or should I add something else to the crystal?" Archibald was actually starting to look like a flea, as he was jumping constantly.

"Not interes-s-sted. Energy is not critical. Fabio is nearby. You bore me, flea-a-a!"

"What do you want?" Archibald would not give up, escaping yet another lightning.

"You-u-u, flea-a-a! You will be my s-s-slave." The necromancer was playing high.

The catorian demonstrated amazing agreeability:

"Fine. Give me the contract with your proposals. We'll discuss terms."

The necromancer stopped shooting lightning bolts at Archibald and screeched:

"S-s-smmart flea-a-a!" It took Archibald no more than ten seconds to bring the terms to a mutually agreeable contract.

"So then, I shall voluntarily stay for one thousand years in mental slavery, and then another thousand with regained consciousness; I shall thoroughly guard my life and health in order to properly serve the necromancer Lumpen; I shall not undertake any attempts to limit his power over me, nor shall I try to terminate my slave service before its due expiration in exchange for complete information to be provided to my teacher Gerhard Van Brast about the way by which the necromancer Lumpen was able to transition to the next era, retaining his full awareness. Last: if I were to be liberated prior to the expiration of the term, the contract shall be considered completed by me. Do you agree?"

"Yes!" Lumpen screeched, rubbing his hands gleefully.

"Then let's not drag this out; I am calling Gerhard." Archibald reached for the comm, but was nearly hit by a new lightning.

"No." The necromancer explained and pointed at me. "He-e-e will tell. Af-f-fter I eat."

"Lumpen, I agree for Yaropolk to convey information, but he must leave here alive and undamaged. I know what really happened to Anna. What's the use of the messenger if all he is able to do is drool? I need guarantees. Otherwise, go ahead, eat, and I will find a way to get out of here.

"I agree!" Lumpen did not think for very long, and his dark light washed over him. The agreement was in force now. "S-s-stand still, my s-s-slave!"

More black lightnings sprang from the necromancer's hands to envelop Archibald in the same way as they had enveloped Iven before. The puppet theater of the necromancer Lumpen received another high- level puppet. Having sent Archibald to keep Iven company, the necromancer proceeded to me. By that point I did not really care any more what my fate would be, because if Lumpen were to breach the agreement there would be no one to point fingers at him.

Without any visible manipulations the necromancer dispelled the field that was holding me in place, and I finally hit the floor. I was shaking as if

I had walked into forty degrees below zero dressed in my underwear and stayed there for half an hour. Lumpen took practically all my strength and Energy. With my arms spread I was lying flat on my back, hoping that the necromancer would give me a few minutes to replenish my strength from the crystal, since at this point I was not even able to crawl towards the door. And I wanted to go out of here not just on my own two feet, but also to try to curry favor with this Dark one. For that, according to Gromana, I needed to take off the anti-grav. What was it she had said? All Dark ones would be friendly to me?

The necromancer's hand twitched, pointing towards the exit.

"Li-i-ight one, run, or you will be-e-e fo-o-od."

"I am about as light as you!" I rasped, pulling the cylinder with the source of Light off my belt.

An invisible force unclenched my fingers, prevented me from putting the looped anti-grav into my inventory. Instead it flew towards the necromancer and floated at eye level in front of his hood. The necromancer raised his hand and, without touching the anti-grav, made it turn in different planes; then he spread his hands and the poor gadget was disassembled into components. The released source of Light was floating in the air right in front of the necromancer together with the parts of the cylinder without doing anyone any harm. If I had had the strength I would have whistled in amazement. How strong one had to be to so easily block the effects of the Light without as much as a grimace!

"Interes-s-sting." I heard a low hiss. After a

respawn and a thousand years spent in confinement, Lumpen had not lost his interest in inventions; I considered that to be a good sign. The necromancer twisted his hand in the air, looked away from the cylinder parts – and they crashed to the floor. The Source of Light entrusted to me by Bernard collapsed and disappeared.

The necromancer inhaled with pleasure as if enjoying the fragrance:

"S-s-small Dark one with one h-h-hundred of Darkness-s-s. Nic-c-ce! How? Not my Darkness-s-s."

Despite the brevity of the question I figured out what he wanted. Guided by his curiosity about the looped anti-grav from our era, Lumpen wanted to know how such a low-level player had managed to reach 100 of Darkness without his artifacts. Apparently, there was no one able to compete with the necromancer among his contemporaries.

"'Shazal' Treatise." I sat on the floor, since it was inconvenient to talk while lying down, and I was still unable to stand up; I spilled the beans immediately. "This new era has strong Dark ones as well."

"Th-th-there were. Before I came along." The monster corrected me calmly, looking at me in a different way now.

During this time I was able to rest some and restore my Energy somewhat, so now it was possible to think of escaping. But there was one question remaining that I had to clarify – my own principles demanded it. I could not just simply run away without finding out the information for the sake of which Archibald had become a slave for two thousand years. It was one thing to be Dark, but being a lowly coward was quite a different matter, as I saw it.

"How will I convey the information to Gerhard?" From all the ways to clarify the situation I chose the most innocent one. As if I had no doubts that the necromancer would share with me.

The necromancer said surprisingly calmly – indifferently, even:

"However-r-r you want."

Cursing silently at damned Lumpen unwilling to help me figure out what kind of actions he expected from me, I found nothing better to do than just keep sitting on the floor.

The necromancer meanwhile seemed to have lost all interest in me; motioning his hands again he was working on Archibald. It looked as if a puppeteer was getting used to controlling his new toy.

At first the catorian was making simple motions in place – turned his head, his body, jumped. Then he said mechanically "Yes my lord!" and goose stepped towards me. I started crawling backward intuitively until I backed against the wall, but Archibald stopped a couple of steps away from me. His eyes, obscured by darkness, looked dead; that turned the catorian's face into a terrifying mask that made you want to look away.

"Used a slave." I suddenly heard Archibald's voice. His mouth almost did not move, which was confusing. Who used a slave? And what for?

"I knew there would be restart. It's always inevitable. And I knew I would not be offered a place in the new era." The teacher kept ventriloquizing, and I realized that the necromancer had found a way to make it easy for himself, and was using thought-speech to comply with his part of the agreement, and convey the information with a touch of irony regarding the tool for this conveyance. Apparently, I was incredibly lucky. Had the necromancer decided to use me as food he could have preserved only my ability to talk and sent me like this, as a living information carrier to Gerhard. At that moment I felt infinite gratitude towards the hundredth level of Darkness, towards Bernard, and towards Archibald. "I found someone to whom a place was promised and enslaved him. Then I transferred my consciousness into an artifact. My slave brought the crystal into this world. He was supposed to find a strong being and resurrect me. But several hundred years passed by uselessly. Then Iven found my slave and killed him. Before dying my slave activated the crystal and transferred my consciousness into the weakest being around so that I could overcome it even though I had no Energy. I destroyed the consciousness of the subject, but I was not allowed to restore myself fully. Iven sealed me within the body and placed the matrix of his descendant on top. You know everything. I have fulfilled my part of the deal."

My video recorder captured the whole story that explained things as they were. Except for one thing.

"Why did Iven only seal you in and did not kill you?"

I did not really count on an answer; I guess I

just bet once again on my Darkness. I wanted to find things out first-hand.

"Passion: that's the lot of morons – that's the reason. It was a deal. My slave was too strong for one Paladin, and he called up his Doll, counting on her help to battle my slave Leguria. But she did not make it. Anna was crazy, and needed to be destroyed. But Iven did not want to let go of that shell with no ghost. So I offered him a deal while grief clouded his mind. I needed life, time, and Energy. He needed his Doll. It was impossible to recover her mind; the only possibility was to replace her with an echo. However, the Paladin was glad to have even that. We bargained. He did not let me resurrect. I promised that I would replace the Doll with an echo that had an aura, and create the binding Reverse, so that no one would find out. He provided me an existence by sealing me in the body of his offspring. Moron! He thought that he conquered me! But he craved riches and power so much that he did not notice as he became my slave. I told him about the weaknesses of his enemies, and he defeated them, gaining respect. I told him about caches and monsters; he found them and gained glory. I told him about dungeons and castles; he entered them and gained wealth. The Light one did not understand that he had long proclaimed to my students that their lord was near. They are already here, ready to welcome me! I sense Don Fabio!"

So that was it! Whether it was the hundredth level of Darkness at work, or simply vanity, now Lumpen considered me one of his followers, part of his army. Of course! A true Dark one would have no other path than to come under the banners of his Dark "God".

"What will happen to them?" I nodded towards Archibald and then at Iven.

"You have heard all. Archibald is my slave. He was an interesting enemy to me for two thousand years. Those are enemies that command respect. I defeated him, and now he will serve me as long as he had the temerity to resist. Then I will let him go – but he will not want to leave by then; I promise. As for the golden Paladin – forget about him. He no longer exists. I have erased his personality; I have left only the memory of his skills in that shell. Now he is my battle puppet. Forever!"

I considered the conversation to be over and was already getting up, when the door flew open, but I was unable to see who entered. The entire room was filled with fire; only around me a wall formed that the flames could not penetrate. The protection saved me even from heat. Frankly speaking, I did not understand who protected me against a horrible death in the fire; nor did I care at the moment. The wave of fire surged and ebbed, revealing my suzerain in full battle regalia. I finally knew what his class was. Bernard was a mage.

"Forever is far too long, Lumpen. Don't you know that?"

"Coordinator," Archibald rasped, now acting as a living shield for Lumpen. The skillful necromancer managed to merge his protection with that of the catorian, and now they were an impressive sight. "You should not have come here. The estate belongs to me.

I am the master here, and you are an unwanted guest. I am within my right."

"I am not about to argue that." Bernard looked around the room; his eyes lingered briefly on the new slaves. "I did not come here to do battle. I came to negotiate."

"It's impossible. I will drain your world. You will try to prevent me. That is your purpose and destiny."

"In this Game anything is possible." A weak smile appeared on my suzerain's face. "You are right – I will not yield the Earth to you; I have my residence here and I am used to it. So I came to bargain."

"What are you offering?"

"Gardish, a world with twenty billion inhabitants, in exchange for the Earth and knowledge.

The necromancer kept silent, waiting for Bernard to present the entire proposal.

"Restart is inevitable. You know very well that Coordinators are never included in the lists. My conditions are: you tell me the method and knowledge to survive a restart, and I give you Gardish instead of Earth. That's not too much for someone who put significant effort into releasing you!"

"Do I owe you too, Coordinator?" Archibald's face scowled in a sarcastic smile; combined with the dead black eyes that looked even more terrifying. "Or are you clamoring for your share because of the vassal's mark of this slave?"

"Not this one. My vassal gained the trust of the Lecleurs, found out everything about you and the blockers. Then he helped Yari with the search. He acted on my direct orders. Are you going to check it?"

"No need: I sense the truth; for that reason I am allowing you to bargain, Coordinator."

Whom did Bernard mean? There was only one person who at the same time was trusted by the Lecleurs and helped me: Devir. You blasted magical son of a bitch, master of compromise! Now I fully appreciated the scope of intrigue of the local players. But I was not allowed to stand with my mouth gaping for long.

"Yaropolk, you will forget about everything you heard here. This is a direct order. No one should ever find out about this." I quickly erased surprise from my face and nodded to my suzerain as dispassionately as I could. "Lumpen, I would like to take my vassal. I do still need him."

"So do I. He must leave the estate alive. Don Fabio will meet him outside the walls. While I have your vassal, I will decide what to do with him next. I need strong slaves... or at least not morons." The necromancer added after a pause, during which he probably assessed my strength.

"Yaropolk, you have heard everything. Go on with those instructions!" Bernard lost any interest in me and resumed his conversation with Lumpen. He could not care less that I was still in the room. "As you prefer. But during restart Yaropolk must be free. He is the Guide and it is too late to change him. It's better to work with what we have."

"Accepted, provided he is worthy of becoming my slave: I will give him to you as a gift for the duration of the restart." Lumpen did not pay me any attention either. Realizing I really had to clear out as fast as I could, I hurried to the exit. "How will you explain to the public that you gave a world of yours to the enemy? They will consider you weak."

"That's fine. No one will dare accuse me openly. From time to time I will hold campaigns to liberate Gardish. I will coordinate them with you. I will organize a small regular army of the strongest players. I will bring them to you as dessert. You are going to like it."

I could not hear what occurred after that, as I turned a corner where I finally was able to catch my breath. My legs turned to jelly and would not hold me. I had no strength after talking to Lumpen, as if he sucked it out of me. I threw up several times and had to use elves' ointment to restore my strength. I still felt sluggish, but at least I could think more clearly. I could kill myself now and respawn in an hour in Bernard's estate. Cons: my suzerain will definitely discover that I am not his mental slave and destroy me. Pros: I will not end up in the hands of Don Fabio. While I had some chance against Don Fabio, with Bernard the odds were totally against me. I downed another vial of the healing potion, got up and started towards the entrance to the estate, passing the players and NPCs frozen in place. The entire estate was under the rule of Lumpen, who had gained control by inhabiting Elizabeth's body; it looked like Sleeping Beauty's castle. Just to think that none of that would have happened, had Iven not followed his passion instead of his duty.

My comm did not work, so I was not able to call

Dolgunata and share the information. Most likely the teleports were blocked as well; besides, I had run out of scrolls. In one of the passages I saw Mizardine floating in midair. The hunter had completed his task of installing the scrolls and returned to the estate to report the good news. The guy ran into bad luck, but I still could do something. There was no honor in letting this player become "food" for the truly Dark one. Mizardine would not be able to withstand that. I took out my draftsman's kit and with habitual movements created three Templar's Blow scrolls, attached them to a broken cornice nearby and popped the force shield that surrounded the player. My idea was simple: it would not be a good idea to kill him by hand. Archibald, for example, did not do it. So I decided not to run the risk either. However, inanimate means worked quite well to accomplish the task; here everything depended on draftsmanship and the power of the explosion. Three scrolls did the job: The hunter's head turned into a bloody mess held in place only by the force field; in a mere ten seconds Mizardine disappeared from the estate. First one gone.

Killing the hunter defined my subsequent path towards the exit. I did not touch NPCs. They were the sacrifice that had to be offered to the Game. However, I did not pass a single player, exploding one head after another. My way towards the exit became a lot slower, but no one had imposed any time restrictions on me. I was only told to go outside. And I was working on that.

Half an hour later I actually did reach the exit.

The gate stood wide open, revealing the line of bewildered players and a group of guards unable to return to the estate because of the force shield. I came right to the edge without crossing it. Those outside did not react in any way to my approach. The dome protected everything that was going on inside from the curious eyes. What amazed me more, however, was that no one could feel my dark aura that was no longer concealed by anything. My complete invisibility provided certain advantages. If I were a believer I could have thought that I had earned that advantage by showing mercy recently to Mizardine and other players whom I had saved.

They were waiting for me: a crowd of necromancers led by Don Fabio was occupying their favorite hill, and methodically infused the space around them with negative emotions. The players were gathering resistance troops from those who wanted to gain additional experience, but in this case it was clearly an uneven confrontation. Don Fabio was creating zombies himself, which made them practically invulnerable to new players. The battlefield looked depressingly like the massacre of the innocents.

Sighing sadly I turned the useless comm in my hands. It was useless not because the dome blocked the connection, but because there was no one I could connect to. My contact list was so short that that the only contact available was now trying to dispel boredom by running in the battlefield among the players trying to defend themselves against the necromancers, and did not have time to talk. Besides, anything I could tell Dolgunata could wait till a better time.

"What shall we do?" I look at my subconscious questioningly. Steve clearly had not expected such a question from me. He scratched first the back of his head and then his chin; the assistant suggested:

"We go to Don Fabio, call Gerhard, convey the information and wait till he frees us.

"Are you sure that someone will set us free? I am not. I can always convey the information later. That can wait; however, surrendering to Don Fabio of our own accord is not prudent."

"So then we come out, take a look around, and set out to help those fighting against Don Fabio. Or are we in no hurry to go out?"

Outside of the protective dome three necromancers appeared in addition to the players and NPCs. They were just standing calmly and staring at the battle. Apparently Don Fabio had decided to send an escort for my humble self.

" Steve, we will come out, or, rather, we will run out as fast as we can, but under cover. On the count of five. But first find me the number for the Paladin Head's office; I will put it in my comm."

I prepared the number and expected that the cover would last long enough to make the call and say a couple of phrases. My backup detonator settled in my hand. I stroked the button carefully. I was counting down moments till time X while making sure to fix in my mind the action positions of all the important parties in the battle.

One: Don Fabio was completing his ritual.

There should not be enough time for him to finish; that was good. Two: A fresh wave of zombies swept the camp defenders and slowed down at the camps, turning colored tents into messy rags. Three: A beautiful panther, roaring gleefully, rushed into the nearest crowd of skeletons. As a true predator she did not give those bones any chance. Four: Ahean, Devir's student, was showing that the effort expended on his training had not been wasted – he cut down enhanced zombies in droves around the druid. That was it. There was no one else worth looking at. Five!

Mizardine had completed his task perfectly. The explosion on top of the hill was so powerful that remnants of zombies and the skeletons were scattered as far as the gate of the estate. The three necromancers instinctively covered their heads with their hands, forgetting that they actually had their shields activated. At that moment I rushed out from under the dome, elated by the success of my trick and the six additional levels I gained from it. My enemies were disoriented and partially disabled. Who suffered more, zombies or necromancers, did not really matter. The thrill of battle and action made my blood rush in my veins.

I pushed the call button and whapped the nearest necromancer so hard I sent him flying. I easily knocked him over together with some players standing behind him. Perhaps they were expecting me, but not at this speed. Without slowing down I rushed towards the hill as fast as my legs could carry me. I did not have much lead, or else the necromancers were too quick. I heard my defense squeak as it dropped a few points from a blow on my back. I realized that each second might be my last one, and listened to the line ring, silently hurrying the answering machine or whatever being on the other end, even though it was pointless There!

"Citadel of the Pala..." I heard the start of the sentence and interrupted it harshly:

"This is Yaropolk! Lumpen is reborn!" Each phrase was an effort. I had to run, breathe and talk. Which is kind of impossible to do well. "He got Iven and Archibald! Gerhard, do something!"

I almost whispered the last words, knowing that I had fulfilled my duty. I was not sure I heard any response; blood was ringing in my ears. The line disconnected.

I was aiming for the bottom of the hill, dodging between the heedless players. Those who were not quick enough ended up paying for it with their lives, as they were directly in the trajectory of the necromancers' attack. My pursuers just blew up everyone in their way. This was fine with me, but only to a point. There were soon no more players, and the hill had not even begun. I had to strive harder if I wanted to get away from them and reach my goal first. Once the necromancers understood in which direction I was running, they stopped shooting at me. If a rabbit is hurrying towards the python to be eaten, why interfere? And I was making a beeline towards Don Fabio. I did not know how many students he had brought with him, but now, after the explosion, he was standing proudly alone on top of the burnt hill, his arms crossed on his chest. There were no students, no zombies, nor skeletons. I could not see Dolgunata or Ahean either. I supposed that they might have been caught in the explosion as well and thought that perhaps that actually was for the better.

"I am just about tired of waiting, Dark one! The master said to take care of you." The necromancer screeched once I approached him. The three that had been chasing me stopped a dozen yards away. Don Fabio's hands started turning dark. Before that "care" took on any concrete form, I caught my breath and used the only trump I had.

"All the way!" The sky settled on my shoulders, bringing ravenous hunger. Leguria was coming towards me.

Each time the transformation was easier. It was the result of experience and me becoming at peace with the essence of that spell. Internally I forced myself to look at Leguria as an inalienable part of myself. Now my shout meant hunger, anticipation and – no point concealing it – enjoyment of my power.

Three vessels who had been incautious enough to stay nearby were filled to the brim with fear – sweet, but quite ordinary. I wound my tentacles around the vessels and realized that I was trembling with the knowledge of how much pleasure eating would bring. Previously I had just satisfied the unbearable hunger; all I wanted was for it to stop torturing me. I ate quickly, neglecting the last bits of the emotions on the bottoms of the vessels, hurrying from each to the next one. Now I knew with certainty that I would enjoy them to the last drop. Today my human side lost its right to interfere with my hunting.

A little intuition, and three bland remnants bloomed with piquant notes of terror, agony and madness. Like a true gourmet, I analyzed the components of the food, noting which flavor I liked best. As I was finishing with the last one I noticed another smell. But as I tasted the air, a hope for new pleasure faded: I encountered the disgusting smell and taste of "indifference". It was as If I had been enjoying exquisite truffles and suddenly came across a stinky old sock. So the reaction was not unexpected: I drew back from the source of the stench to make sure that the air around me would have no trace of that nasty stuff.

Exploring the rest of the territory accessible to me brought further disappointment: there was no more food. I could feel a few potential sources outside of that area, but they were reacting to my call far too slowly or resisted, fanning my anger. Just wait, I will show you the price of resistance! Closer! Faster! Or else my hunger will kill me first. Despair washed over me: they were approaching too slowly. I did not want to die. I decided to return to the "indifference" and try that. I had to fight myself to approach that stinky emotion. Disgust was fighting bitterly against the growing hunger, which was gnawing at me from the inside. Another step, and a wave of contentment washed over me. I even plopped down onto the ground and pulled all the tentacles underneath myself. Hunger and thirst were not tormenting me any more, the smell of indifference disappeared as well, and I calmed down. Calmness. Joy. Sleep. Apparently sleep was a pleasure as well. A palm touched my head and I was immersed in a sea of happiness, as if, after wandering for a long time, I had returned home to loving parents. I craned my neck and raised my head to look in the eye of the person whom I could surely call "father". The one who created me.

"Sleep, my boy," I heard the endearing voice and Leguria disappeared, yielding its place in the game world to Paladin Yaropolk. The memory of the necromancers' death brought nothing other than moral satisfaction with a job well done. I felt myself once again and jumped to my feet. A powerful whirlwind of True Darkness was raging all around. Horrible shadows approached trying to scare me with maws of sharp teeth, then flew off again without doing me any harm. The reason for that was a protective sphere of unknown origin. It easily reflected all of it: the dark lightnings, the superheated lava which lapped at my little island of tranquility. I touched the dome from the inside and felt nothing other than cool glass and the slight tingling of magic.

Darkness and raging elements obscured the view, but I was able to see the culprit of this mayhem: a huge skeleton with xenon lights in his empty eyeholes directed the chaos like an orchestra. In his spread hands he was holding a twisted staff from which dark lightning bolts were flying in the direction of the other warrior. The monster's opponent ignored both this madness and the head-on attack, inexorably shortening the distance between them. There was no mystery. I recognized this player even from the back. His flaming sword blazing, Gerhard van Brast, head of the Paladins of Earth, was advancing confidently towards the skeleton. He was the one that had granted me protection. He was the one who had created Leguria.

"I gave you a chance to leave." The Paladin's calm voice came though the howl of the whirlwind.

"Leave? I am not a rat to run away." The skeleton croaked in Fabio's voice, and attempted to attack Gerhard once again, but the latter just waved him off. The strength of the Head was formidable. He easily blocked the necromancer at a distance. "Our time has come! The Teacher is reborn!"

"You are not a rat, Fabio. You are stupid. Lumpen is only reborn to die again – forever this time. His time is up, and you have wasted yours."

Realizing that he had nothing to counter Gerhard, Fabio tried to kill himself, but Gerhard prevented him from doing that as well. Something that resembled a bird flew off the Paladin's hands, and the necromancer froze in place like a wax doll. The chaos around us stopped immediately, and my protective dome disappeared.

"Yaropolk, deal with the necromancers." Gerhard assessed the situation and issued an order. A portal opened next to the hill, then another, then a third, and necromancers appeared out of them. "Dolgunata will help you. Don't count on the mage, Devir and his student are playing for themselves.

"Devir plays for Bernard." I corrected Gerhard, but he just shrugged in response. This could equally easily signify surprise, skepticism or simply indifference. But I decided not to risk guessing and just share my information. After all, the Head was not obligated to tell me anything, whether he knew or not. "Bernard is within the estate."

Again a brief nod, which I considered to be acknowledgement. A portal opened next to the Head and a gray-haired priest glided out of it, too slowly for the war situation. With a gesture he blessed the space around him. Apparently his own grandeur was what concerned him first and foremost. As if punished for irreverent thoughts, I fell on the ground writhing in terrible pain. The last hours must have killed part of my brain: instead of rapidly running away from a priest of Light I was thinking about his grandness. Idiot. I heard Gerhard's voice through the humming in my ears:

"I look forward to seeing you in the Citadel tomorrow. You will be learning to block impacts from a Light source and hide your Dark aura," Gerhard explained, restoring the same dome around me. Steve analyzed it and stated without hesitation that it would be the next ability I must study. The dome of absolute protection is a great thing. Having made sure that I revived, Gerhard returned to the priest. There was nothing I could do other than stare at them consulting, and bite my lips in astonishment. I recognized the regal white-haired man to be none other than the Pope. What a development! My surprise was exacerbated by the fact that the old man was an elf. Several more portals opened and we were joined by a monk-elf Dalai Lama, a human cleric – the Patriarch of the Orthodox Church – and someone from a class I did not know, but also representing some church. Gerhard greeted the players who came at his call, and pointed at the castle:

"Lumpen is reborn. The entire estate is under his control; he has already captured Iven and Archibald. There are about a hundred living beings in the castle, so he has enough Energy."

"Have you informed the Coordinator?" The monk asked. "When is he expected? I consider it unfeasible to move forward without his support."

"Bernard is already within. The reason for which he had not informed us of the rebirth is unknown. But let's consider the worst: he is on Lumpen's side. There are grounds to suspect that."

"Then let's hurry. My troop will be here in a minute." The priest pointed at the necromancers, who kept arriving. "I consider it's the right time to announce the total Game mobilization. The invasion must be stopped."

"This is excessive." Gerhard disagreed. "I sent out notifications to all the Heads, they promised to immediately send backup from their operative special forces teams. The rest are at the ready, unofficially. Let's not arouse panic so far. If there are no more questions, let's get going. Every second counts. Dolgunata, you coordinate activities outside the estate walls."

The four Heads teleported to the entrance of the estate, destroying one of the necromancers' portals along the way. Gerhard opened a passage in the protective dome, and I felt proud for my class. It's nice when your Head is super tough! All four quickly disappeared within, not bothering any more about how grand they looked, picking up the hems of their robes to climb over the barrier.

Bored from enforced idleness, I could do nothing other than longingly look at another attempt of the minor necromancers to liberate the statue of Don Fabio, standing lonely on the top of the hill. One could praise them for determination and loyalty to their teacher. Good qualities in a not so good class.

"Oh: my congratulations! You have tickets in the front row? Or is this the VIP box?" I heard the druid's mocking voice. The busybody bitch needed no answer. She quickly ran up to Don Fabio – several warriors from the new arrivals covered her – hugged the statue with one hand, and with the second one quickly activated a teleporting scroll. An instant, and the scream of necromancers left with nothing carried across the clearing. Eager to vent their frustration, they switched to me, madly attacking the dome from all sides. The shield wobbled and neutralized all attempts to inflict any damage to me. This only egged the necromancers on, and they, unable to curb their blind rage, rushed at my dome with their bare hands. I was fed up to no end just having to observe all of that, so I hit the nearest one straight in the jaw through the dome. The shield stayed in place and the necromancer sprawled on it and jerked his head from the unexpected hit. There was not enough damage to break through his protection, but I had time: there was nowhere for him to go. His own guys pressed him to my dome hard. A blow. And another, and another. With a disgusting squelch the necromancer turned into black slime. It spread on the surface of my dome and prevented other necromancers from touching it.

They cursed and looked for clean areas, apparently worried about the damage, since the substance easily penetrated their protective shields. Another thing I need to add to my "must have" list: a nasty surprise for my enemies after I am killed. Given my current level, the main problem for the training would be time, because with the constraint of one ability per week it would take me forever to learn.

"May the Light be with us!" the shout nearby rang with pathos and heroics. A ball of light that followed it swept the necromancers aside, clearly demonstrating that pathos without a good attack spell is just hot air. I lifted my head and saw the arriving priests. At the head of the troop there was a white-winged angel pointing his fiery sword at the enemies. The enemies regrouped and black lightning bolts flew at the priests. A great skirmish started, in the middle of which I sat, smeared up to the ears of the dome, had the dome had ears. Periodically a dead body landed next to me, or the ground exploded next to me from a stray spell, burying the dome deeper. The good thing was that there were only players around, so the bodies disappeared practically at once and the spells could not hurt me in any way. At the same time the downside was that no one bothered to invite me to a group. All that free experience was floating by uselessly.

"Don't touch this one – he is sort of one of us." The spells put me so deeply under the ground that Dolgunata had to bend down over my accidental grave in order to see me inside. "I see you have a cozy place here. Almost like a 5-D theater! So we'll just leave you alone."

The druid disappeared, plunging back into the battle. As for me, I was left without even visual input and could only imagine how things were going from the orders I happened to overhear:

"Monks, take out portals on the right! Seraphim, yours are the left ones! Onward!"

The battle drifted down the hill, the noise became more remote and I was left to my own devices. All my attempts to dig myself out were futile. After some time I was concerned that I would be forgotten, accidentally or on purpose. My nervousness was exacerbated by the fact that I did not know how things were going within the estate and around it. Thinking that respawn would be better than uncertainty, I tried to kill myself, but the absolute protection was absolute for a reason: it protected the one who wore it both from the outside world and from himself. During the time I spent in the dome I went through the entire range of aggressive feelings: from irritation to fury to a feeling of helplessness. At some point I just beat at the dome for fifteen minutes or so. I sweated like a pig, I fell an infinite number of times and rose back up expecting that it would take just one more tiny effort and I would get out of this trap. Finally I fell down, and did not have the strength to get up again. So I just stayed there, staring listlessly at the piece of sky I could see through the top of the dome, and at the countdown timer indicating the remaining life of the shield Gerhard had put on me. My confinement lasted for three hours forty eight minutes and some seconds.

From the noise of the battle I could suppose that our people were winning. However, when a particularly loud bang came, so hard that my ears popped despite the protection, I started doubting our victory. Perhaps the necromancers had used the "last resort" weapon, destroying everything around. But my doubts were unfounded. The sounds came back and shouts such as "For the Light!" and "Kill the Darks!" indicated that our troops were pressing the Dark ones hard. Succumbing to the feeling I even joined the general shouts of "Hurray!" and added "For the motherland!", alone this time.

"Get up, lazybones!" Just two minutes before the timer ran out someone remembered me. Dolgunata sounded tired, but pleased. For me it sounded like the bell that would release me. Dirty from head to toe, her armor tarnished by fire, the druid kept shaking her ruffled matted hair, looking more like a scarecrow than a pretty girl. Not at all concerned by her appearance, she was sporting a great white-toothed grin on her dirty face. "While you were taking a nap here, the big boys and girls did all the work. Gabriel, pull him out!"

The winged seraph dived down and pulled me by the leg, releasing me from the trap. As it turned out, the sand around me had baked together and turned into glass, so my grave would have been pretty strong. The seraph carefully returned me to the surface and disappeared into the last active portal, which immediately shut with a characteristic pop. In the middle of a burnt lifeless space there was a huge crater, about two hundred yards in diameter and perhaps as deep. What I was worried about most of all was the fate of the heads of classes.

"I know that's kind of a silly question, but I'll ask it anyway." Dolgunata nodded at the huge pit. "Is the estate your doing? Your scrolls destroyed the hill practically to its roots. So you could have pulled a nasty trick on the Lecleurs as well."

"Vandalism is not among my virtues," I grumbled, stretching my legs. To avoid bickering with the druid, I asked the question that was bothering me: "What happened to Lumpen?"

"I don't know yet. Gerhard acknowledged the report on the outcome of the battle and hung up immediately." Dolgunata responded. "Where is the teacher? Did you get out of the estate together?"

"No." Busy with fighting in the field, Dolgunata had had neither time nor opportunity to find out about the latest events in the estate. " Lumpen took him together with Iven even before the Heads went in. Archibald agreed to slavery on his own, Nata."

"If this is your idiotic sense of humor, now is really a bad time, you cretin!" The druid was looking daggers at me, her pupils narrow like a cat's. She waited for me to refute my own statement, and when I did not, reached for her comm and turned away. Silence was heavy on the ears. The measured beeps were heard very clearly in it. No one picked up. "That's impossible. He must be just busy. He'll call us back later. I have never heard anything dumber than that: Archibald as Lumpen's slave!"

I don't know who she was trying to convince first and foremost: myself or herself. Her voice seemed calm, but it was too high-pitched. This betrayed the alarm she was trying to hide. Thinking about the druid's feelings I wondered if it was simple concern for her teacher or …

"The person in the photograph is definitely not the catorian," Steve heard my thought and shared his considerations right away. *"I am still working, but I can say with certainty – it's a person. Human Paladin. It takes time; the druid tore up the photo too small."*

"What about analyzing which players went across the eras?" I reminded him of another task that was just as important. Steve looked down.

"I am not working on it right now, all the resources were allocated to processing the fragments. I have found only three so far. Archibald, a mage and a shaman. Do you want the names?" My subconscious knew how I felt and did not want to overload me with superfluous information.

"Not now. But searching for the Creator is no less important than analyzing the fragments," I clarified to Steve. "Allocate about ten percent of resources. It may run in the background, but it must be done."

"Will do!" My assistant responded, glad that I had not yelled at him.

"Fine. Let's suppose that you told the truth. Then why?" The druid distracted me from my conversation with Steve. "What did the necromancer promise him in exchange? Archibald always had a backup plan. Always!"

"Archibald wanted to find out in what way Lumpen was able to be reborn in our era." I clarified.

There was no need to make a secret of it. "So he gave herself in exchange for that information."

"He knows very well the way to respawn." I heard a familiar voice. Nata and I turned at the same time and bowed our heads. Gerhard van Brast graced us with his presence. "Archibald was definitely curious about the method Lumpen had come up with, but not to such an extent as to surrender into slavery to his long-time and dangerous enemy. It's something else. Yaropolk, I want to know all the details."

"Certainly." I put together a video up to the arrival of Bernard and offered it to Gerhard. Knowing what the druid's demanding look meant I made her a gift as well. The druid was first to react:

"He was distracting Lumpen from Yari!" she exclaimed in surprise as she watched the video. "He set himself up for Yari's sake!"

"It does look like that." Gerhard was contemplating the horizon. "But he did it not for the sake of Yari, but for the sake of the Guide."

"I don't understand. It's possible to replace the Guide. Could the teacher really value Yari so highly in his role of the Guide that he had to sacrifice himself?" Dolgunata could not accept from any angle that Archibald would make a sacrifice for such an insignificant creature as myself.

"The reason lies not only in Yaropolk, Dolgunata." The Head curbed her indignation quickly. "You are overestimating your teacher. Lumpen's strength is of a higher order of magnitude; breaking the loop of the estate would be beyond Archibald; nor would he win a direct battle with Lumpen. Archibald was first dragging out time, and avoided the fight until he found a solution. Right, Yaropolk?"

"I don't know!" I exclaimed heatedly. I hated the thought that the catorian had sacrificed himself for the sake of me being the Guide once he realized that he could not get out of that. "No one supposed that the pendant would resurrect the necromancer! We had no time at all!"

"Fine. And there were no instructions, quests, indirect comments? There is a reason why your teacher included the line of being released by a third party in his oath." Gerhard kept questioning. I just shook my head for a negative. I did not recall anything like that.

The druid rushed to view the video once again. After a second I decided to replay it for myself as well.

"Here!" Dolgunata shouted. "Look! While the necromancer was burning lady Lecleur, Archibald scribbled something on the wall next to Yari!"

Gerhard and I fast forwarded to the right point. Indeed, unless your goal was to find some sign from Archibald, it would have been impossible to guess that the catorian was actually making some graffiti deliberately rather than just rubbing off the dust. Once I zoomed in real close I saw a lopsided symbol of the scales.

"This is the message for you, Yaropolk." Gerhard smiled with pleasure, and Dolgunata stared at me expectantly. I shrugged my shoulders in bewilderment:

"Why? I still don't get it."

"Scales, Yari, don't be dumb! Scales is a symbol

of justice. You are the Judge!" Dolgunata was stating the things I did not find obvious. But the train of logic was inarguable. I was thinking, not quite sure how my specialty could help the catorian.

"The case that was initiated against the catorian," Steve suggested, *"what if he knew about that?"*

"Is that possible?" I objected uncertainly to myself

"The catorian is a creature from the first era. We don't know how long he lived in it or what abilities he acquired. What if he can see all the cases that have been initiated against him?" My subconscious was saying amazingly sensible things. I was even starting to be proud of myself.

"I think I understand what my teacher was hinting at. Now I have to figure out how to use it in order to free him." I did not want to admit that I had initiated a case against my teacher, and so I asked a question in turn to change the subject. "Were you able to destroy Lumpen?"

As usual, the Head was very shrewd and did not press me:

"He escaped together with his helpers to the world called Gardish. But at first Lumpen swallowed the entire estate and blew it up as the owner. Gardish is outside of our jurisdiction; Bernard went there to warn the Heads of Classes of the new danger. The Viceroy's aides have been notified as well, but I don't have much faith in him. A dozen years could pass before this information makes it to the Viceroy's desk. By that point Gardish will have been wiped out.

Yaropolk, try to understand what Archibald wanted from you as quickly as you can. You realize how much we need him now to fight Lumpen. And another thing; I am requesting a detailed report on what happened within the estate. Dolgunata, the same request for you. I need to understand why I lost my two best Paladins. Present the report tomorrow. Now I need to leave. Duty will not wait."

Gerhard opened a portal and disappeared, leaving me alone with the druid. Nata was silent, thinking of something of her own, and I was turning over the case I had initiated against Archibald, and could not quite grasp how to go about it. To pronounce him guilty? Well, he was definitely guilty, he gave the recruits to the mages for the killing. But what could I demand in return? A respawn? But who would execute that? Lumpen would place such a protective shield on Archibald that a dozen nuclear bombs would not get through it. A fine and stripping of Grandeur points? That would not work; it would not bring the catorian any closer to freedom. A prison term? Again, that brings the question of execution. Who would dare to fly to Gardish? Besides, none of that makes any sense; in order to get rid of Lumpen's control the catorian would just have to respawn once. Just once, but how to arrange for that? That's the million dollar question.

"How long are you going to try to drill a hole in the ground by staring at it?! I don't understand: how could my teacher entrust you with his life?" Inaction was getting to Dolgunata's active character. She wanted the results here and now. But I was unable to give her that. That made her more and more irritated, pacing around me. "Think! While you are trying to search for one little thought in your empty stupid head, they can wipe him out at any moment! If something were to happen to him because of you... Some Judge, aren't you! You can't even be trusted to clean sewage pipes: you'd drown us all in shit!"

The druid's emotional chatter was annoying, and I was just about to tell her to be quiet when I got an interesting thought. Smiling from ear to ear I was staring at the ranting girl as I was saying to myself:

"I pronounce Paladin Archibald guilty of collusion with the mages for the purpose of the premeditated murder of Paladins Monstrichello, Logir and Sartal. I declare the actions of the defendant unworthy of the name of Paladin, and defacing the honor and dignity of the class. I sentence Paladin Archibald to community service within the sewage system of the Sanctuary for two thousand hours, reduction of grandeur by 200 units and paying a fine to the Game in the amount of five thousand granises! Deadline for community service completion: two thousand years. For the duration of serving the sentence all mental blocks shall be removed from the defendant so that he may be fully aware of the gravity of his crime. This sentence is final and not subject to appeal!"

Verdict is confirmed
Verdict is deemed optimal
Case "Improper Behavior of the Paladin" is closed.
The sentence is executed by the Game.

Award for correct verdict: basic Energy level increased by 300

A second later my comm started vibrating.

"Explain to me, my lazy student, why is it that the Game is strongly recommending that I clean the walls within the sewage of Sanctuary for two thousand hours? What, could you not come up with anything else?"

"Verdict was deemed optimal," I parried. It was a pleasure to hear the teacher, and I smiled even wider, thinking of my competence as a Judge. "Fewer hours would have caused unwanted questions and a review of the case."

"What review? Had it not entered into your reckless head that instead of community service it would have been sufficient to sentence me to showing up to Gerhard for repentance and a full report on the case? From the standpoint of jurisdiction it is more correct than sentencing me to that service. Gerhard has the right to punish me at his discretion. For example, to sentence me to a respawn. Why do I have to explain elementary things?"

"Lumpen could have outfitted his favorite slave with protection strong enough that Gerhard would have to wait for you to respawn till the restart came around!" "The winner's triumph" march did not play long in my soul. Annoyance tainted all the joy from freeing the teacher. Enough! He freed me, I freed him. We were even. Everything else according to the deeds!

"He had just resurrected and only gobbled up one estate," Archibald stated with finality. I could practically see him roll his eyes. "Where would he get Energy for that? Great Light, what infinite stupidity! So then. While I explain myself to the Head in view of the depraved imagination of a certain half-baked Judge, you immediately go to the Sanctuary and sit there quietly. Lumpen will most likely want his toy back or to get his own back. So far Fabio, Iven and Gromana are on his side. The rest are waiting, assessing the situation and their chances. But that's my job. I have told you this for information. If you have no questions, get yourself to the Sanctuary, fast!"

My comm went dead, and Dolgunata's came to life. The druid immediately set the silence curtain, which didn't help her much. From her pursing her lips and gritting her teeth it was clear anyway that the catorian was not offering her congratulations on a job well done. I could say one thing: it was better to be scolded by the teacher in company rather than alone.

Having finished the conversation Nata looked at me glumly without saying a word. Apparently what the druid had heard from the catorian was not to her liking, and she hesitated. I nudged her towards conversation with a universal: "So?" The last thing we needed was another phone call, and we had a duel that we still had to work out.

"Paladin Yaropolk, I suggest we make a truce and give up the duel. As conditions for the agreement I offer a verbal apology for words and actions that resulted in a challenge to duel; also, both of us will give up the potential rewards. Do you accept the conditions or do you insist on the duel?"

Anyone would understand that it was not the proud druid's own decision. What could Archibald have said to her that she would give up on the potential victory in the duel and Madonna's Diary, I would never find out. But I was curious as to why she had wanted the diary as her prize.

"I am willing to make peace if you honestly tell me why you need Madonna's Diary. I do understand that it's you, not Archibald, who needs it. Otherwise he would have taken it away from me long ago. Moreover, I think that you forgot to tell the teacher that you wanted to have that thing. Am I right?" I asked, but silence was my only answer. The druid was silent like a statue, just raised her head proudly showing that there would be no amendments to her offer. "Fine. You don't want a duel? Here is my counter offer: either you tell me why you need that damned diary, and we make peace, or you admit that you lost with all the consequences of that. And in that case, if you try, you might get the diary without any questions! Agree?"

"Go to hell, you!" Dolgunata growled through her teeth and turned into a panther. "Duel. Here and now! I don't care it's prohibited!"

The game message appeared that my opponent demanded that the duel be held, and if I disagreed it would be considered that I lost, since the duel had already been postponed and it was my fault. In reality I did not want to fight Dolgunata. I had thought she would share the information, take the Diary and we would set out for the Sanctuary, but she preferred to hide it. I admitted that most likely I had gone too far with my demand that she admit her loss, but I realized that there was no way back, and so the duel would take place. As I was clicking on "Agree" I jumped quickly to get out of the path of the panther. Dolgunata attacked as soon as the "Duel" status came up.

I rolled over to the side, yet got a substantial kick in the side. The protection absorbed the blow, but Steve warned me: a direct hit like that would kill me outright. The chance to win the duel dropped to one percent: that was the probability rating my assistant allocated to Leguria. Everything else Steve considered impossible right away: my shields would be useless against such an attack. Nata was determined, and I felt tired, both physically and emotionally, and just wanted to be done with it quickly. The answer to the question of Leguria was an obvious one for me: winning this duel was not worth letting it out. I considered that was beneath me, even though I knew Dolgunata would not appreciate my motives. So since there was no decent alternative all I could do was use defensive tactics and avoid her blows. I had no strength for attack.

"Go on Yaropolk, call up Leguria! What are you waiting for?" Dolgunata asked, appearing next to me instantly. After pouring a lot of fervor into her initial blow the druid was now playing, mocking me and venting all her pent-up frustration. Grass grew around me and quickly tangled around me into a cocoon stronger than steel cables. My world turned upside down and I was swinging like a caterpillar in the wind. Lush greenery grown by the druid worked both as fetters and as support: I was hanging at about human height. Dolgunata transformed back, came right up to my face and said contemptuously, looking me in the eye:

"You are a pitiful, weak and useless piece of shit! I don't even have to fight you in order to defeat you! What can you do?! Call up Leguria?!"

"I could, but I will not. Even though you do realize that your grass would not hold back Leguria." Contrary to my expectations, I was not angry for being in such a humiliating position for a man. On the contrary, after such a long and hard day I was too tired to feel anything. I regarded the girl, upturned in my eyes with practically Olympic calm and pitied her. This was going to happen sooner or later. At least there were no witnesses, and her breakdown would stay between us. She had been mad at me from the beginning, and now was the ideal moment to find out the true reason for it.

"No, it won't, but your beast won't be able to get me either. Or, actually, you, in the form of that beast won't get me! I know everything about Leguria. One has to be a cretin to rely on it. Why the hell did you even agree to hold a duel at all, you idiot?"As the druid became more excited my restraints tightened more and more.

"Apparently for the same reason that you kept picking a fight," I rasped trying to expand my chest in the cocoon that was hard as steel now.

"Moron, I have every reason to behave that way! I am stronger and more experienced than you. While you have nothing other than your overblown feeling of self-importance. Everything was great until you came along!"

"So that's the problem? Your envy? Someone shoved you off your pedestal without bothering to ask your opinion? At first Archibald was hovering over you and you alone, convincing you that you were oh so unique with your role of Keymaster, your great important mission; and then I came along and all that attention was no longer yours? Dumb bitch sulking – right, Dolgunata?" Frankly speaking I had had that thought before but brushed it aside – it just seemed too unreal. It just could not have been so simple!

Instead of responding the druid removed all her greenery with one swipe of a paw and I fell on the ground. Rolled over at once and jumped onto my feet. The druid was ready:

"I don't care what you think! They think you are worthy of the role of the Guide! They are stupid! You are just a loser who appeared at the wrong place at the wrong time! You need to be replaced!" The girl leaped forward, instantly transforming into the animal.

Another hit with a paw, and my neck was now boasting a precise little cut inflicted purely for demonstration. She got through my block very easily, and with a contented growl, started circling around me looking for a way to play with me some more.

"Fine, you are stronger than I am. It would be stupid not to admit that. But that's not enough for success, Dolgunata. If you were to wipe me out now, you would be thrown out of the Game as trash who did not live up to expectations. Archibald would never forgive your disobedience. And it's as easy to replace a Keymaster as it is a Guide."

The panther kept advancing, her ears twitching. I was hoping to get across to her reason.

"Let's finish with this duel quickly and get down to business. Archibald is waiting." I was trying to play on her feelings for the teacher.

"Do you acknowledge your defeat?"

"No." I smiled. "Never, Dolgunata. I will not surrender to you voluntarily! Those win who don't surrender!"

"If the enemy does not surrender he will be killed!" the druid countered, and the black lightning rushed towards me. A few seconds later I was lying on the ground, without my legs and right arm, tortured by pain and about to bleed to death.

You lost a duel. Pass the reward to the winner.

Dolgunata smirked victoriously, turned into a human and poured an elves' ointment down my throat.

"Sorry, buddy, that's it for now. Give me the reward and send yourself to respawn. I don't want to bother dirtying my hands." She extended her hand, demanding the reward.

I was scolding myself hard for getting entangled in this stupid bitch stuff instead of accepting the peace offer right away. I opened my inventory with my left hand and threw the diary to Dolgunata. Now I really would have to respawn. Not only did I have a hole in my armor, but in addition I had lost almost all my limbs. Why were they all so mean to...

All my thoughts vanished as soon as Madonna's Diary touched the druid. A few messages flashed before my eyes:

The reward is transferred to the winner. The duel is complete.
Player Madonna is resurrected

I did not immediately grasp the point of the message, but as soon as the thought hit the right synapses, I quickly turned my head towards Dolgunata – Keymaster and... Madonna.

The girl's appearance did not change at all. She just kept standing still, smiling, staring at the glowing diary in her hands. But the world around her hastened to change, welcoming the rebirth of the Great One. Right from the druid's feet flowers were spreading like a painted veil, hastening to fill the burnt crater and cover the ruins: all that remained from the hill and the estate. Birds, bees and animals appeared out of nowhere. As I was lying on the ground and observing the magic around me, I saw four rainbows. The world around was filling with bright colors and I was the only ugly crippled patch among all that beauty.

The diary stopped shining and the girl's eyes came to life again. Smiling beatifically she was looking at her accomplishments. It was not clear how Dolgunata's consciousness changed: was that a complete replacement of personality or was that some form of symbiosis? Casting a glance around, the being looked at me and frowned. The diary immediately disappeared; I was lifted up in the air with a slight gesture of her hand.

"Why is the Guide greeting me in such poor shape?" The palms of the creature that used to be Dolgunata flashed brightly, and hundreds of needles stung my body as my limbs appeared in their places again. "That's much better. It's a pity there's nothing else for me to heal here. I could do with some extra Energy."

Madonna waved her hand again and I was carefully placed on the ground once again. So then, since she was the antagonist of the necromancers and Dark ones, she received Energy through creation and healing. That must be appropriate, but what enormous strength she had!

A teleport popped nearby and Archibald was in the clearing, kneeling immediately:

"Milady! It is a pleasure to welcome you to Earth."

"Archibald: good timing." Madonna looked at the catorian sternly. "Why was the previous occupant not erased?"

"It's my fault, Milady. The wrong being was chosen for reincarnation." The catorian hung his head. "The consciousness that is resisting being erased is the Keymaster."

"You put me in with the Keymaster?!" Madonna exclaimed angrily, and Archibald was jerked up into the air. The catorian was obviously uncomfortable hanging in midair, but made no attempts to escape. "You deserve punishment, slave! I do not wish to put up with resistance in my new incarnation! Now I will let the Keymaster step forward so that you can sort out the problem you created yourself. And may the Game help you if you can't do it again and I feel any discomfort! You will accept your punishment later!"

At the end of that scolding the Great one was practically hissing, her mouth curved in an ugly grimace of anger. Archibald landed on his hind legs as soon as Madonna released the body to Dolgunata. As confusion replaced anger on the druid's face it was possible to see the change between the personalities:

"Teacher, I won't allow it! It's my body! I don't want this!"

"Idiot girl, you don't have a choice now. I told you keep away from Yari. You went against my will." Archibald cut her off harshly. "You disobeyed a direct order. This is your punishment. This is your fate. If you don't succumb, your consciousness will be wiped out and the functions of the Keymaster will be passed on to another being. You want to live? Then stuff it and wait for your turn!"

Dolgunata looked at the catorian in disbelief, realizing there was no help coming. Madonna took over, strengthening her position.

At that time several more teleports lit up and the Heads of Classes I had seen already crowded into the clearing. An instant flash of pain from the presence of the Priest, and once again I was covered by Gerhard's protective capsule with which I was familiar. The Heads also kneeled, welcoming the high guest. Madonna waved her hand in the air, and the flash of a positive spell settled on everyone present.

Madonna continued to build her strength.

"Where is the Coordinator?" the Great one said with displeasure, looking over those present. "Why am I being welcomed so shabbily?"

"The Coordinator is fighting Lumpen, my Lady." Gerhard, said, lifting his head. "The necromancer was reborn."

"That's his problem; he should have dropped everything and hurried here. Now he'll have to wait his turn. Priest, you will accompany me to my rooms." "Yes, Milady," the Pope replied, his head still bowed.

"Today I am not in a mood for communication. Because of this slave's mistake," Madonna nodded at the catorian, who was humbly waiting for his fate, "I was unable to take over the consciousness of the subject. Monk and priest, by tonight you need to figure out a way to block the other consciousness. She is a shrew of a girl, and I need none of that. But do not erase her; it's the Keymaster. The rest are released."

"What about Archibald?" The Head of the Paladins inquired as he was opening a portal.

"He deserves punishment, and for this reason I am stripping him of class and rank. He is exiled. Game: I require that the Viceroy be notified of my rebirth. I will be waiting for him tomorrow in the Citadel of the Priests of Earth.

The procession of the players, having not received any grace from the Great One, disappeared into the portal, leaving me alone with the catorian. The Paladin's shining armor disappeared, revealing his furry body. The catorian shook himself, smoothed the fur in a few places, grinned and looked at me meaningfully:

"I hope you understand what happens when you don't obey your parents... or your teacher! The Game must go on!"

While I was thinking over this pearl of wisdom, wondering whether he meant himself or Dolgunata, the catorian opened a portal and disappeared somewhere.

"I have some news." Steve held a theatrical pause which I ignored.

"Fire away." I suggested calmly, expecting that nothing else that happened today would surprise me. But I was gravely mistaken.

"If Dolgunata is the embodiment of Madonna, that explains why she did not have a Doll. Because she used to be a Doll herself."

"That I figured out on my own." I interrupted Steve. "Cut it short and to the point."

"I collected the fragments and completed the analysis. I know who is the Nameless one."

Instead of words a picture appeared in front of me – of a man with the fatherly smile of Sean Connery. Once again that made me remember all the cursewords I had learnt from Sintsov, adding some of my own to boot. The photo explained a lot and confirmed that the Game must go on. Because the only one who smiled like that was Gerhard van Brast, the Head of the Paladins of Game world Earth.

— END OF BOOK TWO —

Want to be the first to know about our latest LitRPG, sci fi and fantasy titles from your favorite authors?

Subscribe to our NEW RELEASES newsletter:
http://eepurl.com/b7niIL

Thank you for reading *The Quest!*
If you like what you've read, check out other sci-fi, fantasy and
LitRPG novels published by Magic Dome Books:

Reality Benders LitRPG series by Michael Atamanov:
Countdown
External Threat
Game Changer
Web of Worlds
A Jump into the Unknown
Aces High

**The Dark Herbalist LitRPG series
by Michael Atamanov:**
Video Game Plotline Tester
Stay on the Wing
A Trap for the Potentate
Finding a Body

Perimeter Defense LitRPG series by Michael Atamanov:
Sector Eight
Beyond Death
New Contract
A Game with No Rules

**League of Losers LitRPG Series
by Michael Atamanov:**
A Cat and his Human

**The Way of the Shaman LitRPG series
by Vasily Mahanenko:**
Survival Quest
The Kartoss Gambit
The Secret of the Dark Forest
The Phantom Castle
The Karmadont Chess Set
Shaman's Revenge
Clans War

The Alchemist LiTRPG series by Vasily Mahanenko:
City of the Dead
Forest of Desire
Tears of Alron

Interworld Network **LitRPG Series by Dmitry Bilik:**
The Time Master
Avatar of Light
The Dark Champion

Rogue Merchant **LitRPG Series by Roman Prokofiev:**
The Starlight Sword
The Gene of the Ancients

Project Stellar LitRPG Series by Roman Prokofiev:
The Incarnator
The Enchanter
The Tribute

Clan Dominance **LitRPG Series by Dem Mikhailov:**
The Sleepless Ones Book One
The Sleepless Ones Book Two
The Sleepless Ones Book Three

The Neuro **LitRPG series by Andrei Livadny:**
The Crystal Sphere
The Curse of Rion Castle
The Reapers

Phantom Server **LitRPG series by Andrei Livadny:**
Edge of Reality
The Outlaw
Black Sun

Respawn Trials **LitRPG Series by Andrei Livadny:**
Edge of the Abyss

The Expansion (The History of the Galaxy) **series
by A. Livadny:**
Blind Punch
The Shadow of Earth
Servobattalion

Point Apocalypse (*a near-future action thriller*)
by Alex Bobl

Moskau **by G. Zotov**
(a dystopian thriller)

El Diablo by G.Zotov
(a supernatural thriller)

Mirror World LitRPG series by Alexey Osadchuk:
Project Daily Grind
The Citadel
The Way of the Outcast
The Twilight Obelisk

Underdog LitRPG series by Alexey Osadchuk:
Dungeons of the Crooked Mountains
The Wastes
The Dark Continent
The Otherworld

An NPC's Path LitRPG series by Pavel Kornev:
The Dead Rogue
Kingdom of the Dead
Deadman's Retinue

The Sublime Electricity series by Pavel Kornev:
The Illustrious
The Heartless
The Fallen
The Dormant

Citadel World series by Kir Lukovkin:
The URANUS Code
The Secret of Atlantis

You're in Game!
(LitRPG Stories from Bestselling Authors)

You're in Game-2!
(More LitRPG stories set in your favorite worlds)

The Fairy Code by Kaitlyn Weiss:
Captive of the Shadows
Chosen of the Shadows

More books and series are coming out soon!

In order to have new books of the series translated faster, we need your help and support! Please consider leaving a review or spread the word by recommending *The Quest* to your friends and posting the link on social media. The more people buy the book, the sooner we'll be able to make new translations available.

Thank you!

Till next time!

www.ingramcontent.com/pod-product-compliance
Lightning Source LLC
Chambersburg PA
CBHW060757030726
47503CB00002B/278